DEFIANT

A "SLAVES TO FATE" NOVEL

J M BLOODWORTH

ISBN 978-1-957943-22-0 (paperback)
ISBN 978-1-957943-23-7 (hardcover)
ISBN 978-1-957943-24-4 (digital)

Rushmore Press LLC
1 800 460 9188
www.rushmorepress.com

Printed in the United States of America

PROLOGUE

Death is a very serious matter—one in which we all must face now or later—though I, for one, prefer later; but it may seem that we don't always get what we want. I never thought it would end like this. There are many ways in which I could picture my demise but being killed by the hands of a demon was never one of them. Everything's a big blur as I lay on the ground, drenched in my own blood. There is something that seems off, however. Other than the crimson moon that stares down at me, the sky also seems to be a bit unique. It isn't the type of darkness you'd expect from a night sky, but a pitch-black abyss being lit by the unnatural lighting of Night's orb.

Here I am, in pain and blind to my surroundings. I'm bleeding profusely through the wounds that are still fresh on my body. I'm partaking in a battle I have no chance of winning. After all, how could I expect to win when I am nearly injured to the extent of immobility? I'm at a disadvantage. Compared to the enemy, I am blind. I see nothing but faint adjustments in positions while he, on the other hand, has eyes that could see as clear as if it were day.

"Get away from me!"

Through the darkness, I can see, only, the silhouettes of what I could only refer to as shadow demons surrounding me, as I lay nearly motionless, unable to stand in my current state. "You will submit and join me in power or choose the alternative. Together, we'll be unstoppable." My legs feel as if they've been broken; yet, I try to stand anyway.

"If you plan on killing me, the least you could do is reveal yourself."

"And for what purpose would you have to see my face?" The only question that stands is what he wants from me. Sure, I've made enemies, but not of the blood-thirsty demon sort. Up until now, demons were nothing more than superstition, spawned by religion. The proof in front of me makes me question where I'm going when I die. What determines where I'd be going after death? Is there a scale that weighs good and bad? If there is, then I'm utterly screwed. I have made some bad decisions in my life, but who hasn't? Are they bad enough to send me to a place in which I'd undergo torture for the rest of existence? I don't know how I feel about that. I believe that faith is something in which one shouldn't suffer in the end for not having. Let's face it. Faith is hard to come by if you have nothing to go off of. How am I supposed to have faith in a higher power that supposedly emanates light when darkness is all I've come to know? You can't magically grow faith by simply saying that you believe. You either do, or you don't, and here I am about to die a bloody death by the hands of a creature I don't believe in. Just my luck.

I am overcome by a sea of emotions, flooding in all at once: the pain that follows my injuries, and the pain that follows the memories of the deceased. Another attack breaks my skin as I remain defenseless. I might as well be dead. Why is he toying with me? Everything that gave me a reason to live was torn from my life. My friends are dead, and Mother disappeared. There is nothing I can do to alter what has already happened, no matter how much I wish I could. He stands over my injured body and continues torturing me. "Please. If you're going to kill me, don't make me wait!" Usually, I am a bit calmer in threatening situations, but given this specific one, I think I'm entitled to lose control over my emotions. After all, everything I had that was my comfort is gone. I don't want to die, but I also don't want to suffer before death. If I must choose one, I choose the quicker path. A second is all it takes for him to disappear from my sight, but I feel his presence creeping up on me. My mind may have given up, but my reflexes are still in survival mode, so unless he pins me down or corners me, I'm not dying that easily. Once again, I try to stand. My legs tremble in pain as I fall forward, landing on my knees. At least this time, I'm not going to lay on the ground, defenseless like a fish out of water. My legs may not work well, but my arms are still active. He takes a fighting stance, and lunges at me, swiping his hand forward, missing my throat by a mere inch. Before I can question what it is he was trying to accomplish, he counterattacks my evasion. I block it, even if barely, maneuvering his hand to the side with my fingers.

"I see you still have some fight left in you. That's quite alright. Gives me the pleasure of ridding you of it." He speaks calmly as if I pose no threat, which, at this point, I practically don't. "You're not strong enough, but with me, you can be. What do you say? Want to be the Jekyll to my Hyde?" He holds his hand out to me, which is a big mistake on his part. I grab his arm and pull him down to my level. With one swift motion, I reach out for his throat. I am quick, but he is quicker. He backhands me with the force of ten strongmen. I fly to the side, plummeting into the pile of corpses that breaks my fall. I slowly lift my body, digging my fingers into the blood-soaked chests of the unfortunate. "Where are you going, I wonder," he says, helping me up, only to surprise me with more unwanted pain. I wince, feeling the first couple inches of some weapon burrow into my flesh. "Why are you crying? Does it hurt? . . . Funny. I don't feel a thing." His face remains hidden from my sight as he pulls the weapon out slowly, licking the bloodied fingers that were, up until a second ago, buried in my side.

I am broken. Not just mentally, but physically—from my seemingly broken limbs to my torn apart flesh. My shoulders and chest are soaked, and the blood, in its lukewarm comfort, drips off my fingertips. "Go to hell!"

"No need. It's all around us. Can't you tell?" He jumps onto me, pinning me to the ground. He has the opportunity to end me, yet he chooses not to. He squeezes my head with both disfigured hands, pushing harder and harder until I feel as if my skull is going to crack open, or crush from the impact. From his touch, I can feel his lengthy talon-like claws sink into my temple. "I need you to see." Out of nowhere, my vision slowly creeps into perspective. I can see, but I can't move my head. There is a slight burning sensation surrounding my peepers like someone rubbed icy hot around them—an overall painful and uncomfortable sensation that I'd rather not live through again. Although I can't move my head, I am still able to observe my surroundings. The scenery changes position from left to right like I am turning my head to perceive, but I'm not. I don't recognize this place at all. There are no structures around us, just open space and destruction. The red terrain surrounding me remotely resembles that of the topography of Mars—the foreign land, painted in splotches of a darker red, being the blood of the bodies that lay scattered around in masses. Was there a war?

The scenery is gruesome, but I can't look away. There are bodies mutilated left and right. There's a woman with her body mangled like a pretzel and a man with his jaw torn apart, dangling loosely from a string of flesh. There's a man with his chest ripped open with no innards to be seen. Not too far from him is a little boy laid out on the terrain like a misused ragdoll with his head, just a few inches away from his body and a little girl that looks as if she's taken a bath in a pool of glass and razor blades. There's a series of pregnant women with their fetuses torn out. Most of these poor, unfortunate souls could hardly qualify as a resemblance to anything remotely human. A certain odor fills my nostrils—the smell of rot and decay, and what I can most-definitely confirm to be the scent of all contents, excrements and company, having been exuded after death. Everyone is dead. There is no question, not even a hint. No doubt that they suffered a great deal before they parted from life. I can only hope that they're in some better place, whatever that may be, whether it's heaven or some kind of parallel. "Are you going to do to me like you did to them? You sick bastard."

"No. A different endgame is planned for you, one that you will see to in the end. It is beautiful, isn't it? This scenery is a perfect depiction of what humanity has become over the years: grotesque, mutilated, callous, and deceitful. Everyone is born with animalistic instincts. Humanity used to act on them and show their true colors, despite the cruel consequences that followed. Through the years, they've been raised to suppress that inner animal. You can suppress it all you want, but the urges are still there, are they not? You've all become ugly with the lies that surround you. Imprisoned psychopaths who take joy in their work are the only people who are true to themselves. Dahmer, Fish, Ripper, Kroll, Trevino, and Holmes were worthy. They provided meaning to what it is to be free. Not locked away like your modern philanthropist, generously giving, and for what? No one in their right mind would give that much to a world that will inevitably be its own undoing. Want to know why the population is steadily increasing and becoming unmanageable? It's because 'survival of the fittest' was taken out of the equation. Look at them, and then, look at yourself." My surroundings begin to spin around until I'm looking into a familiar set of blue eyes—my own. I wasn't looking through my own eyes to begin with. I was looking through his. Everything I was witnessing a couple seconds ago was coming from his own set of peepers. "You have the potential to be a god amongst this filthy collection of insignificant bottom feeders, yet you choose to be a slave. You have power, but it's been kept from your knowing. Why? Was mommy scared to tell you? Everything you've come to know is a lie. How does that make you feel?"

He scrapes his monstrous claws along my chest, receiving a hiss of anguish from by lips, as I try to conceal my current state of pain.

"It hurts me to do this to you. It really does. Your pain reflects my own, but sometimes, getting the message across is worth it."

Suddenly, I see the first notable feature of this demon. His eyes, so wide, so lost, so familiar, stare into mine. I don't know what I was expecting. His eyes aren't black and lifeless, nor are they red. Green? That's a bit more normal than I expected. The only unnatural thing about his eyes is how, given the darkness engulfed around us, they appear so clearly. It breaks the darkness for me, allowing me to see minor features of the face hidden beneath the ever-shifting hair.

A certain light shows up, knocking him back into the darkness and away from me. I close my eyes for a quick second to adjust to the change of lighting, but when I open them, I see an angel. The light slowly fades away, revealing her. Though I can't see her clearly, what I do see draws me breathless. Her eyes are beautiful, a dark shade of purple. Like his, they pierce the darkness, just not as much. She sits with me as she places my head in her lap, running her fingers through my hair. It is soothing. Behind her is the green-eyed demon, just standing there. His shadow army slowly closes in on us, but I am focusing on the purple-eyed beauty. True, I can't see her face, but something about her lures me in, like a siren. She hums a melody in my ear. It's beautiful, but I feel as if I've heard it before. She caresses my cheek with the topside of her hand. "You must open your eyes." Her voice is angelic and kind.

"What do you mean? My eyes are open."

"No, they're not. You must open them now. Any more time here, and you'll be in even more danger. They're tracking you."

"Wait, is this a—"

"You won't remember all that has happened. It will come to you in pieces, but you must be strong. You must make the right decisions. The balance rests on it."

"But, what about you?"

"You won't remember me right away, but that's fine. I am always with you in your time of need, and I enjoy these short sessions with you. You've grown, but something is holding you back. This is the last you'll see of me here but worry not, I'm not going anywhere. I'll be waiting for you where I have always waited. In that world, don't look for me. Time will bring you to me, but till the moment arises, I will wait, my love."

x

"And I will be with you every step of the way. I've got eyes everywhere, in places you wouldn't have thought. You can't forget me no matter how many times you awaken. The scars I've inflicted upon you will make sure of that." The green-eyed man disappears into the darkness. His shadow demons follow him, absconding, one after the other.

The woman's form above me starts to wither away, like a field of dandelions. "I will be with you in the waking world. Keep living and put an end to all—" her voice and body disappear.

I am alone, in this hell. The bodies remain. Something gleams in the distance, but what? I crawl to the item and touch it, but something comes alive. What are those? Snakes? They hiss quietly at me as I back away, not wanting to touch them. The item is a sword, no doubt, but with snakes wrapped around the hilt. A Prussian gem of sorts is embedded into the center, where the snakes intertwine. I hear something. "Hello!" I yell into the night, awaiting an answer. I hear it again, but slightly louder. It's my name. The woman said this isn't real, so how do I escape? Usually, in these circumstances, enough pain would break you from your slumber, but I have already been tortured. What option is left? "Hello! Are you there!" A man shows up in the distance. His body is blanketed by the abysmal night, but his eyes shine through it. They're green, like that demon. "You! Why have you returned?"

"You know not what you speak, boy." His voice is different. It's aged, but not too much. The light coming from his eyes gives me a glimpse of something. What is that over his eye? I can only see a portion of a black shape over it, due to his hair. Other than this highly distinguishable feature, he has a beard. The way he speaks is old world English, or Shakespearean, or something. Either way, it's as if he's from a different time. He has an accent—British or Cockney. Of course, he has an accent. Why wouldn't he? "You must awaken. The world out there is in dire need of a savior; it just doesn't know it yet."

"I don't know how. Reveal yourself. If you are truly the good guy, then you should have no problem showing yourself to me."

"My identity shall be known in due time, boy. Secrets never last." He reaches over me and puts his hand on my forehead. What's with everyone touching me? "Now wake."

Everything starts to vanish, him included, like water-based paints washing off from its canvas, or like fresh blood draining into your shower drain in parting streams.

My eyes pop open and I jolt forward in haste.

"Happy Birthday, Chance!"

I

My heart is racing, but for what reason? I am sitting up in my bed, drenched in sweat. I move my body but get thrown into a state of ache and discomfort. Almost as quickly as I get up, I fall back onto my bed. Mother rushes to my side and removes the blanket that clings to my skin. The reasoning behind my pain is uncovered in a series of scarred tissue. I am drenched in more than just sweat. I am laying in a puddle of my own blood, but why? How? I think I would remember partaking in activity that could spawn such injury. Laid out on my skin are bruises and deep cuts, like I have undergone a sword juggler's mistake. Mother doesn't seem as worried as you'd think one would be. In fact, other than the pain that swallows me, I'm not that worried either. This has been going on for a while. I would wake up occasionally, with new injuries that would overlap the old ones, leaving scars. I've been told that I've been injuring myself in my sleep, yet I feel that is not the case.

Half a year ago, I went for a walk to clear my head. It was late, and while I was walking, I heard a scream originating from a dark alley. I know what you're thinking, but I couldn't just ignore it. I did what I thought was right and entered. The thing is, there was no one there. I could've sworn I heard a woman; actually, I know I heard one. There is no way a scream that loud was mistaken, or in my head. I looked around for a bit, trying to find the source of the sound, but what I found was trouble. I found myself thrown onto the ground as I was jumped by a man the size of a professional quarterback. Three others shadowed him. None of them looked friendly. They wore sweaters that would've been baggy on me, but on them, they looked a bit too small. Their faces were hidden by the overhang of the sweaters' hoodies, but not well enough. One of them had a beard, black like charcoal. The lines on the bottom part of his face indicated that he had to be at least thirty, maybe forty. The other three looked younger. They didn't have facial hair; however, one of them did have hair long enough to drape over his shoulders and fall freely over his chest. The quarterback-looking individual appeared to be around twenty-five, judging by the minimal number of lines his face revealed, and the five o'clock shadow. The fourth was slightly smaller than the other three. He was shaking a bit in his skin, not like a man who feared, but of one who simply couldn't stand the wait.

"Boss wants a word with you." The quarterback's voice was much deeper than expected.

I was pinned to the ground, underneath his unbelievably large foot. "What are you talking about? I have no connections with any sort of gang, or group. Whatever your boss wants, I assure you, I don't have it." I wasn't scared. If I had to be anything, it would have to be "shocked." What started out as a peaceful wandering, turned into an unjustified mugging attempt. Of course, I was a bit dazed in the moment; but who wouldn't be? When it flooded over me—the extremity of the situation—I reacted. I grabbed his foot and twisted. Obviously, it did nothing, given his size, so I did the next best thing. I grabbed onto his ankle as I raised my foot up, kicking him in his backside. His foot fell off me, and I rolled to the side as he stumbled forward.

"Looks like we've got a fighter. It's to be expected. Hold him down."

I jumped to my feet, backing up in a defensive stance. "I don't think so. I'm not going with you guys. Not now, not ever. Now, I suggest you leave."

I was smacked back to the ground, but I didn't stay down. "It's cute that you think you have a choice, boy. What are you going to do to us?

You're powerless, but you don't have to be." The quarterback held me up by the throat, as I fought for air. I held on to his wrist to keep my body from dangling, freely. He was exceptionally strong. "Boss will be happy to hear we've captured you, and with time to spare. He is not one to disappoint."

"That's too bad." With my hands still gripping his wrist, I pressed my thumbs into his radial artery, which got an immediate reaction. "But disappointment plays a big role in life." I punched him square in the face, but he barely budged. I tried again—nothing. "What are you? Steel?"

"You're so much like him. He's really going to love having you. You're both hard headed, but I'm going to have to knock you down a peg. After all," he slammed his fist into my chest as I flew back into a wall, "he only said to capture you alive."

They positioned around me, taking turns. When I crashed into one of them, I felt a pain in my stomach and fell back. "Time to go, kid."

"The hell I will." I grabbed the nearest object and wacked him in the head. One of them lunged at me, but I avoided it. I got in a few punches, but as we continued, I found myself struggling to keep up. One punched me in the ribs. They were quick—almost inhuman. After a while, I was pretty much beaten. I was on the ground with a busted lip and banged up arm. The last thing I saw was the bright flashing of red and blue. I woke up in a hospital room a few hours later and was confronted by an officer. I had to share the details of the situation with him, which was difficult to do since I couldn't see their faces or describe them in much detail. The size was of good help, I suppose. This was months ago. The group was eventually found, separate, and in complete shock. They were either really good actors, or they really had no idea who I was, nor did they have any sort of connection with one another. Bullshit.

Ever since that near-death experience, I have been having a reoccurring nightmare. I don't remember much about it: just a man—a demon. His identity remains a mystery. His appearance was a fog that my memories could not grasp. The darkness refused to uncover any specific features such as a beard or certain markings that could've helped differentiate him from the group. This demonic being is the only recollection of that nightmare that follows me to the waking world. I don't remember anything else. The scars on my skin are a good reminder of what he won't let me forget. Each nightmare was different but connected, like the fragments of a puzzle, leading to the bigger picture.

I keep all of this to myself. No one needs to know about my dreams. There must be a reasonable explanation behind what happens in them and what happens out here. I'd like to believe there is something greater out there beyond our mortal understanding, but at the same time, I don't want to disappoint myself. I have always been one to trick myself into expecting less of something, rather than having higher expectations, so that there'd be less disappointment. The cruelest thing to receive after all, is false hope.

I have always been an easy guy to get along with, which is a good thing. I never had to try to make friends; it just happened— and it doesn't hurt that I'm rich, or rather, well accounted for. I try to keep my money to myself, which is hard to do when my house is three times the normal size of an average one, and my clothes aren't of those belonging to a minimum-wage, household child. Money aside, I am also quite gifted in academics, oddly enough since school is pretty much optional to me. Mother doesn't care, or at least doesn't show concern. You'd think someone would show after my considerable amount of tardiness and absences, but Mother hasn't been fined, nor has she been summoned to court. My life is as perfect as it could get, which, unfortunately means, it can only get worse. Damn. Sometimes, I wish I started at the bottom, so I could work my way up, instead of starting at the top of the heap, only to find myself tumbling down. There's also the possibility that, if I did start at the bottom, I would've never reached where I am already. There are a lot of talented people out there who have yet to be discovered, but that's kind of hard to do when all the attention is being given to celebrities with no talent at all. I mean, c'mon. People get famous for stupid quotes alone, or for disrespecting their parents publicly enough to become a national uproar. Leave some spotlight for actual talent, you dicks!

Anyway, I had just woken up, covered in sweat and blood.

"Come on, Hun. I'll wash the sheets for you. Everyone's downstairs waiting on you." She's acting as if I had spilt a soda-can on my bed, instead of the large amounts of blood that are still fresh in the moment. "Oh, I can't believe my boy is sixteen." She walks over to me and plants a kiss on my forehead. We'll be downstairs, waiting. You should probably take a shower. You smell like defeat and copper."

"Gee, thanks. That is probably the most poetic thing you have ever said to me."

We exchange smiles. "I love you." She pats my cheek and walks out the door with my bedspread in her arms. "And don't forget to use peroxide or alcohol on your wounds. Would hate to see them get infected."

Mother's face may have reflected pure joy in seeing her son turn another year older, but I could detect something else: worry? She is scared about something, but she is keeping it a secret.

I hop in the shower, watching as the shower floor is painted over with the contents leaving my body. I wince in pain as the loofah scrubs against my sensitive wounds. I spend seconds, scrubbing away, cleansing them of bacteria. When I finish up, I dress in my usual clothing, if not a little more formal, due to the occasion.

I make my way downstairs and am surprised to see my aunts. My uncle sits in the kitchen with the rest of them. "There he is! My favorite nephew."

"You kidding me? I'm your only nephew."

"Which makes it that much more truthful." Uncle Carry drove quite a distance: a few hours: to be here for my birthday. "That was by far the longest four and a half hours that I will never get back, but it's worth it to see you growing up."

"Growing up? I've seen you maybe four times in my entire life, all within these last three years . . . It only took you four and a half hours to get here?"

"What can I say? I floored it. Cops had nothing on me." We laugh at the joke. At least, I hope it's a joke. Uncle Carry is tall: six foot-three inches: and has a deep voice, relative to mine at least.

"So, how have you been?" I sip some V-8 from a small, delicate, tea-time mug like I'm sipping tea with the queen of England.

"I am doing great. How's football going for you? Kill anyone by accident, yet."

I started football earlier this year because Stormie, my best friend since playschool, dragged me into it with him. I never thought that, for a second, I'd be playing it. "Football's going well, actually. We won the last game easily. They had no chance against us. I can't believe you drove this far to see me."

"Shit. Of course, I did. Five hours isn't a lot, anyway. I wasn't going to miss this for anything . . . You're really sprouting up, aren't you?" Uncle Carry playfully flexes his scrawny arms, trying to compare them with mine. "I bet you pick up a lot of chicks with arms like those."

"What happened there?" Aunt Joleen quickly darts her eyes to my face. Though, she doesn't specify as to what she's referring to, I know she's talking about the small scar on my cheek. It's not large enough to grab someone's attention from afar, but just visible enough for someone to take notice from a close distance.

I reach up to touch my cheek, feeling the outline of the scar. "Oh, that. You know. Just an ex. She took the breakup a little too harshly." I rub around the mark, remembering how I got it in the first place. It happened a short while ago—about a month. I had just woken up from a nightmare, like the one I had this morning. I don't remember all the details, but some still scratch away at my memory. For some reason, all I can really recall are the colors, green and purple. A man hidden in the darkness. A warrior angel who shows up near the end. That's it. No specifics. Just fragments.

"Ah, that brings back memories." Uncle Carry chuckles at his own words. "My nephew, the lady killer. Did I ever tell you about Judy Rose? Man. She was a looker. The hips on that woman could turn faces from a mile away. The night after prom, I was finally able to—"

—"What are you all doing sitting around? The party's outside."

Outside in our yard—our extremely large yard—by the heated pool, there are at least a dozen underage drinkers, drinking away at the 12-ounce bottles that rest in their hands. Partly dressed girls rest on the poolside and headstrong jocks lay beside them. Isn't it wonderous to think that stereotypes are as such, stereotypes, but still have placement in society? Every good while, you find a jock that fits his stereotypical profile and a cheerleader that suits hers. The basic Justin, living off his jock title and "good looks" with the overbearing father who pushes him towards the edge, and the basic bitch, Brittany—the over sexualized cheerleader idol who has peaked far too early in life and is practically destined to be the single mother of twins from her jock dropout, turned drunk. You think it's wrong of me to profile someone by stereotype. You think it racist, prejudice, or even sexist. I've got news for you. Maybe, stereotypes would lose value, or even purpose, if you stopped enforcing them. Stop being who everyone thinks you should be by origin, and start being who you want to be by choice.

Sure, I am friends with half of the football team, as I am one of them, but even I must admit that it couldn't hurt for a few of them to freshen up on their studies. I may be a lady killer, metaphorically of course, but I do have standards. Couldn't girls have just a little more decency—a little more modesty, when it comes to what they wear? Honestly, wearing a low-cut shirt that reveals what type of bra you're wearing, cup size included, won't make someone love you; sure, they may find themselves attracted to physical appearances, but the love that seeks the core is still absent. It confuses me to see individuals dressed like this in the time of year that you should be wearing a sweater. How can someone respect you if you refuse to respect yourself? The stereotypes don't stop there, not even close. There are the nerds that are so helpless, who refuse to stand up for themselves. There are the self-proclaimed "emos" that wear all black and take pride in their scar display. They're usually the ones that others accuse of wanting attention. They usually cut along the wrists because they "tried to kill themselves," but really, they seek sympathy. Had they really tried to end their lives, then they'd know that cutting horizontally does jack. About nineteen in twenty that say they'll kill themselves don't have the inner drive to do so, and the ones that do, don't go out and yell it to the world. Sometimes, you'll find the one that was truthful to the world about their suicidal intentions, but no one took them seriously. There are the blacks that speak with such profanity and grammatical error that it's an ear sore to listen to. And why is it that, whenever I get called by tech support or some college trying to reach out, I end up getting someone with an accent—usually Indian—that is so thick, it's hard for me to cling on to half of the words that they're selling? You can refuse to believe it all you want, but stereotypes are all around us.

All my "friends" are present at this party: the football team, the cheerleaders, random students that attend my school, my ex-girlfriends, and obviously, my family. Okay, so they're not all close friends—mostly acquaintances. All in all, I have, maybe, two close friends and my mother—the three people I'm able to share anything with. I have a lot of memories here, mostly good. Stormie, being my longest friend, would always come over and chill. Mother was always laid back when it came to my activities. When Stormie and I were younger, we got caught shoplifting a bunch of candy. We were escorted back to my place where mother talked to the police officers. When they left, she didn't punish us. She never told his parents. Rather than grounding me, she taught me the appropriate way to shoplift without getting caught. Why I need to know the skill that is shoplifting, given my lack of money problems, is completely beyond me, but I suppose that it may come in handy, shall I ever lose my inheritance. I don't know why I did it—I mean, I'm rich. I think it was the thrill of getting caught that lured me into it. It was a skill I ended up using multiple times after that day, but I stopped at around eleven. A year ago, we invited a couple girls over to hang out. We waited by the pool with signs, as childish as they may have been at the time, that would say *Adam and Eve's garden*, *Get in the mood and go all nude*, and *Topless babes only*. These were childish tricks, I know, and though they never worked, hey, at least we tried.

"Dude, wicked party, man." Brandon comes up to me and pats my back. Brandon is sort of a friend, but not really. We haven't really hung out in the past, but he's usually up for having a conversation when the timing seems inappropriate. He's the type of guy that ogles girls from a distance. Funny, how the pervs in the background that have their minds in the gutters are usually the ones who don't get laid. Ryley is another friend of mine, sorta. I mean, he's asked me to have a drink with him on many occasions in which I respectably declined. He's known me about six years. I admit, through these last couple years, our interactions have been cut short. He now has his own little group of drinking buddies. There's someone for everyone, to say the least.

After the jumping incident in the ally a few months back, Storm and I tried out for the football team as a joke to impress the girls, not that I needed the extra help with that. Luckily, we both made the team. I became a lineman, and a former friend of mine became quarterback. Unfortunately, his attitude and grades, combined, got him kicked off the team almost as quickly as he started, which transferred the position to me. I've always had some form of luck on my side, which gave me attention, good and bad. I've had people come up to me and claim to be my friend. Then, there's those who call me out and hate on me, simply because they put me in the category of rich snobs who act all high and mighty when, in reality, I'm nothing like those asshats.

"Noice! You have liquor! Bring on the liquor!" Ryley runs past me to the bar that is set up outside. He is an outgoing character, to say the least. Most of the time, he talks as if he's trying to hear himself in a movie theater during the shooting.

"You drink man?" Storm hands me a bottle of Schnapps, waving it like he is just waiting for me to take it.

Hesitantly, I reach out, taking the bottle from his frozen hand. "Uh, not really."

"Have you ever?"

"Of course. I just never made it into a habit." Occasionally, I'll drink something fruity, specifically for the taste. It's more or less like juice, or flavored sprite to me, since I don't recall any memories of ever being intoxicated.

"Well. It's your birthday. If she allows it, might as well take advantage. It's not like you're going to make it an everyday activity and throw your life away." He shakes his bottle, wanting me to tap his with mine so we can drink. I do just that. "That's cool though. Look around at all the underage drinkers. Your mom is probably the most chill mom I have ever met, and I once went over to a girl's house while her mother just sat there, watching her daughter get high."

"I suppose." He's not wrong. Mother is a bit, unconventional in the parenting department. I've never really seen her get mad at me or show anything more than the usual calmness. I smile awkwardly. "Yeah. Maybe she's a bit too relaxed. She's always been more of a friend. Then again, I never really did anything that made her punish me or feel the need to."

"Are you kidding me? You're kidding, right? We got in so much trouble growing up?" Storm nudges me on the arm.

"What you mean to say is that we would've gotten into trouble. Or you would've, had my mother told yours, which she didn't. Sure, we did things, but we still grew up decent. She taught us right from wrong without having to punish us for the wrong. That's pretty damn impressive." I take a swig from the liquor bottle, wincing as the first bit of alcohol goes down my throat. Though, I drink flavored drinks, I don't really care much for actual liquor, such as vodka, or whiskey.

"What, can't handle it?" Storm laughs, shaking me.

"I don't drink alcohol above eight percent."

"Oh, so you're a lightweight. Who'd of guessed?"

"Hey! Who wants to see the birthday boy drink!" I look up to see Ryley with a microphone, pointing at me. "Yeah, I'm talking to you. Care to accept?"

"Really? 'Birthday boy' is a bit 'elementary', don't you think?"

"Is that you backing out, I hear?" He smiles a smug one as he thinks I'll succumb to the pressure.

"I can't disappoint now, can I?" I take another swig as I walk up to Ryley. "Ready when you are, Irish."

"Oh, we have jokes. Think about what you called me, then think about the activity you're challenging me in. Care to back out."

"Care to explain why you're in a mix of wanting to challenge me and wanting me to quit? Is it because you're afraid? It's okay if you are. Happens to the best of us." Sounds are made from the peers watching us. Mostly ones of "Ooooh."

"Best watch that tone, Ryder. I'm Irish. Drinking makes up the majority of my biological makeup." Ryley's grandfather owns a franchise of pubs in Ireland and wants his grandson to take over the family business when he is of age. Not only does he reside in Ireland, but he also opened a few taverns in America, where his son—Ryley's dad—takes co-ownership of. Four generations of Ceallachains have kept their family business alive, and Ryley would be the fifth.

"Stop trying to act smart. We both know that alcohol killed most of your potential brain power. And that cockiness is going to cost you. There are two rules in humility. One: never try to act like more than what you are. Two: Never underestimate your challenger, under any means. You just might come to realize that they're stronger than you think."

There is a crowd around us now, waiting for the actual competition to begin, and in the crowd, rooting me on through her silent approval, is Mother.

"You got this Ryley! Chance winced at the slightest drop of schnapps." Storm looks at me and sees my face that reads, "Seriously, dude." "Sorry bud, but your drinking experience is limited. Usually, I have your back, but not in this event."

Looks like I'm going to have to show him that I'm not that easily beaten. It is true that I don't have a lot of experience, but out of all the times that I've drank, I have never gotten more than a buzz, and I once drank six shots of Sour Apple Pucker, followed by two shots of Tequila. I may make faces, but that's only because I can't handle the taste. My tolerance is on a different level. "Set them up."

Ryley starts it off with a shot of Scotch Whisky. "I took the liberty of bringing some alcohol from home. I should warn you. I don't play around when it comes to drinking."

I mime his first shot, making a face as the whisky touches my lips. "That's alright, I guess. We're just getting started." He takes another shot, and I follow along. After a couple more, he switches the drink to Armagnac, a drink I have not heard of until now. I am six shots into the game, and nothing.

His buzz happened about a shot glass ago. "Another!" He slides me a Rum. To me, the alcohol tastes like rubbing alcohol, if not worse, and the smell unto itself is somewhat intoxicating in the worst way. At this point, Ryley is struggling to stand. It's a good match, I'll give him that. We're tied at nine shots, but I feel he will only last another two, at the most. I, on the other hand, can go another five or six, maybe. Obviously, I can go more, but why risk the damage done to the liver, or heart? "Ok-ay, pal," he fights to speak through his mask of intoxication, "How ab-bout we, we level up? I got a mighty, f-f-fine bottle of Everclear in my sack over t-ther-e." He tries to point over his shoulder at the bag that is behind him.

Fuck that! Do you want me to die! "Dude. I think we should stop. I don't think you can handle any more."

"Ayy, wh-o's try-ying to-oo back out now?" His accent begins to grow thick. "I've sti-ll got fight in meh. I've a decent si-sized," his cheeks puff outward as he holds his fingers to his mouth, "Rectified Spear-ette."

"Are you kidding me? I'm not drinking Everclear or Rectified Spirit."

"Scared-d?"

"Test, man. If you can at least show me that you can stand for five seconds without violently shaking, I'll drink one last shot with you. If you can't even do that, then we're done. You should know when you've reached your limit on drinking, less you want to slumber in a wooden box." I would know. As of this moment, if I take another shot of anything above 15-percent alcohol, I'm going to die. Not in the drunken sense. The taste, back-to-back, of nasty rubbing alcohol, consistently violating my taste buds, is going to make me keel over.

"Looks like we have a winner!" Storm raises up my hand in victory.

Ryley just sits there, half-dozing off, then finally passes out. I grab him by the arm. Storm grabs the other. We drag him to a nice place away from the party so that he can sleep his drunk away. The next issue to face would be the following hangover. Good luck Ryley.

"Hey, Chance. It's been a while." Alycia—my ex-girlfriend— walks up to me in her blue denim jeans and matching crop top, with her arms folded nervously. I don't know if it's the alcohol, but something about her is glowing. Yeah, I'll blame it on the alcohol.

"Uh, hey. Listen. I'm sorry things between us didn't work out. I recognize my mistake. Are you still angry?"

"I, uh . . . I wouldn't say I was angry." She twirls her hair out of habit.

"The red hand print across my face probably told a different story, but okay."

"No, I mean. Yes, I was upset, but I don't think it was anger. Anyway, even though I find it difficult to forgive you, I still want to put it behind us. I just wanted to tell you, I found someone."

"Ohh? How nice." I just look her in the eyes and smile, wondering why she came up to me just to tell me that she's found someone. "And just who is this guy that you smile so brightly at the mere thought of?"

"Is it just me, or is that jealousy I sense from you?"

"Please. You and I both know I don't get jealous, especially since you're the one who falsely left me, because you were too impatient to wait for me."

She raises her hand to slap me, and I let her. "Are you calling me a whore!" This causes some eyes to land on us.

How could you possibly get "whore" out of that? "Hey, you said it, not me."

She raises her hand again, but this time, I grab her wrist. "Who do—" I place my hand over her mouth, telling her to keep it down. "Who do you think you are?" She spits through her teeth. "You're not this god you set yourself out to believe."

"I never said I was."

"Then stop acting like it. What gives you the right to call me a whore?"

"I told you, darling—"

— "Don't call me darling."

"I never called you such a thing, such as 'whore,' but when you look at the origin of our relationship—"

She slaps me once more. "You think you're all that. I got news for you. You're not as hot as you think you are."

"Really? Then, may I ask your reason for pursuing me. I mean, we've never talked, or even got to know each other. You didn't know me at all. So, let me ask you this. Why did you ask me out? . . . If you're going to tell me that you didn't fall for my looks, then you're fooling yourself."

"What if I say I fell for your money?"

I let go of her. "Then, I would say that you're a gold digger, which is, but a couple levels lower than a whore. I never said I was a god, because they don't exist, love. It's just us. I would say I have modesty for someone in my position. You think I'm jealous of you? I could have anyone I want. You forget. We're in high school. If you've got looks, as well as money, then the school yard is practically your oyster. Care to fight on that?"

"You speak so highly of your capabilities. Care to back them up?" She smiles smugly at me, figuring I've lost this little verbal battle.

"Gladly." I look around for a taker. "Ahh, perfect," I think to myself. I walk up to a couple girls that are lounging by the heated pool. One of them looks as if she's sun-bathing, in a white bra with matching shorts, cut high, and a pair of DG shades. The other is sitting by the edge, wearing her baby blue bikini bottoms and a tie-dye crop top. She is also wearing a pair of shades. Her hair is half way dyed a beautiful shade of pink. I walk up to them and start small talk. "So, how are you girls enjoying the party?"

The girl wearing the white bra looks at me and smiles. "It's alright, but it could be better."

"Really. How so?"

"If a beautiful, brown-haired, blue-eyed boy decided to sit with us and talk for a while, I might say this party was worth my coming."

"I like you. There's something about you that I can't place my finger on." I look over to the pink-haired girl who is still relaxing on the edge. "And who are you, if I may ask?" I extend a hand out to her but get nothing in return. I glance quickly at Alycia who is still watching me from a distance.

"You'll have to forgive her. She's shy."

"Really?" I sit on the edge with her and keep my distance. "Hey, I'm Chance. May I know your name?" Nothing. I look her up and down and try to get a feel for what she may like. Her pink hair matched with her tie-die crop top gives me an idea. "So, you like art?" She looks up for a quick second, then returns to hiding behind her bangs. "Yeah, I like art too. What's your favorite piece?" She taps her finger tips on the edge of the pool. "I like the *Discobolus*, *Massacre of the Innocents*, and of course, *The Creation of Adam*. Three different art styles, but beautiful all the same. I take you as a Renaissance girl. Don't know why, but to me, you seem like the type to appreciate true beauty."

"I like Brueghel." Her voice is quiet, soft, and beautiful.

"That's a good choice. Can I see your face, if you don't mind?" She shakes her head, no. I scoot closer to her, to where our shoulders are touching. She turns her head a little more as to avoid my eyes. "I would love . . ." I place a hand on her shoulder, opposite to the one closest to me. I touch her chin and gently turn her face. ". . . to see your eyes." Her friend sits there and watches us, amazed that I could make it this far, probably. Finally, the girl's face is in front of me, but her eyes are still in hiding. "You shouldn't try to hide yourself. Not with beauty like this." Her skin is beautiful and damn near flawless if not for the slight trail of freckles that lines the bridge of her nose. Her vanilla complexion makes her rosy lips that much more noticeable. Now, time for the reveal. I remove her bangs from her face, adjusting them to the side. "Why would you want to hide these? They're beautiful, just as you are? If I had eyes like these, I'd proudly display them." Sappy, I know, but it works for me. Her eyes are a light shade of gray, and conflict with the artificial resonance coming off her hair.

"But yours are." Her eyes widen at her own words and she quickly cowers away—that is, if I'd let her.

"What was that?"

"I'm sorry. I didn't mean to—"

I press a finger to her bottom lip. "It's fine. May you please repeat. I promise, I won't be appalled or whatever feeling you may think I'll show."

"It's just that you said, if you had eyes like these. You may not have my exact eyes, but yours are still beautiful. I think you're beautiful, err, handsome. Sorry."

I give a quiet laugh. "Nothing to be sorry about. You should open up more often. I love hearing your voice." Her lips form a smile and her face, a rosy hue. "I wish you could see how beautiful you are. You know, we don't see ourselves like everyone else does. Our beauty is dimmed." My eyes look down, then back at hers.

"Why do you keep looking down?"

"I'm sorry. I can't stop thinking about, how kissable you are."
Way to go. You blew it.

"Ohh." She turns away. "I don't know. I've never kissed anyone. You wouldn't be satisfied with mine."

Is that an offer I hear? "Is there anyone you like?"

This question catches her off-guard. "Um, yeah. There is. He's sweet. We've known each other for a few years. He is a bit more outgoing though. I don't know where to start."

"Start by talking to him. I've only known you about ten minutes, and I'm not disappointed. If he doesn't see you as I see you, then he isn't the same guy you're making me believe he is." Talking to her is fun and a little relaxing. Her friend continues to watch us without a word, as she "sun-bathes." I assume that's what she thinks she's doing, but given the time of year, the sun is nothing more than a visiting friend of the sky. In other words, she's just hoping someone will come along and pick her up. If not for the heated pool she has her toes submerged in, which in turns, warms the rest of her body, she'd probably be fully dressed.

"What if I do talk to him? It goes well, then we have our first kiss. He doesn't like the kiss, and he leaves me for someone who knows what she's doing."

"If it's kissing you're worried about, what if—and I'm just throwing this out there—I was your first kiss?"

"I couldn't have you do that for me."

I smile at the thought. "Believe me when I say that this wouldn't be just a favor to you. It's a selfish request, but I would actually love to kiss you. If it's also showing you how to properly do it, then it's a plus. But, if you don't, I also understand your sudden placement in all of this. Your first kiss is an important issue." I slowly rise, but her hand grabs my wrist.

"Wait. I want you to show me, but not here. Is there somewhere we could, you know, kiss in private?"

"Yeah. Care to go inside for a while? It seems to be the only place that isn't crawling with underage drinkers and partyers." I extend a hand, and she grabs it, hesitantly.

With her by my side, her friend calls out to us. "You kids have fun now. Show her a good time, Eye-Candy." I look back over my shoulder to see her eyeing me as we walk away. As for Alycia, she looks disgusted, and defeated.

Back in my bedroom, she sits on my bed. "You keep your bedroom rather clean for a boy."

"Uh, thanks. We have to do this quickly. I have a band playing soon."

"What if I can't learn that quickly?"

"Then, we'll have to schedule appointments." I laugh at my own joke. "I'm kidding. With the right training, you should learn the basics pretty fast. Some people have their own signatures when it comes to kissing, so there is no perfect kiss when you're trying to meet everyone's needs. Let's see just how much work you need. Remember, no one has to know about this. What happens in these walls is between us; however, if you choose to tell, I do not care either way."

I sit closer to her and start with one hand on her shoulder. We stare at each other's lips and slowly close the gap. It starts nice, but soon gets a little uncomfortable. I pull away. "Sorry. What did I do wrong?"

"Nothing too big. A quick fix. Don't use your teeth when kissing unless it's a playful bite of the bottom lip. *Hehe.* Just use your lips. Let's try again." With my one hand on her shoulder and the other on the back of her head, I lean in. Our lips touch and we fall into the kiss. It starts out a bit awkward, but she learns pretty fast. Before I know it, she slips some tongue in. My eyes widen for a short moment, but I grow to like it. *How unexpected for her to be the first to pull that move on me.* My hand lowers itself to her upper thigh, then moves to her lower back, right above her buttocks. My other hand supports her neck. I begin to lose myself in the kiss, as my hands are in the mood to explore. With the lack of clothing that she is wearing, it is not that difficult. I push her back on my bed, kissing deeper. I raise her leg and my hand slips into the first inch of the bottom part of her bikini.

She pushes my hand away. "I can't do this. Sorry."

I look at the state she's in, so beautiful, then realize the position I put her in. "Oh, I'm sorry. I was, you know, with the moment and all."

She adjusts her top so that the bottom part of her bra isn't showing. "No, no. Stop. It's fine, really. I should've said 'no' sooner. I guess a part of me was . . . curious, but I'm not that type of girl."

"I know. You're different."

"Is that why you chose me? . . . I mean, you could've chosen anyone. There were many options; yet, you choose me. I'm not outgoing, or flashy. I'm not showy, or even popular. I've seen you around school. I've seen the girls that eye you. I'm nothing like them."

"I know. I think that's why you stuck out to me. It is true . . . that you are nothing like my usual crowd, but is different really a bad thing? You are you, and I admire that. I know I haven't known you long enough to say much about who you are as a person, but what I do know is that you are beautiful, not just on the outside, but where it counts. That is a rarity to find."

"Well, we best be getting back to the party. You did say you were in a hurry. Did you not?"

I escort her back to the party going on outside. I hadn't realized the noise difference until I opened the door. "Hey . . ."

"Delilah."

"Delilah? That name is almost as beautiful as you are. If it is any confidence booster for your plan to move forward with your crush, I would have to say that kissing you was highly satisfying, if you couldn't tell by the possible outcome, had you not stopped me. You'll do just fine. I wish you luck."

She shows me a big cheek-to-cheek smile as she squeezes me and kisses me on the corner of my mouth. "Thanks. Umm, happy birthday, by the way."

She runs off and catches up with the friend that I pulled her away from earlier. They chat and giggle. Her blonde friend in the white bra is pointing at me, and that is followed by a shake of the head by Delilah. No doubt that Barbie doll is trying to get all the details, if only there were details juicy enough to satisfy the curiosity of a girl bent on provocative gossip.

"Dude, there you are!" Storm sneaks up behind me and places a firm hand on my shoulder. "We were looking everywhere for you, man. So, who was that girl you were with? Friend? Perhaps more? I mean, you weren't in your house for long, so nothing happened, right?"

I remember what I told Delilah about confidentiality in the bedroom. "Uh, a friend, kinda. We only just met."

"Oh, I see. So, you didn't, you know, do anything?"

"No, man. She's not like that. She's strong. She's got her heart set on someone. I just hope Highschool doesn't ruin her. It's got its way of destroying everything you stand for, and if it doesn't, the aftermath of graduation, and the realization that grades and the number of friends you make mean close to nothing in the outside world of false hope, will destroy what she's got left."

"Holy shit. I just asked a simple question. A yes or no would've sufficed."

"Hey, Chance!" A green haired man with a black goatee and the tree of life marking his skin, is standing on a stage with a microphone in hand. Behind him: a pale, blue-haired chick with a lip piercing and an axe guitar; a slightly older man with a full head of hair that easily hangs to his waist, a drum kit, and a secondary microphone; and a pasty chick with a crimson red, pixie cut and a Gretsch drum set spread out before her. "We doing this or what?"

I give him a thumbs up, which is his cue to start.

"Hello, everyone. What a pleasure to be performing for an old friend's special day. For those of you who don't know us, we are known as S.S.I.P. I wrote this song specifically for Chance and will be including it in our new album. I call this song, 'Beast in a Cage.' I hope you enjoy it."

I hear the drum sticks tapping against each other to get the rhythm going. A slow, but catchy beat gets the song started. The drums are interrupted by the plucking of guitar strings. The drums beat faster as Nick, with the mic in front of him, starts strumming. His eyes land on the person with the second mic as he nods his head, synchronizing their times.

"He sneaks up on us in our moments of . . ." The second vocalist starts it off with his deeper voice that fits the tone of the song. "G-g-g-giving in! You never give up! Never give up! Wahahah!" He growls into the mic.

Nick joins him. "I'm bein' eatin' alive, eatin' alive! By the monster inside, monster inside! I hear it screaming my name, begging escape. Yes, it's clawing its way, I'm writhing in pain. Too many voices, I'm going insane. Lost through the years, the beast cannot be tamed . . ."

The lyrics are catchy, and the instrumental is hypnotizing. I find myself losing focus, with the music being the only thing filling my ears. Suddenly, I hear something.

"Watch out!"

I turn around and am met with a mysterious outsider, one whom I can only assume was not on the list of invited guests. His appearance is shocking but what really catches my eye is the limp body being dragged in a streak of its own contents. "I'm going to have to ask you to leave," Uncle Cary steps out from the barbeque in which he is already on fifths while the intruder doesn't exactly look as if he is in the right mindset. Courageous as he may be, that doesn't stop him from getting tossed like a ragdoll to the other side of the party. "This has nothing to do with the likes of you. You're of insignificance to me." He turns to look at me, "You, on the other hand are just who I came to see."

"Father? Mother said you left. Did you get the cigarettes you scurried off for?" This is no time to mess around, but I'll just blame it on the alcohol.

"Even in the face of danger, you challenge my wit with these childish antics of a half-drunken sproutling." I'm taken aback by the man who has, without warning, rushed me. I feel a tug at my shirt and suddenly, I am lifted to face the man himself. His face is scarred—wounded, like he's been in multiple wars and yet, has only suffered minimal damage. A scruffy beard outlines his chin. It is a dark shade of brown—the ends, slowly being drained of their youth. His eyes are dark, almost with no color in them. The business he has with me? I wouldn't know. I have never met this man in my life; yet, here he is, lifting me by the shirt.

"Dude! What is your deal?"

He says nothing and just holds me in the air. I have never been one to back out of a fight; it was, after all, my way of establishing dominance. I am never the one to start a fight, and if the opportunity is given to me, I'll try to find another way; however, I will not hesitate to put an end to it if the path of violence is taken.

"Let him go!" Stormie steps up with Brandon a few feet behind him. "We don't take kindly to party crashers."

Brandon, standing within earshot of Storm, bluntly screams, "The fuck! You killed Kennith!" Kennith, being the poor, unfortunate soul who accompanied this madman, unwillingly, since dead men give no consent.

"Believe me." The man's voice is deep, husky, and worn out. "The party is the least of your problems. Let us be and no one else has to die."

"Over my dead body." Storm stands confidently, as Brandon backs up a bit.

"Dude, we should listen. I don't know about you, but I am pretty fond of the life I'm living. Wanna add any more wise cracks like, oh, I don't know, 'At least things can't get worse.'?"

I grab his wrists as he is still grabbing on to my shirt and use his sturdy body as a surface to stand on so that I could pry his fingers off me. Unfortunately, that does not work. He takes notice of this and tosses me into Storm, like the last standing pin in a bowling tournament. We both lay on the ground, breathing heavily, trying to regain the breath lost on impact. "I was given one job, quick and easy, but you've proven to be a hard one to kill."

"I don't even know who you are."

"I wouldn't expect you to remember. You've grown quite a bit from that little sack of flesh that cried on impulse."

"What! That's crazy. What is your reasoning behind this? I never did anything to you. I wasn't even old enough to pose any form of threat."

"Not yet. You've escaped fate once, but the funny thing about fate—it has its ways of working out in the end. I don't mind having your friends' fates happen early, if they so choose."

I force myself back on my feet, waiting for the last bits of oxygen to return to my lungs. "I don't respond well to threats. Would you really kill me in front of all these witnesses? You don't have the balls."

Brandon eyes me in a way of saying, "shut the fuck up."

"I could tell you a whole speech on the various torturous methods I could use on your friends, and how I would dispose of the bodies in ways that couldn't be dug up in any future, but in truth, I don't care about any of them or the surviving witnesses. I have my eyes on one thing, and that is making sure you die. What happens afterward is of no importance to me, so as long as I finish my job." He takes a step towards me. "If you give in, I promise I'll make it quite quick and painless, but if you fight it, I'll guarantee you this. You will live in seclusion, pinned to a wall, upside down by your hands and feet, in a place no one will ever think of looking. Just as you're about to lose consciousness, I'll make sure to keep you alive long enough to keep me satisfied. Your tongue, no more. Teeth? Who needs them? Will it be days or weeks, that the complete weight of the situation strikes you . . . Who knows? As long as you die in the end, I don't care how long you suffer. I'll take pleasure in it either way."

"MMM, kinky. If you weren't my strayed walk-out faughda, I'd consider this little foreplay, ah, but alas, I am but a wee boy living in a world that doesn't yet deserve me." I back up as he nears me. "Ah, but jokes aside, you are one sick and demented dude, you know that." I get pinned to a wall as his hands wrap around my neck.

"Don't I know it. I wasn't always like this. Now, show me what I want to see." His lips are inches from my ear.

"Really," I whisper. "Here, but, but the audience."

"Show me!"

"There are children present!" Storm stands in the background, with face in palm, while Brandon slowly begins to sneak off as in a way of saying, "Whelp, I tried."

"Beg for mercy. Don't be scared to add tears for extra effects."

I elbow him in the gut and as he arches over, I give him a good knee to the face, causing him to turn around. "I don't know your deal, and I don't plan on getting to know you long enough to find out. What I do know is that you're sick. You're far beyond psychiatric help, and too far gone to benefit from prison. I'd put you down myself, but murder is something that people with a moral compass wouldn't resort to."

"Hahahaha." He is on his knees, arched over, covering his mouth with his hand. "Moral compasses are just a way to suppress the beast that lives in us all. I've seen the changes. I've witnessed your so-called evolution, and I must say, what are you proving exactly? Darwin showed us how animals evolved to adapt and even what happened to those that failed to, but what of humans? You evolve differently, it may seem. Rather than changing physically, to adapt to the growing world around you, you suppress different parts of your psyche to appear more tamed. You're all just ticking time bombs. Walking lies!"

"What are you blabbering on about?"

He reaches behind himself and pulls out a weapon. It is a knife-like one with a long black hilt and a relatively short, red blade, curved like a banana, if not a little more so. It doesn't look like a weapon you'd use to simply stab someone, but one used for thrashing. It looks like a mix between a boomerang and a dagger, meant to torture and hook on to someone. He lashes out once at me, as I fall back. The blade misses me by a hair.

"Hey! Get away from him, Creed!" Storm is the only one that has the guts to step forward.

"I haven't an idea who this Creed fellow is, but I like the name. What are you going to do? I have the weapon. You have nothing."

One of the fellow teammates shouts out and tosses my football helmet that I forgot to bring in out of distraction. Storm catches it. "Since no one chooses to step forward, guess I'll have to do," he whispers to himself. He puts the helmet on and adjusts himself into a running stance. He charges towards us. I hit the ground hard as the intruder readies the opponent, crossing his arms together. Stormie headbutts him, causing the psychopath to barely budge. He throws out his elbow, causing Storm to fall in the direction the elbow is facing. Before my friend has a chance to hit the floor, he gets pulled back by the collar of his shirt and thrown into the opposite direction. "What? How did—"

"Hahaha. Nice try, kid, but you still failed miserably. Ahh, I love it when confidence is overruled by the crushing weight of reality's limitations."

This guy is insane. He takes joy in suffering and only sees the bad in humanity. What is his deal? He reaches for me, but I swat his hand away. I slide underneath him, kicking him in the back. He stumbles forward. "You're an odd one. Simply off your rocker. You speak as if you've got no weaknesses, but you do. Everything does, no matter how powerful you think you are." I swing my leg underneath his feet. I roll out of the way as he falls in my direction. Quickly, I get up, but he grabs my leg and pulls me towards him. I position myself so that I don't shuffle on my feet as much, but his pull is too strong.

"You will not best me, child. I have traveled too far to be defeated that easily. To think you have that power is a complete mockery unto itself." He reaches up and grabs my collar again, pulling me in so that I am face to face with him. His breath, repulsive as it is, clouds my nostrils, filling me with the sudden urge to tear up. The taste of last night's dinner gets pushed back down my throat as it so violently tries to let itself out. "What's the matter, boy. Scared?"

I shake my head, not wanting to inhale the fumes leaving his mouth. I reach for his face as he holds me out further. My hands, stretched out as far as they can go, press into his face, my thumbs, trying to dig into his sockets. His grasp on my throat tightens, which is a minor relief, given the circumstances. Everything starts to go black, until it doesn't. I hit the ground, catching myself with my hands. Due to my weakness, as I'm trying to regain my consciousness, I am not strong enough to fully catch my own weight, so I end up falling onto my arms, faceplanting the ground. I roll over to see "Creed"— as Storm called him—bent over, wiping the blood from his forehead. Behind him is Mother, holding a shovel in her hands. On one corner of the shovel are tiny specks of red, splattered along it.

"Don't you dare hurt him." She speaks calmly for the most part, with a slight accent of anger mixed in.

He turns to face her, then smiles. "My, my. You haven't changed much, have you?"

"I don't know you. You have mistaken me for another."

"You don't remember me? Makes sense. I was different back then. A little taller. More defined. Not nearly as many scars as I am displaying at the moment. I have worn many faces over the years."

"I don't care how many aliases you have used. I think I would've remembered seeing your face, with or without the slight disfiguration."

He chuckles. He slowly makes his way towards her. She positions a stance, with the shovel out and ready to attack. Quietly, while looking at her, he makes out a sentence. "It doesn't matter how far you go; I will find you." He stresses every syllable in a song-like manner, emphasizing the word, "you." Her eyes widen, then return to her usual glare. "I always get what I want, dearie."

He charges her, then gets hit upside the head. He spins around, falling onto his knees. Quickly, he gets up, but as he turns to face her again, his face meets the brute force of the shovel. He gets hit with it a couple times more before he gets the chance to get up. He reaches for her and grabs her leg. This is an action that Mother responds to quite quickly with a boot to the face. "Creed" spits out blood. He is arched over on all fours, like a dog, but still keeps that smile. "You made a mistake coming back here. You would've done yourself a great service not telling me your identity."

"Haha. I missed this. I have killed a lot in my day, but you were the first to hide from me as long as you have. Bravo, if I may say. Judging by the way you had to step in to this little brawl, I would have to assume he doesn't know."

"Shut up." She kicks him again in the face.

"I must say, I do love myself a little rough play. One way or another, he'll be mine to slay. Life is a game. It always comes to an end."

"Not by you." Mother strikes down with the shovel, receiving a slight sound of pain from the recipient. Everyone looks away as she does what she does. I watch as the shovel buries itself into his hand. A sprinkler of blood spurts out as Creed raises his hand to his chest, but something is missing. Spread out on the floor in a puddle of their own blood are four fingers, all except the thumb.

"You bitch!" Creed then takes back his words almost as instantly as he gives them, but not from Mother. "I am sorry, Father. I didn't mean it. Please forgive my sudden outburst. You have taught me better." He is arched down at Mother's feet. She does nothing. "Please, miss. Have mercy on me." He reaches out with his unmutilated hand, towards the hem of her shirt. She turns the shovel around and jams the butt of it into his face. He grabs it with haste and pulls it down, using it as a crutch to lift himself up. Mother struggles to take it from him. Still holding onto the butt of the shovel's stick, he swings his other forearm up, breaking the shovel into two. Creed throws the fragment to the side. "Haha, think you have won? A hand is nothing in the grand scheme of things."

Mother drops the shovel head, then punches him in the face. She doesn't stop there. Creed stands still, taking the punches without once trying to defend himself. Even with a broken nose, he does nothing. "You will not have him."

"It's up to the universe to decide that. I am still here, hehe. I am still living. As long as I am here breathing, the more you can assure the boy is in danger."

Sirens are heard from the other side of my house. "Looks like your game is over, Creed."

"That is not my name, and you think a few pesky law enforcers are enough to restrain me."

"They are for most criminals. I don't see you as any different."

"Witnessing your death will be the highlight of my existence."

"Freeze! Everyone! Stay put!" Officers invade my party as they surround the man who has both arms up and a smug grin spread out on his face.

"Greetings, officers. I assume you're here for me."

One of them points at his obvious injury. "What happened here?"

"Oh, this?" He gestures toward his lack of fingers. "Pretty, is it not? I find red to be the most majestic of colors. Crimson to be more precise."

"Quiet, you!" The officer forces Creed's arms behind his back while his wrists get cuffed. "Bandage him up, then put him in the back of the car. I don't want blood in the backseat."

"Right away, sir." The other officer, most likely in training, takes him away, but this does not shut Creed up.

"As long as I don't fight back, they can't kill me and as long as I am living, I have a way back here. Don't get too cozy kid, hehe. I'll be back before you have a chance to settle into your new h-."

The trainee officer silences him while dragging him away.

"Are you okay?" Mother embraces me in a hug, but honestly, I'm alright. This turn of events, strange and nerve-rattling as they may have seemed in the moment, has done nothing to put me on edge, not publicly at least. My outer appearance, for the most part is unfazed, but my mind is racing. Not really fear as much as confusion.

Confusion as to who that was and what his connection is to Mother and me.

"Uhh, yeah. I'm fine. Nothing broken."

"Hey. You the one who called us?" The officer with the nametag, Relic, walks up to us.

"That was me!" One of the party guests shouts out from her location. She runs up to us.

"You called us? Can you point me in the direction of the supervisor of this, party? Or am I to assume these kids are unsupervised?" He looks down at his feet and kicks a bottle.

"I am the owner of this house." Mother steps in.

"I have a few questions about what just happened. That, and the fact that there are numerous varieties of alcohol bottles scattered along the ground of an underage party, but I bet you knew that, didn't you, miss? Come with me, if you would so kindly. I'd hate for this to be in front of your son, which I assume this party is for, or your daughter."

"Yes, officer." Mother turns to me. "Don't worry, dear. We're just going to talk."

"You might want to tell your party guests to leave. This might end with someone else getting a ride from us, if you get the gist," Officer Relic says.

"Don't, Chance. Nothing is going to happen to me."

"The surplus of alcoholic beverages and obviously intoxicated teens might state otherwise. Please don't make this difficult. You know the reality of your predicament. Call the boy a family member or something. High stakes on you going away."

They disappear into the house, leaving me surrounded by the party guests.

"Hey, bud. Everything alright?" Storm pats me on the back.

"Yeah. Why wouldn't it?"

He looks away nervously. "Well, other than the reality that you nearly died by a mysterious and assumingly uninvited guest, then there was your mom cutting that guy's fingers off in front of you.

Now she's inside retelling what went on to that cop. No doubt the cop had to see a few bottles of alcohol on his way in and out of this party, so she's probably . . ."

"Okay, man. I get it. I don't need a recap. If I say I'm fine, then I am. What would I get out of lying?"

"A false reputation that you're completely numb to pain of yourself and of everyone around you, when in reality, you, yourself, are suffering internally for as long as you so choose to keep it secret."

"I get why you think that. I'm grateful to have a friend that cares—"

"I will always be there—" he interrupts.

"—But I am fine. Mother says she's fine, and that's good enough for me. The bad guy is gone. And on the plus side, I think the quarrel sobered me up a bit." *Not that I was at all drunk.*

"He said he'll be—"

"—The bad guy is gone," I repeat, "so let's just move on." I remove his hand from my shoulder and walk into the crowd to be welcomed by a bunch of claps and sympathetic notions.

"I'm sorry this had to happen to you."

"Are you okay?"

"Do you want comfort?"

I'm grateful, I really am, that so many people care. What I really want is to move on and put this whole thing behind me. By tomorrow, this whole thing will be a fading memory. I wave over to Nick who notices my arm. "Hey, Nick. Would you mind if you could play us another song?"

"Are you s—"

"Yes, I am."

He nods as his band sets up the stage to continue where they left off. The party continues to an awkward start, but pretty soon, it feels a bit more like a party, than a pity party. No one questions me of my mental state or if I really think things will go back to the way they were. Okay by me.

"Hey, Chance." A blonde beauty, familiar in her white bikini, walks up to me. "So, my, uh, friend said that you guys kissed?"

I smile at the change of pace. "Yes."

"She denies that you two did anything more than that, and being the playboy that you are, I'd figure you'd give me the answer I am looking for."

"I know who you're talking about. We did kiss. It was more of a lesson, really. We didn't go any further than that, I assure you. She is still the innocent girl I went into the house with."

"Oh. So, you really did nothing?"

I rub the back of my head. "Well, uhh, there was a point where the lesson escalated. It was all me, though."

"What happened?" She has a smile on her face like she is genuinely fascinated to hear the details, not that there are any.

I tell her the whole thing. She just nods her head. "Well, if it was me, I'd let you go all the way, if you get what I'm putting down."

I smile at her. "How could I not?" I wrap my arm around her as she closes in on me. My face is a mere inch over hers as her chest presses up against mine.

"You're so strong to handle that situation the way you did. You barely reacted at all, even in the face of death."

I put my finger to her lip. "Shh, I'd really love to leave that chapter and get to the one that starts with me removing what little clothes you have on." I nip at the lobe of her ear as she giggles.

"Not here, in front of everyone."

"Then, by all means, lead the way."

She leads me to the side of the house that isn't occupied by party guests. She wastes no time as she tugs at the waistband of my jeans, watching as they fall to my ankles.

"Are you sure? Someone could walk into this."

"That only makes it more fun. You still game?" she eyeballs me, already knowing the answer by my obvious approval. I respond by lifting her up and gently placing her on the ground beneath me, not caring about the open space and the ticklish feeling of the grass beneath us. "Ooh, I love how gentle you are with me. Let's hope you're not like that in a few minutes." She leans in, grabbing onto my back and latching onto my waist with her legs, then she trails her tongue along the outer edge of my transverse lobe. She whispers into my ear, telling me exactly what she wants me to do to her. It is almost too much for me to bear. I practically tear off her outfit, lifting her legs above my head. Forty-five minutes or so pass by and we're lying next to each other. "That was heavenly, or might I say, earth-quaking."

"Yeah, I know. But, you know, you could be a tad quieter. Had it not been for the party going on or my hand muffling your screams, we would have been found out."

"And would that be so bad? I wouldn't mind." She tugs on my bottom lip with force. She holds an arm over her chest, looking down at her destroyed bra. "You could have gone easy with that, you know. I liked that bra, and I can't go out like this."

I look to the side and toss her my shirt. "You can have this, if you want."

"Thanks." The shirt looks a bit big on her as it overlaps her shorts by a good inch. "I'll return it, later."

"No need. Have it. I've got other shirts. Count that as an apology for practically destroying your, you know."

She punches me in the arm and scoots closer, resting her chin on my shoulder. "You didn't 'practically' destroy anything. You unquestionably destroyed it. Look at this." She picks up the bra and makes it a point to show me what I have done. "Seriously. Who tears a bra off a woman?"

"I got lost in the moment. I'm sorry. How may I repay you for my misdeed?" I trail my tongue lightly along her neck, enjoying her shutter at the mere contact.

"Down, boy. I'll forgive you this once, but if you ever do something like destroy my favorite thong or something, I will kill you. You hear me?"

"Loud and clear. You know, you make threatening words sound sexy. I almost want to see just what you'd do if I destroyed anything else. Care to find out?"

Her eyes dart down, then back at my eyes. "Again?" Her hand grasps onto my thigh as she straddles me, breathing along my neck. Her lip tickles my lobe as she whispers into it. "Nope. You'll just have to imagine it, big boy."

"Oooh, ooh. You are the devil."

"Sorry, not sorry, but the factory is closed at the moment. Besides, you've got somewhere else to be. Isn't there a festivity that requires your presence? . . . Maybe one for the go." She plants a gentle kiss, then helps me up, patting off her sides.

"My shirt looks good on you. Leaves a lot to the imagination, really. It's as if you've got nothing on underneath."

"Mind out of the gutter, boy. Honestly. I've never met someone ready to go, seconds after spending his load."

"I'm a special cause, what can I say?"

"Special, yes." She smirks, pushing me back with a hand. "I'm sorry, but your friend there," she eyes the certain part of me that is ready for seconds, "is going to have to go without. Now, we should get going."

"If she orders, then I shall obey. Keep those words in mind."

"Honestly. Boys."

We get back to the party. Just when I think no one noticed my absence, Storm walks up to us. "Hey man, where were . . ." He takes notice of my shirtless state and the blonde beauty standing near me, wearing it. "I see you have company. Hey." He holds out a hand to her and she takes it. "I'm Storm. I see you two have . . . bonded."

I rub the back of my neck as the blonde pats down her sides. "Hey, bud. You said you were looking for me?"

"Yeah, but I can see you were preoccupied. I hope you had fun."

"Oh, look at that. I think I see Lily waving at me. Bye, Chance. See you around." She giggles as she runs off into the crowd, not before turning back to say one last thing, "By the way, I'm Shay. See you around, Eye-Candy, oh, and remember what I said about restraint."

"So, how was your, eherm, company?" Storm nudges me on the side.

"Sorry man, I don't do and tell."

"What. Are you kidding me? You always tell me about these things."

"I'll tell you later, man."

The party finally ends, and my yard is a mess. The downfall of a big party at your own house is the cleanup, afterwards. Luckily, some people picked up on their way out. That still leaves a lot of alcohol bottles just laying around. By the pool, there seems to be a stray bra hanging halfway off the side. Storm stays behind and helps with the cleanup. "Dude, that was a nice party. How does it feel, being sixteen?"

"No different than yesterday, when I was fifteen. Haha. Well, I'll see you around man."

"Right, see you tomorrow at school, if you choose to go, that is."

I make my way back to the house and close the glass door behind me. "Mother!"

"Yes, dear."

I walk upstairs and into her bedroom where she is sitting on her bed. "So, I take it the talk with the officer went well. I mean, you're still here, so . . ."

"Yeah. There was nothing to worry about. I just told him what I witnessed. Of course, I had to tell him about the fingers that I, um, butchered, but he wrote it off as self-defense."

"What about the alcohol?"

"He looked it over. I told him it was your sixteenth birthday and that this was your first drinking experience."

"But it wasn't—"

"Anyway, he understood and let it go. As long as we don't tell, he won't. Wild party, huh?"

"Yeah. About that. Who was that guy? He seemed to know you quite well, and from your expression, you knew him."

"I barely know him."

"From the sound of it, it's almost as if he tried killing you before."

"He did. Look, when you were younger, a baby to be more precise, a crazed criminal wanted for the cannibalism of babies escaped a facility. You were his third victim to be chosen after he escaped that prison. He snuck into our house one night while we were asleep. Luckily, he wasn't as quiet as he thought. I woke up to the sound of footsteps. At first, I thought it was nothing, but then I heard your crying. I rushed to your crib to see a man perched over you, drooling like he was eyeing a juicy slice of steak. I fought him off. He didn't get you, thank the gods, but he also got away. After that, we moved. At around five, he found us. That was our que to move again. That's when we moved here. We've been safe, but now, he's found us again. You were the first baby that got away from him. That might explain why he's so devoted to you. He's trying to finish a job."

"He was trying to kill you, though. He said he's never had a challenger like you, or something."

"Of course, he was trying to kill me. I'm the only thing that's ever been in the way of him getting to you."

"But, I'm not a baby anymore."

"It doesn't matter. You may not be a baby anymore, but he still sees you as the one that got away from him . . . I thought here would be safe, but I thought wrong. We'll have to move again, it seems."

"No."

"Chance. He knows where you live, which means that he'll try again."

"Wherever we go, he'll find us. I've made a life here. I have friends. I'm popular. I don't know a lot about my past, which bothers me . . ." Mother fidgets at those words. ", but I'd like to keep the life I have. If he comes back, we'll finish him. He's got a broken hand.

That means he's weaker than the man we witnessed today. He's no match for us."

"That may be, but—"

"We're staying put. Please. I've never really asked for anything, but I don't want to leave."

She huffs, rubbing her arm. "Okay. If you want to stay, then we will."

"I do. Thanks . . . So, you really don't know him, know him?" I ask.

"No. Other than his intentions, I know nothing." She looks away, averting eye contact.

"Oh, okay. That's too bad. Well, I'm going out. Don't wait up."

"Wait. I do know one thing about him. The person you call Creed. Though the reference isn't completely wrong, it's not right either. His name . . . is Artemis."

II

There are many unanswered questions that float around in my mind. It's been quite a few hours since the party, when I nearly died had Mother not stepped in. I've got to say, though, it's just the energy boost I needed. To be face to face with Death was interesting to say the least. To think that a day dedicated to my birth would also be the day that marked my demise. It's a bit messed up. I still feel as if Mother is keeping secrets from me, despite what she tells me. There must be a reason behind these secrets, or perhaps, I'm looking too far into this, and they're really just secrets and nothing more. Everyone has them, and that's totally okay. I just feel that they shouldn't be kept if their main focus is on me. Anyways, I'm just laying on my bed, a lot on my mind. My party definitely won't be a forgotten one. That's for damn sure. People almost died, well, not the party guests, but my mother, my friends, and most importantly, me. I—

"Honey!" The voice comes from downstairs.

"Yeah?" No response. "Yeah?" Again, I receive no response. Damn it. I get up, not wanting to. I just want to sleep, or at least, lose myself in thought until I pass out. I walk myself downstairs to be welcomed by Mother, along with my visiting family.

"Sit."

I do as I'm told, unknowing of what's to follow. "What is this?" I question.

"I know that today may have been difficult and that you have many questions—questions that, in due time, I'll be more than happy to share." Mother meets the glance of my uncle's disapproving stare. The others just stand, not interrupting, yet still looking like they know something I do not. "Trust me. Time is an ally, patience the key." She hands me a small box addressed to my name—a late birthday gift.

"What's this? You didn't have to get me anything." I say, knowing damn well that I could afford anything I set out to buy.

"It's not from us. It's from an old friend. Just take it."

I recognize the signature that has been inscribed into the wood. *Merida Hacket.*

The name brings back memories. A woman whose sole fascination lies on science and technological enhancement. She is, or was a good friend, indeed. She was mostly isolated from the world. The only time she ever left her home was when she needed groceries or some necessity for her inventions. Most of the time, she'd just have it shipped to her. I'd visit her a lot and that always cheered her up. She was extremely pale skinned, a result from not getting the amount of sun she needed. She was a beautiful woman, 33, with curly hair of Irish descent. Freckles lined the bridge of her nose. She was of average height, maybe an inch short of it. Her eyes reflected her heritage, as did her accent. Her home was nearly always filled with the scent of cherry blossom, an aroma I will never forget. For someone who never left her home, she kept the place rather tidy and upheld for visitors. She spent most of her time in the basement, working on projects. Whenever I visited, she changed mode. She relaxed more. We'd sit and talk for hours, usually drinking black tea. I didn't mind. I was never one to drink soda anyhow. The tea was usually spiced up a bit with pumpkin. She loved to hear how I was doing and I, her. We'd exchange stories. Though, older, she and I were good friends. I shared more with her than I did with anyone else. This included my feelings and my thoughts. Storm is a good friend, my best friend, but Merida, she was the only one that I completely turned to when I felt like breaking down. I don't know how, but she completely calmed me when I was younger. I don't know when, but I started to confide in her. She acted as both, a friend, and a therapist. It's almost as if she didn't even have to talk. I just released all my problems and I felt better. I admired her, but last year, something happened. A fire broke out in her lab. She died of scarring and third-degree burns. She died doing what she loved, experimenting. There was a time when I was weak. That was before I met her, of course. Death was always my weak point. The mention of it, even the thought of it happening to someone I loved, was upsetting. I'd break down in tears before I knew it, but my time with Merida helped me grow strong. Now, though Death is still an upsetting matter in my mind, I no longer cry. Well, obviously I cry, but not as often as I used to. To most, Death is an inconvenience, but to me, she's a nuisance. She seems to follow me. I've witnessed too much for her to faze me much longer. Now, someone can die in front of me, but I won't break down like I used to. I've forgotten what it feels like to mourn a loved one's death. I don't know if I miss the feeling of mourning someone or if it's a burden off my shoulders. The memories of Merida stick with me, and they always will.

"A . . . necklace?"

Mother looks over the gift, almost seeming to be surprised by it. "The medallion. I almost forgot I gave this to her." Again, disapproving looks from the family.

"So, this was a gift to her?"

"No. Not really. I lent it to her as a form of, safe keeping. I'm terrible with misplacement. I figured she was a safer location than my own company."

"Why? What's so important about it?"

Her look shifts. "Well, this specific medallion belonged to . . . your father. Before his, untimely death, he told me that, one day, he'd want his child to have it. I only wish, he were given the chance to see who you turned into. He'd be proud, as am I."

Later, when we're finished with our family festivities and games, I get tired. I realize it's probably time that I hit the sack. I reach my room and jump straight into my bed, exhausted. I pull out the medallion and take a look at it. It looks old, but in good condition. A newly refurbished relic of sorts. I place it on my nightstand, having more questions. *She never talks about Father. I've never heard of this medallion 'til now, but that's probably because she forgot. Come to think of it, there aren't many keepsakes that belonged to him in this house, if there are any. An old picture. That's about it.*

I nearly close my eyes when I notice something odd. I walk to my window and stare at the moon. *That's strange.* The sky is lit with the unnatural lighting of the moon. "This looks familiar." The sky is affected by the blood virus. It's beautiful. The wind is roaring, and the trees look as if they're moments away from being uprooted from the ground. The rain is angry and hyper as it constantly falls, drowning its victims, and bouncing off each targeted surface. Suddenly, like a search light, the moon focuses on me. I run downstairs right away. "Mother."

"I thought you went to sleep."

"I was about to, when, well, that." I point towards the window at the moon that pinpointed me moments ago.

Mother looks up at the moon but doesn't respond how I'd hoped. "What? The moon?"

"What?" I walk to the window. The moon is no longer red, nor is the sky. "No, the moon. It wasn't like this. You had to see it. At least a glimpse."

"Hun, what are you talking about?"

"The moon and the sky. They were red. The moonlight hit my bedroom. Out of all the possible targets, it singled me out. I've never seen such natural beauty in a night sky. You should've seen it."

"But I didn't. Are you sure you saw what you claim you saw? You are tired, after all."

"Well, I- it was there, looking down on me. I'm certain . . ."

"Get some sleep. It's good for a boy your age. We see things when we're sleep deprived."

"I understand. Yeah, sleep might do me well." I could have sworn I saw what I saw, but the possibility of sleep deprivation could have been there, too.

"Of course, it will." Mother pats my back as she leads me to the stairs. "Just get some sleep, and when you wake up, there will be a big breakfast before school." She still babies me a lot, but I don't mind it a bit. She allows me to make my own choices and leave when I please, but at the same time, holds a motherly grasp on me, like kisses on the cheek, or a big breakfast.

Halfway up the stairs, I hear a voice whisper, "Soon", in my ear. "What?" I quickly turn around just as Mother has her back turned.

"What, Hun?" Her head is turned so that her ear is facing me.

"Never mind. I thought I heard you say something. I must be more tired than I thought, hehe." I rub my eyes and start heading back up the steps. "Love you."

I flop down on my bed and close my eyes. Finally. Peace and quiet. The warm and welcoming embrace of my bed puts me in a sudden state of comfort. Before I know it, everything slowly drifts away, and I stumble into rest.

"Come to me." The voice is quiet. It echoes in my ears as if I'm in a small cramped box with just enough space for the words to bounce around me. "Awaken." My eyes open so suddenly to the darkness that engulfs my room. I reach for my phone and swipe it open. A bright, blue light blinds me as I force my eyes half shut, still trying to view the screen through the blinding light. I can't take it. One can't just jump from the darkness into the light, expecting their eyes to adjust within the split second they were given before being forced shut. Small steps are to be taken. I sit up in my bed, not without being possessed by the automatic urge to yawn. I walk over to the wall where my light switch is located and flip it on. I blink my eyes a few times to get used to the change in lighting. I take a glance at my home screen for the time. 1:23 a.m. Are you kidding me? Why am I even awake? I hardly had enough time to consider it a baby nap. My ears pick something up, but what? I focus in to test if I'm just hearing things or if I can get a direction as to where it's coming from. Nope. I definitely hear talking. It's quiet enough to where I can't hear the exact words, but I can indeed hear noises, and they're coming from downstairs. I quietly pry my door open and sneak to the end of the stairs. The talking gets louder as I near the source. I stop where the wall turns and listen in to what's being said around the corner, in the living room.

"Don't be stupid!" A female's voice is heard. It's quiet, with a little kick to it, like a loud whisper.

"Shh, not so loud."

"You're running out of time, Deanna. He has to know."

"Yeah. You have a code to follow. We all knew the day was coming."

"It's officially the beginning of the end." Uncle Carry sits with one leg over the other, while drinking a cup of what I assume to be tea. "You must tell him. By not doing so, you risk everything."

"Yes, yes. I understand." Mother's voice is heard.

"No, Deanna. I don't think you do, for if you did, you'd have told him already."

"You've always been the weakest, the most emotionally involved. We have obligations, as do you, but you, unlike us, feel the need to get attached. You think you're protecting him?"

"I know what I am doing, sister."

"I don't think you do, sis-ter. You're selfish. He is the answer. To everything. And you're sheltering him. For what?"

"He is, but a child."

"For how long. Keep this secret from him much longer, and he won't even be able to enjoy adulthood. There are two options that come out of this, sister. One, tell him. He'll either win and live long enough to enjoy the rest of his life, or he'll die along with the rest of us. At least we have a chance, as small as it may be. Two, don't tell him. We'll all be dead anyhow. Go out a hero or go out without so much as a drop of effort."

"Karen's right. He is the key to our destruction or to our salvation. Two choices, fifty-fifty. Flip a coin, we die. Land on the other side, we actually get to have a future. Telling him squat is like having a coin with two tails. We die either way, no chances."

"And just when were you going to tell us you gave away the medallion? We entrusted you with it."

I back up, accidentally tapping the wall with my knuckle. They stop talking suddenly. I hear Mother get up from the couch. I backtrack up the stairs in which I came, to my bedroom. I hear her come up the steps, which puts me in a tight spot. I quickly crawl back into bed and face the wall away from my door. My door creaks as her footsteps tap their way to my bedside. My bed lowers as her weight is placed upon it. I feel her hand run through my hair in slow movements.

"My sweet boy. Eavesdropping is impolite."

I turn over to face her. "You knew I was there?"

"The whole time. I know you. What are you doing up at this hour?"

"Something woke me up, a voice," I say, looking into her eyes.

She pulls me into a hug. "Don't worry about what you heard. It's nothing serious."

"But what—"

"Shh. All will be answered in time, but for now, don't worry. I don't want you to forget about this. By tomorrow, you'll think this as nothing more than a dream."

"What do you mean?"

She suddenly blows into my eyes. My body drops to the point of immobility. I try to keep my eyes open but can't. She plants a gentle kiss on my cheek and pets my hair until I finally fall unconscious.

I feel the warmth around me and the half cold-half hot atmosphere that comes from having one leg in the blanket and the other one out.

"Soon."

"What?" I question half asleep, so my words are more of a mumble than anything.

"Despair." I spring up, catching my heart as it nearly beats out of my chest. I'm going mad. The voices. Is this what Schizophrenia is like? Do I have it? What other answer is there to me hearing voices that aren't there? I hop out of bed and head to the shower. The hot water bounces off my shoulders as I contemplate whether to just fall asleep standing up with the lukewarm water licking my skin.

"Choose me."

I turn around swiftly, nearly falling on my ass. This was a woman's voice.

"The time is near, my love."

"Hello?" I ask. "Ocupado. Who is it?"

"You'll find the strength to strive . . . you'll find your answer in the girl with purple eyes."

"Really." I bang on my head lightly, trying to knock the voice out of my head. Suddenly, I hear a humming noise, a melody. There is familiarity in its rhythm. I have heard this somewhere, but to where, I haven't a clue. I get a chill down my spine and shake it off. I turn off the hot water and grab the towel that hangs over the shower. I get out to a steamy mist that fills the bathroom. I raise my hand to wipe the steam off the bathroom mirror, but some of it is already wiped off. Written in the fogged mirror are the words, "Together Forever-M&M." I smear my hand across the mirror and investigate it, but I do not expect what I see. I stumble back as my reflection smiles back at me. My mirror image looks normal enough, if not for the gaping hole that is placed where one of the eyes should be. I rub my eyes and look back. I'm back to having two of them. I guess it's true what they say—sleep is important.

I jump into the day's clothes, ready to tackle it. I head to the kitchen to be welcomed with a satisfying looking spread of breakfast items. "You really outdid yourself."

"When do I not?"

"You got me there. You really do spoil me."

"You're a growing boy, I mean, if I don't feed you, how exactly will you eat?"

"I could cook."

"I have literally never seen you cook anything in my life. You can't live off noodles and mac, alone. Besides, I like cooking. The least I could do is nurture my loving son properly, so he can grow big and strong, ready to tackle anything the world has to throw at him." I place the dishes in the sink and start the water for them when Mother steps in. "It's fine. I'll get the dishes. Go. You have school to get to. Heaven knows what a rarity your attendance is, hehe."

I walk down the street, about three blocks from my home when Storm runs to my side, "Hey, man." We exchange our usual friend-to-friend fist bump, which usually consists of bumping fists going up, then down, then finalizing it with knuckle contact in the middle.

We usually sit in the back of the bus with the rest of the obnoxiously loud students. They usually throw things back and forth to each other. Of course, the bus driver doesn't do much. He drives us to school. As for getting involved, well, he doesn't. He just drives with one headphone in while we get the usual bus music station. With the activities that happen in the back, the music becomes nearly absent. So much goes on back here. There's enough that goes on up front, but back here, we're kind of hidden from the mirror up front that looks back at us. One time, a couple was getting it on back here. I don't think anything happened. That'd be crazy. I'm not saying they didn't, either. The girls text like crazy with the exception of some guys. Don't think it stereotypical to say. It's the hard truth that goes on, at least in my school. Some try to read, but, as you'd expect, they get motion sickness, and dizziness.

"Hey, Chance?" Becca, a smaller blonde with a red bow in her hair and perky breasts, is sitting in the seat opposite the one in front of me. "That was a pretty cool party, huh? Well, until that, incident. No one got hurt anyway, I mean . . . Did you enjoy it?"

"I did. You don't have to be shy or whatever. Whatever happened, happened. How about you?"

"I did, well, I just sat by the edge of the pool. It was fun, though."

"You didn't hang out with anyone? You could've found me."

"And just what do you think we would've done?"

"Whatever you could've thought of. We could have talked. Walked around. Played around. If you wanted, I mean."

Her face turns a light shade of pink, a good look for her. "Now you're just flirting. I know your reputation."

I lean forward. She does the same, well backwards anyway, relative to where I am to her. Our faces are a few inches from each other. "That may be true, but a reputation is just a reputation. I would have loved to get to know you. Question. Tan lines or no tan lines?"

"What?"

"Would you say your chest is whiter than the rest of you, or . . ." I smile at her. She just covers her mouth, trying to hide the sudden color change in her body, not just her face. Flirting with experienced women is one thing, but there is nothing I love more than the reaction I get from a sexually oblivious one.

A girl suddenly sits in the seat across from mine—Jessyka Sylva. She's trouble, but I can't help myself. She's probably 5'7, blonde, and can be a total bitch to anyone but me, of course. "Hey, Chance. I heard about the party."

"Really, how?"

"Kidding me? That video is all over the tube. 345 views already. Not even twenty-four hours in."

"Nothing I couldn't handle, or Mother, for that matter."

"So, any luck?" She shows me a devilish grin. "You know, with the ladies. A few of my friends were walking when they found you and someone ransacking it on the cold ground. They didn't interrupt of course, which is why you don't know. They did sneak in a pic though. I can't see a face, but I gotta say. She really does look good from the backside."

"So, what? Blackmail. Is that what this is?"

"Heavens, no. That would up your reputation. This is for me." She rests a hand on my thigh and rubs. If you want to watch, you can come over sometime."

"Don't you have a—" I'm suddenly interrupted by an annoyingly recognizable voice.

"Hey, retard. You blind?" This voice, I know. Ashton Hunter, former friend, turned dick. Well, he's always been kind of a dick, but not to me until we went our separate ways. He has extreme anger issues. His jealousy, though he can't see it, is also a flaw in his creation. He was on the football team but got kicked off for aggressive reasons. "First, you take my place on the team, then try to slide into home base with my girl. How braindead are you?"

"Dude, Ashton. Chill. I was just . . ."

"Now stop right there. I'm not going to have your white ass telling me what to do."

"Hey, now. Don't bring my ass into this. It's not that white, is it?" I try to find light in dark situations. Usually, these jokes don't receive a laugh from the one who's verbally or physically attacking me.

Junior High had good memories. Ash and I were friends then, along with Storm and Sam. One day after a school party, Ash found me out of context behind the school. What happened is, his girlfriend at the time fell and got up when I was walking by. She dusted herself off and asked if I could dust off the parts of her that she missed. I ended up dusting her off from the back, which included a few pats on the butt. Selenia and I were friends too, so she didn't mind. Around the time my hand touched her butt was the time Ash came around the corner. I let him get the hit on me. He told me not to see her or even hang around her. Apparently, he thought I was getting in her pants or something. She tried to talk some sense into him. Their relationship ended that day and our friendship was terminated. A few months later, she moved, unrelated causes. Ever since, he hated me. Stupid, right? Don't get me wrong. Had the option to sleep with

Selenia come up, I would've taken it in a heartbeat. She was cute, and I liked her. At least, I think I liked her. Hard to determine until you sleep with them. If they're hard to look at the moment after sex, then it isn't meant to be.

"Stop with the jokes. They're not funny and you're not as jaw-dropping as you make yourself out to be."

"I don't know, man. I never said I was anything. Then again, I might just be modest in words, not so much in action if you get the gist."

He steps toward me in hostility. "You gonna let me speak?" You've talked long enough. You and your friend should move out of my seat before my suppressed will to knock your ass out overpowers my generous option to give you the choice."

Storm pats me on the shoulder. "It's fine, let's move. It's just a seat."

"It's fine, bud. The seat itself doesn't matter. I'm still not going to let someone think they can do whatever they want simply by forcing it." Sometimes, the hard choice is the noble one. Standing up for something, no matter what it is.

"C'mon, man. Can't we do this another time?"

I give it some thought and say, "Hell with it." We get up and make our way to the front, when Ash speaks up.

"Lucky your mom was here to save your ass!"

Storm rests his head in the palm of his hand and mumbles, "Damn, so close."

I turn around and casually move closer to him in slow paces. "I'm going to give you the common courtesy and just dust that remark off my shoulder." I stumble backwards, holding my face. There is a stinging sensation imprinted on my cheek. "Really? Did you really just slap me, out of all things." My hands shake at the thought of putting him in his place. I shake it off and walk back to where Stormie is sitting. "You're lucky I know how to show restraint."

"You call it restraint. I call it weakness."

"I got my ways of getting back at you." I sound confident in the words I say.

"What are you going to do?"

"You'll see. It might not happen today, or even this week, but it will happen."

We get to school and exit the bus in swarms. First are the students who are eager to enter a "fun" day of learning. Then, there are the students who walk calmly, wishing for the day to end so they can go home and skateboard or play COD or do practically anything else except exercise the brain. I'm kind of in between. I'm smart enough as it is. My grades are up there, while at the same time, my mind is elsewhere.

Of course, the first thing, or one of the first things I see, is Brandon creeping. The cheerleaders are getting in a quick practicing session before school starts and there he is, trying to see if there is an angle in which he can see under their skirts. He is what you call, a pervert. People might say the same of me, but am I? It's one thing to get off by looking, or imagining, but I don't do that. The difference is the mind wandering. While he spends his time thinking about what he'd like to do to them, I am busy doing the deed. I don't think about sex, I do it. I'm not a pervert. I'm more of a, sexual deviant? There's a silver lining somewhere. Though similar, I like to think they're quite different. One's scum that defiles women, or men, in their minds while sexual deviants are more of charmers, kinda. An incubus. We're more along the lines of lying, though I try to stick to the truth as much as I can. Masturbation alone, doesn't label one a pervert. Everyone does it. It's normal, but when sex is the only thing on your mind, and it's all you care to think about, then a pervert is what you have become.

Ash is doing what he usually does at this hour, which is finding someone to torture. You know the bullies you see in the movies? The ones that get you thinking, "This hardly ever happens. In all my years of schooling, I've never witnessed as much bullying as the movies single out. Maybe a few name-callers and drama seekers who get videotaped embarrassing themselves." Well, this is Cambridge high, and let's just say, what you see in the movies sometimes happens here. Bullying is more than occasional, and groups are separated into qualities. Stereotypical, I know. There, you have the fashionistas, the drama crew, the rockers, the self-declared *emos*, the jocks separated by sport, and the basket cases who sit alone, waiting to be invited into one of these. Me? I'm not in any of them. It's usually just Storm and me, which I am totally okay with. What's nice about being without a group, is you're not limited. You can be yourself and not worry about the standards they try to force on you. I'm waiting for the day where status quo doesn't matter, and we can all just get along with each other, given the obvious differences that keep us separated. I mean, how can technological use advance so far in fifty years, but when it comes to mental image, or prejudice, we're stuck at an impasse? So, you're gay, bi, or trans. So, you're black, white, Asian, Samoan, or something else, entirely. People diss on anyone who is different from them in ways far too different to unite them. We're all the same. We're here. So, our views are different. So what. As for sexuality, people only think anything other than heterosexual is wrong because public standards decree. Religions think anything other than straight is a sin amongst itself. Who has the right to throw hetero in as the default? So, Adam and Eve happened to be opposite genders. Just because something happens earlier on, that doesn't make it necessarily right, or better, even. And why is Christianity the only option for salvation? The bible's been around longer? Who cares? Every religion—Norse, Greek, or Christian—has the same chances of being real, as does it the opposite. God wrote the Bible? God encouraged the Bible? Hard to believe. By this point, there's probably a bunch of hardcore believers who think me the antichrist for having such beliefs. Nowadays, everyone is thought to be the antichrist: Le Vey, Dahmer, Manson, et cetera. You're lost, I get it.

For example, people tend to hate anything new. You grow up with certain music or television, so that is your default definition of good, because it's something you know. In the newer generation, everything that happens is just a reboot of a previous idea. The music doesn't seem to show as much effort. You might have some certain criteria for what sells rap or pop as being good because the rap you grew up with is slightly different than the rap you witness now, as are appearances. Rainbow grills? Personally, I think that's stupid, but that's my opinion. Probably a popular opinion, but still an opinion. I guarantee, if something new that you hate was around in the time that you grew up, your opinion might be different. Not everything old is good nor is everything new bad. Personally, television has gone down in quality and effort, but that doesn't mean every show is to be hated. In a group of twenty shows, there might be a solid three that are decent, and out of those three, one might be on par with what your childhood held.

Ash gives me a disgusted look as I pass him by. I make my way to the field behind the cafeteria and walk around, waiting for school to start, oddly enough. The sooner it starts, the sooner I can leave.

"Hey, Chance." Jenny waves as she walks up to me. She's cute. Her hair burns with the fire from the sun and the beauty marks on her cheeks add to her looks. She's modest, and I admire that. She's a bit on the shorter side, maybe 5'4. I used to date her sister and since then, we talk occasionally. She has a bit of a crush on me, this I can tell. Then again, I'm pretty sure there are probably quite a few that have a crush on me. Jenny hides her beauty, her curves, with a couple layers of clothing. She wears a thinner material, gray sweater with a glimpse of a purple V-neck underneath and a pair of blue slim jeans. They're a bit tighter on her thighs, but as they go down to her ankles, they flail out like bellbottoms, being not as exaggerated. Her hair is curlier than straight and her eyes, gray. I've always loved gray eyes, the way they truly reflect at you. Blue eyes are overrated, especially with the addition of blonde hair.

"Hey, Jenny. You look lovely."

She runs her fingers through her fiery curls and twirls a few strands between her index and her thumb. "Thanks. Are you just saying that, though? I mean, it's just basic clothing, nothing fancy."

"Yes. Modesty looks good on you. Many girls hide behind excessive amounts of makeup and show too much skin, what with the shorts that rise to the upper thighs and shirts that show more than they hide." I put a hand on her shoulder. "It takes a true, natural beauty without makeup to make average clothing look desirable. You're beautiful, is what I'm saying. Never think you must show off to get a guy to notice you, or a girl, whatever preference. If skimpy clothes are the only things that attract someone, then they're not worth your time." I step a little closer to her, her head being under my chin, and her eyes looking up into mine. "Excuse me if I'm overstepping my boundaries, but you deserve someone who knows what they want out of life." Her face glows bright with a rosy touch. Without her knowing, she slightly purses her lips, like she's expecting me to go in and close the gap. My head lowers as I feel the light touch of her lips rub against mine, then the bell rings. That infernal interrupter.

She backs away with a smile. The bell interrupted what almost became a kiss. "Well, um. I guess we should head to class. I've got a test in Statistics and I can't miss that." Her eyes roll, telling me she really doesn't want to take that test. "Well, bye Chance. Until next time." She props her sweater up like a princess gesturing a "good day, sir." Her hand runs down my arm, as she backs away. Once her hand reaches mine, I quickly grab onto it and pull her in to a quick kiss. Her eyes grow wide with surprise, but they eventually close as her body melts into mine.

"Okay, okay. Get to class. There's plenty of time for that after school." One of the security guards looks at us and continues patrolling the campus.

"That was, um—"

"Yeah," I interrupt. "Not bad. Definitely enough for me. I spoke true, though. About your soulmate."

"Someone who knows their place in this world? Like you?" She smiles as she slowly backs up, getting a small start at her way to class. We have maybe three minutes till the late bell rings.

"I'm probably not the ideal choice, either. Not for someone like you." Her head slightly rotates out of confusion. "You're pure. You have goals. Me, on the other hand? I just go with the flow. You deserve to find love, if that exists. I'm still in and out of relationships. Love isn't in the cards for me. I wish I could have that Disney ending, without death being involved, somehow. I'll always be your friend, no matter what. As for the kiss, I'm not sorry. I enjoyed it, as you did."

"But . . ."

"Trust me. There are many better choices for you than me. I'm far from pure."

"Maybe, I need a little darkness."

"Sorry, Jen. Not if it ends with you, having a broken heart and a sudden drift in the belief that love is still possible." I look at my phone. "I say we have about fifty seconds before the bell goes off a second time. Her look is a mixture of confusion and regret. I pull her into a hug, resting my chin on her chin. "Don't give up. True love takes time, trust me."

"How can you know so much about something you don't believe in?"

"Gotta be open-minded. I may not believe in it, at least not for me, but I've read a good deal as to what true love should feel like. I gotta go to class. You too, huh? Text me whenever. I'll always have time to talk if needed." We part ways and head to our classes. I think I may have made a big mistake kissing her, I mean, I enjoyed it. Usually, I go for girls that tend to move on. It is high school, after all. Time to live and not be chained down. I may have just taken a first kiss, and from a girl who still has some connection to finding love. Way to go, Chance. Still, the kiss was passionate, unlike some I've shared.

As I head to class, I come across a puddle, a result from the early morning rain storm. I usually look down when I walk, so that I don't trip. I still have some peripheral vision as to what's in front of me. If I had not looked down when I walked, then I wouldn't see a foreign face stare back at me through my reflection in the puddle. This reflection shows my face, but like this morning in the bathroom mirror, something's missing. Almost as quickly as I see it, I look back into my own face.

In an instant, I get pushed into the brick texture of the school building. "Told you to stay away."

"What the hell did I do?" I try to pick myself up off the ground, but Ash forces me back down.

"You, you . . ." His face becomes dumbfounded. "How about I just make something up and get your ass in trouble."

"Oh, yeah. Smart. The bruises you give me will definitely show someone, I've been up to no good."

"Don't be a smart ass, Ryder."

"Hard not to be when the person confronting me is anything but. And referring me by my last name? C'mon, Ash. You're better than that."

"You're all jokes. How can you be so calm in situations that would freak anyone and still find the audacity to joke about it? I saw the video of your party, as did many others. You're calm as can be. How is that?"

I shrug my shoulders. "Death is only Death. Can't ask for much better than a quick one."

"He threatened to make your death long and excruciating."

"Well, I guess. You're asking why? 'How' is also a valid question. To tell you the truth, I don't know. As to why I'm not shaking right now, well, that's because I'm not in danger with you. Let's say, in hypothesis, that I show my emotions like anyone else. With you, I still wouldn't fear you."

He slams me harder into the wall. "I'm going to break your arm."

"Go ahead. I'll just pop it back into place. My pain tolerance is quite high, depending on my emotions. The reason I'm not scared of you? You're, for one, not a killer. You can hurt me, but I know you. You wouldn't kill me no matter how much I pissed you off. You're a school bully, nothing more, nothing less. You're not a school shooter, a bomber, a terrorist, or even a threat, not to me anyway. Tell me again why I should fear you."

"You say you're not scared of me because I'm not a killer? Look at the video! That man was a killer, and were you scared? No!" I get knocked to the ground in a swift punch with force behind it. "It almost sounds as if you're scared of nothing. I got news for ya. Everyone, no matter how mighty, has at least one fear. What is yours?"

I smile, the taste of blood in my teeth. "About that. To a man with only one fear. If that one fear is erased, would it be replaced by another, or would he simply be fearless? Think on it. Take your time."

His boot crashes into my chest, not without my hand grabbing hold of the boot, making the impact a little less powerful. "You stole my girl in Junior High, and now, you attempt to steal her once again."

"Ash, buddy. When it comes to women, you're blind. You can't see they're stringing you along. The girls that you speak of, their anything but loyal. Gotta heighten your standards, or lower them, depending on how you level women. Do standards go by looks or loyalty. They come together at some point."

"She spoke of your name when we got off the bus, even when you were a distance away. You've poisoned her mind."

"Really? She said my name? What context are we speaking of?"

"I'd watch it. You're really pissing me off."

"Weren't you already there?"

He picks me up by the collar of my shirt. Why the shirt? I mean, come on. I hold on to his wrists and quickly jab my thumbs into them with force. He quickly releases his hold, dropping me. "You bastard."

"From what I hear, you're not wrong." I pull him in for his gut to make contact with my knee. As he kneels to the ground, I make my way to class.

"You're in a world of hurt, Chance!" His voice lingers behind me as I turn the corner and enter B-hall. I enter a class full of eyes that can't help but turn my way.

"Oh, lovely of you to join us. Take a seat." Mrs. Greenbrier isn't amused by my seven-minute tardiness. I sit next to Alex—a math whiz—and Tyler—a moron. Alex loves school from what I can gather. Tyler, on the other hand, is totally oblivious as to what class this is. He's usually passed out in a textbook. The teacher doesn't care. To her, it's your loss if you choose to snooze during a lecture. It just means that the night's homework will be that much more difficult. She finds no trouble in helping someone out who actually tries to pay attention, but with someone like Tyler, she shows no sympathy. She'll simply guide you as to what pages to read from. If you show no interest in learning, she'll show no interest in trying to catch you up. It's your responsibility.

"Chance Ryder, please come to the office. I repeat, Chance Ryder." The voice is heard clearly over the intercom. I rise to eyes that follow my every step. Vultures. It's just an office visit. Focus on the teacher for Christ's sake.

III

I walk past the other rooms, getting a glimpse of what's happening in the other classes through the clear rectangular window on the top of each door. Mr. Steinbeck's Algebra 2 class is having a quiz. Judging by the students' faces, none are prepared. Miss Nordeis' Statistics class is doing a recap on what has been taught this semester, getting a head start to prepare for next month's semi-finals before school lets out for winter break. This school separates its buildings into courses. As you might have guessed, B-hall is the Mathematics building. The office is by the entrance gates to the school and B hall is one of the first buildings you pass coming in, along with A-hall, so I don't have much of a walk. I walk into the office building. No one's here. I expect to find at least an administrator at the front desk, but it's empty. A noise is heard shuffling around in one of the rooms when an older man walks out.

"Mr. Ryder. You may come in."

Mr. Jenson, the principal, has darker eyes, almost black, and brown hair, underlined with the beginning stages of middle age. "I didn't do anything, sir. Ashton started it."

"Ashton?"

"I assume that's why I'm here. My early confrontation with him."

"None of the sorts. Though your 'confrontation' will later be discussed, you're here because of a certain video I saw recently. I'm guessing you know the one." I nod. "How are you doing by the way? An event like that might cause some stirring. If needed, I can assign a counselor, or—"

"Mr. Jenson. I don't need a counselor. I'm doing just fine."

"Mr. Ryder, I highly believe you should get some form of help. I mean, you can't be fine. Not like that. No one could remain unchanged after an incident such as that."

"Well, I am, so can I go?"

"I didn't want to have to resort to such measures, but if you refuse my offer to find you help, I might have to bring your mother into this. She must want what's best for you."

"Go ahead."

"I pardon?"

"Mother will agree with me on this. We don't do, help. We've always tackled everything alone, without it."

"I recall you having a counselor at one point. What was her name, uhh, Miss Hackett? Merida?"

"She was more of a friend. Who happened . . . to . . . counsel me."

"See. everyone needs help at one point or another. Shall I make an appointment with the school counselor? What day would work for you?"

"I said no."

He has a stern look in his eye. "You can display the whole macho 'I don't need anybody' look all you want, but deep inside, your inner child is screaming out for help."

I stand up, already tired of this confrontation with the principal. "Well, if you don't mind." I walk over to the door. Mr. Jenson doesn't move. I turn the handle, well, at least, I try. The door is locked.

"Sorry, but I can't let you leave."

"You can't do this."

He chuckles lightly. "Of course, I can. I'm the principal. I'd try not to fight it. Turning the knob won't do anything." I turn around and Mr. Jenson is standing right there, hands behind his back, mere inches away from me. "The boss won't be happy with my actions, but pretty soon, he won't be a problem."

"The School Board definitely won't agree with this much force."

"Funny. I'm not talking about the School Board." He removes his hands from his back and lunges at me. "A mere child doesn't deserve to have so much power. To hold so much authority. Soon, that won't matter."

"What are you saying?"

His hand presses my face into the ground while his other hand holds a sharp object to my throat. "Any last words?"

"Yes, actually." He moves his head closer by a small inch, so he could hear the last words. "Why do the bad guys always ask that stupid question, as if giving the enemy one last chance to escape?"

He smiles a genuine one. "Always end with a joke. Nothing personal, Kid. Oh wait . . ." I grab onto his wrists to prevent him from moving any closer with the blade. My legs wrap around his waist and I throw myself to the side, flipping our positions. "Wait, this isn't—"

"Like I said, never ask the question. It causes distractions." I grab the blade and throw it to the side. I give him one good punch to the jaw and watch as he spits out blood. I release him and stand. He slowly gets back up, wiping the blood off his lip.

"You're unusually calm, Kid."

"And?"

"Oh, nothing." His eyes look black for a moment as he throws his body at me, wrapping his fingers around my throat. I feel a slight prick under my ear and a small trail of something wet slowly run down my neck. "For someone hard enough to kill, you bleed quite easily." I headbutt him in the face. His immediate reaction is to let go of me. "These bodies are fragile things, are they not?" Blood leaks from his nostrils and the bridge of his nose slightly leans to the right.

I grab his arm and pull his body in, balancing his weight on my feet as I ball up and launch his body behind me. He makes a loud thud noise. I flip over to see him holding on to his side as a puddle of his own innards overflows through his fingers. The corner of his desk is stained with his own blood. "You think that's enough to kill me."

"I'm not trying to kill you." I look back at the door and make my way towards it. Mr. Jenson gets to me as my hand grabs the handle of the door. He pulls me back, but I hold on to the handle. His pull becomes too strong as my body gets lifted. The handle ends up breaking and I fly back. "Damn it! What's your deal?"

"You're naïve, child. I wouldn't expect you to understand what's going on, not when there are many secrets being kept from you. You are too far in the dark on this one. A very dangerous place to be, indeed. Either way, you can't leave now, what with the handle being broken and all."

His eyes turn black again. "You have the power of the dark one in your blood, yet, you know nothing of it. What a shame." I hear a crunching sound coming from him when his arms seem to elongate. His arms thin out as they do this. His joints dislocate, giving him the grotesque appearance of an abstract drawing. His back is arched over as he supports his weight on his horridly disfigured arms. His fingers sharpen to a point and his teeth are replaced with fangs.

I stumble back, raising my arm in defense. "The hell are you?"

"There's the fear I was looking for. Welcome to a world of existing nightmares." His voice seems darker. He crawls up to me, backing me up into a wall. "Where the only way to wake up . . . is to die . . . The amount of uncertainty in your eyes is delicious. Am I sleeping? Is this a nightmare? Am I going to die? You must be in a world of shock right now. Am I wrong?" His smile surpasses the natural threshold of a realistic one. He licks his lips. He slashes his fingers at me. I duck under his arm, hearing his fingers scrape the wall. I back away as fast as I can, trying to think of a reasonable explanation as to what is happening. So far, I can't think of anything.

"What are you!"

"I'm the thing that keeps you up at night." Somehow, I knew he would say that.

He crawls slowly towards me. His arms pop every step he takes. Saliva trails down his chin, mixing with the blood that is already there. I have nowhere to go. Nowhere but the great unknown. He nears me. The suspense might just kill me before he does, but I choose to not give up, given the circumstances of the impossible situation I've been placed in. I jump to the side, trying to be anywhere except right in front of it. Like a cat to yarn, he keeps lunging at me. With every move it makes, I make a countermove to throw it off. I finally screw myself as I find myself underneath his desk. Why does his desk have to be so damn close to the wall? I mean, the chair barely has enough room to move on its own without bumping against it. I back up into something uncomfortable, as I jump. I reach behind me and pick up the microphone used for the intercom. Perfect. The principal ducks his head under the desk, limiting my moving space. One chance. I lift my leg and kick him directly in the eye. He recoils, giving me the time needed to get out of the tight spot I'm in. I turn on the mic and speak into it before I get interrupted. "Storm Friezone, you're being called to the office. I repeat, Storm Friezone, you're being summoned. And quick!" The mic gets taken and chucked against the wall.

"You have become a pain in the ass." His words are distorted, but the message is clear. I find the strength to get up, only to be knocked down. He crawls on top of me. I wrap my fingers around his throat to prevent him from closing the gap between us. He opens his mouth, making a screeching noise, while revealing his needle-like fangs. Slowly, he starts to overpower me. I punch him square in the jaw. That does nothing.

"Stop. Stop. Get off me!" The handle on the door makes a noise from the outside. He looks behind his shoulder just long enough for me to throw him off. A cracking noise is heard as his back hits the wall.

The door opens and in walks Storm. "Yes Mr. Jen-Chance?"

I breathe heavily, trying to capture my breath. "Let's get out of here." I rush to the door, but he doesn't move.

"What happened in here?'"

"Are you kidding me? He tried to kill . . ." I look back, but there isn't a monster. Laid out by the wall is Mr. Jenson, struggling to get up with his torn clothing.

"That boy is crazy! He tried to kill me!"

"What!" I run up to him and lift him up. "He's lying, bud. Can't you see?" The room is a mess. The contents that were on his desk are now spread out on the floor. His shirt is soaked in blood and clings to his side. This doesn't look good at all. "He tried to kill me. He . . . He transformed."

"What?"

"Transformed. You know, changed. I know what this sounds like, but—"

Mr. Jenson chokes up blood. "You need help. Seriou—" I press tightly against his throat, making it to where he cannot breathe. His hands flail out, trying to release my grip.

"Chance. Let go of him! Now!" I do as I am told. Mr. Jenson falls onto the floor, holding his throat. Storm runs up to him, holding him up. "Principal Jenson. Are you alright?" His hand comes up behind Storm, still resembling the disfigured claw it had before Storm arrived. "I'll be fine. I'm lucky you got here just in time, or I'd be a goner." His claw closes in on Storms back.

I push Storm out of the way, punching the principal in the jaw over and over. "Tell him the truth, demon. Show him what you are. The grotesque abomination you displayed before we were interrupted. If you don't, I'll force it out of you."

"You're delusional."

I grab his chin, forcing him to make eye contact. On the edge of his stern expression, there seems to be a . . . a grin. "And you're driving my patience."

Storm grabs me by the shoulders and pulls me off the principal. "Dude, what has gotten into you?"

"Nothing. Let me threaten him long enough and he'll reveal himself in time. Give me a minute. That's all I need."

Storm raises his hand and slaps me hard across the face. "Sorry, but you're losing it."

I rub my cheek, feeling the warm hand print that has been placed on it. "Yeah. Yeah. Maybe, I have gone a little crazy in the moment. We should go." I lead him towards the door. "Wait here, I have to apologize to Mr. Jenson."

"That would probably be smart. I can stand in here. Maybe, he'll go easier on you or something. I can talk him out of any, harsh punishment?"

"That's okay. I got this."

"Don't do anything stupid."

That is exactly what I plan on doing. Stupid and risky. I close the door, letting Storm wait outside.

Mr. Jenson sits smugly at his desk. "Well, I'm waiting for my apology, boy."

"Look, I'm sorry for what I was about to do." I slowly walk over to him. He retreats slowly in his seat until his back is against the wall. Being forced to apologize to a creature like this. It's below me, but I must do what I must do. "I may have almost crossed the line with the whole, about to skewer you, thing."

"As if you could come close to accomplishing such a feat."

"As I was saying," I grit my teeth, trying to remain calm, "I am deeply sorry. Put this behind us?" I hold out my hand in good graces.

"Boy, I know a false apology when I hear one, and that is by far the best attempt I have ever heard, but if you think I'm stupid enough to reach out and grab your hand, you are highly mistaken."

I withdraw my hand. "What do you think is going to happen? I'm just going to pull a knife out of thin out and repeatedly stab your hand in the same spot until the pain causes you to reveal your true nature?"

"That's very specific. Is that what you were planning?"

I turn to face the door. "Well, with apologies out of the way, I leave you to your plotting."

I hear his hands lightly tap the desk. "I beg your pardon."

I swiftly turn around while his hands are still pressed against the desk and grab something from it. As I plunge down with the first sharp object I see, he removes his hand with haste. As quickly as he draws his hands back, I grab one of them, elbowing him in the face in the process, then I plunge the sharp weapon-like object through the middle of his hand, hearing his bones crack on impact. His screaming fills the room as his body begins to deform as I'd anticipated. His fingers crack and dislocate as the blood that was recently pooling in the center of his hand starts to absorb into his new-found skin. His skin begins to tear away at random spots, revealing a gray, more defined muscle underneath. His lips begin to shrivel up to nothing, revealing only teeth that sharpen to a point.

The office door opens and in walks Storm. "Dude, I said . . . what the hell!"

Mr. Jenson is almost completely gone. In his stead is a humanoid beast with limbs grown out to unproportioned lengths. Each hand now consists of four razor sharp claws. His leathery skin is grayish-black with tinges of brown in between. His face holds close to none of his original features. His eyes are sunken in and one of them glows red while his nose is no longer a nose, more like two holes representing his nostrils. His hair slowly regresses, and spikes start to appear along his back, starting from the top of his head. His neck can only be described as a mass of muscle with a head atop. All in all, he, or it, resembles a nightmarish demon from religious folklore. Kind of like how a minotaur has the head and legs of a bull and the body of a man, this new creature definitely shows signs of more than one creature. It has the upper body of a man with the arms slightly larger than the rest leading to rather large nightmarish claws, the legs of a bull, and the head, which is starting to resemble that of a tyrannosaurus rex if the flesh was torn off.

I was expecting something unusual, but this is a bit more than I bargained for. "What the hell are you?"

"I . . . my weak . . . am a . . . Chasmm . . ." His words are cut off by animalistic snarls and growls until that is all that remains. The creature slowly starts to lose its former humanity as it leaps onto the desk and roars. Storm and I run to the door, but the creature is too fast on its hind legs.

"Dude, what the hell do we do? It's blocking our only way out. What kind of office doesn't have a window?"

"We just have to distract it long enough to escape?"

"What!" he exclaims.

"We're not going to fight it! Look at that thing! You distract it!"

"The hell I will!"

"Fine. I'll distract it. Get ready to head for the door." We part ways as the demon follows Storm. "Hey! Hell spawn." I pick up the first object I see and charge the monster, jamming the pen into one of its orifices. The monster shrieks as it uses its unusually large claw to pull the pen out of its punctured eye. "Ha! That'll show you." It swings its arm back, flinging me into the closest wall. Luckily, my back broke my fall. I'm arched over with my bangs in my face. An intense pain has overcome my body as I try to stand, not without the jolt of discomfort in my spine. The beast draws nearer, leading me to a corner. It swipes its claw at me. I duck as the claw misses my head by a measly inch or two. It opens its mouth and clenches its jaw at me. It charges me like a bull to the color red, pouncing as I jump to the side. The room is filled with a loud siren-like noise that deafens the ears when too close. The creature sways its head back and forth, banging it against a wall, attacking anything near it with its piercing claws.

"Chance!" Storm stands in the near distance with the door open. I jump up and charge towards it. The demonic hybrid shakes its head and rampages close behind me. I practically dive out of the office as Storm quickly slams the door shut. We exit the building that holds the office in it and see swarms of students leaving their current class halls in room-assigned lines. "Okay, it's obvious he's no longer following us. We best get to our classes. Act as if nothing's happened."

"I don't know what the hell that was, but it wasn't nothing!"

"Storm! Relax. This is no time to freak out."

"This is the perfect time to freak out! I'm surprised you're not freaked out! What the fuck was that thing!"

Now, it is my turn to slap him. "We mustn't lose ourselves. You think I'm not freaked? Of course, I am. That was a fucking monster, but I must remain calm. Now, here's what we're going to do. We're going to go back to our assigned classes and act as if this never happened. You hear me? Nothing. Just try to avoid him until I come up with a plan."

"And how the hell do you suppose we do that, Chance? He. Is. Our principal. Now that we've seen what he is, do you think he'll just leave us alone? Who knows how many other demons are living in plain sight? What if this entire school is run by those damned things? We're in a trap of their own design. I might have to switch schools just to survive."

"Storm, Storm! Breathe. We've wasted enough time. We have to get back."

"Are you seriously worried about attendance? You? The student who plays hooky and comes to school when he damn well pleases." He takes a deep breath and tries to calm himself down. His hands slightly shake. "I'm sorry. I don't know . . . I can't do this, man. I'm scared."

I place a hand on his shoulder, "So am I. I'm terrified. As of yesterday, religion was a fucking joke, and now, I don't know which one to look to. I'm scared shitless, but I won't let the enemy know that. Our fear fuels their gain. The moment we lose ourselves in doubt, they win. Do you want that?" He shakes his head. "Good. Are you good?"

"You're surprisingly good at this 'talking sense into someone' shit. I'm still scared, but I can at least stand without shaking, now."

"Great. Go back to your class, bud. I'll think of something. Don't worry. We'll expose that hell spawn for what he is. We will defeat that son of a bitch."

We head in separate paths, walking to the classes we left behind. Honest to God, I don't know how the hell we're going to defeat that thing, but it helped Storm, so now, I must think.

"Trisha Quartez?"

"Here."

"Alexis Ramírez?"

"Here."

"Chance Ryder?" Mrs. Greenbrier is taking role call as I find my place in line. "Aww, Chance Ryder. Perfect timing. Is Timothy Valentino here?" The fire alarm finally shuts off and the intercom picks up.

"Sorry for the unscheduled fire drill. May I please have everyone meet in the bleachers? Thank you."

Everyone gathers around, sitting next to friends and tolerable peers. "Yo, bud!" Storm sits at the top, waving at me. I make my way to the top row.

"Okay, okay. Quiet down." The bleachers silence as someone makes their way to the middle. He wears a black suit with a red tie and has his hair slicked back with a few short bangs curled over one eye. This man is Mr. Jenson. He doesn't look beaten up at all if you don't count the minimal scratches on his cheek and maybe some slight bruising. "It appears we have some pranksters in this audience." He smiles as his eyes direct to us.

"Fuck, shit, he's looking at us."

"Act oblivious, bud. Keep your guard up. We're not out of the ballpark, yet."

"False alarm? What about the howling we heard!" One of the students yells from the bleachers.

"I was getting to that, thank you. These pranksters thought it'd be funny to let loose a wolf on campus, then tricked the fire alarm. Rest assured; we caught the mongrel. Luckily, it was tamed. As for the pranksters, they will be punished. You know who you are. I will have to meet personally with your parents. Chance Princeton Ryder and Stormie Windyl Friezone, will you come up here?" Unbelievable. Additional to him telling us we know who we are, he has the audacity to spotlight us, anyway. Everyone looks back at us as we slowly rise, making our ways to the middle of the field. Everyone's eyes are on us as we head down the aisles. I spot Ash along the way. Rather than the smirk I'd expect to see, he appears genuinely shocked, and a little in disbelief.

Principal Jenson firmly grabs onto our shoulders. "Everyone else, get back to your normal routines." Everyone leaves the bleachers, leaving us with this disguised beast. "Boys, did you honestly expect I'd let you run out on me?" He leans into us, so that we could clearly hear his threats. "I own this school. The moment you walk onto these grounds, you're mine. I own you. Obviously, I can't attack you here, and I'd rather not drag you away so publicly." He claps his hands. "I've got it. I'll keep you after. That's normal for detention, yes? I could suspend you, but why give my prey time to plot." He squeezes Storm's shoulder, "I bet you wish you'd just leave Chance alone when you had the chance, don't you?"

"He's my friend. He's my brother. Whatever pain he has to go through, I'll gladly endure with him."

"Brother's going a bit far, isn't it? I mean, can you really call him a friend? How long have you known him?"

"That's none of your business."

"I suppose I could suspend you, Friezone, but you're not a normal student. Not anymore at least. You're a part of this, now. There's no escape for either of you. You could switch schools, but no matter where you go, you'll be watched. I'll call your parents. Inform them that you'll be coming home late. Not like you can tell them our little secret, can you?" He stares at me, intently.

Lunch arrives and I'm sitting alone until a girl confronts me. "Uhh, hey."

"Hi, Ariel. How are you?" Ariel is an ex of mine. I broke up with her a few weeks ago, and though, at the time, she was emotional, we started talking again as if nothing had happened. She's pretty cool, a bit out-going at times with her attempts to get back together with me, but I'd say her persistence is one of the admirable traits about her. She doesn't know how to give up.

"I'm doing alright. So, is it true? You let a wolf on campus?"

"Sure you don't want to talk about something else?"

"I just can't believe you'd do something like that."

"I had nothing to do with a wolf. It's a mix-up. Please, another topic."

"Sorry, so, umm. About the party." Perfect. The one thing other than the current scenario that I don't want to discuss.

"Did you enjoy it?" I smile, though I want nothing more than to just leave.

She nods. "Oh, yeah. It was great. I had to leave a little early. Something came up, but someone sent me a video. Do you know what I'm referring to?"

You would bring that up, wouldn't ya? "Yes. I do. Before you say anything else, I'm fine. It was resolved."

"Really? Just like that?"

"Yep. Anything else?" *And by anything, I mean anything at all that isn't one of the two topics you've managed to bring to my attention.*

She twirls her hair. She's not as shy as a few of the girls I've been with, but I've always loved variety. Though shy is my more-leaned-on preference, I'm okay with a little perseverance. "Oh, yeah. So, a few of my friends are going to a movie. I was wondering if you'd like to go."

"Are you asking me on a date?" *Not that I'm against it, but why?*

"You don't have to call it that if you don't want to. Just a social gathering of friends attending a movie. Nothing more. I mean, I would love it if you ended up asking me out in the end, but if you don't, that's cool, too. I'm not completely certain as to what I did to make you dump me, but that's a hill we've come to pass."

"Exactly, Ari. We dated once and stayed friends afterwards. If we date again, that friendship may not be easily resolved."

"We can be something else." I stay silent for her to finish the idea she started. "You have urges, as do I. We can stay friends as you want, but at the same time, we could also be intimate."

"Why, though? I'm never single for long. I'd soon enough have someone to fill that want." *Or need.* "Even if they don't partake in those acts of union, I'll still respect their space."

"Whatever happens between us stays secret. Before you say anything, just think about it."

"I don't need to. I don't cheat. It's wrong."

"Okay, okay. I get it. That's a respectable trait in a man. Many would jump at the opportunity, though many aren't like you. You have a line of women waiting to fill up on you. I do have to say, your morals confuse me."

"How do you mean?"

"You don't cheat, though, you did date my two sisters simultaneously."

"They knew about each other. It's true that I don't cheat, but that doesn't necessarily mean I stray from a polyamorous relationship. Life is too short to be bound to one. Sometimes, they're not for that, and I'm okay with it. Sometimes, I do pick up a few that are up to it."

"You're like a drug. Most guys don't have the amount of luck on their side, but you, you're intoxicating. You're the drug to their addiction. Rather than a single beverage, you're the entire bar, fitting to a variety of specific and entirely different desires. Some go for daquiri. Some do Vodka. Sex on the beach. Smirnoff. From the most diluted of drinks to the most savory of tastes, you adapt to fit everyone's needs. Almost like you're auditioning to fit the man they seek, then you find a new toy." She scratches her palm, nervously. "You're playing them. Using them. Is there a single girl that you've been truthful with, about who you are?"

I smile to myself. "Funny how you say these things. You seem to understand me more than most. You accuse me of deceiving girls, but here you are, subtly asking me to take you back, as if I wasn't using you. You intrigue me."

"I mean, I don't care if you use me. Even though you lie to attain girls, it's not as if they care. I can sense that, through the thick fog you use to disguise your true self, there is a true part of yourself that you do display. You're caring. You just can't be tied down, I get it. Anyhow, can you at least join us in a movie? That's all I'm asking." She touches my hand, awaiting an answer, an answer that I don't give right away. "Oh, that's fine." She smiles a fake smile and turns to leave with her friends. She walks slowly as if she knows I'll stop her.

"Hey, Ariel," I say as she already starts to leave me. "So, what time should I meet you? You know, for the movie."

Her smile shifts from a fake one to a genuine one. She turns and runs up to me, jumping into my arms, tying both legs around my waist. She is, but a couple inches shorter than myself, yet she manages to get to my level. You'd think by my level, I'd mean face to face, but no, that is not the case. My face gets buried in her chest as her arms wrap tightly around my head. "Thank you, thank you." She extends her arms, forming some space between us until she leans down, pressing her lips against my own. I lose balance as her body shifts, making us land on the ground, her above me. Our lips don't part, though. The scent of cherry fills my nostrils and her long, milk chocolate hair curls around my cheeks. Suddenly, out of realization, she stops. It was only a couple seconds, but they weren't seconds I'd choose to take back if I could. She stands up, pulling me up with her, and dusts off her skirt. "Sorry. I didn't think." I place a finger to her lips. Before she can say anything else, I bring her lips in for another kiss. Her eyes stare into mine at first with surprise, then they close. My hands trail down her sides, closing the gap with our hips.

She's a bit confused at this. "I thought . . ."

"Sorry. I slipped up." I smile warmly at her. She returns one. "Just between us, and your friends." I instantly look at the girls in the background who are giggling amongst themselves.

She runs back to her friends. "Is Friday fine?"

I can't remember the reason I broke up with Ariel. She is beautiful. She's definitely not stupid. Her slight accent is appealing. She has three sisters, all living in the same house. I can imagine it could get a bit dramatic in her house. I've been there a few times. Her mother is chill. No father is in the picture. Her house isn't super big, then again, my judgement may be a bit biased. I get along well with her sisters. Her youngest sister is almost as outgoing as Ariel. The other two are a bit gossipy. When Ariel invited me to her house for the first time, I sensed someone was watching me. Angel is pretty cool. She's the younger sister. Just like Ariel, she's persistent. She came off a bit strongly when she introduced herself. Her handshake was firm. Angel doesn't know the meaning of personal boundaries. At Dinner, she'd scoot her chair next to me and start immediate conversation. She talked about the usual girly things, like favorite spirit animal and such. Hers is apparently an alicorn, whatever that is. Only when Ariel intervened did Angel back off, for the time being. She has Ariel's eyes, if not a little more goldish. There are three bedrooms in her house. The mother has one and the four sisters divide into two bedrooms. Angel and Ariel happen to share the same bedroom, which is the same bedroom I stayed in when I spent the night. Other than my interrupted showers, I'd also awaken with Angel, right in the middle of Ariel and me, clinging to my waist. All in all, Angel may be a bit clingy, but she's definitely interesting to listen to when she gets into a conversation. Sometimes, she'd be caught in a one-sided conversation until she catches my attention.

An average height Indian boy runs up to me and tugs on my shirt from behind. "May I help you?" I ask, turning to face him.

"Ashton wants you to meet him at 3:00 p.m. Saturday night. Mountain View Park. Don't be late."

"And if I don't?"

"He didn't say." Just like that, the kid leaves.

"You're going to fight Ash?" Brandon pops up out of nowhere. "Can I sell the tickets? Five dollars a pop. Crap, I gotta make the tickets."

"Where did you come from? Are you just snooping around, eavesdropping?"

"What, no. Pfft. I was just walking around when I heard that you were going to fight Ash."

"Well, you heard wrong. I'm not . . ."

"Hey! Fight on Saturday! Ash or Chance! Place your bets! 3:00 p.m.!"

Why do I bother with this moron? "Stop, I don't want . . ."

I feel a hand on my shoulder as Storm's face appears. "Dude, I'm not usually one for violence, but the word is out now. You can't back out. Your reputation could plummet."

"Doubt it. I don't fight for attention. I'll show up, but not to fight. I'll turn it around."

When School ends, I try to stuff myself into a filled bus. I trip over a foot, heading to the back.

"Klutz, much?"

Rather than laughing, some students just look away, or stare.

I hop up to face the accused—Ash. Storm rushes to my side and turns me around. "Grow up," he tells Ashton, "Everyone knows this is just your attempt at a petty cry for attention."

"What would you know about attention, slave boy. You stand beside him, keeping him out of trouble; meanwhile, you don't receive any attention from anyone. You cower in his shadow. Facts are facts. He's a fighter. You're a runner. Stick with what you do best and observe."

"Wait!" Storm tries to stop me as I find myself face to face with Ashton.

"He's not an observer. He simply stays out of harm's way. Nothing is wrong with that. And, I'm not his only friend. How about you, though?"

"I have friends."

"No, you don't. You have suck ups. You're just a sorry excuse with an anger problem. Best enjoy your time here because if you keep up with this, the only place you'll find yourself is behind a mop. I'll be there, making sure you never run out of things to clean."

"You listen here. I have the potential to be the best. I was a quarterback."

"Was. Now, why do you think that is?"

The bus gets to our stop as Storm and I step off, together, eventually parting ways. I open my door, smelling something cooking. "Mother."

"In here, honey." I sit at the kitchen table. "How was school?"

"It was fine. The usual."

"Hehe, I doubt that." She puts down the frying pan and removes her apron, turning to sit with me at the table. "The principal called. Something happened at school today? Do you want to talk about that little incident? I'm willing to hear you out."

"I didn't do anything wrong."

"Obviously."

"What?"

"He could have come up with a better lie than that. Who ever heard of placing a wolf on campus as a prank? It's such an obvious stretch. As to where you'd even get the damn thing, that is beyond me. I know you did nothing wrong. I just need to understand a few things."

"You're not going to ask me to go back to the school and serve my punishment?"

"For what? Punishment is served by the ones who did something wrong. I suppose I could just call him up or invite him over here to clear the air. I'm very persuasive."

I shake my head in disapproval. "I don't think that would be a good—"

"Don't worry. I'll handle this. Mrs. Friezone called me. I have to go over there and work my magic on her. Just go up to your room or something. Play a game, have a friend come over, vandalize things. Have fun." She kisses me on the forehead. "I'll be home shortly. "And help yourself. There should be plenty to fill you up."

I head up to my room and immediately pull out my phone. I dial the familiar digits of a girl.

"Hey, Chance. What's up?"

"Hey, Ariel, about Friday, I have a game—"

She cuts me off. "You don't think I know that. I knew my message to you came to be a little vague."

"So, when do you want me to show up? After the game?"

"When do you play?"

"Late."

"If you want, I can reschedule with the girls for Sunday. What are you doing on Sunday?"

I think for a moment. "Nothing. I'm free."

"Sweet. Hey, I heard you are going to fight Ashton. Are you sure that's a good idea? He's a bit unhinged."

"I know, I know. It kind of just happened. There's nothing I can do now about it. How did you hear about it so soon?"

"You kidding? Gossip spreads. I wouldn't be surprised if the whole school knows by now. I just hope you know what you're getting into."

"You don't think I can handle him?"

"I know you can. Just, don't go too far."

Confused, I say "You make it sound as if I'm the one that's unhinged."

"Don't take this the wrong way. You do have a bit of an anger problem, and before you say anything, hear me out. Don't get me wrong, you're really good at suppressing that anger, and putting it off as if nothing's wrong. That scares me. You show everyone the side of you that you want to display but has anyone ever actually . . . gotten to know you? Really. I know you're not a bad guy, but anger is a hard thing to control once it's been unleashed, and a fight is the perfect setting to lose control."

"Where is this coming from? Have you always thought this about me?"

"Sorry. I should've spoke up sooner."

I clear my throat, "Hey, Ariel? If you thought these things about me, why do you still . . . I guess what I'm trying to ask is, why do you want us to get back together?"

"I guess a part of me is curious. To be honest, I don't understand my feelings for you all too well. Maybe, it's the sex. Maybe, I like you. Who knows? You never really liked me, liked me anyway, right? So, why does it matter, as long as it benefits you in the end?" I've never heard Ariel speak like this. I don't know how to respond. She makes it sound as if I'm this trashy guy who uses women. Is this how everyone thinks of me? "Well, I've gotta go. Dishes and chores to do."

"Okay, talk to you later, then."

"Wait! One last thing. Kick his ass."

Oh, hopefully I don't need to, but if need be, I'll do more than that. I sit down and turn on a system to pass some time. Maybe some first-person shooting will help. I'm not a gamer, but that doesn't mean I don't play from time to time to ease stress. Only when I look at the clock do I realize just how long I've been killing Jackal snipers and grunts. I hear the door open downstairs, knowing that Mother has finally returned, but there's someone with her. He's male, that much I'm sure of. I walk downstairs and come face to face with the guest. He's dressed nicely. He wears dress shoes and plain black pants with the shirt tucked in.

"Chance, Mr. Jenson and I need to talk. Do you mind making up some tea?" I do as I'm told and bring a couple mugs to them.

"Naughty boy, ditching school like that. Stormie, too. Such a good kid caught in your act." Mr. Jenson crosses his legs, giving me a look like he owns the situation.

"Please, Mr. Jenson," Mother begins, "I'd greatly appreciate it if you didn't taunt my son."

"Why, of course. My dearest apologies, Miss Ryder. I mean Miss Winters. Why don't you have his last name?"

"Keep to business. My choices are my own. Chance, dearest. Why don't you head to your room while we talk?"

"You don't want me to stick around?"

"We'll be okay. Just talking like adults. Turn on some music or something. We're not talking till I can hear the music from here." Something in her eyes tells me that she's got this under control. It's not like the principal would just show himself now. He's probably waiting for the moment we're alone once more.

"Why—"

"Please, baby. Just do as I say."

I eye Mr. Jenson. He does the same.

"You're mine." The voice is in my head. This much I know is true because his lips didn't move, though the voice doesn't sound like his anyway. I head up to my room and do as told. I blare the music until I could hardly hear myself think. I lay on my bed for what seems like hours, but it's only been fifteen minutes. I hear something downstairs through the music. It is quiet compared to the music, but loud enough to vaguely pierce it. Suddenly, I hear a window shatter. I rush downstairs, and the principal is gone. Mother is bleeding along her arm.

"What happened?"

"Nothing I couldn't handle."

"You're bleeding."

"Just a man with control issues and a slight anger problem trying to tell me how to raise my son. I handled it. Now," She claps her hands together, "who's hungry?"

"We've got to call 9-1-1."

"Just leave it alone. If you can, try to steer clear of that man. I know that's a lot to ask, since, you know. Something is off about him."

If only you knew.

The table spread looks appetizing, though a bit much: a bowl of macaroni shells; a bowl of salad, put together with leaves, olives, egg chunks, and bacon bits; and a plate of Medium rare steak, brownish mashed potatoes, and buttered up corn on a cob. The smell of the steak, peppered and coated, can be tasted through the air. "This looks great." If this were a cartoon world, the aroma would have lifted me up.

"When do I ever make a meal that isn't?" She has a point. "Speaking of, why didn't you eat while I was out?"

"Sorry, I had some thinking to do." Not a good explanation for why I didn't eat.

"Thinking? And what, if I may ask, would a boy your age have to think about? Is it a girl?" I just take a bite of the steak, refusing to say anything. When's the last time I really thought this hard on something someone said? "Girls?"

"What?"

"Does your thinking have to do with girls? I can't think of anything else you'd have to worry about." She sips her tea, staring at me from across the table."

"Mother, that isn't, is this really appropriate to talk about with you?"

"Is it a crime to want you to open up? So, is it not girls?"

"No, I mean. I don't know."

She smugly smiles, "I see. What's her name?"

"Ariel."

"Oh? How is she doing? I didn't know you guys still hang out. That's good. Are you guys back together?"

"It's something she said. And no. We're not dating. Her feelings for me are still there, but I don't know how to respond."

"Boys, never knowing how to appropriately respond to a girl's feelings. Be honest. Now is not the time to hold anything back, not while you're young. Live your life to the fullest with no regrets and remember . . . don't forget to wear a condom."

I place my mug on the table after a small sip, raising an eyebrow, "Mother?"

"Grandkids are a blessing, but I don't need any right now."

"Mother?"

"Yes, Dear."

"Can we not casually converse about my intimate relations with the girls I've been with?"

"Okay, okay. I'm just saying, one slip up, and you'll have more on your hands than you can handle. I just want you to be safe."

After Dinner, I phone one of my friends.

"Hello?"

"Hey, Sam." Sam is one of my older friends as well, not as old as Storm, but a good friend all the same.

"Hey, Chance! What's up?"

"Nothing much. Just wondering if you are doing anything right now."

"Are you asking if I can hang out?"

"I suppose I am."

"Yeah, sounds fun. When?"

"How's now?"

She grows quiet on the other line. "Oh, now? Um, now, I'm, can my sister come?"

"Isn't your sister old enough to look after herself?"

"Yeah, but I don't think I should leave her alone right now."

"Sure, be there shortly. Bye." I grab one of my mountain bikes I haven't ridden in lifetimes. Come to think of it, when the hell did I ever ride this thing?

A few corners, blocks, and a few stoplights later, I finally make it to the sidewalk outside of Samantha's house. Her house is nowhere near the size of my own. It's got a couple bedrooms and a bathroom. It has a backyard, small as it may be.

Sam walks outside with someone shadowing behind her, trying to go unnoticed, but it isn't working. "C'mon Danielle, say hi. This is Danielle, my sister. I know you've met, but why not make it official?"

Yeah, she's usually in her bedroom when I come over, but I see her when she comes out to eat or grab something. I extend my hand out to Danielle. "Nice to meet you, officially, I mean." She just nods. She's got headphones in, so I doubt she can hear much of what I'm saying. Slowly, she lightly grabs my hand with hers, well, my fingers anyway, like she's grabbing a piece of paper. Time to note that as one of the awkward moments of today. "My name's Chance," I rub the back of my neck, "but you already knew that." *Idiot.* She lightly giggles and I must say, it's adorable. Guess she can hear me, which makes me wish I'd thought of something else to say. She murmurs something so quietly, while hiding halfway behind her bangs. "What?"

"I'm Danielle." She speaks louder, but is still quiet to the human ear, especially with the car that decided to drive by at the exact moment she opened her mouth. If I had not already known her name, I would have probably asked for it again, but instead, I pretend that I heard it so we could move on from this awkward moment.

"Nice to meet you, officially. So, you're going to hang out with us for a couple hours?" *Again. Stop stating the obvious, you fucking tool. You're hopeless.*

"Mmmhmm." Her shy nature shows her adorable side in ways. Someone who doesn't talk as much and just listens, or it might be because I'm new to her. Friends are usually quieter around their first interactions, but as time passes, they show a more energetic, off-the-walls personality and share a certain humor that if any random bystander happens to be walking past, they'd assume we are crazy or something.

"So, what do you guys want to do?"

"We can walk around or something." Obviously, Sam hasn't a clue, nor do I; otherwise, I would have just offered something, waiting for an agreement.

"Get on my bike."

"What?" They both answer at once.

"There's room. Don't worry. I'll go slow." My bike only has one seat, but one of them could sit on the handlebars as the other tails along.

Hesitantly, they near me and my death trap. Surprisingly, Danielle gets on first, probably because her sister insisted it. It probably sounded safer in Sam's head if Danielle was at least sitting. "Are you sure about this?"

"Yeah, of course. I'll be careful. Remember to hold on." Danielle lightly tugs at my shirt. "You have to hold tighter than that. I don't bite."

"Oh, really?" Sam asks right away with humor and outburst. "Are you sure about that?"

"Okay, fine. Have it your way. Your sister can sit on the handlebars."

"Nope. Not happening. No way." Sam hops on as her sister clings to me with dear life. "You have to have a little grip to at least stabilize yourself." Danielle's hands lightly grip my shirt like holding onto a bouquet of roses, while trying not to crush the stems. Sam, on the other hand, enjoys the wind in her hair. "So, is it too late to ask if you even have safety gear? A helmet? Pads? Bubble wrap?"

"We'll be fine. Probably."

"Wait, whaaa—" Before Sam could finish that word, I speed away. Danielle's hands release themselves from my shirt and, instead, find themselves on my stomach as her arms are wrapped around me with her face pressed up against my back. I assume her eyes are closed, simply because what she is doing is an act of fear, in which case, she wouldn't want to see what is happening. Some people are like that when riding a rollercoaster, usually closing their eyes, and tightening their grip on the metal bar that is placed firmly above their waist when they hit a series of loops.

"Hang on, this is going to be a bumpy ride, ha-ha! First-time passengers, please fasten your seat belts in the slight possibility we lose course." Danielle's arms tighten around my torso as her chest is pressed against my back and her face is buried in the area between my shoulder blades. We ride a few miles until we reach a cooler location, near a river, like it isn't cold enough this time of year. "Okay, we have reached our destination." Sam gets off with her hair slightly aiming towards one direction. "Okay, Dani. You can let go."

Her arms release themselves from my waist as her hair is a tangled mess, looking as if she walked into a windstorm. Her face is white from fear. "So, how was—"

"That was terrifying! I thought I was going to die. How can you j-just g-go off and d-do something as c-c-crazy as . . ." She raises her voice to the average volume, as her own is a bit on the quieter side. To me, it's a bit humorous.

"It got you to open up a bit. You were holding on tightly. I say that's progress."

She turns her face to the side and puffs out her cheeks a bit. "Well, don't do it again."

"Okay, okay. I promise, I won't do something that crazy again, not unless you give permission." I hold my hand out for a handshake. A little less hesitant than the last, she grabs hold of it, tighter than last time, but still light in comparison to others.

"Well, I'd say you two hit it off right away."

"What?" Her sister goes back to hiding behind her bangs.

"Aww, you're so cute when you're flustered." Sam pats her sister on the back.

"I'm not cute. And, I'm not flustered, either."

"Chance. Be my second opinion and be honest. Would you say Dani is cute when she's flustered?"

I nod. "If I'm being honest, I'd say she's cute when she's mad, too." Easily embarrassed girls are the best to mess with. I can't be the only one who thinks that.

Sam and I laugh at Danielle's embarrassment. "Well, anyway. What are we doing here? I know you're not going to have us swim. It's way too cold for that right now."

"Of course not. I thought, maybe, we could walk around a bit. Talk and junk."

"Orr, we could . . ." Sam shoves past me. "Bet you can't beat me in a race!"

"Oh, you're so on." I chase after her, as Danielle tries to keep up with me. It doesn't take long for me to pass Sam. "You're losing your grip, Sammy. Thought you were faster than that, haha." I look behind me to see Dani tailing near and Sam behind her. What the . . . I lose focus, trying to figure out how Danielle caught up this quickly. As I slow down, she doesn't. I slow down too fast for her to change direction as Dani runs through me. As we lose balance, falling to the floor, my first reaction is to hold her in my arms so that I take the fall with her, just along for the ride. I land full force on the ground, holding on to her back. I open my eyes to see Sam finally catching up to us.

"Did I forget to mention that my sister used to be in track? Ha-ha."

I let go of Dani as my arms just fall to my side. Danielle opens her eyes and lifts her head from my chest. "Why did you slow down?"

"Hey, sorry. You caught me by surprise. I wasn't expecting you to be right behind me."

We hear a flash as we look to the side to see Sam with her phone up. "This is going to make an adorable screen-saver."

I look at our positions as does Dani. She takes notice of me staring. Her hands are still placed on my chest with her body straddling mine. She quickly throws one leg over to stand, patting off her butt. She turns to her sister and reaches for the phone. "Give me that." She tries to take the phone, but Sam hides it away.

"Not a chance."

"C'mon. That picture is embarrassing. What are you going to do with it?"

"Relax. It's just going to be my screen saver. Maybe, a few friends will see, but it stays on my phone. You gotta admit, you look adorable in the picture. Why would I delete this? I'll probably never see you in such a state again. It was a perfect position to land in."

"Make sure that picture doesn't leave your phone. It could be taken the wrong way."

"Please. There is nothing wrong with the picture. It's cute, nothing else. There's nothing sexual about it. You have clothes on, as does he." Dani turns her face, turning red. "Why are you blushing?

Is it something I said?" She smirks and nudges her sister. "Perhaps, it's the last statement that's got your mind wandering into, dangerous territory, heh?"

"I don't know what you're talking about."

"Oh, my Goddess, it is. You closet perv. It's always the quiet ones, I swear."

"Stop it. I'm not a pervert." I admire this sisterly bond that they've got going on, here. It almost makes me wish I had a sibling of my own. Someone to play jokes on.

Sam laughs a bit at her sister's current state. "It's fine if you are. Everyone has perversions from time to time. It's normal. Nothing wrong with it. I bet Chance has a whole book of them."

"Um . . . You two are very, how do I say this, close for sisters. Well, not close, but, very open about things."

"Most sisters are. If there's one thing you should know about girls, Chance. It's that we gossip. Sisters share everything. Their love life. Things that happen. There are no secrets, at least, not between us."

"That's actually admirable. Sweet, kind of."

We walk along the riverbank, talking and sharing stories. We exchange a few shoves, playfully of course. Sam manages to push me into the ice-cold water.

"Oh god, I'm sorry. Did I shove too hard?" She pulls me out of the water, almost as quickly as I had fallen in. I can feel my body temperature go down, slowly as I shiver to death. I am now officially an ice cube. Sam wraps her arms around me. "Oh my, you're ice cold. You need a towel, or a blanket, or something."

"I'm fine. Really."

"Either way, this gives me an idea. Uh, take off your shirt."

"What?"

"Don't argue. Just do it." I do as I'm asked and hand my shirt to Sam.

"Next, you'll ask for my pants. My, my, what dark fantasies underly that imagination of yours? I'd very much like to know."

She shakes off whatever thought pops into her head, "Your shirt is what's cold and damp. Without it, you shouldn't be as cold." Sam hands my shirt to her sister and starts to pull her shirt up to reveal a black push-up bra.

"What are you doing?" *Oh, thank the gods. I've only read about this scenario from fanfiction.* Stop judging me. I'm entitled to read that sort of stuff.

"Oh, please. A bra is no different than a bikini top. I have to warm you up, somehow. Now, um, this next part might be a bit, awkward." My eyes widen at the realization of what she means. She pulls me in, chest to chest. She is a bit shorter, so I have to kneel a bit, but not too much. I can feel her bra pressed against me with her exposed skin contacting mine. Her arms wrap around my back. The nice warmth of her skin feels comforting, but not enough. "He needs more heat. Dani. Take off your shirt."

"What?" She reacts by crossing her arms over her chest.

"We have to warm Chance up, so he doesn't get sick."

"Really, you're overreacting," I say, "not that I'm complaining, or anything."

Dani huffs. She walks around me so that I don't see her. I feel a second set of arms wrap around me and a second bra press against me, from the back. It's a bit softer in fabric, and from the feel of it, her breasts feel a tad bit larger than Sam's, not that I'm thinking of such things while they're "helping." About ten minutes pass, and we're comfortably intertwined in each other's' embrace. Their combined body warmth nearly makes me doze off, while at the same time, I try to fight off whatever naughty thoughts attempt to ruin this otherwise innocent moment. Meanwhile, I'm waiting for this fantasy to end at the worst time, but it doesn't. This is very much real.

On our ride back to their house, Dani holds on to me, but doesn't say anything.

"Thank you for that. We had fun." Sam pulls me into a hug. All I can think about is the event that took place moments ago with her breasts pressed against me, though they were covered.

The fuck is wrong with you? She's a friend. "No problem. We should do that again, sometime." She raises an eyebrow. "The hang out part. Not the skin contact." *However, if you'd like—*

"Sounds fun. Just say when." She plants a small kiss on my cheek and ruffles up my hair with her hand in a playful manner. "See you around. C'mon, Dani."

Danielle confronts me, holding on to one arm with her opposite hand. "Well, I had . . . fun. You know, with you, and stuff."

"Yeah, same. Look, Danielle . . ."

"You can call me Dani, if you want."

"I'm sorry if I did anything to make you uneasy. I had fun. Maybe, next time, you could join us again. I hope I didn't come off too strongly. No hard feelings?" I extend my hand. Faster than the others, and with a twist, she grabs my hand and pulls me down to her level where she plants her lips lightly onto my own. Like that, she rushes back to her house without as much as another word. Sam stands at the door, staring. Is that a smirk planted on her face? Her eyes follow her sister as she runs past Sam into the house. She closes the door behind them while keeping eye contact with me.

I make it home and face plant onto my bed, exhausted.

"Time is running out." *Aww, shit. Not again.* I know I heard the voice, but at the same time, I'm just far too tired to care at the moment.

"Go away. I haven't the patience . . . to deal . . . with . . . you." I start to lose myself as I begin to fall asleep. As for the voices, they're not going anywhere.

Iv

The aroma of a freshly made breakfast fills my room. My eyes open to streams of sunlight pouring through the blinds of my window. I have a good feeling about today. Waking up to the smell of a hot breakfast, rather than the faint whisper of a voice in my head. I'd say that's a good start to a normal day. I hop out of bed and do the usual routine: shower, brush teeth, make hair, and dress.

I enter the kitchen to a spread of biscuits and gravy, along with scrambled eggs with buttered toast and sausage, spicy. There are pieces of sausage submerged in the steaming gravy, which means this is her famous hot and spicy, Italian sausage-style biscuits and gravy platter.

"You spoil me, you know that?"

She sits on the opposite side of the table, smiling, waiting for me to sit before she eats. "You're the only one I have to spoil. Making you happy is the very thing that gives me purpose, ever since your father, well, let's not talk about that. Please sit."

I do as she orders. "Do you miss him?" I never got to meet my father, or if I have, I was far too young to be given the faintest memory of him. I've seen pictures of him. I have his eyes and his squared jaw. A picture of him holding hands with Mother is in the living room, near the television. Half of the picture is torn, which just leaves Father with a severed hand holding on to his. No doubt that the hand belongs to Mother, but as to why she cut herself out of every memory of him is beyond me.

She swallows a bit of the biscuit as she gathers up what words to say. "Yes, I do. He would have been proud of you, you know. To see who you grew into it. As for me . . . he might have some doubts in choosing me."

"Choosing you?"

"Your father was a loving man; yet, he caught the eyes of many. The moment you were born, he knew you were his new-found purpose in life. To help you grow into a remarkable adult. He got caught up in some trouble, though. That trouble followed him, and everyone he cared about. For that reason, he, umm, had to leave. It was the saddest moment in my life to watch him go, and I fought to keep him. No matter the problem, I'd be there with him. He had other plans. He let me keep you, and I never saw him again, until I found him dead. Though it was heart-aching to believe, he made the right decision. If he had kept me by his side, I might have wound up dead. You could have. I lost someone I loved, and I couldn't save him. He figured, that with me, you could turn into the man he knew you could become."

"But, why would you say that he would have doubts in choosing you? Are you saying that I am not the man he would've wanted me to become?"

"Heavens, no. You're twice the man he would've wanted you to become. As for the man that you'd need to become, well, you're not there, yet."

"That I'd need to become? What do you mean?"

"In due time, sweetie. Everyone has a purpose, big or small. Your purpose has the potential to change how we see the world. Now eat your biscuits." She gives a forced laugh. "Though, he's been gone for so long, the mention of him still brings sorrow."

"I'm sorry for bringing him up, Mother."

"No need for apologies. Every child deserves to hear about who his or her parents are or were."

I delicately eat what she has spread out before me, like I'm savoring the taste, which I am. "This is really delicious. You really do make the best food."

"Aww, that's kind, but there is always someone better. A lesson you should come to realize."

"And I have."

"Have you, now."

"Well, yes, I have." I look down at my empty plate and stand to place it in the sink.

"Oh, honey. I'll take that."

"It's fine, I'll—"

"Nonsense." She takes the plate from me. "If you stand around and talk all day, you'll be late. You do plan on attending today, don't you?"

I smile and run up to my room. I grab my bag and the bike that, up until a while ago, I forgot I had, and head out the door. "Bye, Mother. I love you."

"I love you, t—"

I speed down my street and around a couple corners before I meet up with Storm, waiting at the bus stop with a few others. "Yo, Storm. Get on."

"When did you get that thing?"

"Good question. I wish I knew, now get on."

"Yeah. I think I'll pass."

"C'mon. It's just a bike."

"With one seat," he says, raising an eyebrow.

I sigh, flipping my hair to the side. "You gonna get on or not?"

He turns around to the others, kind of hesitant in doing so. "Well, it's been a glorious chat, ol' chaps, but I must be on my way in style." He gets on the back and puts his hands on my shoulders. "Don't think much of this. With you steering, better safe than sorry."

"No need, bud."

"What do you meaa-e-eannn. Holyy shiiittt!" He screams in my ear as we pass twenty going downhill. Twenty may not seem like a lot, but when you've got no walls or protective layers around you, and you feel the harshest of winds whipping you at all angles, twenty may feel faster than it is. It doesn't take long for us to reach the high school. We come to an abrupt stop in front of the entrance gates. Storm is locked in terror mode, with his hands clenched tightly, like he just got done riding the scariest of rollercoasters. He slowly breaks his fingers loose as he takes a deep breath and stumbles off the ride.

"You alright?"

"What is wrong with you? I nearly died!"

"Exaggerate much?"

"I am not exaggerating! We . . . could have . . . died!"

"Probably. You wouldn't have died. It's perfectly safe. Do you want to ride it home after school?"

"Umm, well. We'll see. There are a few things on my phobia list: creepy crawlers, intense darkness, the Grudge, rollercoasters, and now, thanks to you, that death machine we rode to school on. It's going to take some intense consideration before I come close to getting on that thing for a second time in one day."

"Hehe, fair enough. For a football player, you're pretty soft, aren't ya?"

"Not soft. I just care about living."

"When I think about it, you've changed a bit from when you saved me years ago. Always quick in fights and standing to protect people. Now, you steer away from them."

"I could easily win in fights."

"I know that. It's just that you, don't fight."

"Just because you can fight, doesn't mean you should go looking for one. If there's a chance to avoid conflict, I take it. I'm a freaking pacifist for Christ's sake. Violence leads to nothing good. Besides, you can handle yourself now. That scared, defenseless kid from years ago is no longer easy to trample." The school bus enters the campus and comes to a stop as it lets out a swarm of students, some who want to be here, and the rest, ehh. "Hey, bud. Speaking of football, a couple of the teammates have been talking and—"

I stop him. "I think I know where this is going. No need to worry about them."

"They're thinking about benching you."

I scoff at the thought, "You can't bench the quarterback."

"Look, man. As a friend, you know I'll always have your back, but you haven't been coming to practice."

"I go to the games."

"Yes, you do, but without you at practice, there's no teambuilding. I'm not asking for much, but with you choosing what days to come and with your absence at practice, the coach, no, the team is considering the thought that maybe, they should choose another quarterback. They've been considering me, but I can't do that to you."

"Congratulations, man."

He steps in front of me as we walk and stops me in my tracks. "No, that's not what I want to hear. Look. We started this together and I can't think of being on that team without you, man. They need someone who's, you know, reliable."

"Do you agree that I'm not?"

He rubs his shoulder, "When it comes to this, you're not. If you're not interested in football, then you should quit. Hell, I'll quit with you. Football is a commitment, and your head just isn't in it. Do you hate me for saying this?"

"I could never hate you for speaking your mind. Do you remember why we joined in the first place? The thing is, I don't know if that was the full reason why I did join. Maybe, I joined because it'd be something we could dominate together."

"And now, it's just me. Sure, you're present at the games, and you do one hell of a job at making up for your absences, but it's not worth it. To be uncertain whether the quarterback is going to show? It sets off the mood. And the coach also wanted to consider someone who, shows up to school. I know your grades are somehow left intact, but your attendance poses an issue. Please, just show up to practice. There aren't that many practice sessions left, so could you at least finish strong? Show him that you're serious about this."

"That's just the thing, Storm. I'm not. Serious, I mean. Besides, the coach is an ass. How he hasn't gotten fired yet is beyond me. He abuses those players. His whole identity is toxic. One more outburst from him, and I might just make him have no choice but to bench me."

"I mean, you're not wrong. To be honest, if you decide on quitting, I won't hesitate in following. With everything that's happened with the principal, I can hardly focus on my studies, anyhow. My dad is starting to pick up on my, demeanor. How do I tell him that my principal is literally from hell?"

"I said I'd deal with that."

He looks away. "Yeah, and I want to believe you. But, we're human, and he's obviously not. I don't see an easy way out of this."

Students start to pass us by as they step off the multiple buses that have parked behind one another. The first person to truly catch both eyes is a black kid with a charcoal "Bad to the bone" U-neck and a chain necklace with a fake dagger on it. His faded glory jeans are torn from the knees down and his chucks are definitely worn in. He glares at me as he walks my way. "Let's go, Storm."

He takes a glimpse as to whom I'm referring. "Oh, yeah. Probably a good idea." We walk in the opposite direction, trying to put in some distance between us.

"Yo. Bitch. Where are you storming off to in such a hurry?" He grabs on to the collar of my shirt as he pulls me back towards him, letting me fall to the ground. I pick myself up and start walking again as if I didn't just get thrown to the floor. "Hey, Princess. I'm talking to you." He shoves me a couple times before Storm slaps his hand away from me.

"Not today, man. Don't you have a puppy to kick or a kitten to plant in a tree somewhere?"

"I'm sorry. Are you trying to be funny, or . . .? I can't tell. Listen, Raincloud, you talk when asked to speak. I'm talking to him."

"And he's not talking to you. Why do you keep picking on him, when you know he can stomp yo ass in the ground?"

"I'm giving you one more chance to leave this situation alone. Trust me, you'd be smart to take it."

"I'd be a bad friend if I took it. Best if you—" Storm places a finger to Ashton's shoulder and instantly gets thrown on his ass. This doesn't keep Storm down. "You wanna go, Dickwad?"

Ash's nostrils flare. I step in between them as he steps forward. "No, no, stop."

His eyes burn with hatred for us. He angrily huffs and forces through me, turning around to face me. "Remember, Saturday. Show or die." His words lack intimidation, at least, to me. I know I can take him. Truthfully, I'm sorry for him. He likes to play the bad guy. He always has, even when we were friends.

In third period, I sit, bored in AP English. Mr. Amor has us reading "Nineteen Eighty-Four." I've already finished the book the week he handed it to us. I already have the essay written that's due in three weeks, so for now, there's nothing to do, but wait for class to be over.

Lunch comes around, but in all seriousness, I just want to leave. "Hey, bud!"

"Hey, man."

He looks me up and down. "What's wrong?"

"Nothing. What brings you to that?"

"Something's off."

"We can't all act the same, every moment of every day. It's normal to act completely different one moment to the next . . . You ever wonder if there is someone out there for you?" I ask, noticing his smug reaction.

"Oh, so there is something wrong with you. Why do you ask?"

"Oh, it's nothing major. Just caught up in thought, I guess."

Storm chuckles. "All these years and I didn't strike you as the affectionate seeker . . . Look man, I believe there is someone out there for everyone. You just have to look. Hehe, in all honesty, I'm surprised you haven't found 'the one', given your history of relationships."

"In all honesty, I probably passed up 'the one' as I was caught up in not being lonely."

"I don't believe that. There's a group of girls we could socialize with."

Near the cafeteria is a group of partly recognized individuals. Sarah is sitting down against a wall, lost in a book. The others tower over her. Brittany is laughing, giving hand gestures, and pinching her fingers together as to indicate size. The girl next to her is texting while listening. The blonde beauty, Jessyka, is chatting and laughing with a slim guy with perfectly quaffed, blonde hair and a pair of DG shades placed atop his head. He's laughing and having a good time as he stands, holding on to his elbow with the opposite hand as the other hand curves into a fist pressed against his chest. He's wearing a pair of red and black chucks and a pair of plaid capris with no pockets.

Storm and I walk towards them. Jessyka is the first person I turn to. "Hey."

She looks at me and smiles, "Uhh, hey. Didn't expect you to come by. Chance, this is Sci."

"Sci? Is that a nickname, or . . .?"

He delicately holds out a hand to show good bonds. I take it and give it a firm shake. "No, it's my name. My, it is true what they say. Your eyes do shine under the sun."

"Pardon?"

"Ope, there I go again, moving too fast. Hehe, I'm sorry if that was a bit, out of the blue."

"No, that's fine. Just a bit sudden. Not to sound, uh, rude, but are you . . .?" I give a pause, hoping he'll finish the thought.

"Gay?" I turn away out of discomfort as he says that. "Dahling, there's no secret about it. As for your question, yes. Is that a problem?"

"No, not at all. Just wondering."

"Now that that's in the clear, have you ever tried being with a man? Not to sound forward." I shake my head. "Pity. Rumors spread about you. Personally, I'd like to get to know you and see if they're all true."

Jessyka stands in front of Sci. "I'm sorry. He can be a bit, him. He doesn't hold back."

"No worries. It's fine. I was wondering."

"Wondering?" Jessyka replies.

"Yeah, if you'd like, if you don't mind, to go do something sometime, with me." I was a bit hesitant at first, I mean, this is Ash's girl. I don't want to start trouble, but then, I start to think, and I begin to realize that I don't care. Jessyka is up for anything. I can tell she doesn't want to be with Ashton, and quite honestly, I don't blame her.

"You're not just asking me this because you know it'd tick off Ash, are you?"

Busty and intelligent. Good to know. I stutter, trying to find the right words. There are none because that is exactly what I'm doing.

She laughs. "My, when did you resort to this? So, what do you have in mind?"

"I didn't think you'd be okay with this if you knew."

"What your true intension is? Please, I might not, like, be in smart classes and such, but I know a set up. So, as for the plan?"

"I just wanted to know if you're doing anything later. We can improvise. You know, wing it."

"Dude, what are you doing?" Storm nudges me on the shoulder. "Are you trying to piss Ash off even more?"

I turn my head and talk quietly as to only speak to Storm. "I said I'd get back at him. At least this way, it'd be fun for me, too. It's not like I'm interfering with true love or anything."

"Dude, that is so low, but I'm not complaining. You do you, man."

I smile and focus again on Jessyka. I reach out for her hand and she takes it. "So, what do you say? Wanna hang out with a real man?"

"I'd love to. When do you have planned?"

"How is Wednesday, or Thursday?"

"Sounds good. We can meet at my house on Saturday, 6 P.M." Figures she'd choose a day that I didn't give the option to.

"Your house, uh huh. Isn't that a bit . . ."

"Scared? It's just Dinner. It's not like we're going to do anything daring—unless you want to. Hint. Hint."

I rub the back of my neck. "Right. Thanks for that clarification. So, your house it is."

Stormie waits for me near the buses once school ends.

"Hey, you don't want to get a ride on my bike?"

"God no! With your steering—"

"Yeah, yeah, yeah. It nearly killed you. Don't be a baby, man. We've got to conquer fears at some point."

"Easy to say when it's not your fears being conquered. What are you scared of, by the way?"

"Everyone's got fears, even me." I reply.

"Commitment doesn't count."

"What? I'm not scared of commitment."

Storm stifles a laugh. "Whatever you say. You don't fear commitment. You steer away from it. You'd rather take a long road of obstacles than a short one of commitment."

"That makes no sense. Commitment is a long road unto itself. Anyhow, how did we even get to that? We were talking about my steering, and how you're too chicken shit to ride with me."

"You want me to tag along on that death trap? Fine. Let's make this quick. I swear to God, if I die . . . I am never speaking to you again."

"I can live with that."

We curve the corners as we head to Storm's house, avoiding cats that jump in the way. Though, my first thought is to go through them, I don't exactly know how my bike would handle the impact.

I know it wouldn't get damaged, but that doesn't mean we wouldn't fly. We part ways as I set course for my house.

I enter my home and am automatically welcomed by Mother's voice. "Dear, is that you?"

"Yeah, that it is." *What. Were you expecting someone who isn't me to just walk through the door?*

"Oh, lovely." She pokes her head out of the kitchen. "Dear, it seems I made a little too much alfredo. How about you call over your little girlfriend. Maybe, with her help, we can put away all the food."

"Girlfriend?"

"Samantha. She's a charming girl, a bit boyish, but cute, all the same."

"Sam is just a friend."

"Who's a girl, hence, she's your girlfriend. Do you have to put your guards up at the mention of such a possibility? She'd make a perfect girlfriend for you. She's smart and independent. She dresses appropriately."

"I know what you're doing."

Mother tries to hide her smile with the angle of her stance, but I can hear it in her voice. "And what would that be?"

"You're trying to set me up with her."

"No, no I am not. Setting you up with her would involve getting you guys to talk. Getting you two to hang out and become something bigger, to be . . . yeah, okay. I guess in your eyes, that sounds like matchmaking. I'm just looking after my boy. Call her up. I made plenty."

"To eat?"

"Yes, that is what I said. She's better than those so-called friends of yours. Not counting Stormie, of course."

"You don't like my friends?"

"What you call friends, I call conveniences. You never hang out with anyone, other than Samantha and Storm, unless there is a party going on somewhere. At least your two friends actually go out of their way to hang out with you, not just when you're around. Am I being clear?"

"Yes, you're being clear. Fine, I'll call her, and see if she wants to eat over, but not because you told me to. This is strictly my decision."

"Yes, of course it is, Mr. Initiative."

"Are you kidding me? I always make the best of a situation. You've met a few of my girlfriends. I'm definitely not a stranger to romance."

Mother chuckles at this. "Oh, my boy. My sweet, clueless boy. Yes, it is true, you've always got 'company', but as for romance, you've got no clue. You act like the gentleman you want to be, not that you aren't, not for yourself, but to simply adapt to that woman's standards. You are a gentleman at heart, yet you choose to be anyone except who you truly are. You're caring, you've got morals, you're smart, but your inability to be alone keeps you from finding that one special person. You've got to make peace with solitude before you can truly appreciate the opposite company. If you hide behind multiple masks, you'll forget who you are, and you'll ultimately fail to find a girl who fell in love with you. The real you."

"Nice speech, motivating, really." I look down. She's not wrong. She sees right through me, she always has. Through my thickest of masks, she always managed to know what I was thinking, to know how I was feeling. "I get what you're saying. You believe that if I date a girl that loves me for me, then I'll start to see her best attributes. My path will change. Rather than picking up whoever I deem beautiful enough or unique enough for me to use for my public image, I should find someone that I don't need to put on a mask for."

"Like I said, you're a smart boy."

"Smart, maybe, but I don't think I'm ready to put my masks away. I don't think I could settle for one girl for long. I know it may seem wrong, but it's me."

"You're still young. Real love is still a foreign concept."

"Like you and Father." She looks to the side. "I guess I should go call her, then." I make my way to my bedroom, closing the door behind me.

I find Sam's number in my contacts and call her up. The phone rings a few times then, "Hey, Chance."

"Uh, hi. I was wondering if you were doing anything. Mother made a little too much alfredo, so, I was thinking, hey, why not have help eating it all."

"Yeah, I could eat. Mom is out at the moment, doing who knows what."

"That's fine, I'm sure Mother won't mind picking you up."

"Do you mind If Dani joins us? I know it's a lot to ask, but . . ."

"Sounds good. See you two in a bit." I toss my phone to the side and lose my jeans. I throw on a pair of Faded black "Tony Hawk" Skinny jeans and a tight-fitting top. "Hey, Mother!" I crack my door open a bit so that she can hear me.

"Yes?"

"Do you mind if you can go pick up the girls?"

"Girls?"

"Sam invited her sister. I figured you wouldn't mind. Do you?"

"Sure, Hun. I don't think I have met her sister. Can you be a dear and set the table while I am out. The food is ready. I won't be long."

"No problem."

I rush downstairs to quickly ready the table before she gets back. She wasn't kidding when she said she made too much, but with only two people living together, I can't see how she would've messed that up. If there were five people under the same roof, then I could find where she went wrong, but with only two, she shouldn't have even come close to this, unless she planned on inviting an extra guest, while making it look like total luck or convenience. Yep, she planned on feeding more than just the two of us. I placed the bowl of salad in the center of the table, and portioned the alfredo into four plates, putting exactly how much I assumed they could eat as individuals into each plate. There was still alfredo left in the serving bowl. Mother made sure to leave some for seconds, but I'm sure she didn't mind cooking it all. Cooking is a hobby of hers, at least, that's what I assume. I never really see her doing much else. God, the role of a mother seems like a handful. I put the dressing sauce near the salad. Perfect, the table looks ready to go. Wait, nope. I rush to the kitchen counter and reach into the first drawer, grabbing some silverware and napkins. One fork and one knife per plate, neatly wrapped in a napkin, kind of like how a restaurant presents them on each individual table. Now, we're talking.

Mother should be getting to their house right about now, so I have another ten minutes, estimated, until they return. With nothing to do, I just reach into my desk, pulling out a stack of papers, my unfinished projects. I like to write, but I can never seem to finish a song. I always either get the beginning or the end of a song but can never seem to complete one. I guess I could just write eight fire verses and just repeat them with a line or two in between to set the mood. That's what most songs do. In all honesty, writing a song shouldn't be as hard as it is, not when repetition plays throughout. The instrumental is probably where the challenge comes in. I grab one of my lyric sheets and try to write down a few more lines. My songs are usually about sweet, caring themes, like death, or mutilation. Like I said, they're pretty calm. Right now, I'm stuck on a word. Fuck, what do I rhyme with orange? Syringe? No. Foreign? God, no. Got it! Door hinge. Nope, never mind. I mean, it rhymes, given the right syllabary, but I don't think I could find a good use for that. In case you haven't figured it out, I'm writing about blood stains in the walls. Why blood stains, you ask? Who knows? I write the first thing that comes to mind. I don't write often enough. Between school, when I go, and the other things that fill up my days, I don't really do much. I write when the mood hits, which isn't often. Other than songs, I also write short stories, or at the very least, excerpts from what could potentially be short stories had I had the drive to write one. They're mostly fantasies I have with numerous girls I've encountered, and end with me, dominating them.

I hear the door close downstairs, and a pair of feet rush up my steps, leading to my room. "Hey, what you doing?" Sam peeks her head into my room. "Oh, what are you writing?"

"A song. It probably won't get finished anytime soon."

"Oh, cool. How many songs do you have written?"

"Can't say I have any. They are partially written. Every one of them."

"You just need motivation. Every writer needs that. Anyway, we gonna eat or what? By the way, you look nice, but you didn't have to change into new clothes for this. It's late, anyhow."

"What makes you say I just changed? For all you know, I could've been wearing this all day."

"That could be the case, then I'd be asking why you'd just leave your discarded clothes, laying on the floor." Her eyes dart towards the pair of pants I had on moments ago, just chilling by my bedside. "But I won't judge. Kay, bye. I'll be down there, eating, so get your butt down there and enjoy with the rest of us." Her head disappears as she closes the door behind her. Not much time passes by, maybe a couple seconds, until I jump off my bed, practically skipping towards the kitchen table.

"You prepped the table wonderfully. You even went extra with the fancy napkin folding." Mother sits, hands folded, waiting for me to take a seat.

"Thank you both for inviting us over."

"No problem, Samantha. You're practically family, anyway." Mother turns her attention towards Dani with a smile. "Dani, is it? It's a pleasure to meet you, it truly is. I hope my son treats you right. He has a thing for silent cuties."

"Mother."

"He can get a bit carried away in the bedroom, though."

"Mother."

"And I'm the one who has to hear it."

"Okay, that's enough of that. So, how do you two like the food?" I speak prematurely, taking notice that no one has taken a bite out of their food, yet.

Sam hides a smile behind her hand. Dani looks a bit flustered, not knowing how to react. As for Mother, she seems pleased with herself, looking smug, while slowly taking the first bite.

"This is really good, Mrs. Ryder." Dani takes the second bite, enjoying it, hiding her face in embarrassment.

"Thank you, dear, but please, call me Deanna. And my last name isn't Ryder."

"Oh, sorry."

"Nothing to be apologetic for." In the end, Dani ends up eating way more than I had anticipated, given her small stature. I guess that shows me that I shouldn't be one to assume. She has thirds, while I myself only had seconds. She was a bit hesitant to grab seconds herself, so Mother took charge and filled her plate, telling Dani that there was nothing to be embarrassed about. Sam barely finished her first plate. Then again, I did fill it pretty full. I offered to help with dishes, but Mother shooed me away with the girls. "Go play, or whatever," were the words she used.

We run up to my room and close the door behind us. Dani is still a bit speechless. "What's the matter?" I ask.

"Think she's a bit embarrassed about what your mom said earlier, hehe."

"Oh, that. Nothing to be embarrassed about. She was kidding."

"I don't know. Sam has told me about you. From what I hear, you're quite the lady killer. She likes you, but she doesn't want to ruin—" Sam jumps onto her sister, while pressing her hands against Dani's mouth so she can't speak. I already heard enough of that sentence to figure out the last unsaid words.

"She doesn't know what she's saying." Sam eyes Dani, as in telling her through eye contact, "Before you finish that thought, remember that I know where you sleep."

I smile, confidently, sitting next to her on my bed. "No point in hiding it now. If it wasn't true, then you wouldn't have reacted the way you did. You would've been caught off guard, then disagree with whatever was said. So, with that said, how long have you liked me?"

"No, really. We can literally talk about anything else right now."

I move closer to her where our shoulders are touching. "What if I don't want to talk about anything else. What if I want to discuss the infatuation you have with me?"

"Oh no." She places a hand on her face. "Here's the egomaniac I've heard about."

"What? Egomaniac? That's not me. Humble is what I am. Yep, humble. The average monk."

Sam lets out a cute giggle. "A monk, huh? Who's rich and has pretty much everything going for him."

"The money doesn't define me. In case you haven't noticed, I don't use my money often. I live my life like everyone else. I don't expect to be put on a pedestal. So, are you going to answer my question? How long have you liked me? Serious question. For all you know, I might feel the same way."

"It's hardly an infatuation . . . If you're going to push the subject, then fine. I've liked you for a few months now. We hung out more than usual. I got to know you more: your humorous side, your protective side, and your serious side."

"I guess all that's left is the compassionate side."

She nudges me on the shoulder. "Be serious for a little bit. I'm pouring my heart out to you, and if you can't even, talk to me about it, then, I don't know. Maybe we can talk about something . . ." I turn our bodies to face each other, and while she's confused as to what I am doing, I decide to kiss her. I watch as her eyes widen, but she doesn't pull away. They never do.

Our lips part as she's left in a state of dissatisfaction, like she wasn't done, but she's definitely surprised. "Sorry, you were rambling."

"Y-you just kissed me." She raises her hand as if she's thinking of slapping me, but then lowers it, like the thought disappeared.

"I did. Do I wish I could take it back? Nope, not unless that kiss just put a big fat crack in our relation—" Her hands press against my shoulders as we fall back with her on top of me. Her lips find their way to mine. My hands roam along her back as we take in each other's scents, then we hear a grunt noise. We forgot that Dani is in the corner of my bed, just watching. Her hands are both covering her face with the fingers parted, revealing her eyes, so really, she wasn't really looking away. She doesn't say anything. Her face tells it all. "That, was, something." My hair is a bit messed up from her hands constantly running through it.

Sam scoots up to Dani and pulls her hands away from her face. She whispers something into her sister's ear, receiving a shake of the head from Danielle. "I don't know if I can do that." Though quiet, I can still hear partial words. Dani is dragged over to me by Sam.

"What is this about?"

"So, Dani told you that I liked you, yet, she failed to share one crucial point: she also likes you. It started out as a simple crush. She's seen pictures of you online and has heard some stories about you. I think it was the first time she hung out with you that made it official. She got to experience hanging out with you, and that moment you two had at the end. She's shy and a bit closeted, so, as her sister, I am going to do the sisterly thing and help her out with this little steppingstone to speaking the mind."

"So, you like me too?" She taps on her legs, trying to avoid the question.

"You're going to have to take the lead on this one. Just go in for a kiss," Sam tells her, while holding her hands.

"Excuse me. I don't think that's the right approach. I mean, you and I kissed. Wouldn't it be weird if I kissed your sister?"

"Only if you make it weird. If I remember correctly from what I've heard, you've done more than kissing sisters. Now kiss mine." She grabs our heads and tries to force us to kiss, which results in my head bumping into Dani's.

"Oww!" Danielle backs away, rubbing her head as it throbs.

"Oh my god, I'm sorry." I lean in closer and rub her forehead. "Are you okay?"

"Yeah, I'm fine. Nothing bad, it just hurts." She looks up into my eyes as I focus on the place I hit her, rubbing intently. She grabs onto my wrist and pulls herself up. Without notice, she presses her lips against mine. Too quick to grasp, I fall into it, reaching for her shoulders and pressing my body into hers. My hand falls to her back and trails downward till it reaches the spot right above her butt. I know this is wrong, them both being sisters and all, but I can't stop myself. Actually, I'm not completely certain them being sisters is the problem, but the fact that they're my friends. Usually, I'd be game, but I try to keep separate, my best friends and my intimate relationships. Friends are good to have, and real ones are hard to find. Though the reality of the situation is thick in my mind, my body can't seem to find the strength to push her away. I want to, or do I? I'm in a difficult bind. It's hard to do the right thing, especially when a different part of me is starting to take the wheel. I release my lips from hers in order to catch my breath, realizing our positions. I have her on her back, with me above her, while my hand is on her bare skin under her shirt. Luckily, I stop in time to where my hand isn't high enough to squeeze her breast, but, instead, rests on the bare skin right above her naval. She shivers at the sudden feeling of my fingers rubbing against her.

Samantha stands to the side of the bed with a big smile behind a hand. "Oh my. I wasn't expecting you to move this fast. And on my poor, defenseless sister."

"It was the heat of the moment, I swear."

"I bet. I mean, a brain is a powerful thing, but if there is one thing stronger than the human brain, it's, well, you know." *Crap, she noticed.* I cross my legs, acting as if nothing is wrong. "So, how far were you planning on going with her before you stopped? Just a question. Be completely honest."

"Okay. All lies aside, I was planning on going all the way."

"What stopped you?"

"Other than you watching us like a hawk? For one, I needed to breathe, and two, I felt it'd be wrong to go through with it. Don't get me wrong. I like the both of you. Sam, I've known you awhile, and hearing how you felt about me might've opened a few doors. As for you, Dani, I only just met you recently, so my feelings towards you are almost strictly by looks, not to sound like a complete douche. So yeah, if you two were anyone else, any girl that I just pass by in the hall or any girl that passes me looks in the field, I'd go all out. Us being friends kinda puts a damper on things. At least for me."

"Wow. I know I asked for the truth, but that was more than I expected to hear from you."

"What'd you expect?"

"I don't know. Something a guy would say, like 'I'm not in the mood,' but what you said sounded a little sincerer than I had expected, you know, in a fuckboy type of way."

"Oh gee, thanks for that."

She laughs in a way that tells that she knew what she said could've been misinterpreted in a way. "I'm just saying, there's a lot of talk about you. How you act. The different variety of women you've messed around with. Tell me something. Would you ever consider settling down for someone? The right one."

"Have you been talking to Mother?"

"What?"

"Nothing. It's nothing. Maybe, I don't know. Funny thing about finding the right one. You don't know she's 'the one' until you've had time to know her. I had a conversation similar to this one, recently. As for settling down, I don't know. I may be experienced in dating, but I don't cheat or anything like that. I usually date one person at a time, but at the same time, I'm polyamorous, if that makes sense."

Sam takes in a deep breath and moves closer to me. "I'm risking it right here," she mutters.

"What?"

Again, I find myself pushed down further than I already am on my bed. Sam shifts her hair to one side and straddles me. "I hope you don't think any less of me for doing this. I'm kinda putting myself at risk here."

"For what?"

"Losing you as a friend. Part of me wants to stop, but another part of me wants to know."

I find myself breathing in and out, trying to balance out my emotions of lust and calmness, but another part of me has other plans, and Sam notices this. "Know what?"

"Would you ever stop being my friend?"

"Why would you ask me that? I'd never stop being your friend. If there was a problem, we'd be civilized and talk about it."

"Even if we were to do something that can't be taken back once done?" My eyes widen just a little bit out of realization of the given situation. A part of me knew what was going on as soon as she threw both legs on either side of me, but my morals kind of hoped I was overthinking things. "I don't want you to think I'm taking advantage of you, being in the state of lust you're in." She leans into my ear, "I can feel it."

My first response to that is to switch positions. I grab onto her waist and flip her over so that my face is hovering over hers. "Please. As if you could take advantage of me. If anything, I'd be taking advantage of your good nature."

"I won't tell if you won't. Take advantage of me. Bend me to your will. Make me forever yours."

I hiss through my teeth. I feel as if I'm losing all control. "I'm warning you. This will be permanent, Sam. This is a serious matter. And what about your sist—"

"Shh. I know it's serious. And quite frankly, I don't care. If there is one thing I'm certain about, it's you. I'm willing to go to any length to show you just how much I love you."

"Lust and love are two—"

"Shh, let me finish. I've been in the friendzone for a while now, and it's been painful, watching, hearing stories about you and other women. I feel that the only way I can get over these feelings is to connect with you in a way that only I can. We're friends, have been for a while, which means that we have a connection you didn't have with those other bimbos. The longer I go, not being able to touch you, may just part us, out of the pain it'd give me just to see you every day. Doing this will give me a sense of satisfaction. I will know if you were meant to be with me or not, no matter how awkward future meetings may be. We will get through this together. As for my sister," she smiles seductively at me, "she'll join in when she feels the time is right." It's like she's a different person, entirely. She's so dominating in this situation, it surprises me, and if I must say, it's a complete turn-on. Her hands reach between us as she begins to unbutton my jeans. "I've watched you take charge, go after what you want. You're so dominant, but for once, I'd like to see you play the opposing role. I want to see you in your most vulnerable state." With one hand still on my crotch, her other one rubs against my face in slow notions. "I can tell by the look on your face. You're nervous. Maybe, this is just what you needed. A goddess to take you as her servant. You crave someone else to make the decisions for once, don't you? Or maybe, a mix of both. Come on, baby. Tell me what you want." She is now a completely different person. She has reached god-complex status, or in this case, goddess-complex. Like a German seductress without her tools of sexual torture, it seems Sam has found a certain fire in her heart that is giving her the strength to act on impulse, rather than on rational thinking. Her last words throw me as she forcefully strips me of my jeans. "Take me now, Adonis. Show me that the rumors aren't rumors." The fact she goes to a private girl school makes this situation way more tempting.

I finally snap as the beast I was holding in finds its way out. If I'm Adonis, then that makes her my Aphrodite, the woman who awakened my deepest desires. I lift her up by her legs as she responds by putting her arms around my neck, leaning in for a kiss, a kiss that I'd return with twice the force she exerts. She wants me, the real me, then that's what she's getting. I feel throbbing in my head and my vision starts to fade in and out, cutting some fragments out of this memory, then it just stops. I fall onto the bed with her under me, her legs still around my waist. "You are so beautiful." I kiss her neck as I slowly begin to disrobe her. I feel a second pair of hands on me. Dani comes in slowly and unsure of her actions, so I help her out. I place her next to her sister as I tend to both of their unspoken desires, well, one of theirs anyway. Sam was pretty open about what she wanted. My left hand holds Dani's leg up as it wraps around me. My other hand fondles her breast. Dani releases a few small moans but is still red with embarrassment. I sit up and remove the shirt off my back, revealing my toned body. I wouldn't say I'm ripped. I don't have Johnson's biceps or build, but I am definitely fit. My shoulders are broad, and my chest sticks outward. I am completely aware I have good upper body definition, but that doesn't mean I go to school and brag about it. A lot of girls find out on their own. It fills me with pride when I see their expressions. Girls who only see my face, handsome as it may be, usually don't expect me to have the body that I have, but when they see it, it makes me want to show them what I can do with it. With my shirt off, I crawl out of my jeans, so that I am just in my boxers, as I hover over both girls. Dani's first reaction is adorable in my eyes. She tries to cover her eyes but finds herself staring anyways, like a pup waiting for the bone to be thrown. Her hand jerks towards my pecs, feeling along the semi-hard surface. Sam, on the other hand, while she looks at my body, traces her hand along the fabric of my boxers, feeling everything, from the material to the obvious bulge that has formed underneath. Her thumb rubs against my neatly trimmed happy trail, starting from the origin at the bellybutton to the endpoint where something else begins. I take this as a "Take them off," and I do exactly what I imagine she's thinking. Sam stares with locked eyes while Dani bites her lip, growing hot by the experience. My hand reaches for the hem of Sam's shirt. I try her first, thinking that Dani would loosen up, being the last to disrobe. I pull her shirt over her head, revealing a purple laced bra, which complements her fair skin tone. I reach my hands behind her back, undoing the clasp that holds the bra in place.

I gently message her bosom, circling the areolas, which prove to be one of her sensitive spots. Good to know. Her body bucks at this. Her back arches and her legs tighten. She's right where I want her to be. I aim her legs towards the ceiling, removing her pants in the same manner I did the shirt, revealing a matching set of panties, purple and laced, revealing certain areas of skin that reside underneath. I lick my lips at this, going in for the attack. I rub my hand against her side, feeling the fabric of her lace while visualizing what's underneath, although her panties leave little to the imagination. The state of her undergarments makes me question if she's ever done something like this before, so daring, but at the moment, I don't care. I crawl down her body as I go in for a kiss, right below her belly button. She's just as beautiful as I imagined she'd be. My face hovers right above her most sensitive of spots. She takes advantage of this and tightens her legs around my head. My hands hold on to the inside of her thighs as I tackle the situation with sureness and initiative. I know exactly what I want. I want her to beg. I want her to regret pulling out this part of me, but at the same time, I want her to feel satisfied as I do in the moment. My eyes dart to the side as I eyeball Dani with pure lust in them. Luckily, I've still got some conscience left. I know Dani is a bit more fragile than her sister. She's also a little more sensitive and shyer, so I must approach her differently. I leave Sam hanging, but by the looks of it, she understands. She may be in lust mode, but a part of her, the sisterly part, still wants this to be a good experience for Danielle, and it is my obligation that I make this one not to forget. "How are you feeling?" I breathe hot air, causing Dani to tense up. Sam holds me from behind, with one hand along my scarred chest and the other, reaching lower.

"I-I don't know. I feel hot, like I'm going to pass out."

"That's just your body telling you that it needs sustenance. Don't worry. It's normal. The first step to cooling off is removing these clothes. Let the cool breeze kiss your body." I pet her belly, lifting her shirt just a little, waiting for confirmation to continue. She doesn't say a word, which is the right amount of confirmation I need. "Don't worry, really." I kiss her bare skin. I crawl on top of her and kiss her neck. Her body jerks at the sudden feeling of a certain appendage of mine, jabbing against her stomach. Sam remains as is, directing my love towards her sister.

"Oh my, I-I don't know if it'll—"

"Shhh. You'd be amazed at what your body can handle. Don't worry about a thing. It's your first time, so it's only natural you'll feel a little pain. Tell me, dearest, have you ever, popped your cherry?" She blushes at this. For some, it'd be hard to tell, with how red she initially was, but I notice a difference in hue. "You know, have you ever bled?"

"I know what it is." She cuts me off in haste. "And yes, I have. I was playing a bit too rough with—it's embarrassing."

I smile at her innocence. "Dani, there is nothing wrong with masturbation. It's completely normal. That just means it won't be as painful for you as it could've been, had you not popped it."

"I popped mine too, accident, of course." Sam says.

"That just means there'll be no blood shed tonight." *Damn.*

"I don't know about that." She runs her fingers along my sides, meeting the slight traces of scars on my skin. Her hands stop on them and her fingers rub the swollen areas. "What happened here?"

"I don't really know."

"Do they hurt?"

"No, they never did." In truth, my scars did burn a bit whenever I woke up with them. The first few days, they were usually inflamed until the swelling went down. "Are you concerned?" I rest my hand lightly on the inside of her thigh.

"A little. They look like they were initially deep. One just doesn't get injured like that and go without realizing it."

"Hey. I'm fine. You needn't fret over something that inflicts no pain on me."

Samantha balances on her knees and falls over on her butt, removing her panties, both legs extended outwards, then she drapes over me, once again, rubbing my chest as I'm arched over her sister. In her barest form, her breasts press against my shoulder as I can clearly see them with my peripheral vision. I manage to remove Dani's top, revealing a cute white bra with pink flowers on it. Adorable. The bra isn't too showy or seductive, but it squeezes her breasts together to show off her cleavage. She has natural beauty, Sam too. They don't need excessive amounts of makeup to create false beauty. She's skinny, with just the right amount of baby fat on her stomach, not enough to bulge outwards, but enough to have her not be a complete twig. She has dimension, something to grab onto. Her breasts are slightly larger than her sister's, but her body is more petite. She's like an anime character, with her size being that of a girl, but her body being that of a woman. I remove her bra in the same manner as her sister's. I hold her close to me, so that she can feel me against her. Her body trembles with need. My lips graze against hers. My hands work on her shorts. I pull them down just enough to show off a pair of white panties with some sort of design on them. I take this moment in, wanting to remember everything. I can't believe I'm doing this. There's no going back once I continue. If we quit now, we'd know exactly what we look like naked, but we'd still be in the dark of what we feel like, truly. I lift Dani's legs up, towards my body, her barely covered butt rubbing against me. She can feel it, and that causes her to vibrate a little. I definitely feel this as I hold in the desire to plow her mercilessly. She's a friend. She's a friend, which means I must show her who I am, while also trying to hold back, resulting in as little damage as possible. With her shorts and panties off, I kneel in front of both, Dani and Sam. I grab onto Sam's legs and drag her towards me, like an animal going in for the kill. I feel her, bare skin against bare skin. My head begins to ache again, and my eyes burn up. I decide to end the tease fest. I pull her up in sitting formation as I kiss her without warning. With one plunge, she moans into my mouth. I can truly feel her, wrapped around me in a certain comfort that a hug couldn't provide. Dani salivates at this, awaiting her turn. She decides not to wait. She crawls behind me, putting her arms around my body as I'm in an embrace with her sister. Her hands squeeze tightly at my inner thighs, a little higher where a certain part, or parts, of me encounter them. She kisses the nape of my neck as I am one with her sister. I have slept with sisters before, but this is different. I know these two, and that's a bit stimulating. About an hour and a half passes by and I'm lying, exhausted of breath, on my bed beside two equally exhausted sisters. Sam is huffing, and Dani tries to catch her breath. Their bodies feel warm next to mine.

"My, my." Sam breathes between words. "The stories are certainly true. You are a Ryder, pun completely intended."

"What stories have you heard, exactly?"

"Enough. That you are a force to be trifled with. Even in your most vulnerable state, you're hard to control. I initially wanted to dominate you, but that backfired. You truly have enough stamina, to handle two at once. You, Chance Ryder, are an amazing specimen: sexy, smart, fierce. You have that fire that a girl just can't help herself but jump into. You're dangerous."

"And don't you forget it. How about you, Dani? Was I, enough for you?" Odd question to ask when I already know, but I do enjoy the various answers received. There is never a tiresome moment in the relinquishing of a girl's virginity—not for me, anyway.

Danielle takes a deep breath to speak. "I was expecting a lot, but you proved to be more than I could handle. Sorry if I screamed a little too loud. The stories about you are no lies. They are usually vivid, with so much depth, that I couldn't help but imagine it as a movie in my mind, but only till I experienced it myself did those tall tales prove to be legit." She rubs her side. "I feel like if I lay here any longer, I won't be able to move." I think the aftershock is starting to hit, like an extreme exercise where the next morning proves to be the most painful.

I laugh at this. "Chance? About what I said—about our friendship—"

I cut her off. I turn to face her, holding her hand. "We'll never stop being friends, ever. No matter what. I promise you that."

She smiles and nuzzles my neck with her face. "I love you."

My eyes widen with surprise. Those words aren't just words; they're genuine. I can tell, but I don't know if I can say them back and feel what she wants me to feel. "I love you, too." She isn't looking at me, so she can't see the dead eyes I give to the ceiling. I care about Sam, Dani too, but if it's love that she's seeking, I'm afraid she'll have to wait until I can find it myself. "Look, Sam." I hear snoring as I look to the side. Both, Dani and Sam, have fallen asleep on my sides. They're warm, this I can't deny. They're comfortable, a little too comfortable. I find myself dozing off, then everything goes dark.

V

I wake up early, ready to tackle another day. The sun is fairly new in the sky, and the birds are hardly awake, themselves. Everyone is usually asleep around this time or beginning to wake up for either school or an early work shift. Luckily, it's the weekend, which means no school, like that makes any difference to me. I like waking up early for some "me time." Like most days, I decide to follow a routine. I jump in the shower, washing yesterday's scent off my body. I end up finding myself in thought. About what? What can a sixteen-year-old male, high school student possibly have to think about? I hear my phone go off while in the shower. I reach out of the curtains, shaking off my hands so they're somewhat dry when touching my phone. Have you ever tried operating your touchscreen with wet hands? It's difficult, that's what it is. Your fingers stick and hardly slide across the screen. The drops of water that smear on the screen provide a challenge. You must dry off the phone and wait for it to dry completely, because if it isn't, your fingers don't slide fluidly. I look at the notifications. A text from Sam. The last few days have been a bit much. I told Dani and Sam that what we did wouldn't affect our friendship, and I stayed true to that word. It's what happened after, what Sam said just before she dozed off. It was a bit awkward to face Mother the next day, because, not only did she hear that night's activities, she also had to turn off my light. You may be thinking, "Who has sex with the lights on?" or "What's so bad about that?" When your mom has to pop your door open after hearing no response, to turn off your light while you're on your bed, sleeping with two girls, stark naked, with the blanket barely covering your legs, it can get weird fast. She was kind enough to let us sleep in that state. She even called their mom, asking if it was alright for the girls to stay the night. Something about a movie night. Mother truly is the best. From what Mother said, it's almost as if the girls' mom was completely clueless of their absence.

As for yesterday, I ditched my football game. The coach is going to be more pissed than usual when I see him next. He already believes that I don't belong on the team, that if I don't believe it's my obligation to show up, then I have no right to play. I feel like the only reason I'm still on the team at all is because of Storm. Storm is his favorite. As a coach, or even a teacher, you're not supposed to show favoritism. Let's face facts. Even if it's not shown, there is always a favorite. There is always going to be someone you like more than someone else or someone you don't like at all. Of course, a teacher is going to like the student who actually tries to excel, a lot more than the student who sleeps constantly or who pays attention to practically anything else but the lesson. I'm a different case. I barely show up to school, but I still keep my grades up. In the case of football, Storm plays his ass off. He gives his 110%. As mathematically incorrect as that is in my head, he gives his all. I barely show up, if at all. Storm, being the coach's favorite, talks to him. Honestly, I don't care if I'm kicked from the team. I agree with the coach.

I skim over Sam's text message:

> "Heyyy ☺ Sorry, I don't usually use emojis. My cousins got arrested last night shoplifting. Idiots. They made it worse by resisting arrest. They ran and even cracked a bottle of stolen

alcohol over the cop's head. God, why
do they have to be so stupid. They're
lucky they're still underage. One more
month and they better straighten up."

I text back in a few simple words:

                            "God, that sucks."
"So, anyways. What r u doing??"
                            "Shower. You?"
"Just laying here. Woke up not too
long ago.
What are your plans for the day?"
                  "I have to fight Ash today,
                        so that will be fun.
                  Dinner plans at 6. You?"

Sam is a fast texter. Honestly, I don't know how a lot of girls do it. While I'm typing a text, it almost always seems like they've got the next answer figured out, followed by more conversation.

"I'm going to a birthday party later
today. A friend's brother. Other than
that, I don't know. Dani's staying home.
She rented a few movies to watch. Hey,
can I ask you something?"
                                  "What?"

I wait for what seems like minutes, the longest pause between texts in this whole conversation, then the phone rings. I answer. "This question requires a phone call?"

"Yeah. Have I made you uncomfortable the last few days?"

"With?"

"I mean it when I say I love you, but a part of me wonders if those three words are too much for you. You say it back, but I feel the emotion isn't behind them."

"Look, Sam, I was meaning to talk to you about this earlier, like yesterday, but I couldn't bring myself to. What we did, we can't take back, and I'm okay with that. However, I don't know if I'm ready to love. I wouldn't even know what it would feel like. You're a close friend, and I didn't want to tear us apart if . . ."

"Let me stop you right there. I'm not going to stop being your friend. It's going to be painful, but I will fight for your love. We had a moment. A moment I wouldn't take back for anything. I'm okay if, what we have is strictly physical."

"Woe, Sam. I couldn't do that to you. I can't use you like that."

"My sister and I talked it over." The fact that she talked to Dani before confronting me about this is a bit of a shock. I didn't even get a part in the decision. "You made me feel good in a way I've never felt. I was able to escape the world for that moment, and I'd be happy to continue doing that. Well, I gotta go do something. See you later. Love, uh, sorry. Bye."

She sounded a bit down, but she doesn't want to give me up. A part of me feels bad about that. In all my relationships, I was able to say, "I love you" with ease, but with these two, I can't bring myself to be untruthful.

I wipe the fog from the bathroom mirror, getting a look at my face. I dress and groom myself, but what do I do while it's so early? I quietly leave the house, taking a look at the very few cars driving down my street. Boxes are piled up next to a Movers van next door. I wave at Mr. Baldwick. He waves back. "Hey, Mr. Baldwick. You're moving?"

He rubs his prematurely balding head as Gwen, his five-year-old daughter, clings to his pant leg. "Hey there, kid. Yeah, we're moving to Georgia. I have a job opportunity there. It's been nice here, but it's been hard for me to find work. The wife and I will make it work."

"I hope things go well for you and Heather. Gwen too." Gwen runs up to me and I kneel. She runs into my arms and I pick her up. Gwen is young, which means she's highly impressionable.

"Thanks, Chance. I hope things go well for you too. You're a brilliant boy. You have a future, and I'm not just saying that because you're starting off well-placed. If only all teenagers acted like you: kind and respectful to their elders."

All teenagers being like me? Those words ring in my ears. If only Mr. Baldwick knew who I really am, what I really think. I don't think he'd want more teenage boys like me, boys who use women. I may be aware that what I'm doing is wrong, but I don't stop doing it, and that unto itself is even more wrong than not knowing. "Well, I got to get going."

"Oh, somewhere to be?"

"Not really. Just walking around."

"If that's the case, I can spare a few minutes. Want to come in? I'll have Heather make us some tea."

"Uh, yeah. Sure. That sounds nice." The Baldwicks' house isn't too big, but it's the appropriate size for three, maybe even four. The house, itself, is brown with a picket fence in the backyard. The walls are salmon, which totally clashes with the outside. Personally, I don't like the color scheme. The house has a staircase that leads to a bedroom and second bathroom. Steve Baldwick sits across from me in a reclining chair, making small talk.

"Sorry to intrude, but I couldn't help but notice the police at your house a while back."

"Yeah, um. It was just an incident with an unwanted guest. Nothing to get into."

"Fair enough. Sorry I couldn't show up to your birthday. We were boxing up our things. Lots to do, you know. Hehe. I remember when we first moved here. An energetic, 8-year-old boy running around the streets. The first thing you did when we showed up was run over and introduce yourself. You were kind then, just as you are now. I hope you never change. This world needs kind souls like yours. I don't know if you're noticing, but this world is going to hell, pardon my French. All the shootings, the muggings, the cults."

"I don't know. I'm not, how you see me." I say.

"Don't say that. You've got a future. Keep up with what you're doing." A certain smell fills the air: cinnamon.

"Tea is done. And I noticed my dear husband didn't say it, so I'm going to. Happy belated birthday, Chance. You're growing up. Just don't grow up too fast."

"I was getting there, Hun."

"Uh huh, sure you were, well, I'll leave you to it."

"Mrs. Baldwick? Don't you want to sit down and talk?" I ask.

"Oh my, yes, but, Gwen and I have to clean her room of the scattered boxes, don't we?"

Gwen rubs her dress in an innocent manner, digging her foot into the carpet. "Yes, Mommy." Heather grabs her daughter's hand and leads her away. She uses her free hand and waves it at me. "Bye, bye."

We sit, drinking cinnamon spice tea. The temperature of the tea can be seen clearly as steam escapes the mugs. They rest on coasters on a glass table between us. I cool it off with a few blows, as I take a small sip. "This is pretty good."

"Yeah. She grew up in England, so tea is her specialty, hehe. No, but really, she does all the cooking. I'm lucky if I can make a top ramen without burning the noodles."

"Well, you're lucky to have a woman who cares."

"Yeah. She's too good for me, but I try. How about you? Is there a girl in the picture?"

"Nope. That there isn't." *There's multiple.*

He slowly takes a sip out of his mug, burning his lip in the process, wiping it with a napkin. "You're still young. Find someone smart. Someone who doesn't settle. A real go-getter. I bet you catch a lot of eyes."

If only he knew. "I guess. I'm not ready for love."

"At your age, it's rare to find. Give it time." He looks at the clock. "Oh, look at the time. I'm sorry to cut this short, but I got to get back to what I was doing."

"No apologies. I hope things go well for you at your new job."

"As for you, too. Be good, that is. Don't get in trouble with the law or anything. One more thing, those parties. They can get a bit loud, but I let you enjoy yourself. Your next neighbor may not be as forgiving. Keep that in mind, Chance."

"Thank you for the tea."

I continue on my little stroll, passing by a few homeless guys with grocery carts and the gangbanger-looking types. "Watch where the fuck you're going, kid?"

One of them nudges me on the shoulder with his. A real looker: ragged clothes that reek of alcohol abuse and sewage; a scarred hand; and yellow stained teeth, most likely from years of smoking. A switch lighter hangs partly from his pocket and in the other, a knife. "Fuck you looking at, money bags." He holds one hand on the handle of his knife, then lets go, pulling his torn shirt over his pants. They walk away as a police car drives by. A tattoo of a gun can partially be seen where the collar part of his shirt begins, on the back of his neck. Scarring can be seen on the back of his hairless head as he walks away.

"Dicks," I think to myself. Men, or people like that in general, are what's making this world go to shit. I'm not against tattoos. Some of the nicest people I've met have tattoos, as well as the cruelest, prickish people I've ever met being inkless. There is always something going on in the world, whether it is a shooting in a school or a church, a suicide displayed in a public venue or a tree in the backyard, or even criminals on the run, leaving bodies dead in their trail. If there ever was a time for the devil to rise, now would be it. Sins are everywhere: teachers sleeping with students, parents bruising their children, and cruel kids posting nudes of the one that broke their hearts online for the world to see. Bitches, nudes are private. If you're childish enough to pull that card, then maybe your heart was meant to be broken. Break you down, so you can build yourself up, hopefully in a good way. As for where I live—Poshe, CA—blood stains the streets, literally. If you walk along a sidewalk, there is bound to be orange mixed into the gray. Poshe is between Bakersfield and Fresno, and just like both of their reputations, Poshe has its beauty as well as its ugly. Funny. You'd think that, with a name like Poshe, it'd be in-between Los Angeles and Beverly Hills. In a way, my home portrays the gothic and bleak display of mobster territory in the 1940s, without the mobster overrun and with the exception of higher technology. This is the place where vigilantes and rap gods are made. Why Mother moved us here a while ago to make a home, I have no idea. Surprised that no one tried to rob us, though. If they did, then I don't know what I'd do. A part of me would say, "Hey, they needed it more than me," but the more practical side of me would think, "If they have to steal to get what they want, then maybe they deserve less than what they have." May sound like shit coming from a boy who's never known what it feels like to be poor, but it's how I see it. It's my opinion. An opinion is really the only thing anyone is truly entitled too. Names, too. No one can take your name forcefully, without your consent.

A cop car rests on the side of the road with one tire missing and the airbag inflated. I see the slight glimpse of a head behind the airbag. Somebody's in there. The fact that no one's done anything proves what I say about this place. I run up to the car and try to force the door open, finally tearing it from its hinges. A hand drops down, skin torn from the palm. I try to pull the body from the car. Nothing. I grab the pen that I keep on me and prick the airbag, deflating it. The officer is already gone. I notice blood, still wet, on the collar part of his uniform. His hand is glued to the steering wheel and one side of his face is bruised. I pull the collar down a bit. I should really leave this for the cops, but I'm curious. His body is right in front of me. How could I not observe before the scene is kept behind yellow tape. I see one of his eyes flicker. He's still alive, barely, even if there is only a spec of life left in him. I pull down the collar of his uniform, revealing a gash, not deep enough to automatically kill him, but deep enough to not give him much time. This is fairly new. This had to have happened within the last hour. I turn his face. There, in a neon pink smudge, is what looks like lipstick. I hear sirens coming, which is my que to book it. This early in the morning, and I have already come across gang bangers and a dead, or dying, cop. All in all, I'd say this day is going to be eventful. The police cars are followed by a firetruck and an ambulance. The fireman looks directly at me and I nod. If I did anything but, then I'd look suspicious. More suspicious than I already do, one street away from a dead cop. Shit, this is going to come back to haunt me. I just know it.

I pass by what looks like a robbery in a convenience store, and even a pink Volkswagen, shaking and vibrating, with a pair of legs on the steering wheel. Just going to let them have their privacy. All of this, and it's not even sundown. Honestly, the best time to attempt any of these acts would be in the bleak blanket of nighttime. Kids skateboard past me, nodding their heads in acknowledgement. At least, not everyone's a dick in this Gotham rip-off. I walk towards the park. It's around that time. Time to get it over with. I see a crowd as I make my way through them. Of course, Ash is centered, right in the middle of it all.

"Didn't think your ass would show up." He grinds his teeth and a look of complete seriousness is drawn on his face. "Let's get this over with, Ryder."

"Last name. I don't know. That's such a low budget villain thing to say."

"Which would make you the low budget hero."

Good comeback, but I have one even better. "Low budget movies usually never have a plot twist and are straight forward. If I'm the low budget hero, then that means this will be quick with no climax. Guess who wins in low budget hero films." I finish that sentence by pointing at myself, smug about it. "The ones who start the fight usually end up regretting it."

"No, the ones who start the fight know what they're doing."

"And are beaten down in the end by the very person they underestimated. LaRusso, but that's just one example."

Phones are taken out as everyone backs up just a little to give us room. "Kick his ass!" *Animals. That's what they are.*

"Look, we don't have to do this. You can still back out. I won't think any less of you."

"Good to know." Ash slowly makes his way up to me, both arms up, guarding his face. He throws the first punch. I dodge, without moving my hands. He tries again but gets the same result. I fluidly circle him, not moving a hand as I avoid contact, repetitively. "Fight back."

"I'm not fighting anyone."

"Because you're a little bitch. Backing out of a fight can ruin that false sense of bravado you're trying to show everyone. Now's your chance to show how tough you are." He shoves me. "C'mon. Don't you want just a little blood. In respect to our past friendship, I'll even let you throw the first successful punch."

"Oh. How very gentleman of you. Would you like an award? Listen." If I'm going to fight, then I'm fighting in a way that tires him out. There are ways to fight that don't have to end in black and blue.

"Enough. You think people want to videotape this? They're going to have to edit the video to the point where you throw your first punch."

"Gonna be a boring video, then."

He continues throwing his punches, tiring himself out with every attack. He starts to move without pattern, which starts to catch me off guard. It gets harder to dodge when he has no rhythm. He finally manages to contact skin, causing me to stumble back. As I'm caught off-guard, he strikes me in the gut, causing me to grab my stomach, bent over. As I'm in this form, he takes no time to knee me in the chin, grabbing my hair. "How about now? Had enough?" He throws me to the ground, kicking me a couple times while I'm down. I take it amongst myself to grab hold of his leg. He tries to release my grip. "Stop. What do you think you're doing?"

Storm rushes into the scene but doesn't get involved. He stands on the inner circle, standing next to the scum holding their cellphones. "C'mon, man. You got this. You're holding back."

"Is that so? Show me, Chance. Get riled up for me."

I spit out blood that clings to my bottom lip. My head starts to ache, but not because of Ashton. It's more of a migraine. I cling on to the ground beneath me. "Stop, my head."

"You want me to stop, then do something, pretty boy." His foot goes back and kicks me in the ribs. With force, he places the foot on my face. "Fitting end for a place mat." With one hand ready, I grab his foot and throw him back on his ass.

I crawl to my feet. I grab Ash by both legs and pick him up, while facing away as he hangs on my back. I use my strength to swing him around a bit in midair, then let go. He slides a distance, hitting his head on a rock. On the landing, he appears to have also landed on his arm. He grits his teeth, throwing his head back as he conceals a scream. There is no point in commencing any further.

"I think we're done here. Oh, and by the way. Refusing to fight doesn't make me weak. Having the internal struggle to keep from pounding you to a bloody pulp even though I want nothing more than to do so makes me a stronger man than you." I push the nearest viewer out of my face and swim through each layer of bastards.

Ash yells after me. "Get the hell back here! We're done when I say we're done."

Storm follows me. "Looks like they're going to have a boring video," I say.

"Oh, I don't know about that. You swung him around pretty good. That might be the only part of video that's worth watching. Sorry I didn't get involved."

"That's fine. It wasn't your fight. It was ours."

"Yet, you involve yourself in other affairs."

"Funny," I smirk to the side. "I seem to remember a kid who ran into a problem that wasn't his, because he felt that it was the right thing to do. This was my fight, scheduled, too, so I understand. If it was a kid that's just getting picked on, that would be the time to intervene."

"Like that one kid who gets bullied, constantly. You've jumped into quite a bit of those ordeals."

"Kyle. Yeah, good kid. He has to stand up for himself. For as long as he doesn't, I will."

Storm pushes me to the side, playfully. "You'll throw yourself into a situation and beat someone up senseless for someone else, but you refuse to do so for yourself. I don't get you. I truly don't. For anyone who does, I applaud their strategic, puzzle-solving skills."

"I have to go, man. Dinner thing. Unless you want to come."

Storm starts jogging away. "Nah, I'm good. Have fun for me, won't you?"

I show up at Jessyka's house but am surprised to see a few cars parked outside. I knock on the door and with no hesitation, the door opens. I find myself face-to-face with an older woman with dark hair, obviously dyed, and an outfit that shows she's trying to look younger than she is. She's not too old, maybe in her mid-forties, but her clothes resemble that of a girl who's preparing for her first date. Red lipstick and generic hoop rings. "Hi, I'm—"

"Chance Ryder. Yes, my niece described you. I didn't know how accurate she was. So, are you her boyfriend?"

"Um, no. I'm not."

She sighs. "Weird. She hasn't told us who he is, yet." *I wonder why. He's completely inappropriate and doesn't know how to present himself to parents, or adults in general.* If he acted as himself in front of any responsible parent, they'd turn him away. If they could read my mind, they'd probably turn me away, too. Thank God, they can't. I know how to act in public. "Do you know who he is?"

First word. "Nope."

"Hey, Chance. You made it." She takes my hand and leads me to the back.

"Crap, sorry. If you told me you were having a party, I would've gotten you a gift. I thought this was just dinner. I can run to the store right now."

She grabs my arm as I turn around to head for the door. "You don't have to do that."

"I'm rich. The least I could do is run and get you something."

"If you stay till the end of the party, you can give me another gift. C'mon, the party's back here."

There aren't too many people here. Thirty-five, tops. There's music going on as everyone settles in, doing their own thing. There's a couple sitting back, drinking punch. A few people are dancing to the music, off key. "Hi, you must be Chase. You are a looker." An older woman, slightly younger than the aunt who opened the door for me, walks towards us. Her hair is curly and blonde, and her lips are pink. She looks like an older version of Jessyka in the face. She holds out her hand to me and I take it.

"My name is Chance."

"Oh, I'm sorry. I'm Jessyka's mother. I hope you enjoy the party, kids. I'll leave you two be. Don't do anything daring."

"Hey, Jessie!" A male with a guitar on his back calls her over. She leads the way.

"Hey, Austin. This is Chance. A friend of mine."

"Hey, man." I hold out a hand.

He hesitates a bit before he returns the gesture. "Aww, yes. Chance. Rich boy. Didn't expect to meet you amongst us mortals."

"Sorry? What's that supposed to mean?"

"This doesn't seem like the type of place a rich boy would take part in." He pinches my hand with his thumb and his index like a picky child picking the peas out of his soup.

"I'm just like you. I don't go to Galas or fancy, snobbish events."

He gives a face like he doesn't believe I'm just like him. "Right. All you rich guys are the same. You have money, so you don't have to worry about work or any actual responsibilities to make up for it."

"Well, I guess, if you look at it in that lighting. But—"

"But nothing. I've met a few rich kids in my life, always showing off. You all come from money, so don't you even think you know what it feels like to work your ass off to barely get by." He glances over to Jessyka. "Why'd you even invite this twink? Are you two close, or what?"

I lightly move Jessyka out of the way, then step up to Austin. I grab him by the shirt and pull him in so that his face is a couple inches from mine. "Don't even, for a minute, think you know who I am. I don't use my money as a crutch to get by. I don't shove it in people's faces. Any other rich kid you've met, I assure you, I'm not them."

He doesn't look amused. "So, you going to be a big man. Punch the kid who has no intension in resorting to physical violence. Just get it over with."

I release his shirt and lightly push him out of my face. "I think I said what I needed to say." I shove by him, nudging his shoulder. Jessyka follows me, while Austin tries to ask why she'd run after someone like me.

"Wait, Chance. I'm sorry about Austin. He can be a bit, unfiltered about his biases. He's actually a nice guy when you get to know him."

I'm sure. "If he's judgmental about certain groups, then, does that mean he's judged you? Does he know the real you, or even the context as to why I'm even here?"

"What are you talking about?"

"He judged me as a 'rich, spoiled brat.' I bet he's pointed out your flaws. Commitment issues. You stray from loyalty. After all, you did bring me here to make Ash jealous, did you not?"

I'm met with a slap across the face. "Are you suggesting I'm a . . . a whore?" She says the last word silently, so no one hears. Some eyes are on us, including Austin's. He shows a toothy grin. He's certainly enjoying this.

"I'm suggesting—" I'm slapped once again.

She grabs me by the ear, then grabs my arm with force, a pissed off look in her eyes. "Come with me." She drags me into her house. "Don't bother us! I have to talk with him!" Her aunt, mother, and other relatives stare at us as she drags me upstairs. She shows some strength as she throws me into her room, closing the door behind her.

"Look, I'm sorry, but it's my truth. You're—" Again, she doesn't let me finish. She slaps me in the same spot as the other two times, then, to my great surprise, clashes her lips to mine. She parts them almost as quickly as she combined them. She raises her hand, but I don't flinch.

"I'm going to tell you what you told Austin. You don't know me, so let it go. You can't just call me a whore and get away with it."

"I didn't." The stinging sensation on my cheek returns, getting more painful as each blow overlaps the previous one.

"You were pointing towards it. Do you think I sleep with every sad soul that gets the opportunity to date me? Newsflash. I don't. I'm not some floozy. Some one-nighter bimbo that screams the night away, then uses the morning to find a new night project." She raises her hand and slams it down, only to be caught by my hand.

"Will you stop with the—" The sweet taste of watermelon from her lips returns to mine as she shuts me up with one small move. I grab her shoulders and pull her away. "What's with you? Are you bipolar? I don't get you?"

The stinging on my cheek has been worked in, so the next blow begins the numbing process. It begins to feel good after a while. "In a way, I'm kinda like you."

"How are you like me? And don't even think about slapping me. That's getting old."

"It's funny." Her arms are on either side of my body, with her face above mine and her legs straddling me. "You say I have commitment issues and that I'm not loyal. Are you sure you weren't using words that describe you to describe me?"

"I'm loyal. Just not committed."

"You can't have commitment issues and be loyal. If you're going to play the field, you can at least own the role you've taken. Chance Ryder: local eye candy, free-for-all deviant."

"I wouldn't say free-for-all. I do have standards."

"Do I fit them?"

Crap. This situation only has one ending from the way things are playing out. Should we just quit prolonging the inevitable and get it over with? "You do."

"You were right about one thing, though. I did bring you here, so that you could get back at Ash. Not me, you. Is that a problem?"

Her hair slowly slides across my face as her head moves ever so slowly, following the movements of her body on mine, trying to find the right bodily reaction needed to continue. "Nope." Without any more hesitation, she loses her shorts and undies, and I lose mine, getting to work with our sexual desires. Turns out, she likes getting her hair pulled, hard. Time slips by, the whole thing a big blur. Her lips can still be felt along my neck, and her powerful moans, still heard. Her hands were quite adventurous, frisky if you will, as were mine, and I loved every second. The parts I could remember, anyway.

We return to the party, our minds still in the room. How long were we in there? Thirty minutes? Some spots are blank, following the head-spinning headache that overpowered me. I remember having to hold down on her mouth multiple times, trying to muffle the screams that echoed in my palms. Her nice, slender body matching the rhythm of my more toned body. Her eyes ran along my physique: the scars that marked my chest and abdomen. My eyes traced over every curve of her, remembering the moment, like I do with every girl I sleep with. I remember Monica who wasn't too skinny, with fat in all the right places and the tiny moans that marked the night. Sheila and her adorable, Australian accent that hummed nicely in my ears; her body was toned, her chest a bit smaller than some. She had the riding skill of a Texan champ during bull-riding season. There was Rebecca, Tiffany, Marylyn, Crystal, Misty, Diyanne, Beverly, and so many more. They all have places in my memory, each one given a signature that marks our moment, but none have come close to Sam and Dani. It's not that they were better, but more along the lines of, *they are friends*, which allowed me to appreciate them more.

"Hey, Jessyka. Where were you?" A tall, lanky male with baggy clothing and slight scarring on his face walks up to us. "Hey, man.

I'm Dustin. You are?" He holds his hand out to me, waiting for me to do the respectful thing and grab his hand in return.

"I'm Chance." I take his hand in mine and shake it firmly.

"Far out. Any man of Jessyka's is a friend of mine. Wanna join us in our little circle? We're just exchanging poetry."

"About?"

"Anything, really. Whatever speaks to you." He sounds a bit space-bound, but altogether, a nice guy.

"You write poetry?" Jessyka asks, looking at me, her fingers dragging along my arm. "You don't strike me as the type."

"Cool, man. Wanna share with us? I'm sure they'll welcome you in." We walk over to a small group of teens reciting poetry or self-written lyrics. Austin happens to be in this group as he is the next one to go while we walk up.

"One mustn't strive for approval to be accepted, for as long as you be yourself, and nothing less. That is all one can ever expect from another. No mask. Just your face. No guise. Just who you are: unfiltered and without secrets. Whether homosexual, heterosexual, or something in between, you are beautiful and should be treated fairly. As long as you accept yourself, others will as well. You are you, and that makes you perfect." Austin sees me in the crowd, and the mood changes. "Dustin, man. Why'd you have to invite him over here? He's not like us. Does he even play?" Austin's eyes don't leave my body. It's obvious he hates me, but why? Because I'm rich? That seems like a piss-poor reason to hate someone. "Whatever. I can't do this, not with him here." Austin walks out of the circle, dramatically.

"So, I'm guessing his whole 'be yourself' thing was a guise."

"I'm sorry. He can be a bit—"

"Yeah," I interrupt, "I've heard."

"So, about that poem. What speaks to you? Love, money, what?"

"I should warn you. My poetry is a bit different than you'd expect coming from someone like me." Dustin rotates his hand as a gesture, telling me to proceed. "Pardon me if there is no beat. I mainly write lyrics, so the instrumental is absent."

"That's fine. Poetry doesn't need a beat, man."

I take a breath as to ready myself. "—Blackness roams inside my soul; a dark, relentless part of home, that pulls me further down the road, a path into the great unknown. To be unsure of what's to come, to know for certain how it ends; a prolonged death that's none too far, that follows these untold events. I feel them eating deep inside, the demons that refuse to go. The thoughts that echo in my mind, the feeling of being alone."

I pause for a few seconds. They wait in silence to not interrupt any last words that may follow. "Wow, that was . . . deep."

"It didn't take long to write. It's unfinished."

"No, really." One of the girls speak up. "That was good. With the right music and pace, that could be a song. It's better than some songs that play repetitively on the radio."

"Thank you . . ."

"Haylee."

"It was average at best." Austin walks up out of nowhere. "Poetry is supposed to have heart. Soul. What you said were just words. Empty words at that. Was there even any meaning behind them? I mean, in the lyrics, you said you're alone. From how I see it, you're popular. You get all the girls you want and to top it off, you're rich. How the hell are you alone?"

"Come on, man." An average height male jumps in the middle. "Can't you just admit he's not too bad and get on with your life?"

"Yeah, Austin." Jessyka defends me. "You can have company and still be alone."

"Do you know how stupid that sounds? You can't have company and be alone. You can be lonely, I guess, but that's a different subject. Jesus. Why are you all taking his side on this? You don't even know him."

"Neither do you."

"Forget it. I don't need this. Sorry, Jessyka. I have somewhere to be. Happy birthday." Austin walks away, heading for the house.

"Wait, Austin. Don't go."

I put my hand on Jessyka's shoulder. "I'll go talk to him. Yo, Austin. Wait up." I catch up to him, outside of Jessyka's house while he's near his car.

"Oh my God. Won't you leave me alone, you spoiled sac of—"

I punch Austin square in the jaw as he falls back against his car door. He holds his face as he picks himself up. "What the hell, man." He swings at me, but I catch his fist, throwing his body against his car. I pin him to it, facing the vehicle.

"You don't know me. You don't know what I'm thinking, nor what I'm capable of. People like you are close-minded. You're so quick to judge someone. Maybe, you're due for a change."

He elbows me in the gut and turns around to face me. "Get your filthy hands off me. You're even crazier than I thought." He turns to get in his car when I grab the guitar case off his back and whack him upside the head with it. The weight of the guitar makes a crack sound as he falls to the floor. He rests his hand over his head and looks at it. Red covers his fingertips. "What the fuck!"

My hands tremble as I try to fight the headache that sends me into a state of intense pain. Everything starts to fade when, "Is everything alright?" A female's voice is heard when I slowly turn around. Jessyka's mother is at the door with a concerned look in her eyes. Her face, though blurry at first glance, starts to come into focus.

"Uhh, yeah," I call out, "Austin just fell. I helped him up. No worries."

She waits a few seconds while observing us, then she turns and closes the door. Austin's car door closes as he slowly begins to drive away. Small traces of blood can be seen clearly in his blonde hair. "You're buying me a new guitar, rich kid. Ya fuckin lunatic." His car speeds away.

I get home late and head straight to my room. The rest of the party went by quickly. All the drama left with Austin. I may have lost it just a little when confronting him by his car, but what's done is done. There's no point crying over spilled blood, or whatever the saying is. In this case, blood is accurate. Something inside of me, a part of me that I've never succumbed to, wanted him to suffer, and for what? Having his own opinion of me? If I were to do what I was thinking in the moment, I'd be no different than everyone else: the ones who punish those they disagree with. Everyone's entitled to their own opinions, even if the majority of those opinions are wrong.

I plop down on my bed, feeling something rub against my leg in my pocket. I pull out a phone, but it's not mine. It's got a gray case with a music note on it. I push down on the side button and the screen turns on. No lock screen. How unsecure. There's a pic of a boy on it. A boy and a girl. The girl, I don't know, but the boy, I do. Blonde hair over a pale face. One eye visible for the camera and the other one, hidden behind semi-long bangs. The one that can be seen is hazel in color. The neck of a guitar can be seen rising above his head as it hangs from his back. I have Austin's phone, but how? I don't remember grabbing it, so how'd it get in my pocket? He could've planted it there, but I don't see the point of doing that. That just means he'd have to come by and get it, but he doesn't know where I live. Guess I have to go to him, but not tonight. I rest the phone near mine on my dresser, taking notice of a thin, yet deep gash on my palm as I begin to doze off into slumber. My vision fades steadily as well as my hearing. The last thing I hear before I turn in for the night is quiet, but clear. The words sound ghostly and send a shiver down my spine. "You're not strong enough."

√I

Nothing says, "Wake the hell up!" quite like breaking my neck on a three-foot fall. I wouldn't really call, falling off my bed, a delightful awakening, but it does the job. Almost as soon as my eyes open, I hear a notification on my phone.

"Hiya. I don't think we made out a clear time schedule for when to meet up. Text back when you get this."

"Hey, Ariel. So, what time do you have in mind?" I text back.

No more than a minute passes when my phone dings. She is quick at this, no doubt. "Hi. Would it be okay if we go sometime during lunch? There's a movie showing at 1:25."

1:25? That isn't too far off from the time now, maybe three hours. "See you then."

She responds with a smiley face. Three hours to do whatever. What the hell am I going to fill the time with? I hear knocking at the door, so I rush to see who it is. "Hey, Storm. What brings you by?"

"Just stopping by. Did you just wake up?"

"Yeah. Late day, I guess. Why?"

"You're still in your boxers."

I step aside, allowing him in to wait as I dress. A young woman is walking her dog when her eyes come across me. I raise my hand and wave. "Hey."

She does the same and raises her hand to mimic my greeting. She does it slowly. Her eyes try to decide whether to look directly at me in the state I'm in. I slowly close the door as I reenter my home. That was a bit awkward, but it's done.

"Honestly. Answering the door like that? You never did have shame. Then again, I never really taught you to have any." Mother enters the room, moving a pile of laundry with her. Do you know that girl?" I shake my head. "That would explain the shocked expression on her face. She was cute, though. I bet she thought so, too."

"Mother. She's like 21 or something. There's no way she's in high school."

"And? That's not too far off from 16. Usually, a 21-year-old is bound to make the same mistakes as a 16-year-old. What I'm saying is, five or six years isn't a lot. A 21-year-old is still a teenager, mentally. If you brought home a twenty-year-old, I'd allow it. I kept you long enough. Get dressed and go outside. You two enjoy yourselves."

"Thank you, Miss Winters." He looks at me, "Have I ever told you that you have the coolest mom ever?"

"Only a lot."

We walk down the street, talking nonsense. To any random bystanders, our conversation would sound a bit crazy out of context. "So, you don't know how you got them?"

"I don't know. I wake up with cuts and sheets clinging to me. Mother says I lash out in my sleep."

"And cut yourself with what? Your fingernails aren't long enough to break skin. Maybe, there's another explanation."

"Like what? I have a few melee weapons, like steel talons and daggers, but they're still in my closet when I wake up. It's not like I sleepwalk, harm myself, and place them back where they were."

Storm stops in his tracks. "Oh, I got it! What if, when you're asleep, another personality takes over. It's like a co-possession thing. When you're asleep, he or she is awake. Maybe, your other personality is suicidal, but still sensitive to the touch, which is why it hasn't fully done the job. It just could never cut deep enough."

A few people passing by look at us like we're deranged. "I said this a couple times, but I'm going to say it again. You need to join a creative writing class. Oh, and you've got some issues to work out."

"Don't most artists, kidding. You're the one who should join art classes, or creative writing or something. I've read a few of your poems and short stories. They're good. I had no idea you had a thing for Jenny, or Delilah, or Becca, or even Sama—"

"You read those? Damn."

"A few weeks ago. I didn't know you had those feelings for them."

"Those were just some erotica shorts. Scenes, or whatever. There're a few girls that I can't sleep with. Those are usually the ones that don't want to give up their virginities, and I don't want to be the man that forces them and is too weak to turn back. So, I write down my fantasies and what I'd like to do to them, given their personalities and quirks."

"Damn. Why don't you jerk off or something like the rest of us? Gotta say, though. That is a creative way to use lust. Your fantasy for Jenny was extremely detailed. You should publish them. You know. Change their last names so that you don't make them public."

"I have thought of it. I don't know. Who'd read something as saucy or X-rated as a bunch of short stories about a boy getting laid by many different women?"

"You'd be surprised. Everyone has their fantasies, and some people just like to read for pleasure. It's good to have a plot, but sometimes, it's good to just get straight to the point, ya know. Men and women get the urge to release, and the sooner you're able to do so, the sooner you can move on with your life. As you may know, it's hard as hell to concentrate on anything when your sexual urges and lust control your every thought." I nod in agreement. "All I know is, if you were to publish those works of yours, I'd read them."

"You're just saying that because you're a friend of mine. You'd have bragging rights, not that there'd be anything to brag about."

"I don't have to say it's good. I'm your best friend. I'd tell you if your work sucked. I wouldn't want you to embarrass yourself in public. That'd ruin my rep." I nudge him playfully on the shoulder.

I glance at the time. "I have somewhere to be."

"A date?"

"Something like that."

"Say no more, man. You do what you gotta do. I'll just stop by Gwendolyn's house. She lives nearby."

"Who?"

"She doesn't go to our school. You wouldn't know her, unless she knows Sam or Dani, but I doubt it."

"Thanks, man." I run off into the opposite direction. "Don't do anything I would do."

I find myself outside a salmon-colored house with purple lilies out front. Before I reach the door, it opens. I find myself looking into a pair of cloudy eyes with short black curls that barely reach her nose. She sucks on a lollipop and wears a semi-tight fitting, off the shoulder T that lowers to about three inches above her knees. She smiles and removes the usual cherry lollipop from her lips, "Chance. It has been forever." She comes in for a hug and I return it. "Do you not like us anymore?"

"It's not—"

"I tease . . . Sis! Your boy candy is here!" She looks me over once again, "Mmhmm. Boy, wouldn't I love to replace my lollipop with you. You just keep getting hotter."

"Good to see you, too, Serena."

"I kid, really. You're so easy to make uncomfortable." *Like hell I am.*

"You'd be surprised as to what I could handle without being uncomfortable."

She steps a little closer to me, placing her hand on my side, lowering it. "Is that a challenge?" Serena is hot, like her sister. By her sister, I mean Ariel, not to say her other sisters aren't cute either. Ariel lives with three, not counting her mother, of course. Serena, in terms of sexual outgoingness, stands a little taller than Ariel. Angel is at the bottom, but she is still clingy when she finds what she likes, in an adorable way.

"Boundaries, Sis. What are you trying to do? Seduce him in public?" That part is what gets me. Rather than saying that what she is doing is wrong and too out there, she says that it's wrong to do it in public, meaning that if we were in the house, it'd be fair game. "Sorry about her. Come in." I do as I'm told. I enter the living room. Angel, the youngest, is arched over the couch, looking at me. "My friends are on their way. When they get here, we'll head straight to the movies. Oh, it's probably a little late, but Angel wanted to go, so . . ."

"Yeah, okay."

"That was quick."

"If Angel wants to go, she can go. Though, she's a bit sensitive to these movies if I recall."

"I can do it. I'm not as scared as I was." Angel lowers herself on the couch and pats the seat next to her, motioning for me to sit. "I may need to sit next to you, though. For reasons unrelated."

The doorbell goes off and three of Ariel's friends are invited in: Faye, Peyton, and Juniper. "Okay, my mom is waiting. Is everyone ready?"

We follow Juniper outside to the 69' Chevy Nova that awaits us in front of the house. "Hey, kids. Y'all ready?"

We hop in, one after the other. It's a bit of a tight fit. Putting seven people in a vehicle as small as a Nova can be difficult, depending on the size of the individuals. Luckily, we're all skinny, or at the very least, not fat. Angel has to sit on Ariel's lap to make room for me as I lower myself to get into the small, compact car. Of course, I hit my head just barely getting in. Don't get me wrong. This is a very nice car, but trying to fit seven people may not be the best idea. The front can fit maybe two people: the driver and the right-side passenger. The back can fit three—four if lucky. Juniper sits in the front with her mom. The five of us squeeze in the back. Peyton sits on top

Faye, right next to me, with Faye having one leg hanging over mine. Our shoulders squeeze against each other until we get to the movies, where we try to get out of the Nova. "Bye, mom," Juniper says as her mom drives away.

"Six tickets to see 'Grave Robbers,' please."

The guy at the window looks at me with unamused eyes, "Uh, like, this movie is rated R. Do you have an ID?"

"Crap," Faye says. "We can watch something else if you'd like."

I wave my hands, "No, I've got this."

"You don't have to buy the tickets. I invited you."

"It's fine, Ariel. No point wasting your money."

I slip a hundred under the window. "Are you trying to bribe me? What kind of guy do you think I am?"

"Everyone has a price. A hundred doesn't seem bad if you're just letting a few teens into a rated R movie. Just take it. Not a word. I won't tell."

"Look, kid. Take your hundred back. You can either watch another movie or leave. I'm not going to deal with this. A hundred dollars isn't much if I get fired and lose my income." Great. Out of all the ticket salesmen, I get the one that's difficult to bribe.

"It's okay, Chance." Ariel puts her arm on mine. "We can watch 'Under the sea' or 'The Rising.'"

I lean into the window, "I understand that you're just doing your job, and I respect that. There aren't a lot of people that take their job seriously like you. I'll just leave it at that. I mean, smoking marijuana in the booth probably isn't allowed, but hey. Who needs to know, right?"

"I have no idea what you're talking about."

"You know exactly what I'm talking about. Please sir, just let us in. No one has to know."

"Are you blackmailing me?"

"No. To blackmail you, I'd have to have physical proof that can be used against you. I do not, but I can tell your boss that I first-handedly saw you smoking. That could result in inspection, which could lead to termination."

He taps on the desk, thinking. "Fine." He prints up a few tickets for us, "That'd be $44.95."

I hand him a fifty, "Keep the change." This asshat would have received more had he been cooperative.

I hear him muttering as we walk away, "You underhanded, little teenage mother—"

"That was amazing. Were you really going to blackmail him?" Ariel says.

"Nope. I would never blackmail someone for something as small as marijuana. I was just hoping it'd work. What they do to pass time is their problem."

"How'd you know he smoked weed?" June asks.

"I smelt it, faintly. It was either him or someone nearby."

The theater is half packed, mostly in the middle and the back. Luckily, the back row is empty. We take seats in the back-corner area of the cinema. The back is nice because you don't have to worry about the screen blinding you intensely, but it can still get bright. As for the sound, it can get loud during some movies. That's always a part I hated when movies come out on DVD. The sound can flux so dramatically that you must keep changing the volume on your remote. I just wish the editors or sound people could make it to where the noise could always be somewhere around the same volume, where you could still tell if they are whispering or screaming, but that'd probably confuse some people. Plus, in the back, you don't have to worry about the constant kicking on the back of your seat.

Three guys sit directly in front of me. They're a bit taller. Tattoos cover the one guy's neck. They each have shades that cover their eyes. A bit odd since it's dark as hell in here, or it's about to be. I tap on one of their shoulders, "Excuse me. You're kinda in the way and there are so many different seats around."

He looks back at me, smiles, then turns back around. The lights dim further, and the movie begins. Just as the movie starts, a man walks up to the front of the movie. His face is hidden behind shades, and his hair, if he has any, is covered with a beanie. He has on a backpack and reaches into it, pulling out a weapon. He aims it towards the ceiling and shoots. "So sorry to say that your movie has been delayed!" He shouts so that everyone can hear him. The doors open and a security guard barges in, gun ready in hand. As soon as he enters, he drops. "Any hero gets shot. You hear me! You will all sit quietly, or you die. No exaggeration. If you want to test me, then, by all means, try to stand."

The three guys sitting in front of me stand, pulling out guns of their own. Part of me wonders how four guys carrying guns got past the system. Sirens can be heard outside. "May I have a volunteer to stand?" No one moves. "I don't want to pick and choose, but if no one stands up, I will start shooting aimlessly. Who wants to die? Huh?" Angel shifts in her seat, trying to hide, but the man speaking sees her. "You there. Little girl trying to hide her face, come up here, now." She clings to me. The man loses patience and walks towards us. He grabs onto her arm.

I grab his wrist before he can pull her in. "Touch her only if you want your wrists to get snapped."

"Don't speak such words unless you plan on following through." He jabs the gun into my side, "I recommend letting go of my wrist." I do as I'm told.

"Freeze!" An officer enters the scene with gun ready. Drop your weapons and come willingly. No need to make a mess of things."

"But, I like making a mess of things!" One of the guys upfront aims his gun, only to get shot before he can fire. The other two drop their weapons.

The last one pushes me out of the way, grabbing Angel. "Shoot me, you kill her. Now, drop your weapon." The cop hesitates to drop it. "Now, fat boy!" Slowly, the cop lowers his weapon. "So easy." He raises his gun and shoots the officer in the ear, missing his body by a little. "Damn it!" Once more, he shoots him. This time, he hits the cop in the side, ripping off a good chunk of love handle. The officer drops to his knees, then falls over. "Anyone else!" He rubs the side of his head with the gun, removing the beanie and messing up his hair. "Look what you all made me do. If you just listened!" **Sigh** "Okay. New plan." He points his gun point blank at a little girl's face. The mom screams as she tries to pull her child away, but it's too late. The gun goes off, leaving a lifeless body with a sobbing mother over it. "Everyone dies!"

"You bastard!" The mother leaves her dead child and jumps at the maniac, grabbing onto his wrist so that he can't shoot her. "You killed my baby. My poor defenseless—" She gets knocked back.

"Don't you touch me, Bitch!" He holds the gun to the bottom of the woman's throat and aims upwards, blowing her brains out through her scalp. "Want more? I can bring it." He has a field day, leaving at least nine bodies dead and three injured, bleeding out on the ground. A security guard and two cops lay dead near the entrance. If I had known there'd be a shooting at this movie, I would have chosen another one, or not come at all. Angel sneezes, and the guy takes it as a threat or something. He points a gun at her, but I intervene. I grab Angel and leap just before the bullet leaves the weapon, missing us both. I hold onto her as we hit the floor. I break the fall, and she lands on top of me, face in my neck. I roll over, so that she is on bottom, giving me space to react. As he aims his gun towards one of the other girls, I kick his kneecap in. This throws him off guard as he shoots at the ceiling. "Fuck!" His hand trembles as he tries to aim his gun at me through the pain. "You will pay for this." I grab his hand with the gun in it and fight it off.

Little do I remember that the other two are still in the room as one of them sneaks up on me. "Enough." He holds me back by the throat. "Lights out." I feel the gun being placed against my head. Rather than fight, I close my eyes. The gun shot temporarily deafens me as I fall to the floor, looking up. The man was overthrown by Ariel. I would have been dead right now if she hadn't pushed the gun off trajectory. He takes back control, throwing her to the side. "For a bunch of kids, you've proven quite a handful. Let's empty the load, shall we."

"We have the place surrounded! Come out with your hands up! If we see so much as a weapon in hand, we will shoot!"

"Well, kid. If I'm going down, then why shouldn't I bring a few with me?" The door gets slammed in as an officer with a shield barges in.

"Drop the gun, scumbag!" The cop nears the scene with shield ready to deflect incoming ammo.

"Any time, guys . . . Anytime, meaning now!" The cop drops the shield as one of the forgotten thugs shoots him in his blind spot.

As a last line of defense, and a cheap shot, if I may admit, I punch the nearest thug in the crotch. He automatically lowers his hands. I take action and jump him, retrieving the gun. Without so much as a thought, I hold the gun up to his head and pull the trigger, right in between his ears. He falls to the floor, with his brains escaping out of one side, making a mess of the ground beneath him. One down, two to go. "I'd leave if I were you. You're at half the number you came in with."

"Sorry. We don't leave until the job is done."

"What exactly is this job of yours, that you're willing to die for?"

"Wouldn't you like to know?"

"Yes. That's why I asked."

"Silence! I will not be made a fool by the likes of you: a child." He gets thrown back by something.

"Get out, everyone!" Two cops enter the room. They aim their guns directly at both criminals. "Now!" The last fifteen or twenty people leave the room in a clump. I grab the girls and we follow. As we make it to the door, both the cops shoot at one of the thugs as he was about to shoot. This leaves an opening for the last remaining to fire while he's not being looked at. He manages to drop the officer nearest me, splattering some of his blood on my face and my shoes. With only one cop and one murderer in the room, we stand on equal terms. The remaining cop raises the weapon, only to have it get shot out of her hand.

"This will all go by smoothly as long as you don't interfere."

She steps forward without her weapon. "Sorry. I joined the force to help those in need. And, I've read about you, Theodore Finch. I understand where you're coming from."

"You don't understand shit!"

"You've only ever known one parent, but he was an abusive drunk. By age eight, he died of an overdose, leaving you an orphan on the street. You ran away after that, fending for yourself, starving. You started hanging out with the wrong crowd. Eventually, you found a new family: a bunch of thieves and drug addicts. They took you in. You were so grateful, you took the fall for one of their actions, giving you time in Juvie. After counseling, you were placed in a foster home. You did well for three years, until you came across the same crowd that got you in trouble to begin with. You stole from your foster parents. You took advantage and gave away their food to your friends."

"My family!"

"You stole two-grand so that all of you could escape and start new in a new country. The place may have been different, but your antics weren't. You felt neglected everywhere you went, except for when you were with them. All you ever wanted was to be loved. The attention your dad never gave you, but you had a family."

"That foster care wasn't my family! Even with so many new-found brethren, I was never noticed. I had to fight for food. They never thought a good for nothing brat like me belonged to be part of the family. I guess, in the end, they were right. Do you know what it's like to be closest to the youngest in a group of twenty? We had to fight to get what we wanted. There were so many of us. None of us got the attention we rightfully needed."

"I didn't know that."

"Of course, you didn't. Your kind never asks questions. You react before you know the bullet points. If you knew as much as you do, then you should also know that the last of my family was just killed, meaning I have nothing else to lose." He points his gun at her.

"Listen, Theodore. You're still young. If you go willingly, I can talk to them. Within ten to fifteen years, you can get out on parole from good behavior. Don't let your past define who you are. Only you get to decide who to become."

"Thank you for the therapy, but . . . I've already decided."

I jump at the police officer, getting her out of the way of the incoming bullet. She tries to move but can't. I look at where the pain is: her leg. "Crap, I'm sorry."

"Don't be. You may have just saved my life."

"How cute." I get up as he shoots. Fortunately for me, I dodge it just in time. I zigzag towards him, barely dodging bullets. "I don't have to shoot you!" He aims his gun, once more and for the last time, towards the girls. "Time to choose."

My head throbs as my eyesight goes blurry. A buzzing noise echoes through my ears. A flashing light gets thrown into my eyes as I come to. When I realize what's going on, I'm outside, sitting in the back of an ambulance van, having a light get shone into my eyes."

"Oh good, you're reacting." A doctor pulls back the mini flashlight. "Tell me, do you know where you are?"

"I'm at the movies."

"Good, good." He jots down some notes, "Do you have any history of concussions?"

"What?"

"Concussions. Blackouts. Seizures. Have you ever had problems with loss of consciousness?"

"Uh, no."

"Odd."

"Umm." I put his pencil down so he can look at me. "What exactly is happening? I was just in the theater. What happened to the criminal? Is the police officer alright?"

"I see. You remember the events leading up to . . . Do you not remember what you did to Theodore—the intruder?"

"I was walking up to him, then I got a headache." I reach down to my soaked shirt. "What the . . ." I rub my fingers together, feeling the wet, sticky, red liquid that covers my fingertips. "Am I—?"

"You got shot. In the side, saving one of your friends. You don't remember feeling pain? Did you say, you had a headache when all of this happened?"

"What time is it?"

"Don't worry, Chance. It's only been ten minutes or so since we arrived."

He continues writing notes when Mother enters the scene. "What happened?"

"Ma'am. Are you this boy's mother, or legal guardian?"

"I am."

"Chance!" The girls run over to where I am. "Are you alright?"

"Sorry. He has to be left alone right now." The doctor says.

"No, I'm fine, really."

"Son, as a responsible doctor, I would highly advise against moving right now. We still have questions, as do the cops now that you're awake."

Mother motions for me to go and talk with my friends while she talks to the doctor.

Angel and Ariel practically jump in my arms. "Oh my god! You scared the hell out of us!"

"I'm fine, really."

"Are you? Even if there's no official diagnosis, you must be out of your mind to even do what you did!"

"Like saving your sister? I admit that it was reckless, but I'd do it all over again."

"You could have died!"

"If I would have let you or your sister die, I'd still be having this conversation with someone else. You must realize that by doing this, you're telling me that I'm stupid for risking my life. If you died, I'd be hearing it from someone else, telling me that I was weak. How could I let you die? I would have been a coward. Both would be bad circumstances. I chose the more heroic path. Besides, none of us are dead, so I'd say it's a win."

"You really are crazy," Faye says, "but, I think it's hot."

"Faye! Death isn't funny." I chuckle at this situation. "What the hell are you laughing at!"

"Sorry," I wave my hands, "It's just nice to have people that care."

Angel tugs on my soaked shirt. "I really am grateful that you risked your life to save me, but I don't know what I'd do if you died for my sake. I would have felt at fault."

"You shouldn't think those things. It was my call."

"Can I—can I see it?"

"What?"

"Your wound, I mean, in case you thought I was talking about—"

"Sure." I slowly raise my shirt, unsticking it from my flesh. It's still a bit tender, but it's tolerable. The bullet's been removed, and right where I apparently got shot is a bloody padding bandage, held tightly to my skin with hospital tape. All I know for certain is, it's going to suck later when I remove this.

"Does it hurt?"

"Honestly, I didn't feel it. I—"

"Chance Ryder?" A couple cops walk my way, separating me from the girls for a while to answer questions. "We'd like to discuss the situation at hand with you." I nod my head as in a way to say, "Sure thing, officer." "We heard that you don't exactly remember what happened in there. The events that transpired in the end between you and Theodore. That might be troublesome if this continues in the future. I guess, firstly, I'd ask if you've ever witnessed something like this before."

"No."

"Okay, okay. Wait. Chance Ryder? You live in that big fortress of a house a few miles off, don't you?"

"Yes."

"To my understanding, an incident like this happened then, too. Not the blackout, but a psychopath intrusion. Kind of weird having two incidences revolve around you, isn't it?"

"Are you suggesting I'm at fault for both?"

"Heavens, no. Not to say you were of any affiliation, or connection to the events that happened."

Mother comes from behind, separating me from the officer, "Excuse me. If I understand correctly, Chance is still underage, meaning you shouldn't even confront him without my presence."

"Sorry, ma'am, but your son, uh, Chance, just got involved in—"

"I'm well aware, Miss . . . officer lady, but he is still underage."

"You're entitled to a lawyer if that would appease you. Trust me. He may need one."

Mother gives a small, annoyed laugh, "Excuse me. You are way out of hand. I don't care what position you hold, or what you thought happened, but he is a victim in all this; yet, you treat him like a suspect."

"Miss, this is a serious matter. Yes, he is a victim, but the way he reacted, and being part in an ongoing investigation, he didn't act in a way a kid should. It's almost as if he was prepared. He didn't hesitate—"

"It was self-defense. I'm sorry, but whatever happened to those delinquents was well deserved. My son shouldn't be held accountable for protecting his friends."

"You're also a suspicious character, Miss Winters."

She's taken aback, "Excuse me?"

"The officer that was sent to your house a while back. Did you bribe him?"

"What are you talking about?"

"Nothing at all. Just that, he was sent to your house after an incident was called in, but when he returned to the precinct, he didn't recall a thing. It's almost as if he was paid to omit what truly transpired. I saw the video of what happened at the party, and your kid treated it like a game. I don't know what you did to prevent him from sharing the details, but I will find out. I'll remember this."

"I wouldn't be so sure."

I interrupt them, truly curious as to what happened when I wasn't exactly present. "What exactly did I do to the crim—to Theodore?"

She rubs the back of her head. "Yes, that's the other thing I need to discuss. I'm not going to ease this on you. Your reaction to this revelation can piece some things together. You killed him. Do you remember how?"

"I what? I don't think I'd forget something like that."

"For someone who doesn't remember it, you're handling it quite well for your first time around."

"How, exactly, did I kill him?"

"Ooh, you're good. You can act like this and say you don't remember, to save your own skin, but you know something. What kind of boy your age would react as you do to this news?"

"I just take death differently than some. But, when I say I don't remember doing it, I mean it."

"Spare the bullshit. This isn't some Norman Bates scenario. How odd for you to black out just in time for you to murder someone and be innocent. Let me tell you something. I don't believe in mental illness. I mean c'mon. Bipolar? ADHD? ADHD is practically diagnosed to everyone now days. Is there really something wrong with being active in high doses. I mean, it's diagnosed when you're young, when, in reality, kids are just naturally hyped up. Why do we have to make it bigger than it is? You remember. Like them, you're using blackouts as a way to make attention for yourself. It's like a free card. It's sick."

"Hey, Veronica. Give the boy a break." Another officer confronts the situation.

"He's faking it."

"Why don't you go. I'll take it from here." Veronica takes her leave, leaving me with the officer I saved. "Sorry about that. You have nothing to worry about. Even if you did remember, you'd most likely be let go. We were in a situation where there really was nothing to do but to react. He was the one with gun, after all. It's not the fact that you killed him that raises questions. It's how it went down. Do you want to know how he died?"

"I'm not sure, now. I'd rather know everything."

"Okay. Well, just know that what you hear, you did it to save us. Don't worry about jail. These questions are just protocol. It was self-defense."

"Okay."

"They said the last thing you remember is zigzagging towards him, right? Well, you dodged most of the bullets, only getting hit by a couple. No fatalities done. When you reached him, you snapped his wrist before he could act quickly enough. I thought you'd stop right there, but you didn't. Neither did he. He moved just slightly, adjusting to the newfound close proximity fight at hand, before you swiped the knife from his hands. You tossed the knife aside and, what happened afterwards shocked me."

"What happened?"

"You devoured him. You leaned into his neck and tore it up. Even after death, you didn't stop. I had to listen, hearing the gurgling noises he made up to the point where he finally choked on his own blood. The thing that gets me is, you didn't spit the flesh aside. You ate it. By the time you finished, he was practically just a body and a head. His neck was mincemeat. By the time the rest of the officers barged in, you had already finished the job. One of them went to question you, but you didn't respond. Not until now. Do you honestly not remember any of that?"

"I can honestly say that I don't. Sounds graphic."

"I'd count you lucky for the fact that you didn't see it. To witness that at your age would screw some people up. To hear about it is one thing, but to be there while it's happening is another. Well, if that's all, then, I guess you're free to go." She sounds uncertain. "Don't worry about consequences, though, you will probably be getting something in the mail that requires mandatory counseling sessions. Not to say that you're crazy, but having these blackouts isn't healthy."

"This was my first time. I swear."

"Even so. If this is your first, then more likely than not, it won't be your last."

"I see." I slowly back away as to leave this conversation.

"You're free to go. This may not be the last of this, though. Expect a visitation later on, to further legitimize the story."

I catch up with the girls. "So?" They leave close to no breathing space as they close in on me, wanting to hear what they most likely witnessed themselves.

"So, nothing. I was let go. If it had been a different scenario, then I'd be handling a different approach."

"They let you go? So soon?"

"Geez, Ariel. Don't hold back at all."

"Sorry. It's just . . . unusual. I had a friend who came close to killing someone for self-defense, and that lasted for about a month, so that they could get the story straight. To let you go so soon. It makes me wonder how many people, how many true criminals, got past the radar due to lack of investigation."

"He's free. You should be happy."

"I'm not saying I'm not. It's just that, we all saw what he did, almost with no hesitation. He ate a man, not to mention the guy he blew the brains out of. He's not even fazed by any of this."

"Ariel?" Juniper rests a hand on her shoulder. "He saved us. We could have met the same fates as many in that theater, but because of Chance, we get to see another day, now . . . I must call my mom. She doesn't know what happened."

"Let's get you out of that shirt." Angel tugs at the hem.

"I don't have anything under this."

"So. You're a guy. It's not like you've got breasts. Besides, better to be shirtless than to be caught in one that looks like you escaped a murder spree." *Which I kind of did.*

I can't argue with that logic. "It doesn't matter. Mother's here, so she'll probably be taking me home after this, anyway."

"Hun. Let's go home." Right on que. "You can hang with your friends later. I need to take a look at the wounds."

"Coming. This was eventful. Maybe, we can hang out again sometime."

"No doubt. Maybe, we can do something other than a movie."

I laugh at this, "What are the odds of this happening again?"

"Don't jinx it."

On the way home, the ride is quiet, until Mother breaks the silence. "So, did you have fun?"

Hell of a way to undermine a tragic moment. "Uh, yeah. I wish I actually got to watch the movie, but, oh well."

"From what I hear, you handled the situation." She taps the steering wheel. I can tell this isn't a conversation she pictured having with me.

"Yep. Tore his throat apart. I wish I could remember it."

"Count it a blessing that you don't."

"Mother. Am I broken?"

She chuckles at this. "Whatever would make you say that?"

"This isn't the first time I've come out of a situation without memory." Come to think of it, the first time I could recall not having recollection of an event, I met Storm. "You seem to handle it well, too. You're always calm."

"No, I'm not. I do worry about you. I always will. I just express it differently, as do you."

"Am I a bad person? I chewed that guy's throat apart, but I don't feel bad. I mean, I know that I should, but I don't. How can that be possible?"

"I knew we were going to have this conversation at some point. I was hoping that'd it be later . . . Look, these blackouts? As they're calling them, are—"

"Stop the car!" The car comes to an abrupt stop as I nearly fly into the dashboard.

"What is it!"

I get out of the car, closing the door behind me. I run over to an old beater, crashed into a tree. The car smokes from the front, as well as the back. I use my elbow to smash through the window of the side that isn't caved in. "Sir. Are you alright? Sir?"

The man raises his head slowly. His nose faces one direction and one eye is swollen shut. A cut runs down his split lip, blood dripping off his chin. "Kill me. Don't make me suffer anymore."

"I'm getting you out." I reach for the seat belt, but it's almost as if it's been glued tight. The sudden smell of gasoline fills my nostrils. "Come on! Try."

He extends his good arm, putting his hand in mine. "Give this to the first person that comes to my aid."

"What?"

"Get out, now."

"Stop speaking nonsense. I'm not going to just let you die."

"We live in a world where we're constantly dying." He lights a match and drops it.

"Chance!" Mother jumps as we both go flying to the ground. As we hit the floor, the car blows up with the man inside. "What were you thinking?"

"That I could save him. Guess I couldn't."

"You asked me earlier if it makes you a bad person that you can't express the appropriate sympathy for certain situations. That man earlier didn't deserve your sympathies, but just look at what you did. You came to the aid of someone that you didn't know. The fact that you know you should feel something should tell you that you're a good person, even if it looks like you're heartless for not crying or feeling bad. Knowing is enough."

"Wait. Say that again."

"Knowing is—"

"No. The aid thing."

"You came straight to his aid?"

I guess I did. I feel something crumple in my hand. It's a piece of paper. He must've slipped it into my hand when he grabbed it. I take a look, but what I find puts me in a new place.

At home, I pace around my room, looking over the piece of paper. This is all a game to someone. Whoever it is knew I'd be there, but how? "Good luck, next time." These are the words that repeat on the piece of paper. To anyone else, this would be nothing more than happy thoughts. I know better. The words that he said tell me that this was planned. Are these words describing the theater incident? Did he plan, but how? I smell a setup. Who hates me enough to go that far?

VII

I find myself in a situation where I'm running. Running from what, exactly? Fire surrounds me. I feel the heat of it swirling around me, sucking away the very breath I breathe. I take deep breaths, trying to retrieve my lost wind. "Nowhere to go. Nowhere to hide."

"Who the hell are you?" I speak through the fumes choking me out, stripping me of my ability to speak. My words are forced. I raise my arm up over my eyes as I squint, trying to see past the tears. I can barely see, nor can I find the words to speak. I'm blind all over.

"This is your destiny. Our destiny. Only when you come to terms to who you are will you finally begin to see where you stand. What choices you'll have to make. Friends or survival? You will find that you can't have both."

I try to force myself off my knees as I stumble through the vicious flames until I'm out of the fire's domain. I cough up the last remains of the smoke that forced itself down my throat. I hear sloshing noises with every step, then I feel the wet stickiness between my toes. I look down. The entire ground is puddled with blood. I look at my hands. Blood covers my fingertips just as it soils my toes. I am bare, with red smeared over the majority of my skin: my legs, my arms, and my chest. I come across a wall, a red wall with a stranger staring back at me. I touch the surface, but my hand goes through it. Only now do I notice that this wall is entirely comprised of blood, not exactly solid. The stranger staring back at me copies my movements with perfection. Bangs cover his eyes. His hair is clumped together by the thickness of the red substance that covers everything else. He looks familiar. His skin is a bit scarred. The wall comes down, splashing to the ground, leaving me with both: a metallic taste in my mouth; and the sense of something foreign, clogged within my throat where I'm forced to try to regurgitate it. I gag, trying to get the taste off my tongue. I hear crunching and tearing. I turn around to see a man hunched over another man. The man on top drips with this stuff. He keeps lowering his head over the other, until I realize . . . he's eating him. I see so clearly, the skin being separated by strands and torn apart slowly, blood gushing out of the underling's neck in small spurts. The thing on top looks at me. Just when I start to turn away, it returns to eating, then it stands, tall and full. It tears off an arm and drags it on the floor behind it as it limps towards me. I back away slowly, but it doesn't look as if this thing wants to harm me. It stops face to face with me. His blue eyes stare into mine. He has my face. He holds out the severed limb, offering it to me. I raise my hand to gesture that I don't want it, but before I can say anything, he puts the messy butcher work in my hands. He vanishes before my eyes, and so does the arm. I feel something coming up. I drop on my knees to throw something up, only to feel the familiar metallic taste escape my mouth. Something can be seen in the little puddle of blood I made. I reach out for it and lightly pick it up. "A . . . finger?" Realization hits and I hold my hand to my mouth. I'm going to be sick. "Is this some kind of sick joke!"

"You are more than you are. You are ineffective. Broken, but you can be fixed." A dark figure steps out of the shadows. The blood washes away and I find myself in a black abyss with nothing, standing in front of what I presume to be a hidden man. One eye can be seen, but just the color of the iris. Out of the dark shines a green light. His eye. "Just take my hand. This will be over quick." I swipe at it.

"Get the hell away from me." My hand phases through his and I find myself alone, again, with just his voice bouncing all around me.

Something pushes me down. I look up as my vision is full of shadows: demon-like beings hovering over me, extending their claws. Something's off with these shadows. They have no distinct features like mouths, eyes, or even ears, yet there is blood dripping from where their mouths should be. "You're imperfect. Luckily, I'm here to fix that. You're split between emotions. Rather than controlling them, they do you. Notice a pattern with those headaches you get? They're not random."

"How?"

"I have my resources."

"You're my conscience. That's it. My conscience is trying to tell me something in what is obviously a dream."

"You have a pretty messed up imagination if this is a dream. What of the blood bath? What metaphor can your conscience possibly be trying to show you?"

"I-I don't know. This isn't real, though. I'm going to wake up any moment." I pinch myself harder and harder, trying to end this terrible nightmare.

He flinches slightly at the pinching of my own skin. "You leave when I say you can. Why would I let you leave when I still have some things to enlighten you with? Your insentience is when I get to play. Kind of a one-sided relationship, really. You see, I don't sleep."

"What do you mean, my insentience is when you play?"

"Well, not me physically. I'm trapped here, but only temporarily. My spirit though, mmhmm, it's very much alive. There's a part to you that you, yourself, don't realize. Tell me. What do you think happens in between your little headaches, when you come to, and don't seem to recall exactly what events have taken place in those questionable moments? You're starting to get them more frequently now. Have you noticed?" I attack him, but I'm not able to touch him. "You're weak, but with me, you can be more. You can be stronger."

"I'm fine, thanks." I don't know what any of this is. I know that none of this is real; it can't be. As for waking up, I don't know what's keeping me here. I know dreams are pathways to the subconscious part of the mind, but what could this dream possibly be trying to show me?

"The blank expression on your face says otherwise. You're confused. You don't know what you're doing here. More importantly, you don't know what I'm doing here. Either way, you haven't much time. Sooner, much rather than later, you will have a very difficult choice, indeed, to make."

"This is a dream. You mean nothing to me. None of this means anything. When I wake up, it will be as if none of this ever happened."

"In that case . . ." He confronts me, slowly, then grabs hold with his demonic claw. Not allowing me to leave, he scrapes his treacherous nails down my wrist, slicing the veins with every passing moment. "Ooh. That looks like it hurts. Let me get a closer look at that flesh wound."

"Keep dreaming."

"That, I will. Given how weak you are, I could slay you with ease, but I won't. I still have hope for you, yet."

"I'd rather die than be anything like you."

"Oh, trust me. Those are the only options there are."

I get pulled into the darkness by three shadowed creatures. I get pushed down to my knees as I'm forced to look upward towards the sky.

"No, dear. Don't do this. You're better than—" A woman falls to the floor at my feet. Her familiar curls, greying out into thin strands. I watch as the light exits her eyes and her once beautiful brown hair falls dead onto her bony complexion.

"Mother?" I turn her to face me. Her gray eyes. Her dead stare.

"How could you?" A voice from behind speaks. I stand to face the owner of this voice. A tall man with darker skin than I, steps up.

"How could you choose him over your own friends?" Two women appear behind him.

"I-I didn't. I chose you. All of you."

"You killed your own mother, man!" Storm's words are filled with betrayal. Sam and Dani back up, avoiding eye contact with me. "Face it. Everyone who comes into contact with you is fated to die."

"No, why would you say that?" I jump at Storm, holding him in my arms. When I'm met with a few seconds of dead silence, I choose to face him. I stare into his eyes—dead like my mother's. I back away,

feeling something crush under my feet. I look down at the wrist I have come across. More importantly, whose wrist I snapped. "Dani?" My eyes widen at the magnitude of bodies that lie motionless in my wake. "No," I silently say under my breath.

"Oh, yes." I spin around to face the monster who forced these images upon me. "Gotta face facts. You're better off, alone. At least that way," he looks at me, "no one gets hurt." My hands begin to shake, then it rains. "Don't tell me you're crying. Over this? Man up. I thought you were tougher than this."

I can't even feel the tears leave my eyes. I reach up and swipe my finger under one of them. On my finger, as plain as day, is a liquid, but not of tears. Not mine, anyway. "Is this?"

"You guessed it, haha."

I put my hand under my cheek as more drops of this black liquid puddle in my palm. "Why is this black?"

"Corruption is a beautiful thing. Try to fight it, but you're meant to become like me."

"I'm nothing like you."

"Not yet."

My hands begin to shake as the familiar pain can be felt pressing on my brain. "Shut up!"

I'm curled up in a ball, squeezing my head, staring at the ground. "I'd watch that temper if I were you. You might do something you'll regret." His voice echoes in my head. I crawl towards him, but he disappears. I come across a wall. The pain recedes as I find the strength to pick myself up.

A brick wall? What feels like stone is beneath my bare feet. I follow a path that has obviously been placed for me. My brain screams "trap", but there is literally nowhere else to go. I come across a sign that reads, "POSHE: when there is nowhere else to go." This has to be a joke. Everything looks tinted, like I'm looking at a black and white picture frame through a blood-red looking glass. Blood seems to be the theme here. Tomb stones can be seen for miles, each one with a different name: Sara Stone, loved mother, dear wife; Terra Armstrong, alive through her voices of plenty; Dan Nickels, coach, husband; Kyle Shine, deceased; Jenson; Ashton Jay Hunter, had it coming; Chance Princeton Ryder, yet to be determined—the list goes on. Where the tombstones end, a line of ruins begins. I walk up to a run-down elementary school. Smeared on one of the one-way mirrors in red is a handprint with the words "help me" underneath it. "What is this place?"

"This is where every self-proclaimed hero and heroine goes when they die. Everyone who steps up to the role eventually ends up here."

"I'm serious."

"As am I."

"Oh, really. If this is where heroes go, then one can only dream where villains go."

"Evil doesn't die. The fun thing is, to be a hero, you must have hope. Something to fight for. One can only fail enough times until that hope dies. Villains don't carry around the burden of hope. There's nothing chaining us down. Haha. Villains fight for themselves. As long as they remain living, they don't stop."

"That doesn't answer my—"

"Heroes follow morals. Guidelines. There isn't a handbook on what it takes to be evil. You just do it. There are no limitations. Villains, like demons, just get reborn. There's no keeping us down."

"Is that your religion? Rather than believing you'll die someday, you believe you're immortal."

"In the end, beliefs are all someone truly has." Those words. They're familiar. Where did I hear them? Here? No. Out there. These words sound like something I said.

"Do I know you?"

"You don't know me, but you've seen me, hahaha. As fun as this has been, I need an answer."

"You want an answer? Here it is. Go fuck yourself."

"Such language. And you were supposed to be the civilized one. You say that this is all, but a dream. None of this is real. How do you explain the unexplainable scars on your body?" A type of black gas begins to stem from him, like an aura. "Don't worry. I'm not going to kill you. I need

you, but one of us will have to make a difficult choice." He backs away as his three shadow demons move towards me. "This won't harm you physically, but you will feel like you're dying, slowly. I'll be here awaiting an answer. Make it quick." He motions with his hand and the three nightmarish ghouls latch onto a different limb.

I scream out as their teeth bite into my flesh. I feel my veins being pulled at and my muscles being separated. The pain is more than anyone could bare while being awake. Suddenly, the pain stops. I open my eyes. I am no longer in pain. My body has no marks on it, nothing extra to what was already there. A hand grabs mine and I take it.

"You've got to leave, now." It's a woman. There are no visible features to her physique. No skin tone. Just a shadow, like the rest, but she's trying to help me. The only thing that resembles human qualities on her face are her eyes. A pair of beautiful, purple eyes stare into my blue ones. "C'mon. Follow me." Her shadow resembles that of a fit young woman with curves and long flowing hair. Her hands are small in mine and her voice escapes her mouth in an angelic manner. "Before it comes back."

"How do I know I can trust you? You're a shadow, like them. What's to hide?"

"I only appear as a shadow to you. Only when you uncover the truth will my appearance be known. Last time was supposed to be the last time, but he's getting closer to where you are."

"What's your name?"

"Really! That's what's on your mind?"

"Haha." My mysterious tormentor steps out of the shadows. "Thought you could leave so soon?"

He gets pushed back by a man with long hair. A familiar man with green eyes. He looks back at me, "Won't you please tend to your personal questions in safety, boy. Now, leave while I have him."

"Who are you?"

"Just listen to him?" The woman whose hand I'm still holding asks.

I don't know if I can trust her, but if she wanted to do me harm, wouldn't she have done it already? "Just go with her." This voice is feminine. It almost sounds as if it's in my head. I hesitate no longer as I get up and follow her to a cliff.

"Just see yourself waking up. You ready?"

"Ready?"

With our hands still attached, she falls back over the cliff with me trailing closely behind her. "Ahhh!"

VIII

I spring up in my bed, drenched in sweat. "Oh, sweet mercy. What the hell." I try to move but retreat in pain. My hand presses against my soaked chest. Blood? Not again. I look over at the time: 8:45 a.m. Great. I'm late for school. Not to worry, though; I'll just show up late. I tend to my wrist, which appears to have been damaged in my sleep. I take my time getting ready. After all, there is no point rushing to be somewhere in which you can't possibly show up on time. It's not like I'm falling behind in any of my classes. I watch as my own blood separates into streams and retreats into the shower drain. It always was fascinating to watch, calming even. I stare at myself in the bathroom mirror once the fog dissipates, running my finger along the fresh cut right above my belly button. Wonderful. Another scar to add to the collection of mysterious wounds that snuck onto my skin. I don't know how I keep getting these marks, but they all share a common denominator: my nightmares. I know it sounds ridiculous, but weirder things have happened, just not to me. My face is drained of its usual color and a shadow overlaps my eyes, like I haven't slept in days. I reach into the cabinet to retrieve some of Mother's foundation. Desperate times. I'm not going to let a worn-out appearance get the best of me.

I show up on campus and sign in. I enter second period near its end. Luckily, not many turn their attention near me; they just keep their faces down towards their desks. Mr. Douche, the history teacher, gives me a look and continues back towards his deskwork. "Okay class. Time's up. Please pass your quizzes forward." Everyone complies with instruction, some irritated that they didn't get to finish. "You have only yourself to blame if you didn't finish. Maybe if you studied, time wouldn't be an issue. It may just be me, but 45 minutes should be plenty of time to answer twenty-five multiple choice questions." Some of the students show no emotion towards the relinquishing of the quizzes, probably because they studied. "As for you, Chance. You will have to make up for the quiz."

"Whatever."

Lunch arrives, and I spend the first fifteen minutes taking the quiz that I was late for. Mr. Douche was a bit surprised that I chose to take it so soon. I guess he expected me to wait, so that I could study. He was a bit more surprised that I managed to finish within a fifteen-minute time slot, while it took the majority of a period for the class to nearly finish at all. I meet up with Storm shortly after.

"Where the hell were you?"

"Taking a quiz."

"You were late to school, weren't you?" What can I say? The man knows me. We keep no secrets from each other, or at least, we try not to. He closes in on me, squinting his eyes. "Dude. Are you wearing makeup?" He smudges his thumb against my cheek, wiping off some foundation.

"I, for one, think a man who has the guts to wear makeup in public is hot. Most rock stars use it, after all." Shay gets in between us with her gaze on me. "My, my. Just when I think I've seen all of you. What other surprises lurk beneath that bravado? Will we ever know?"

"Hey, Shay. Eavesdropping is hardly noble."

"Neither is eating a man. And it's hardly eavesdropping if I just so happened to hear you while walking over here, handsome."

Storm stares off in another direction, awkwardly. Meanwhile, I'm concerned at the fact she even knows what I did at the theatre. In retrospect, I should have foreseen it. "And what is the nature of your visit?"

"What? I can't just talk. Why does there always have to be something in it for someone? Well, I guess I'll just leave, then. I have friends to get back to." I return to face Storm, but this isn't the end of Shay's conversation. "Oh, and by the way, I heard of yours and Jessyka's little interaction. Bad boy."

"How did—"

"Nothing happens without at least one person taking notice." She reaches for her pocket and swipes the screen. She reveals a pic that has been sent to her via text message. It shows the backside of a male overlapping a woman's figure. The woman's foot is covering the male's buttocks.

"Wait, this is—"

"Looks like you two weren't alone, after all. What will Ash think when he sees this?" Honestly, with this out in the open, I'm surprised he hasn't confronted me, yet.

"How long has this been known?"

"Not long. I just got this message, which means that this person hasn't made it completely public, yet. I can't be the only one who has this pic, though. There must be a few others. I'd bet that Ash has it. It is his girlfriend, after all. Other than that, I wouldn't worry. This picture really does you justice." The pic doesn't reveal anything too graphic. Jessyka's face is visible, given she is under me. Her feet wrap around my waist, covering any graphic nudity. My shoulders cover her chest, so other than the identities of the two, our bodies, for the most part, are kept covered. "See you around, player." She walks around, swaying her hips when Storm's phone goes off.

He checks to see who it is. "Oh, a picture message." He pulls up the picture that Shay showed me. He immediately puts it away.

"What is it?"

"Uh, well. It's not important. What with what happened on your date and everything else, it's not really—" I hold out a hand, and he hands me his phone, not without commenting on my bandaged wrist. "Is that from the incident?"

"No. That's . . . something else." I'm now staring at the pic that Shay showed me, displayed on Storm's screen. "I'm fucked." I don't know who could've taken that picture, but by the angle given, he/she had to be standing at the doorway.

"I knew you went to the dinner, but this is foul play. She's his girlfriend, man."

"It just happened. Aww, this is going to bite me on the ass."

"Nice view, Chance." I turn around as Sci walks by with a few friends. "I knew you were fit, but this, woo. I'm saving this as a screensaver."

A few others walk by: Lily, Becca, Alycia: as they exchange glances at me. Alycia smirks at me. "Dude!" Brandon slaps me hard on the back. "How could you do this to a brother?"

"This wasn't even supposed to be public. At least, not in this format."

"Either way, I'm jealous. Hey, do you do squats, or—" I walk away from this conversation. So many things transpiring, simultaneously.

I spot Jessyka Sylva across the yard with Ash. Ash looks pissed. His eyes land on me. He starts moving towards me, getting quicker with every pace. It almost looks as if he's about to strike, but a security guard can be seen nearby. He forces himself through me, telling me that this confrontation is going to happen one way or another. I continue walking towards Jessyka.

"Hey, Chance. Can I talk to you really quick?"

"Hold that thought, Jenny. I have something to do."

"Hey, Chance." Jessyka doesn't look as upset as I'd expect her to be.

"What happened between you and Ash?"

"He dumped me. Well, it was more of a mutual dumping."

"Oh, I'm so sorry." I put a hand on her shoulder; however, I feel she doesn't need the comfort. She's taking this pretty well.

"Don't be. I knew what I was getting myself into the moment I chose to sleep with you."

"About that. I don't know who did it, but I will find whoever snapped that picture of us."

She snorts a laugh, holding her hand to her mouth. "No need. I had my sister take the picture. She was a bit hesitant at first to do that to me, but I manipulated her. Sorry I didn't tell you before. I mean, it is your body, as well as mine that's being displayed. I made sure she did an angle that didn't reveal all our assets. Hope that helped."

"Gee, thanks." I roll my eyes. She notices. "Why, though, would you do this? This was secretive."

"Says who? I did this for you. You did say you wanted payback at Ash. How would it be payback if he didn't know?"

"But the whole school? I could get in trouble."

"No, you can't. It's not like you sent the picture around. You can't get in trouble just for being in the picture . . . cheer up. You can't get in trouble for fucking in your free time. I don't know why you're upset. I thought you were a man who liked any attention that showed this side of you. I mean, you've been with quite a few girls. It's definitely no secret."

"I guess, but—"

"If you were anyone else, maybe it would've been embarrassing, but you're you. If you were Kenny Shire, then you'd be the laughingstock of the school, but you're hot. You have a nice bod. Who wouldn't want to display that? Besides, if you thought you were popular with the girls before, consider this a highly unneeded boost."

"Kyle."

"What was that?"

"It's not Kenny Shire. It's Kyle. Kyle Shine."

"Right." She rotates her wrist. "Whatever. See you around. The bell's about to ring and I can't be late." She looks down at her phone as she walks away. "Damn. Still no reply."

"What was that, Jessyka?"

"Nothing you should be concerned with. It's just Austin. He hasn't returned my message. He's usually quick at responding." You've got to love how women tell you that it's no problem, but then they decide to share every detail, making a big deal out of nothing. "By the way, Chance. If you ever want someone to vent to, about the other thing that happened, I'm here for you. You've got to be one of the most cursed students here, to have to deal with all this bullshit."

The bell rings and everyone heads in different directions to get to their classes. I, on the other hand, decide to take a walk. I circle around the security guards, incognito, until I reach a certain corner of the school. A few students can be seen smoking. This is the one place in the school that's camera-free. This is where students go to do most of their acts against regulation: smoking, quickie before school, a small hit—whatever the act may be. The guards don't come back here too often, which is of great surprise, knowing that this should be the one place they should watch more than others. As to why security cameras haven't been placed, I'll never know. I wait here, enjoying the cool outside air until I'm alone, or so I think.

"My, what a surprise to see you here, in the blind spot of campus grounds." A middle-aged man walks out of the shadows with grayish, brown hair slicked back. "Something on your mind, son?" He sits next to me on the faded brick wall I sit on.

I move over, trying to get distance between us. "What the hell do you want?" I stare at him, trying to figure out if that last meeting was my imagination. It couldn't have been; I mean, there was a drill afterwards. Storm remembers, doesn't he? It feels so real, but, at the same time, it's too absurd to be real. I'm having nightmares, receiving scars, and hearing voices. Perhaps, my reality is starting to clash with imagination.

"Why, I'm here to take the pain away."

"What pai—" I fall back as he swings at me.

"You'll know when you feel it, hehe."

"That wasn't a dream, was it?"

"My dear child. Who says it isn't? Anything could be a dream. You just need the right wake up card."

"You're demented!"

"I'd watch that tone if I were you. Can't we communicate in an amicable manner, boy? To call me demented? You? The boy who's hardly fazed by death, as if it's a drunk, passed out on the sidewalk outside of a grocery store. You looked at that police officer with fascination, not horror." Perhaps, Mr. Jenson isn't completely wrong. There is something wrong with me, but one thing I know for sure: I'm not a demon. He picks me up and throws me. I land on my side.

"It's over here." Footsteps can be heard as two security guards enter the scene. "That's weird. I thought I heard something."

"What are you talking about? He's right there. Are you blind?" They don't acknowledge the fact that I'm talking to them. "Hey." I reach for the security guard, but my hand goes through him. "What the."

"They can't hear you or see you, thanks to my cloaking."

"Cloaking?" I get knocked into one of the guards, or rather, through him.

"Did you feel that? Ugh, I just got a chill. Nothing to see here." They leave the scene, giving us the privacy, I wish I could avoid.

"Tell me, young man. For someone who fights through pain, but doesn't show it, do you even feel it? I'm desperate to know."

"Stop the small talk, demon. I know I'm not crazy. Our last meeting wasn't in my head, was it? . . . Wait. How did you know I came across a police officer?"

"That's not all I know. I know what you did in the theater. You killed two people, and with vicious intent. You tell yourself it was all in the name of protection, but you enjoyed it. At least, you would have, had you remembered it, even a little. Those darn blackouts. You wish you could remember, while most would find relief in not knowing."

"You don't know a damn thing, demon."

"Sure, I do. It is you that knows not. You ready to open your eyes? The world is so much bigger when you account for all the creatures that live in it. The world is much darker than you know, infested with secrets you'd much rather forget. You just stepped into a world you'll wish you never took part in. Several grievances will be felt on this long and heart-shattering ride. Are you sure you want to meet what's on the other side?"

"I'm sure my 'yes' and my 'no' will have the same outcomes."

"Smart boy. You grow stronger with every experience. Shame you won't be around for . . ." Mr. Jenson grows slightly taller, his voice crackling into a husky, incongruous, animalistic growl. His skin tears open, revealing the veiny muscle that lies beneath. He falls on all fours as he arches his back, like a cat that has been scared white. Blood drips down his face as his hair starts to fall out, revealing small spikes that grow into larger ones that start at the top of the beast's head and end where the shoulders begin. His eyes bug out, and his teeth stab through the bottom of his mouth. He reaches for his ear and clearly tears it off, leaving strands of mangled flesh behind. His arms dislocate, dropping to the floor beneath him, claws rip out from his fingertips as the original fingernails peel off. His feet resemble hooves of some sort and what seems to be a bull-like tail, drags beneath the legs of his newly transformed figure. What has just transpired before my eyes can't be explained fully in words alone. It's truly a sickening sight, to see such a gruesome transformation. Have you ever seen a snake shed its skin? What has just happened is far worse, but like a snake shedding its skin, I can't look away. It growls at me. It's as if this new, muscular form robbed him of the ability to speak clearly or speak at all. As it nears me, an odor like none other follows. I look at this sickly, grey creature, wondering how such a being exists. It makes me rethink religion in all sorts of ways. Though, I'm not a character of Christianity, I have heard of great deals of torture displayed in the Bible. Plagues brought upon unbelievers. Locusts. Even walking on water or turning it into wine, but I have never heard of a being that resembles what I'm seeing. Is it possible that this is the true appearance of Lucifer, himself? Has he come to punish me? This looks like something from Greek mythology, which raises more questions. The possibilities of such things give me a new perspective on life. Where do I stand in this universe? Are there more of these atrocities out there? Am I going to Hell when I die? So many questions that race through my mind when I should be thinking of a way to kill this thing.

Its enormous hands stomp on the ground as it readies itself to charge. It salivates profusely. Its eyes are set on me as it runs on all fours towards me. I jump out of the way. One thing I could gather from this little experiment is that it doesn't stop on the dime. It skids as it changes direction. That isn't much, but it's reassuring to know that this thing can't turn as quickly as it charges. This gives me somewhat of an advantage. I just have to avoid its impact long enough to gather information. That's going to require me to get in the way and jump right before collision, like a game of chicken. It howls towards the sky and makes snarling noises. Here goes nothing. As it charges, I run towards it. It picks up speed as it locks in on its target. I jump to the side and it skids, trying to turn. As it comes to a slow stop, it swipes its claw at me. Another weakness I pick up: given the size of this unearthly monstrosity, its movements aren't quick. Its arms are long and lanky, which means it can't aim right for its prey. It has to have distance in order to grab onto anything. How do I kill this thing, though? I don't bring weapons to school. It screeches once more and has another go at me. I leap as it digs at the air. As I fall out of the way, a new obstacle gets involved.

"What was that growl?"

"It came from this direction."

Two security guards enter the scene and the beast takes notice of this. As I avoid it, I'm not sure the unsuspecting guards will be able to. "Get out of here!" I wave my arms around, trying to ward them off. "Leave!"

"What the hell is—"

The guard gets cut off, literally, as his top gets separated from the bottom. The guard's organs spill out over the land as the beast picks up the top half, throwing it into its mouth. "Durland!"

"Get out of here. You can't fight this thing." I'm not even sure if I can fight this thing.

The second guard stands, frozen. The sight of such an impossibly grotesque abomination has rendered him speechless. A thick strand of saliva gets dropped on his head. The saliva, alone, gives off the foulest of odors, like rotting corpses that were locked in a small, contained space. If you were to keep the smell growing for about three months in a closed off area, then open the door to let out all the stink, you'd get approximately what this beast's saliva is giving off. The smell alone makes my eyes water. The guard turns around, only to be freed from the joyful prison that is life. He fights for about three seconds, but that isn't enough. He disappears into the monstrosity's awaiting tomb. The beast leaves no traces that he ever existed, physically speaking, of course. Obviously, he must have pictures or belongings that are his, or at least, a kid. Maybe he has a wife, or a husband, perhaps. Who knows? Looks like his family is going to be mourning over an empty coffin.

The former principal charges once again, not giving up. So far, the only weaknesses I sense off him are his turning reflexes once he's started running, and the obvious fault in having long arms. I can't pierce through it, even if I had a knife on me, given the two inches of thick muscle that cover the thing. It opens its mouth, giving a loud banshee-like sound that pierces the eardrums at close range. Oddly enough, this gives me an idea. If the thing has muscle surrounding it, then I'm just going to have to hit it where it hurts. The only place I can think of that I can't picture having muscle, are the over-exposed eyes, maybe even the inside of the mouth. This is going to be tricky, perhaps even stupid. I try to move out of the creature's vision, but like a predator to the prey, it moves with me, making sure that I can't leave its line of sight. Maybe, this thing does have brains if it knows not to look away. The copious drool leaves its mouth while it savors the last moment with its meal, staining the ground it lands on. I could almost see the stench coming off it. It shakes its head like a big dog washing away a bath, as the drool hits many near-by objects. Its long, curved claws dig into the ground before it takes off with a quick start. I do the same, running towards it. I take notice of the long strides it takes, hoping that it'll be enough. I'm less than three meters away from it when I duck and slide. I cover my face as protection as the beast's hind legs barely miss my flesh, contacting the ground just behind my head. Before it has time to adjust its position, I jump on its back, using the spikes to climb up. Like the most insane bull ride I've never been on, I hang on for dear life, trying not to jump around as much. If I manage to fling in the air and come crashing onto one of the spikes, there's a high possibility, around 100%, that I'll be impaled. I tense my muscles as I climb up, using the spikes, until I'm resting on its neck, or rather, the mass under the head. The creature tries to violently shake me off. I'm just barely holding on for my life until my grip loosens. I get flung into the air and crash down, just barely holding on to this demon's nostrils. It growls as I try to reach my arm up. I'm screwed. How do I possibly win? How can I? All hope is lost. It finally shakes me off and I come to a painful stop as I hit the ground. I try to get up, but my leg jolts in pain. It's not broken, though, it does feel intensely sprained, like the worst sprain I have ever had in my life. I don't have enough reach to get to its eyes. I look over to the mutilated, bottom half of the first security guard, just lying on the ground, surrounded by a puddle of blood. I notice something sticking out of the pocket. I quickly roll over to the severed half of a body, pulling a stun gun out of his pocket. "This might work." The beast lowers its head, flaring its nostrils. It's now or never. Before it has a chance to raise its head, I aim the stun gun at its eye, but it moves too quickly. The school alarm sounds, and the beast goes haywire. The sounds of students leaving their classes can be heard as the creature starts to take back its original form. The animal slowly shrinks down to a formidable size, when suddenly, a bared principal Jenson lies on the ground, taking deep breaths, "You did well, Mr. Ryder. Taking on a beast such as I, and living, is not an easy task. Such a shame for the security guards, though." He licks his fingers and picks his tooth with a sharpened claw.

"So, you do know what's going on when you turn into that thing?"

"Do I know what's going on? Yes. Can I control it? Not so much. Basic instincts are something that can't be controlled." He raises up his hand, "Best be on your way. We'll do this again, sometime. Oh, what tragedies await us." I start to walk away, wondering if leaving him here, alive, is the right thing to do. "Who knows? Maybe, next time, your dear ol' mom will be the object of my focus."

I stop in my tracks. Voices get louder, but I don't care about that right now. I'm face to face with him, but he just smiles. "Who says there will be a next time?" His eyes change as I grab him by the throat and slam him into the ground, slightly hearing a crack. I grab the nearest object I can and slam it into his sternum. He lunges forward with a deep breath as I force him back down. I hold him as I continue to jam the pointed rock into the same spot until he begins to bleed out. He manages to stay awake, even if barely, just to tell me something.

"C-c-congr-gratulat-tions." He tries to catch his limited breath. "You're a-a mur-derer-r." He slowly drops his head and his eyes close. He lies motionless with a fractured sternum, bleeding out profusely as the indent in his chest puddles with his innards.

"It came from this direction!" A group could be heard getting closer. I find somewhere to hide as the students pass me. I get out from behind the tree and run in the opposite direction of the students that just passed me. One of the students can be heard screaming, which is followed by the others. Security guards run past my new hiding spot towards the incident.

I notice Storm walking to his next class. I pick up a small rock and throw it at him. "Ow! What the . . ." He looks down at the rock near his feet and picks it up. "Who threw this!" I wave my arms out of the bushes so that he can see. He walks towards my location and I pull him in. "What the—Chance? Why did you . . ." He takes notice of my current state. Scratches, though, not severe, outline my skin, drawing some blood. My shirt is torn a bit and splotched in foreign blood. "What happened to you?"

"I'm in a predicament. I got caught up in something."

"Did you kill someone? A big wolf or something? What else could make you look like this?"

"Attention, school. Classes are to be cut short due to circumstances that can't be discussed publicly. Everyone, head to the front of the school." The intercom goes off. At the same time, police cars enter the school yard in pairs. "An incident has happened, so the school is letting everyone go. School will be out of session for a couple days. Before you leave, you will be searched for any weapons or anything that could put you at the crime scene, such as certain stains on your clothing, or even in your bags. Don't fight it. That will be all."

"Dude!"

"Shh!" I hold my hand up to his mouth to silence him.

"What did you do?"

"It wasn't my fault. It was me or him."

"What? You . . . Who'd you hurt?"

"Yeah. About that."

His eyes widen. "You killed someone?"

"Gee. Do you want to say that any louder?" I hiss. "Why are you mad at me?"

He runs his hands through his hair. "Look, I'm sorry. I'm stressed. I'm not mad, I swear. I just want to know what's going on."

"I killed Mr. Jenson. Is that what you want to hear?"

He's taken aback at this. "You killed—"

"Yes."

"Did he, you know, change?"

"You remember that?"

He looks at me in disbelief. "Of course, I remember that. I've been having nightmares for, like, a week now." Students line up at the entrance/exit of the school, getting searched by the officers at the gates. He tears away at my already torn shirt.

"What are you doing?"

"You can't go out in that." He removes his letterman jacket.

"You always wear that. Don't you think people will recognize me wearing your jacket? It'll be suspicious, especially if I have no shirt underneath."

"That's why you'll be wearing the shirt underneath my jacket." He throws his T-shirt at me and puts his jacket back on. "Like you said, I wear this jacket a lot, so it has to stay with me. I had it zipped all of today, which means, for all they know, I could have been shirtless under this thing all day."

"What about me? This isn't the same shirt I've been wearing all day. Even if we get away with that, how the hell are we going to hide this shirt? Finally, what about the scratches? The blood that is stained into my arm."

"We'll just have to pray that no one notices your shirt change. We'll have to put the shirt somewhere. Frame someone. As for the scratches . . . did you by any chance ride your bike to school today?"

"Yes. What does that have to do with, ohh."

"You already have random scars on your skin that are older than the rest. Just show the officer the scars. You ate shit riding to school and got banged up pretty badly. You took a moment to recuperate before you got back on."

"Dude, that's brilliant. Now, that just leaves two things. Where are we going to put this shirt, and how do I clean up the blood on my arm? Lick it?"

"God, no." Storm reaches into his bag and pulls out a large bottle of water. "Thankfully, I bring water for practice. Looks like I'll just have to drink tap for today. Pretty sure, practice is cancelled, anyway." He holds out my arm and pours water on it, wiping away at the blood. "Good. Now, we just look for a place to hide—"

"Move it, Jew!" In front of our hiding spot is Ash, picking on, yet, another of his underlings. He drops his bag. "I said, move it!"

He shoves the kid in front of him: a younger, brown eyed boy with dark, curly hair.

Storm grabs his bag and places the shirt in it. "I don't think you'll care if he's the one framed."

"I don't know, man. Ash knows it's not his. He'll look for the one who put the shirt in his bag."

"And when that time comes, there will be no cops around. You just have to keep denying it." Storm quickly throws the bag back into place as a voice is heard.

"Hey! Kids!" Shit, we're found out. I stay put just to make sure. "Is there going to be a problem?"

"No, officer. Not at all. Young Kylie here was just concerned about what's going on," Ash quickly says.

"Well, get back into line."

When no one is around, Storm and I rush to the growing line, not being sensed. Thank God.

"Hey, Chance!" A girl runs up behind us. She's perky in nature towards some people. Her bright, orange hair, which is caught in my peripheral vision, automatically gives her away. I turn around, looking into her beautiful gray eyes behind a pair of cute, designer glasses.

"Hey, Jenny. How are you doing?"

She twiddles her thumbs in shyness, tripping over her words, trying to figure out the right ones to say. "Weren't you wearing another shirt earlier?" *Shit.* I open my mouth to speak, but—

"Actually, he got in another fight with Ash. His shirt got dirty, so I lent him mine. He couldn't go home to get another one. He'd be even more late than he was if he had." He holds out his hand, "By the way, I don't think we officially met. I'm Stormie, Chance's best friend."

"Pleased to meet you. I'm Jenny."

I get the conversation back on track, "So, all you wanted to ask was why my shirt is different?"

She shakes her head, "Um, no. I was, or still am, curious as to why—"

"No! Give it back!" The student in the front of the line that is being searched at the moment refuses to hand over his bag to the officer."

"If you don't hand over your bag, I'll have no choice but to assume that you're guilty of the crime we're investigating."

"No, it's not that. It's—" his bag gets pulled, but he pulls the bag back towards him, refusing to let go. "Give it back!" The bag goes flying, releasing the contents inside. Everyone snickers at what's found in the pile. It wasn't what the officer was expecting, but, instead, a bunch of magazines devoted to naked girls. "No, no." He tries to gather his things when a teacher helps pick them up but refuses to give them back.

"Pornography on school grounds will not be tolerated." Funny, since the dress code isn't that strict.

"No, give them back. They're not mine."

"You still shouldn't have brought these to school. It disrupts the learning process."

"And the broken dress code doesn't!" The teacher walks him to the principal's office, where he'll most likely have to talk to the vice principal. "Those are my dad's magazines!"

"Then, he can pick them up." This causes the student to break out in tears.

"Wow." Storm breaks the awkward moment of silence. "That's embarrassing."

The line gets back on track with being dealt with. "You were saying? Jenny?"

She breaks out of her trance, "What? Oh, yeah. I was wondering about you."

"Really?"

"Yes, I mean no. I was thinking about the other day, you know. Two weeks ago." I realize the moment she's talking about. "I was wondering how someone like you could do what you do. You kissed me like you cared, but, you're always with someone else. Why is that?"

"That's a bit difficult to describe. Or explain."

"I'm willing to listen. I won't hate you!" She waves her hands around, dramatically punctuating her point. "I just want to understand why you are the way you are. I feel that, if you were to let your love shine through, you could find someone that you could devote all that love to."

"What makes you say that I want to find love?"

She gives an awkward smile. "Everyone deserves love. Do you feel that you don't?"

In less than half an hour, Jenny went from being a friend—kind of—to being my psychologist. "It's not that I feel I don't deserve it. I just can't have it. More specifically, I can't feel it."

"That's a lie. The kiss you gave me had all the emotion in it. You can feel it. You just don't want to risk opening your heart to someone because you think the moment will never last. You opened your heart to Stormie to be your best friend. Do you honestly think he'll be by your side forever? Eventually, he'll get married. He'll move. Whatever the reason, nothing is permanent."

"I-I don't really feel comfortable talking about things like this."

"Sorry for intruding on your life. I was just wondering why you beat yourself up."

I place my hand on Jenny's shoulder. "Don't be sorry for caring. I'm grateful that you care like you do."

"So, did you find out who took the picture of you?" An automatic change in conversation.

"What picture?" is what I was going to ask, but a reminder of this morning came flooding into my head. "Oh god. You saw that?"

"Yes. I got a message earlier."

"I'm sorry. That's probably something you didn't want to see."

She shakes her head, "It was certainly a surprise, but I didn't mind it. You're actually in better shape than I thought." Jessyka was right.

The first thing that enters my mind is, "You think about my shape?", but I discard the thought. "I already found out who took the picture."

"You did? Who?"

I'm about to say who did it when Ash is heard a few people ahead of us. "You gotta be shittin' me. I don't know how that got in there!"

An officer pulls out a torn, bloody shirt from Ashton's bag and automatically pins him out of instinct. Ashton fights the law, arguing that he didn't do it. I should feel sorry, but I find this a bit amusing. "Everyone, stay put," one of the officers says, "The search continues in case there's anyone involved."

An officer looks at me, up and down, mostly focusing on the scratches on my neck, arms, and cheek. "What, exactly, happened to you?"

"I was biking to school today. Kinda ate it. I've crashed quite a few times, actually. I have older scars if you want to see them." I say what is needed, but not too much as in to make my argument too forced. If I say too much, it'll sound as if I'm hiding something. The officer allows it, so I lift my shirt to show him some scars.

"Do you have the bike?"

"I do. It's in the office." An officer escorts me to the office so that I can't run. Luckily, the woman at the desk isn't looking, so she doesn't question my scars, herself, since she would have been the first to see them earlier, had I eaten shit on the way to school. Though, her not paying attention helps me in this instance, it makes me question my bike's security.

The officer allows me to leave through the office door, where I meet up with Storm on the other side.

Mother opens the door before we get to it. "Hey, hun. I got a call from the school. What happened? Did you see anything?" Storm and I both shake our heads, but Mother takes notice of this, "I see. Did anyone else see anything?"

"They're investigating students right now."

Mother walks around me, observing my attire. "Hmm, I don't remember getting that shirt for you, or even seeing you bring it home. It kinda looks like one of Storm's shirts."

"Yes. That's what it is."

"And the scratches?"

"I ate crap on the way to school. It took me awhile to get up. As for the shirt, I got in another fight with Ash. My shirt got pretty messed up, so Storm lent me his."

"How kind of him. I won't keep you. You two head up to your room. I'm making Dinner. It should be ready in about an hour. Storm, do you want to stay for Dinner?"

"That would be delightful, Miss Winters."

I take a deep breath as we head to my bedroom, grateful that she didn't ask any more questions. I close the door behind us, then plop down on my bed. Storm follows, sitting on the edge, near my feet. "I can't believe this is happening. It makes me question everything I've ever refused to believe in."

"No kidding."

"You didn't see him, Storm. Last time was a partial transformation. This time, he was huge. I could hear his bones mending, breaking. His body was recreating itself from the broken bits and pieces. His skin went inside out. I can't believe that our principal was this, demon."

"I can't believe you killed it in the state it was in. How'd you do it?"

"I didn't." Storm opens his mouth to say something, but I interrupt, "I mean, I did. I didn't kill him in his demon form. The class bell went off, and interfered with his form, somehow. It was a temporary truce, but he threatened that, next time, he might hurt someone that I love. I guess that I snapped and killed him while he was weak. Do you think I did the right thing?"

"I don't want to be the one to say that killing is right; but, in all honesty, I don't think there was any other way. Either way, someone would've died. If you showed mercy on him, who knows who he would've targeted? I don't think you did the wrong thing. Does that help at all?"

"Yeah, I guess."

"I'm sorry. I'm just not one for violence. Usually, I'd say murder is wrong, but, under these circumstances, I don't know."

I walk over to the bathroom, "It's fine. I understand. I mean, I don't feel sorry for him, but, I don't, not, feel sorry for him, if that makes any sense . . . I'm going to hop in the shower and rinse off this feeling. Feel free to turn on the TV or whatever."

"Mind if I read your fantasies?"

"Uh, I don't know. Something about my best friend reading into my sex life sounds a bit invasive."

"Better me than your mother."

"Better none of you at all . . . Whatever. Put whatever back where you found it, though."

I turn the shower on hot, feeling the nice steam bathe me in its gaseous form. I hop in the shower, not literally of course, and feel the nice hot droplets of water ricochet off my neck. My hair grows thick with water and clumps together, hugging my shoulders. I lift my head up, catching some of it in my mouth as I swish the water around my teeth, kind of like a quick wash. I feel as if I'm not alone, so I open the glass door of my shower. No one's there. I feel a slight shiver down my spine but shrug it off as being my nerves acting up. I step out, once turning the water off, and step in front of the mirror. My eyes must be playing tricks on me because, in the mirror, staring back at me, are a pair of blood-shot eyes. The pupils are black as usual, but the irises are not the usual baby blue that they usually are, but, instead, a certain shade of green. I blink, then they're gone. Strange. I turn away, but quickly turn back. Through my peripheral vision, it's almost as if my reflection didn't move with me. I lean in and am surprised to see my reflection smiling. The smile begins to fade away with the skin. The Chance in the mirror presses his bloody hand against it and starts shaking from the inside, violently. The whole bathroom begins to shake. Chance starts to bang the mirror with his head, breaking skin with each impact. In a banshee-like scream, he says, "Get out!" He starts to tear away at the skin surrounding his eyes. My vision begins to be lost as I find myself completely at a loss for sight. I can feel the blood drip down my cheeks along with the cool air on the sensitive pink under-flesh. I scream out, that being the only thing I could think of. I fall to the floor and rush to the door, opening it to feel all the hot air leave the bathroom.

"I can't see! Storm! Stormm!" I collapse to my knees, feeling around the floor.

"Chance!" The voice isn't Storm's. "What's wrong!"

I hear footsteps pass me when I feel something drop down on my shoulders. "Who's here! Back away!" I lash out, attacking whatever's trying to harm me, but get held back.

"Chance! Snap out of it!" I feel a pair of hands grab my face and aim my focus at a specific direction.

"Storm? Is that you?"

"Snap out of it!" I hear him mumble something, "Sorry." I feel a nice, firm slap across my face as my vision begins to come back. In front of me are Storm, Dani, and Sam. Storm is directly in front of me, looking worried. Sam and Dani are in the same state, but to the side. "What happened?"

What do I tell them? Do I just be honest, saying I lost my eyesight temporarily? My reflection attacked me through its own body harm. "I don't know. I lost my vision for a second." I look at what's on my shoulders—a towel—and quickly realize that I'm sitting on the ground stark naked. I quickly grab my towel and wrap it around my waist.

"What do you mean?"

"My reflection tore off his face and, I sound crazy. I wouldn't just say something like that if it wasn't true."

"It definitely does sound bizarre, to say the least."

"Don't call me crazy!" I throw my hands onto Samantha's shoulders, receiving a surprised look.

"Dude. Are you feeling well? I think you should—"

"Don't, Storm. You're going to just tell me to lie down. I know what I saw. At least . . . I think I do."

Storm places a gentle hand on my shoulder, "How much rest have you gotten?"

"What happened?" Mother enters my room, worried about something, "I heard screaming."

"It's alright, Miss Winters. He just had an episode is all." I don't like the way Storm said 'episode.' He makes it sound like I have schizophrenia or seizures or something. I did not just have a psychotic break. I know what I saw, despite what they say, but a part of me also says the opposite. Isn't that what a psychiatric patient would say. They know what they saw, when they really don't, not to say that they don't see it or hear it. Our minds play tricks on us in cases of stress or intense circumstances, like when a kid who's afraid of the dark sees a pair of glowing eyes attached to a demon with a tooth for hunger, when in actuality, it's a stuffed rabbit lying on a couch in the dark with a giant carrot in its mouth, acting as the tooth for hunger. Obviously, I could come up with a better example, but I don't want to. Maybe later. Is this really my mind playing tricks on me? I did just kill the very thing that I've refused to believe in my whole life. Storm has a better chance of believing me than the girls. He was around to see the demon. To them, it'd be nothing short of a fiction writer's crazy illusion.

I feel a tap on my back as I look to see who it is. "Are you alright?"

"Yeah, sorry for the scare, Mother. It won't happen again."

"That's not what I was going for. I just want to know if you're fine." I nod my head. "Okay." She ruffles my hair with her hand, messing it up. "You never know how long your hair truly is until it's soaked." We exchange smiles, "Well. Get dressed. You can't eat like this. Dinner will be ready in a few." She closes the door behind her, leaving the four of us, once again, alone.

"Sure you're fine, man?"

I nod at Storm, to reassure him that I am. I head back to the bathroom, hoping to see everything back to normal. Blood is splattered all along the inside of the mirror with a handprint that drips from the fingertips. I reach my hand towards the mirror, watching as the mirror begins to crack around my face. The whole left side of my face shatters, revealing something that is underneath. It's like two different people staring back at me. One of them is me. The other has familiar green eyes. I've seen them somewhere. Come to think of it, I've seen them quite a few times, but where? The iris may be green, but that isn't the crazy thing about this. Surrounding the iris, being the sclera, it's pitch-black. There is no white, but a bright green eye floating around in the pit of Tartarus. Half of my lips form a serious line, while the other half reflects my current state of being. One thing that's the same is the scarring that stays the same on both sides. "What is going on?" I say to myself.

My concentration is broken by a voice. "Chance? Are you alright?" Dani's reflection stands next to mine in the mirror. I turn my head to find out if she's really here. She rests her head on my shoulders and puts one arm around me. I look back at the mirror to find out that everything is normal. Somehow, this feels like the beginning of a villain's tale. Why a villain, you ask? What hero would be seeing these things? This is like the beginning of a bad guy finding out what his true intentions are through a separate personality. Dr. Jekyll, calling Mr. Hyde. I repeat, will Mr. Hyde come forth. Someone set me up an appointment with Arkham. As if the demon wasn't enough, now I'm seeing hallucinations, and really vivid ones at that.

I put my hand on hers, "Yeah. I'm fine." Her hand trails down, following along the obvious scar that runs across my back. "It's nothing. Really." She says nothing, and just kisses my shoulder.

"If there ever is something wrong, you better tell me or my sister. Don't go toughing it out like a man who tries to keep all his struggles bottled. That will break you. I want to be the one to make you better. You hear me?" I nod. "I'll kick your butt, otherwise."

I smile at her through the reflection. She returns one. "Look at you, trying to be cute."

"I'm warning you. I'm not a force to be crossed."

"Right." I position her to face me, rather than us just exchanging looks through our reflections. "Do you want to, maybe show me a sneak peak of what you'll do exactly, if I refuse to comply with your terms?" Her body is firmly kept in place against the bathroom sink, with mine pressing against hers. My face is hovering above hers.

"Chance." Her voice is low. It's cute. I go in for a kiss when her body tenses up, "Your towel."

I look down to see my towel, resting at my feet. Danielle's body is mere steps away from being one with mine. "I'm sorry. I can't help myself around you." My hands tremble slightly.

She grabs hold of my wrists, feeling the shock waves flow through her body. "Chance? What's wrong? What's gotten into you? You're usually not like this."

I lightly grab hold of her chin and make my way towards her awaiting lips. "You're what's gotten into me. Please, Dani. Help me." My lips crash against hers in a semi-violent, semi-gentle manner. Her hands grab onto my relatively broader back. One of my hands sneaks behind her and pulls her in from the buttocks. The other hand rests barely on the inside of her shirt, where her bra strap is found. She stiffens as a certain part of me presses against her. Her eyes open to look into mine.

She breaks apart from me. "What the . . ."

"Something wrong?"

She stares into my eyes, as if she saw something foreign. Something that wasn't supposed to be there. "Uh, no."

"Good." I breathe down her shirt, causing her knees to buckle. "Because, we're just getting started." I reach for her pants, curling my fingers around the waistband of them. I feel the nice silk material of her underwear rubbing my knuckles.

A knocking at the door breaks the moment, "Chance. Are you done? Is my sister in there?" The door opens as Danielle pushes us apart, pulling her pants all the way up where they were before the door completely opens. "Chance." She stops as the door fully opens, revealing Dani, fully clothed against the sink, and me, in the barest form, a few inches away from her, standing in my obvious display of arousal. "What are you two doing?" Her tone isn't enraged, but it isn't calm, either. Before either of us have a chance to answer for ourselves, Sam grabs her sister by the ear.

"Ow, ow, ow."

"Let Chance get dressed in private."

Everyone sits at the table, quietly as I make my way. "You were up there an awful long time, Hun. Everything alright?"

Sam turns her head and eyes me down. "Yes. Nothing wrong. Food looks delicious."

"Why, thank you, but I'm not convinced."

"Honestly. Not to sound redundant, or like a broken record, but I don't know how you do this every day. Making food as good as this, day after day, night after night. Taking care of me."

"The job of parenting isn't an easy task. I just make it look easy. Honestly. I'm just doing basic parenting. If you can't handle as much as nourishment and care, then you are already unsuitable to be a parent. To know what's right and wrong, and to pass on your knowledge and experience to the future is the only way we can move forward, while also letting them experience their own. Always add to the old. Don't just empty the slot and start anew. Look at you. You grew up rich, but you never thought of yourself as superior to anyone who didn't share your wealth. You don't even flaunt your money. That's success as a parent. I've outdone myself with you." She picks up a fork, "Now. I feel we've waited long enough. Let's eat."

As she scoops into the peppered corn, I speak up, "Wait." She stops hastily, as if something happened. "Let's say grace."

She shows a small smile, then it turns to concern, "Is everything alright?"

"Yeah. Why wouldn't it be?"

"Well, we haven't prayed since you were seven."

Something happened recently that, turned my point of view on religion. None of us are entitled to see tomorrow, and I just wanted to regain what I've lost. If I happened to die, I don't want my lack of faith to be the death of me, in more ways than one. "I just feel like saying grace."

"What's gotten into you? Why are you so, different, all of a sudden?" She places her silverware down and folds her hands, motioning for me to start. The other three do the same.

I have forgotten how to pray, but the reason I'm doing this remains. "Lord, forgive me for my time away. I call to you in hopes for insurance. Assurance for my protection after death." So far, this sounds like a terrible way to start off a prayer. It sounds more like a beg for mercy than a change of heart, which it probably is at the moment. Faith is hard, after all, to achieve. It can't be achieved through words, alone, but the belief that there is something greater. Something good, that pulls you along the right path. It is up to you, whether or not to stray from it. Obviously, this is one example of faith. There is more than one religion. To say one is right and all others aren't would be a bit, shortsighted. To have faith means to open your heart to all possibilities. Not just the close-mindedness of Christianity at its worst. Oh, you're gay. You're going straight to hell. Shut the fuck up you prejudice sacks of hypocritical dictators. Believing that you deserve better because you "know" Jesus. You can't just go home and drink. You can't sin all week, then go to Church and act like all sins are washed away like that. It's like Mother's Day in a way, or Father's Day. You can't go all year, ignoring them, then once said holiday appears, you act like they're the center of attention. They should be treated like they're loved every day, every week at the least. Having a day dedicated to a parent is like saying they're meaningless every other day of the year. "If you are up there, somewhere, then you can understand the unsaid words that I can't seem to find. I'm sorry to have to call to you under these circumstances, not just faith. I'm not sure if I do believe, but this is a start. Thank you for everything you have given and for the free will to act for ourselves. Amen." I open my eyes. Everyone does the same. "I know it wasn't the best."

"It was alright. Definitely an honest one," Sam says. "It wasn't the worst one I've ever heard."

"What's with the sudden change?" Storm asks.

"Nothing wrong with a man who is in the beginning stages of finding faith."

Sam looks over to Dani. In return, Danielle turns away, avoiding the daggers flying her way. Dinner comes to an end, and Mother starts on the dishes. Storm has to leave, so I walk him to the door. "Hey. This whole faith-seeking wouldn't have to do with a certain demon who died, would it?"

"Yes, it does. That opened my eyes. I was ignoring it all these years, only to be presented physical proof of the lie I was living."

"I understand. Seeing that would turn many atheist heads. I'm not judging. It's actually nice to see you take part in something like that. Does this mean you're going to be going to Church?"

I shake my head, "No, Church isn't for me. One can simply pray at home and keep faith in heart. Church is for two people: those who believe you must go to one in order to prove your loyalty, and those who have it, but find themselves in a moment of weakness where they need a third party to help them remain on the right path. As long as I occasionally show him, or her, that I am worthy of his or her mercy, I'm good."

"Hope that goes well for you, man. Well, I'll see you later." We exchange a handshake and he heads home. As for Dani and Sam, they're here for a short while longer, but how to spend the time?

We head to my room and sit in awkward silence for about five minutes, so I break it, "I'm sorry for what you walked in on." Sam says nothing, but huffs. Dani faces a window. "Will you at least look at me?" I turn Sam to face me.

"Okay. I'm looking at you. Now what?"

"I said I'm sorry. What more do you want? For me to get on my knees?"

"It wouldn't hurt."

I do as I'm told. I kneel before Sam, slowly looking up to look into her eyes, making sure to make this as awkward as possible. "I, Chance Ryder, humbly apologize for any present, as well as future, transgressions I have and will make. I only hope, that in due time, you will find it in your heart to accept this well-given gesture." Samantha shows a sign of a smile, which turns into a giggle. "I knew you couldn't stay mad at me."

"I'm not mad at you."

"You have a funny way of showing that you're not mad."

"Well, I am, but not for the reason that you think." I stare at her, as if trying to make the moment more awkward than kneeling like a knight to a princess. "It's not that you were naked with my sister."

"Odd way to start a sentence but continue."

"To do it in secret. You didn't—"

"Wait a minute." I cross my legs and scoot closer to her. "You weren't mad because of what we were doing. You were mad because you weren't a part of it. Are you jealous?"

"No, maybe. I don't know."

"Don't be embarrassed. I think it's adorable. As long as jealousy doesn't swim into sabotage to one's relationship."

"You didn't even confront me. I thought we agreed, at the start of this, that we are a package deal. No favoritism towards one. I mean, I did like you before she did, so . . ."

"Sam. I find both of you attractive." She moves a little closer to me, until our knees touch. "This won't ruin our friendship, as long as we try to hold it separate from our sex lives. Agree?"

"Only if you agree to the terms of—"

"And I'll always come to you or Dani when getting closer to the opposite sister. You are a package deal, after all."

Sam rubs her hands down my chest, "Glad to see you seeing things my way. We still have some time if you want to apologize, correctly."

I know you may think it unrealistic that I get laid as easily as confronting the situation, but for some, it is as easy as that. In high school, sex is almost a necessity. For some, it takes extra work. For others, it comes easy. That's usually because of money, or popularity, or even looks. For the rest, it may seem like an impossible task to get laid by senior year. It's high school, people. It's practically the beginning stages to figuring out who you are and what love is. If you're lucky, you know what it is by twenty-five. People in these environments most likely don't know what love is, but they've already lost their virginities by sophomore year, either by a crush that broke their heart, a quick fling, or even an uncle or two that got too drunk. Here, all it takes are good looks, charms, or status. Luckily, I've got all, so you can only imagine how I get the girls. For those that none of this works, that is because she is saving it for "the one", which isn't bad either. Notice how I implied this one being a girl. That's simply because guys don't care about chastity, usually. Their goal is one track-minded, being sex. No matter what, though, always use a condom—birth control does not always work—unless you plan on your life being ended too young. If you don't have one, then at least make sure your pull-out game is strong. This may have actually been offensive to some, but it sucks to suck. I'm sorry if my words of truth shoved that stick further up your ass than it already was.

I grab Sam by the shoulders and nip at her collar bone, receiving small moans in the process. I motion for Dani to get involved. She does what is told of her. I sneak my hand into Sam's slim fitting V-neck and trace her belly button with my finger. I pull up from the hem to reveal her nice toned stomach. I trail small kisses down her stomach, leading to her V-line that disappears into her lengthy, black ruffle skirt, while rubbing the insides of Danielle's thighs. I crawl on top of them, having one knee in between each of their legs. I swiftly remove my shirt, tossing it aside, revealing my fit physique. I shadow Sam's hand, tracing down my own skin, while Dani follows shortly behind. Her fingers disappear into the waistband of my pants. I unbutton, slowly, teasingly until I find myself kicking the pants off my ankles. Impatient as I am in the current state I'm in, I'm unable to wait for them to remove their own clothes. I undo Sam's ruffle skirt, leaving her in a pair of black panties and a black bra to match. Dani wears a pair of white boy shorts, which look as amazing on her as the black, seamless panties look on Sam. Sam bends down to remove her stockings, but I interfere. "You don't need to remove those. I like them." We all lay naked on the bed. As Dani trails her tongue down my neck and nips on my ear, I try to hold myself back from violently squeezing onto Sam's supple breasts. I begin to lose control.

"It's fine, Chance," Sam moans, "I can see you're holding back. No need to." She removes my hands from her breasts and moves them south. I feel her arousal, which triggers my dominant side. I grind my pelvis against hers, hearing her cute whimpers. I take initiative and plunge in. She raises her hands and holds onto the headboard behind her for support. I place one hand gently around her throat and the other one grabbing onto a hip for control. I shift front and back as her breasts bounce ever so slightly at impact. Dani gets behind me and wraps her arms around me, grabbing onto my boys as she steers me into her sister. She lightly bites into my neck, only making me wilder. I pick up speed. The only sounds, being the slapping of skin and the moans and gasps coming from the girls. Sam's hands tighten on the headboard as her head rocks back and forth into it. Dani grabs a little harder, too, tugging and pulling as to hear me whine out of pleasure. I stop mid-thrust. "What's wrong?"

"I almost let loose. I've gotta save room for your sister."

Dani takes Sam's spot, but Dani takes a different approach. She gets on all fours and faces away from me. "Go easy." I stare, hungrily at the perfect, yet delicate peach that's spread out in front of me. I reach around her, holding onto her mounds, like I'm going for a bull ride. I align myself and dive in, no restraint. She screams at first but settles into a series of light moans. Sam hugs me tightly from behind, with her breasts pressed against my back as she gives me a firm slap on the rear, causing me to plunge a little deeper into Dani's unsuspecting flower, causing her to yelp. Sam rubs herself against me, her hands held together around my base as Dani's rear keeps slapping into them. "I don't think—I can handle any more."

"Don't worry, baby. I'm almost there, then I'll pull—"

"No! I mean, you can switch places if you want to let go." It takes me a while to realize what she means. Oh. I release her from my clutches, only to regain dominance over her other asset. I enter slowly, as it is more delicate and a new-found territory. She bites her tongue as her eyes water.

"I can stop."

"No! Don't hold back." She cries out.

"Are you—"

"Do it, dammit!" I plunge in as her hips buck and her back arches. She lets out a whine and looks towards the ceiling, like her soul is leaving her body. I go faster and faster, until I make one final thrust, holding in my grunts. Quickly, I pull out as I let out all my dying children onto her stomach and chest. I collapse over her, taking in her hair's aroma. The room, alone: a mixture of watermelon and sex, the watermelon, being that of their perfumes. I roll over onto my back, taking deep breaths. Suddenly, I feel a certain pain down below. Sam begins to milk me for everything I'm worth, not leaving a drop unsplit. The pain is that of when a man simply has given his all, in terms of release, but keeps going anyways. The girls lay on either side of me, rubbing circles into my chest with their index fingers. Sam is the first to get up, walking towards the bathroom, swaying her hips side to side. My stamina may have been used up, but, damn! It always hurts when an erection tries to regain its posture after being used up.

"We best be getting in the shower if we're going home, not smelling like a couple of marathon runners."

Dani grunts, not wanting to get up. "Fine." She slightly moves, grunting in pain, "Oww!"

"What is it?"

"It hurts a little. My butt. It stings to move."

I laugh at hearing this, "You better get used to it now, because, come tomorrow, you're not going to want to move."

She slaps me on the arm, "You knew I was going to end up like this? Douche."

"Never ask a guy if he wants to try new things when the sex has already begun. Our rational thinking is at an all-time low during those stages. Did you enjoy it, though?"

"Shut up."

"Alright. I guess I deserved that." I prop myself up and step off the bed, grabbing onto Dani's arm, "C'mon. Time to shower. Best be movin' while you still can." **snicker**

Thoroughly, we wash each other's hard-to-reach spots which mostly consists of the smalls of the backs; however, they want to do more, so we end up washing the other side. When we're done with one side, we turn around so the one who was in front transfers to the back, making sure we all get cleaned in the process. "Well, we gotta get going."

"Yeah, okay. It was fun having you over."

Sam leans her face in closer to mine, staring into my eyes. "What's wrong with your eyes?"

"What do you mean?" I look into the bathroom mirror, after wiping off the fog. Mixed in with my natural blue, are little green swirls, spiraling around the dominant color. Odd. Cool looking, but odd.

"Do you have some rare disorder?"

"Actually, this is the first I'm seeing this." I look back at the girls.

"It's gone." Just like that, the green spirals disappear. What a shame. I thought they'd add to my looks. We don't seem to question what just happened. We just go with it.

"Is your mom here to pick you up?" Mother leans in the doorway of my room, without making a sound, until she speaks.

"We were going to walk. Mom's probably still at the casino." Sam says.

"What. No. I'm not letting you walk in this darkness. This is a dangerous place to walk around at night." These words catch me off guard since she usually lets me walk around this late. "I'll get my coat. I'm driving you girls home."

"You don't have to go through the trouble of—"

"No trouble at all." Mother walks out, letting us say what we need to say before they leave. We don't say anything, but exchange kisses.

"Bye, Chance. See you later."

"Absolutely."

Just like that, I sit in my dark room, alone, tired as hell as I drift off into dreamland. I don't bother to undress, so I just position myself into a comfortable one as my eyes refuse to open till tomorrow.

Ix

Huh? What's going on? I find myself staring at a body, arm over the side of a bed, and hair, brown and unkempt. I reach for him, unable to make physical contact as my hand passes through him, like a projection. I take a closer look, only to be slightly surprised as to who I'm staring into the eyelids of. Is this—me? Is this what I look like when I'm sleeping? How did I get here? The last thing I remember is being drowsy and closing my eyes. I must've fallen asleep, but that still raises the question as to how I got here.

Is this a dream? If it were, I'd be able to touch whatever I dream about, wouldn't I? I only remember bits and pieces of my dreams. Nightmares, too. I remember certain quotes, but not who said them. I remember being scared, being happy, but as for the reason I feel such emotion, I haven't a clue. The predicament I'm in, somehow, feels like this would be a dream, but why would I dream of watching myself sleep? Dreams reflect your inner most thoughts and how you feel about certain things. Dreams are the subconscious part of the mind's way of trying to tell you what you refuse to accept. It usually works that way. The subconscious mind knows you before you know yourself. In other words, every decision you make, every path you take, is already known to the inner mind before you have a chance to say it out loud. That doesn't necessarily mean that you will follow what it is trying to show you. It may know your true intent, even if you choose a route that's the complete opposite. It's a confusing concept, really, so there's no point in trying to understand how it works.

What else could this be? To dream or not to dream, that is the question. There is only one thing that I could think of as to what this is. I've read up on it, but not a lot. It was in one of Storm's dad's books: *Conscious Sleep*. It is a neuroscientific text, which focuses mainly on escaping. Reading about the mind was interesting, but what caught my undivided attention were the diagrams and passages that focused on astral projection.

Unfortunately, it wasn't written in depth. It was written in theory, so it practically explained nothing. There were diagrams, drawn, of a body leaving a body while asleep. It explained how the mind is capable of observing, while the host body lays unconscious. I didn't believe any of it, of course. Out loud, it sounds ridiculous. Now, I'm having second thoughts. One: How do I get back into my body? Does it just happen naturally once I awaken, or do I force my way back in? Two: Am I going to remember any of this once I'm awake? I guess now's my time to explore, to figure out how this concept works. I step towards my door, reaching for the knob, nearly falling through, forgetting that my intangible state makes the action of touching anything impossible. I use this time to observe what happens on the streets while I take refuge in my dreams. After all, one's truest self is only visible when all eyes are absent, meaning complete seclusion. Not to be completely isolated, but to be free of any second or third-party involvement.

So far, nothing's changed. There's a homeless man sleeping on the curb, and a man in a trench coat, pickpocketing. How long will it take him to see that the man he's trying to steal from probably doesn't have anything valuable? Amazing that, even though I'm technically asleep, the intoxicating aroma of abused hard liquor and chewing tobacco still holds power over my sense of smell. I hear a gunshot from a couple blocks away, so I rush to see what the commotion is all about. A man with a beaten-up face comes running my way. He refuses to hide the gun in his hand as he runs openly through the street, not hiding his face. Stubble covers his chin in an inconsistent pattern, like a hack job with a razor. His hair is short, revealing a small scar above his eye. I come across a body in the middle of the road. There are a few homeless low lives nearby who refuse to confront the situation. They treat the dead body as if she's garbage, simply tossed to the side. Even I must admit that that's despicable.

My sympathy for the woman is at its minimal, simply because I don't know her; but at least I know I should feel something. That's got to count for something, right? I can't see her face, but I can see that this woman is a bit on the small side. Her face is turned towards the street. Her arms and legs are covered in filth, making it nearly impossible to determine an exact age using the number of lines and wrinkles on her skin. Her hair is entangled in knots and twigs. Her height is above three feet but can't be higher than five. Her scent is of urine. Her wardrobe is a collection of rags and filth; no doubt, she's without a home, too. A tin can gets tossed through me, landing in the growing puddle of blood around her waist. One of the homeless bystanders is obviously drunk as he laughs while walking towards the woman in a zigzag motion, trying to keep on his feet.

"Hey, pretty woman!" The drunk man mumbles as he zombie-walks his ass up to the scene.

"Hey, back off, man!" This is what I would've said had he been able to hear me, but since no one can, I feel my only option is to observe. I wish I could do more, but the gravity of the situation prevents me from doing so. I want to leave, but a part of me is curious as to what he's about to do to this poor woman who's already met her fate. He stumbles to the ground, near the woman's face. He places his unwashed hands under the woman, turning her over to reveal a face. Looking at it, I come to realize that this is not a woman, but a girl. She can't be more than nine years old, eleven at the absolute most. He licks his filthy finger and wipes away some of the dirt on the girl's face, revealing a rather pale complexion.

"My, my. What are you doing out here, pretty girl?" He pets her head, getting a finger caught in her nest of hair.

If I could do anything, I'd kick him square across the jaw. I'd grab a hammer and personally knock away each tooth. Better yet, given the undergoing circumstances, I believe a better punishment could have been on its way. Using a nutcracker to crush his testicles under the forced pressure would do nicely. I'd be satisfied to just hear the noise that is made when a testicle proves no match for the applied pressure. Obviously, I can't do anything, but rant internally. He drools from the mouth. As for the other drunks, they watch. This man, if you can call him that, tugs away at her wardrobe, disrobing her of all that she wears, leaving a dirty girl in her barest form. The skin under her clothes is still white, being cleaner than the parts of her that were initially exposed, like her face, arms, and legs.

"What the hell are you doing!" I know he can't hear, but I can't sit here and watch a little girl get defiled. I turn away, hearing a zipper being undone. Almost as quickly as the zipper is undone, I hear grunting, then the sound of skin slapping against each other. What kind of world do we live in where there are no boundaries when it comes to these sorts of things? I can't be here. I can handle a lot, but witnessing, or at least hearing, a little girl get raped is one of the things I don't tolerate. If there is a God, then there is a Satan. If there's a Satan, then, there's a Hell. I believe that there's a special place for pedophiles and rapists in the depths of Hell if there is one. Even more so, the act of necrophilia is a different case, entirely, yet, it's equally disturbing, if not more so.

I leave the scene, trying to get it out of my head, which, by the way, is going to be impossible to completely forget. I find myself three blocks away from where I was in a matter of seconds. *How'd I get here?* No one seems to be on the street. A beaten up, yellow Volkswagen with a busted taillight and a shattered windshield is parked on the corner of St. Vista Drive. "Parked" is an understatement, really. The vehicle only has two tires, placed in the front of the car, letting the back slope down. This car's going nowhere.

"Fuck you!" A door slams at one of the nearby houses. A woman in sweats and a shirt that's almost too small for her already small figure storms outside in tears.

"Where do you think you're going, wretched bitch!" A tall, husky man with a beer in hand storms after her, stopping dead at the porch. "You leave, I kick you and your poor excuse for a son out on the curb! Where will you run! Huh?" His voice is thick with German descent and he is obviously not the least sober.

"Good! I'm moving out!"

"Mom!" A boy around my age runs midway towards his mother, tears flooding his eyes. Freckles are placed randomly along his cheeks and his curly, brown locks dangle just above his eyes.

"Kyle, please!" His mother begins to cry as she tries to muster up the words to speak to her son. "Don't do this. Just come with me. We'll find a better place."

The male adult laughs drunkenly, "Where to, exactly? You don't have any money. You don't even have a job. I'm you're income. I pull the weight around here, so tell me, bitch. Where do you think you'll be running off to?" He takes a step towards Kyle, "Take him with ya if you're leavin'. If you don't care about where you end up, surely, you'll care about where he ends up. Your chances of surviving are slim enough without him slowing you down!"

"Go to hell! Kyle!" She angrily points her finger to her side, "Now. Come here!" Kyle hesitantly steps towards her, making quick stops in between every couple baby-steps.

"You listen to your mother, boy." He takes another swig of his can, crunches it, and throws it to the side. "Maybe, she'll make money doing what she does best. Sucking dick. Do you want that for your mother?"

"Stop fighting!" Kyle throws his fists to his sides. Both parents stare at him and he cowers back into his shell, "Sorry."

The surrounding neighbors can obviously hear this ruckus but refuse to get involved in any way. That's how this neighborhood works. Everyone keeps to themselves. Someone could get shot outside of their house, and they'd just let the police officers find the bodies. There are a few good souls that aren't going straight to Hell when they die, but the majority is definitely going down. They should just call this neighborhood "Hell's Lot" for Christ's sake.

I've seen this boy around school. He's one of the other recipients of Ashton's school-level torment. I've stepped in a few times to protect the kid. Kyle Shine is of fair height, maybe 5'7, but his muscle could use improvement. He isn't scrawny, like a twig or anything, but he has close to no muscle, either. I thought his life at school might have been different than his life at home, but seeing what's going on, that has proven false.

"You think this door mat will protect you out there? He can't even stand up against me." The husky man looks over at Kyle, "C'mon, boy. You may be useless, but the least you can do is talk some sense into your dear old mum. Die in the world or stay with me and man up to the terms."

"Don't talk to him like you're his father!"

"I've got news for ya, Princess. I'm the only father figure he's ever had that didn't walk out. You want to talk about fathers, take him to his. Oh, wait! You don't know where he is! So, shut the fuck up!"

Kyle runs to his stepdad and punches him. Unfortunately, that doesn't do any good as his hand flings off the older guy's beer belly. "Don't talk to her like that!" He keeps flailing his arms around, not causing any damage.

The abusive dick raises a hand and swipes it across Kyle's face, causing Kyle to fall to the floor, holding his nose. "You're finally taking initiative, but you're still weak. Wipe that up. I don't want blood on my porch." He throws a cloth at Kyle and slams the door behind him.

Kyle's mother helps her son up and they leave the premises.

Wow. I had no idea Kyle had this life at home. I turn away thinking, *I wonder what the girls are up to,* when I take one small step, suddenly showing up on a new street, entirely. I'm standing in front of a small house, a familiar house. *How'd I get here? To Sam and Dani's?* I was about to walk here, when, suddenly, I just showed up. I see red and blue lights coming from their window. *Are they really still up? What time is it?* I walk through their walls and enter their room at my own risk. Sam and Dani are sitting on the ground near their bed, with controllers in their hands. *So, this is what they do when it's late.* They're playing COD with the volume blaring and the lights off.

"Aw! You killed me!" Dani moves her fingers with haste as she randomly runs in zigzags to dodge any gun fire that may be coming her way.

"You got to do better if you want to defeat me." Sam is definitely not new at this. "Eat lead."

I like this side of them. They're just relaxing in their room, playing a game, dressed in their pajamas. Sam is wearing a loose, black midriff and a pair of black, skull sweats. Dani is dressed a little more comfortably, in a loose-fit T that barely covers her thighs as she wears a pair of faded gray boy shorts. Maybe, one day, we'll have to relax a bit in my room, playing games, laughing. Nothing to see here, so it seems.

I wonder what—Now, I'm standing in front of a decent-size house: Storm's house. I think I'm getting the hang of this astral projection thing. Rather than walking, I can simply imagine where I want to go, which can prove useful in the future, if only I can figure out how to astral project at will. All the lights are off, telling me that they all might be asleep. I phase through the walls into a comfortable little living room with a library on one side. Storm's father is passed out in his work room at his work desk. He's a carpenter, but in his free time, he writes. He has a few published works that aren't too bad, but he doesn't make enough money in royalties to afford this place, so he uses his writing to make extra cash when he can. He has a little over a few thousand readers, which isn't a lot when you consider how big the world is. Right now, it looks as if he's fallen asleep while writing one of his new stories.

Storm's mother is peacefully asleep in her room, half submerged in a pile of blankets. I check on Storm. Like his parents, he's asleep, with his door not completely shut. His arm hangs off the bed, like he's about to tumble off it. I know the feeling. Only thing is, my bed is a bit bigger. I sit on the side of his bed, not thinking. Surprisingly, I don't fall through. I find it strange that I walk through the walls and doors, but somehow, am able to sit on the bed. I hop around, but the bed doesn't shake. It's like I'm able to sit, but not make any adjustments to Storm's sleeping body. Good to know. I watch as he stirs in his sleep. *What are you dreaming about, man?* I wave my hand over his face. I don't know why. I just do it. As I do so, it looks as if my hand begins to get pulled in. I don't know how to explain what it looks like, but it's like a magnet trying to reel my hand in from a distance. I retract my hand hastily. *What the hell.* Slowly, I move my hand towards him again, fighting the pull as I try to steadily move in without the sudden force. As my hand nears his forehead, it tingles as small threads escape my fingertips. The feeling is strange. It's like a shock that won't stop. Grab a ballpoint pen, or any pen at all, and scrape your palms with the tip of it. It tickles for the first few seconds, but the longer you do it in the same place, it starts to sting for some reason. That's exactly what this feels like, but in all areas of the underside of my hand; yet, it's oddly alluring. I welcome the feeling. It looks as if thin strands of hair get pushed out of my fingertips, tugging at the skin, as they link my hand to Storm's forehead. Storm's head grows hotter as I can feel the semi-painful, yet welcoming feeling of the threads moving around in his head. Suddenly, I feel like I'm dropped. I scream as I free-fall in a void until I come to an abrupt stop outside an enormous estate.

I don't know how I got here. I wasn't picturing a place to go, and even if I was, I have no idea where this is, exactly. I've never seen this mansion in my life. I confront the gates that have a massive "S", only to be stopped by a couple body guards.

"Rete!" A muscular, Haitian man with a thick accent confronts me from the gates. Two other men can be seen atop pillars, like prison guards aiming their weapons at escapees. "Èske ou gen yon rezèvasyon?" Apparently, they can see me. I'm no longer an astral projection, which makes me question further as to my whereabouts.

"What? I can't understand what you are saying."

"He is American." The secondary guard isn't as muscular but is still pretty built.

"You are far from home, are you not?" His accent remains, but at least now, I can understand him.

"Can you tell me where I am?"

"I would turn back if I were you, traveler. No one passes. Not without his permission."

"Can I pass?"

They look at each other, then the Haitian looks at me, "Not from us. Enbesil."

"Te dakò."

"A reservation. Èske w pa konnen sa sa vle di? Ya need one by da owner of dis estate."

"How do I get a reservation if I can't see him, or her?"

"Dat is for you ta figure out. Now, leave. You have overstayed ya welcome." The Haitian puts a hand on the gun that hangs on his back.

"Can you at least tell me where the hell I am?"

"Underground if you don't move now." They have no emotion on their faces, if you don't count the natural anger that hasn't left them since I arrived. These two definitely take their guarding duties seriously.

"I'm just asking where I am, nicely. You don't have to be a couple of douche bags under the weather."

"What did you call us?" His gun is now in his arms. Seriously, who carries around an AK-47 to guard a house? I understand a handgun, but c'mon.

"Turn back. You cannot fight us. You are, but a puny white male, after all."

These words catch me a bit off guard, "Woe, woe! You don't have to bring color into this. How would you feel if I called you a couple of dumpster-born degenerate thugs?"

A gun gets aimed at my chest. An Ak-47 could do the job from a distance but holding it point-blank is overkill at its finest. "Calling you by skin color, and racist slurs are two different things. Your being white has nothing to do with the fact that you're still puny." Obviously, I know this. I'm not racist; I was just talking in the moment. My best friend is black for crying out loud. With his voice deep and his eyes focused, he says, "Leave."

"Yeah. I heard you. Leave or you're going to end me, yada yada. Kinda hard to not hear with those thick accents." I turn away. Where am I possibly going to go? This mansion is in the middle of nowhere for heaven's sake. All there seems to be are a lot of sand, pillars, and rock formations. If there were pyramids, I'd say I was in Egypt. If I wanted to go anywhere, I'd die before I got there. "I was just looking for Storm, but damn, you won't even tell me what state or country I'm in."

"Isn't that why you're here in the first place? To see the Storm King?"

I quickly turn around, while they quickly point their weapons. "Storm lives here? Wait, I said Storm. Not this so-called Storm King."

"Whether the answer is yes or no doesn't change our stance. You can't enter without proper approval of King Storm himself, or a reservation."

"King Storm! He's not a King! He's . . ." Then again, this is a dream. Storm could be a fucking centaur for all I know.

"You dare besmirch his greatness? Pou sa, ou dwe mouri. Ekzekisyon! (For that, you must die. Execution!)" All four guards aim their guns at me, about to shoot, when a bald man with no shirt, wearing a layered neck piece and what looks to be a golden man dress, walks up to the scene.

"ما هذا الهراء؟ (*What is this nonsense?*)"

The guards stiffen up, arms to sides, "Mesye. Sa a Ameriken te tache non ou. *(Sir. This American has tainted your name.)*"

"American?" This king looks familiar. His accent is different than his guards. While theirs is Haitian, his is something more along the lines of Arabic. "Move aside. Let me git a good look at American visitor."

"But, sir. You said—"

"Now, I'm saying to step aside."

They do as instructed as the king takes a good look at me. "Chance? Is that you?"

No way. I take a closer look at this man, only to realize that he is Storm. His semi-long dreadlocks are replaced by a clean shaved, reflective dome, making his shoulders appear as more broad than usual. His face is covered in tribal tattoos, as are his eyebrows. A thick, black goatee is visible beneath his bottom lip. Along his chest are scarification patterns, appearing as a bunch of dots that form designs. His fists consist of multiple golden rings, at least three per hand. The gold dress around his waist is silk and decorated with many engraved patterns. His physique and face resemble a man who is in his early twenties. "Storm. What's going on? How are you like this?"

"Come old friend. You must come in. I am sorry for any troubles you may have had to get here." The guards open the gates, allowing me in. The inside is much vaster than I may have believed. The doors are enormous, but the inside is like a kingdom unto itself. Pillars line the halls and chandeliers dangle from the high ceilings.

"Storm. What is this? Where am I?"

He chuckles, "Where are you? Where else would you be? You're in the Saharan Desert."

"I'm in Africa! How? There are, like multiple countries in the Saharan Desert. Which one am I in? Egypt?"

"No, no. Dat is our neighboring country. You are in Libya. How can you be in Africa and not know it?"

The last thing I remember is placing my hand on Storm's head and falling, which means, "Storm! I don't know how you're—"

"Storm is only a nickname given to me by the punishments I give to everyone who crosses me. You may call me Abdal. It's short for Abshir Abioye Ade Chidubem Abdallah III, after my grandfather."

"I don't know how to tell you this, Abdal, but you're dreaming."

"You speak nonsense. Come, come. I will show you the bathhouse and spa."

We enter a big room with half a dozen, half naked women lounging by a pool that stretches about half a mile around the room, leaving a huge moat around a stretch of land in the middle. A woman in an abaya walks over to Storm, giving him her respect as she bows. "My king, I didn't know we'd have visitors."

Her face is covered by a niqab, only revealing to me, her beautiful eyes. "Chance, this is Anaya. Anaya, Chance." I hold out a hand, but she steps back a bit. "Anaya. It is okay. You can express welcome." She holds out a hand. I take it in mine as we exchange smiles.

"Nice to meet you, Anaya."

"Indeed." She retracts her hand from mine and returns it to her side.

"Anaya, dear. You don't have to wear that indoors. How many times must I tell you?"

"I apologize, master."

"Master?" I look at Storm as he looks at me.

"Yes. These are my concubines. I thought I mentioned that."

"Concubines? Mistresses? How many do you have?"

"Seventeen. These are, but a few, of my women that I keep around for company. Anaya?" Anaya straightens up, chin up and speaks nothing. "You are surrendered to my good friend here, so please, show him a good time." Storm walks off into the distance, being greeted by a few of his other women. These women come in many shades, from dark to light.

"Wait! St—I mean Abdal. Where are you—" and he can't hear me. Anaya stares at me with awaiting eyes like she's awaiting an order.

"What do you wish, master?"

"You don't need to call me that."

"Not doing so will dishonor you. I must show you where I stand."

"I am not above you, so . . ." Storm settles in the far end of the oversized pool with the other five women as they take turns flaunting their assets in his pleasure. "Hey, does Abdal—never mind."

"You wish to speak of the other master? Do I not please you?" She refuses to look me in the eyes as she bows towards the floor, "I apologize. I must be punished." Usually, these words would excite me, but my mind is elsewhere at the moment.

"No, that's not it. I was just wondering, if Abdal shares you often. It doesn't seem like a life for anyone. To have little meaning. To be shared without consideration for your own feelings."

"Master Abdal has never shared any of us. You must be special. As for me, my sole purpose is to please the man of my dreams. Master Abdal is kind to us. He shows mercy. When we are tired, he lets us rest. There is no one I would rather be serving. I have not known you for long, but I see some of him in you."

This flatters me. To hear that I remind her of the only male she'll ever let order her around. "Can I ask you something?"

"You needn't ask. Anything."

"Why do you wear that? Your eyes are so beautiful. Your voice is the sweetness that my ears have been longing for. You hide your body like you're ashamed of it. I understand that it's probably a culture here, but you're indoors now; yet, you're the only one to be covered head to toe."

"Are you insinuating that you'd prefer my body disrobed, Master?" I open my mouth to answer but can't find what words to say. This is a dream, after all, so why am I not taking advantage of it? So what if Storm thinks this is real? If I tell him, then it might kill the mood for him. I'll let him have this. Anaya removes her niqab, revealing a young face that's slightly older than mine. She can't be any older than twenty-three. Her lips are plush and have been kissed by beauty incarnate. She removes her abaya, revealing a nice, curvaceous body with round, perky breasts and hips that bow slightly outwards. Her body is unmarked by ink but has a few piercings on her nipples and naval. She wears diamond anklets and a rhinestone headdress tiara frontlet that mixes with her long auburn hair. Though, she is topless, her bottom half is covered by a pair of black, low-rise, cheeky, laced panties. She gives a quick spin, showing me a quick glimpse of her firm buttocks. She tugs at the hem, revealing some skin underneath. Her underwear is laced around the whole waistband and hip sections, only hiding her private section. "Does this attire please you?"

I nod as she takes my hand, leading me to the pool. She sits me down at the step awaiting a notion to continue. I swiftly pull off my shirt, allowing Anaya to work with the bottom half, leaving me in my boxer briefs. "You are so beautiful." It's a shame that this is a dream. I'd have loved to do this in the waking world. I snap out of it and throw my clothes back on. She's like a siren. For a split second, I forgot where I was. To share a wet dream with my best friend? It sounds a bit, odd.

"Did I disrespect you? For that, I apologize."

"This has nothing to do with you. You're perfect, but none of this is real. Wait here. I'll be back." I leave the pool, looking over at Storm enjoying himself. This is his dream, so I shall leave him to enjoy it. How the hell do I get out of here?

"Friend! Is she not to your liking? What is it?"

"Nothing of that sort. I just need to find—the restroom." *That is the first thing I think of? Wonderful.*

"Out the door, to the left. Keep walking for about a quarter mile and you'll come to one. Be back quickly. They've been practicing a dance. It'd be a shame if you missed it."

I leave the bathhouse to be met with a hallway that probably stretches for a good mile. I'd kill to have a house half this size, and for someone under my living arrangements, that's saying something. I open every door I come across, hoping that one of them gets me out of here. What do I have to do? Die? I try to think of Storm's bedroom, but nothing happens. I step outside of the estate to find the guards lined up against each other on the ground, soaking in their own contents as their heads rest separately, mantled on spears sticking out from the ground, relative to the bodies. Their eyes are gouged out, but the expressions of pain and agony remain on their faces.

An arrow flies past my head. I drop to the floor and quickly try to get a glimpse as to who is trying to end my life. "What the hell!" I turn around to see five men, in what appear to be cloaks, make their ways towards me, slowly, with spears and axes in hand. They speak in a language I do not understand, but from the tone in their voices, I can tell they don't have friendly intentions. I grab hold of the nearest spear, tearing off one of the heads that are impaled, and using it to fight back. "Back, you savages!" One of them steps closer to me, not slowing his pace at all. As one of them nears me, the other four part ways, encircling me. I step forward, aiming with the spear, only to have it defeated with one simple swing of an ax. They close the circle, approaching me in a hostile manner, spears and axes battle-ready. I feel myself get pulled back by a force stronger than the one I'm able to exert in the opposite direction. The force tightens around my throat as I'm forced onto my knees, trying to move forward. One of the tribesmen grabs the top of my head and pushes it down so that I'm looking at the ground. I hear the grinding metal, knowing that he's readying his ax. I should feel fear, but, in all honesty, I don't know what to feel. In one's own dream, if he or she is to die, then they are forced into waking up in sweat. That, or they die in real life, too. What happens if I'm in someone else's dream and I die? If I were to die here, would my body forever be lost inside the mind of my best friend or would I be expelled from the dream? I feel the sharp edge of the ax graze my neck, then I feel myself free-falling once again.

Before I know it, I'm lying on the floor of my best bud's bedroom. I guess death is the answer when trying to escape a dream that I've astral projected into. How unfortunate. I leave Storm to his dreaming while I let myself out. Something tells me that he's going to be waking up really soon.

I notice that the sun is beginning to rise, so I decide to call it a night. I picture my destination, appearing in front of my house. I head to my bedroom, passing Mother's, then an idea comes into my head. It's a bad idea, probably not one of my best, but I decide to try it anyway. I peek my head through her bedroom door, making sure she's asleep or decent. She looks so peaceful when she's asleep, not that she doesn't look peaceful when she's awake. She always seems so easy-going and tranquil when awake; now's my chance to see what goes on inside that head of hers. I take a deep breath and rub my hands together, contemplating whether I should do this or not. I reach my hand out, only to be stopped. I push down on my hand, trying to close the gap between my hand and her forehead, but it feels as if I'm trying to move my hand through a waterjet's exerted power in a hot tub. I add force, finally getting there, as I feel the tingling sensation grow stronger the closer I get. It wasn't this difficult with Storm. I wonder why it is with Mother. Unlike my experience with Storm, my whole body begins to drown in a shockwave of jolts until I finally get the result I was looking for.

I look around, not recognizing what I'm seeing. The streets are different and, somehow, everything seems to lack color. Horses roam the streets, pulling carriages, and people walk the streets as if there is no worry of getting hit by a vehicle. I feel a sudden tug at my shirt and look down to see a little brunette girl in a dirty, white dress.

"Mister? Do you know where my mum is?" She looks as if she hasn't bathed in a couple days; yet, her clothes state that she comes from money. Her hair is a mess but looks as if it was styled a few hours ago. I kneel to say something, but an older woman calls out.

"Dora!" This woman looks as if she's in her thirties. She dresses wealthy and carries around an umbrella. "Dora. You had me worried to death. Don't you run off like that."

"I'm sorry, mommy."

"Look at you. You're filthy. Hurry home. We must tidy you up at once. You can't just run off and talk to weirdly dressed guys. He could be dangerous."

"I don't know. I like him." She pulls the child away into the opposite direction. "Bye, bye, strange man." She waves her hand as they disappear behind a building.

That was strange. I take a stroll, observing the new whereabouts that I have fallen into. I hear distant conversations. The accents mixed with the weird clothing gives me the odd feeling of being out of my territory. This isn't America. This is England, but where in it? I turn a corner and am met with the familiarity of nightfall. Sobbing can be heard from a distance. I enter a darkened ally that lies vacant for all except one crying body. I confront the person. The closer I get, the more the person begins to come into focus. I'm standing behind a little girl. Her identity stays hidden due to the lack of light. I kneel to comfort her; yet, I don't know how a complete stranger will be able to do such a task. Part of me says to leave her be, but the other part says not to leave her here all alone. A flashlight can be seen from the end of the ally, getting nearer.

"Aye! Who goes there?" The light reveals to me what I couldn't see before. The little girl isn't alone. In front of us lies the bodies of two grown individuals: a woman and a nicely dressed young lad, who may only be a decade older than I am. The woman, I've seen before. Both bodies lie motionless, soiled in their own contents. Blood puddles around the man's neck. The woman's top half is turned, exposing the red handprints covering her breasts. Her dress is lifted, revealing to me, more than just blood splattered along her wardrobe. I'm no blood analyst or detective, but from the visible evidence handed to me, I can tell that she's been molested or raped. Only question is if this little girl was around to witness it, or if she came across them. I extend my hand to her shoulder, contemplating whether I should touch her in the state she's in.

"Uh, hey," I start slowly, as to not speed things up, "I'm sorry for—"

Without a second to process, she turns around and buries her face into my stomach, letting out all her tears. I don't really know what to do, so all I can do is pat her head as the light shines in on us. "Bloody 'ell is goin' on 'ere?" We take a few to process. "Well, speak up." I continue to embrace her in my arms, while she continues to weep into my stomach. I can handle death. I can handle watching people die. For some reason, I can't stand by as children cry. It's one of my weaknesses; though, if you think about it, does caring for a child when they have nobody around really count as a weakness? I mean, think about it. Most can't handle blood when face to face, or the extended drama coming off one's suicide, and I can. If anything, I've got less weaknesses than most, emotionally speaking. The light passes me and the little girl, and rests on the two bodies. With the light shone past us, I can see the identity of this little girl. The flashlight quickly drops as I hear the man behind me screaming in the other direction, "'elp! Crazy loon is a psychopath!"

Two new voices can be heard stomping towards us, "You there! Put yer hands where we can see 'em!" The little girl tugs on my shirt, telling me that we should book it. I pick her up and begin to run when a bullet flies past me, chipping the corner of a brick wall. "I said stop! Now, put 'em up, I say." I comply, putting the girl down and turning around. I keep her behind me as we step forward.

"You got it all wrong."

"Tell me, then, the reason behind yer cowering. If you believe yerself to be innocent, then you would have obeyed the first time."

"True. I would if cops weren't the idiotic brutes that they are."

The officer forces me to the ground, bending my arms behind my back. I feel the tightness of my shirt being pulled back, until it stops.

"Honestly, young lady. You don't pay attention in your classes. You don't do your work. Your grades need major improvement. I should call your foster mother right this instance, but I won't. This is your last warning." I'm sitting in a hallway, a fancy one at that, as students cross the halls, getting to classes. I can hear a woman talking to someone behind me. The door is slightly open, letting me hear some of the conversation between the two. "Dora, you are a smart, young lady. I can see that, but you refuse to work towards your full potential. Honestly, fooling around in class. You've gotta separate your hobbies from your curricular activities."

"But I want to paint. I'm really good at it."

"That may be so, but it will never get you anywhere. Our job is to push you. Discipline and focus make the woman, and, though you are intelligent, you lack both. You don't do as you're told, and that can get you in trouble, someday. Your focus lies elsewhere when in class. I understand that you have dreams, and dreams are good, but you shouldn't try to run for 'em. You'll only get hurt. Try to stick with the books, okay? Knowledge is power. The only power that you'll ever need."

"Okay, Mrs. Cambridge. I understand."

"Glad to hear. You may take leave." The door opens fully as a girl a little younger than I, walks out the door. She must be in her teens, at the most, fifteen. She locks eyes with me for a split second, smiles, then walks off in the opposite direction. I've never met her, yet, she gave me a look of familiarity. Her eyes, I recognized. The blueish gray, like the foggy shores of the vast ocean, looking me in the face. Her face shows some form of likeness to someone I know, only younger. Come to think of it, she looks like the little girl from earlier, aged about seven years; but, at the same time, resembles a younger version of a woman I've come to know for some time. A woman that's been with me through it all. Yes, I'm talking about Mother. If it wasn't for the name, I'd say they were the same person. Another woman walks out of the office. She's older, most likely the one running this school that I've somehow stumbled into. "You there." I look up to meet the face of the principal. I only assume she's the principal, given that she was speaking with authority earlier on. "Yes, I'm talking to you. This is an all-girl's school. Mind elaborating to me the reason you've stumbled onto school grounds? I assume that there's some reason." Her eyes look me up and down, as if she's observing my state of wear. "Why are you dressed like that?" She shakes her head, "Out, out. No boys allowed."

I stand and bow, politely. "Sorry, ma'am. I apologize for my trespassing. You will not find me on school campus again."

"Hmph. Excellent manners. May I ask, though, about the state in which you dress. I don't know of any school that enforces such dress-code."

"Oh, yes. This. It's, uh, homemade."

"Marvelous patchwork. You are quite gifted in the art of sewing." She shoos with her hand, "Well. Off you go, young man."

I walk the halls, passing by a bunch of prep students staring at me. I come across a girl grabbing books from her locker. "Uh, hey, Dora." She turns to face me, with a big smile spread across her face, like a girl whose crush asked her out after three years of waiting for notice. "Do you know who I am?" She nods. "Have we, ever met?"

"You have traveled a great distance to get here. Do you know what you are looking for?"

"What? No. I mean, I was just thrown here. What year is this if I may ask?"

"You must stay focused on the big picture. I can tell you're a bit confused on what's going on. You're being here alters actual events without the consequence of change."

"What are you talking—" She places her fingers over my lips.

"This is just a sneak peek. You're digging yourself into a hole that's already been dug. Leave it alone and I promise, you'll know all."

"Not until you tell me where I am. When am I? Who are you? How do you know me?"

"Meddling with one's dreams is a personal matter, as are memories. One shouldn't try to snoop without awareness and approval."

"Are you aware that this is a—"

"Bye, Chance." She shoves me, as I fall into another void. Images fly by me, like sped-up video clips, being shoved down my throat. I take a hard blow, crashing into a solid surface. I hear a woman's voice. It wakes me from my temporary unconsciousness.

"I should tell him; but what if he resents me for lying. Years of growing closer."

"If he finds out on his own, he'll be more upset than if you told him yourself. Secrets are a plague that keep bonds from being made."

"I don't know what to do." Two voices can be heard from the other side of a door. "Just a little more time. He won't understand." I've heard both voices before.

"You give him too little credit. He's a clever boy, thanks to you. You've given him the education, along with the freedom to grow. He's experienced. You haven't failed yet, but this unorthodox connection for the boy needs to end if you plan on him moving forward. Compassion isn't a bad thing, unless it intervenes with the overall plan, and—" The talking stops.

"Chance?" I stop in my tracks, slowly turning to walk away. "Don't you know eavesdropping is an unattractive trait?" The door swings open on its own, revealing the two that were previously conversing. *Mother and Dora? They know each other? How?* Mother steps towards me. "You can't be here." She extends her arm, contacting my forehead with her fingers. "We'll discuss this later, Chance." Everything begins to deform and fade away, like a resolving acid trip. Before I know it, I'm lying on the floor of Mother's bedroom. I notice light shining through Mother's blinds. *How long was I in Dreamland?* I make my way back to my physical body. I lie down to match my body's sleeping form, feeling the tingling sensation of my bodies coming together.

My eyes pop open as I just lay still. *What the fuck just happened?*

X

Everything from the previous night, leading into early morning, rests freshly in my mind. It feels like a dream, if not for the total recollection of events. I don't usually remember dreams so vividly, yet, how could this not be a dream? Mother hums a tune while finishing up with breakfast. "So, how'd you sleep?" She asks this question with her normal tone, nothing added to it. Maybe, she doesn't remember what happened, or maybe, it didn't. I want to ask, but, if it didn't happen, I'll just look stupid.

"Pretty good. I had a dream. Nothing out of the ordinary." I try to act as if it were only a dream. If it was, she'll shrug off my answer out of normality. If it did happen, she'll bring it up, maybe. This would be a good plan, unless she does think it was a dream also, in which case, she won't even bother sharing. "How about you? Dream anything?" If she shares that she dreamed of me, then I'll know what I did, happened.

"Mmhmm. Are you sure you didn't dream anything special?"

"I'm pretty sure. I mean, even if I did, I probably wouldn't remember it. I never do. Not completely."

"Good to see that you didn't hurt yourself in your sleep, though. You've got quite the collection of scars." She glimpses at my upper body, then looks back at the food she's preparing. "I gotta say. They've healed quite well. You don't really notice unless you get really close." She turns off the stove and moves the food over to the table. "Breakfast is served." She sits across from me, "But, before we eat, let's get down to the issue at hand."

"Which would be?"

"Dream jumping." I slowly put the fork down. I had a feeling she was going to bring it up if it actually happened, but I wasn't expecting her to be so blunt about it. She is not turning corners. "Your father could do it too, among other things. In fact, that's how he met . . . that's how we met. I was astounded at first."

"He could dream jump? And I'm just hearing about this now?"

"Most refer to dream jumping as astral projecting. As to the second question, you never asked. Besides, would you really believe me unless you did it yourself?" She has a point; however, being face to face with a shapeshifting demon opened my eyes a bit. I probably would have believed her, regardless. "Was this your first time?"

"It was."

"Do you know how you did it?" I shake my head. "Well, I can honestly say, this won't be your last time."

"If I don't know how I did it, then how did I do it? And if you know about astral projection, then you must know how I was able to do it."

"Good observation. I do know how it works; yet, I can't do it. There are books that can explain better than I can."

"They're just books, though."

"Yes, they are. Many are false and gravely exaggerated superstitions; but, out of the vast majority, there are a couple that are based off fact. There are a few books in our private library that might help you. You're taking this surprisingly well. It's almost as if you're not new to this type of thing."

"No. This is a first for me. Maybe, I just handle certain things differently than other people."

"Boy, is that the truth. You hardly batted an eye to that serial killer at your party just as you shrug off what happened this morning like it was nothing more than a dream. Normal, you are not. That's not a bad thing."

"So, what do I do, now?"

"What do you feel you should do?"

"I don't know. Maybe, I should take a look at those books later. Do a little studying on the subject."

"That is a fantastic idea. Who knows? Maybe, you'll pick up a few tricks," she says.

"Wouldn't that be great. I don't know, though. A part of me feels like I'm going to wake up at any moment. This is all one big dream."

She smiles, "I would imagine that it'd feel like that. Finish your food. You've got to get to school."

"Hey. How did you push me out of your dream? It was as if you knew that I wasn't supposed to be there. Then again, you figured I was dream jumping. Did you know when you pushed me out, or did it cross your mind when you woke up?"

"I don't really know how to explain that. While we are on the subject, what did you hear? While you were eavesdropping."

"Not much. I mainly heard voices. I knew someone was talking, but I couldn't make out the words. I did recognize the girl you were talking to, though. Dora?"

"You've met her, then? In my dream?"

I nod my head, "I didn't know it was the same girl, though, until a little later. It's as if I was going through her life."

"May I ask how far you got into that girl's life?"

"She was a teenager. Principal visit. Something about drawing in class. She knew who I was. That's what surprised me. I'm curious as to what connection you two have. She said that I was meddling."

"You were in my head. In a way, that is meddling. I used to know her, but that was a long time ago."

"From the looks of it, it's almost as if it took place in the 18th or 19th century. From the accents, it was somewhere in England."

"It was a dream. Dreams aren't always accurate in terms of time and place. They're practically a cluster of all your thoughts combined. Any who, we'll talk about this later. Feel free to skim the books. As for time and place, you should be heading to school if you don't want to be late."

She was right about one thing. I show up to school a few minutes late, having come up with an excuse. Luckily, the front desk is used to me by now. They just slide me the sign-in slip, no questions asked. Nothing special happens for the majority of the day. Students roam the halls, talking about the incident of the week: Mr. Jenson's sudden demise. Obviously, only Storm and I know the true actions that took place. No student was held accountable for the murder, due to lack of evidence. Ash was let go after denying everything. There was also the proof of his whereabouts during the incident. Occasional locker checks are done, in hopes of finding the culprit with their pants down. Our school was displayed on the news, with some student witnesses who were the first to come across the body.

Come Lunch, I walk around observing the students paying zero attention to their surroundings as they fiddle with their phones. "Chance!" An average-height beauty with long, flowing blonde hair rushes to my side. "He hasn't responded to any of my calls."

"Who hasn't responded?"

"Austin! Who else? I went by his house and his mom said that she hasn't seen him since the party. She's worried sick. She put out flyers and hasn't heard back yet. What if something happened to him?"

"Jessyka. I'm sure he's fine."

"I'm not so certain. He wouldn't just vanish without telling someone. We should look for him."

"What, exactly, are we going to accomplish? If he's been missing since the party, do you honestly think that we're just going to run into the guy? For all we know, he could be miles away. A new city, even."

"You've got to help me. We have to at least try."

"Maybe, and this is just a thought, but maybe, he doesn't want to be found. Think about it. He tells no one and doesn't answer his phone or his messages. Maybe, his life wasn't the best. There are many reasons why people run away." *Shit. I knew I was forgetting something.*

"Sure, he can be a dick. I know you didn't hit it off with him, but he has a good life. His mom loves him dearly, as does the rest of his family. You can't even call him. His phone doesn't even ring. If my messages don't get read or responded to, and my calls don't go through, then that means his phone is off. He could very well be—"

"Dead? Kidnapped? Unconscious?" *Way to go, Chance.*

Jessyka tears up. "How could you be so calm about this? He could be in serious danger. Never mind, if you won't help me, I'll find someone else."

I grab onto her wrist as she turns to storm off, "Wait, Jess. I'll help you."

"What's with the sudden change of heart? You don't care about Austin."

I wipe one of her tears away, "You're right. I don't care about that asshat. I won't lie about that. I do, however care about you. If you feel you should look for him, then I guess I can accompany you, even if the chances of finding him may be close to none."

She thanks me with a hug. Ash can be seen from a distance, eyeing me down with murderous intent. Usually, he confronts me, but, this time, he keeps his distance and walks away.

School comes to a close and I find myself in the school yard where football practice takes place. "What a surprise to see you show up for once!" The team is lined up for exercise, leaving me to the side, being barked at by Coach Nickels.

"Sorry Coach, I was—"

"You've cut practice too long for any excuses to be acceptable. You're lucky I haven't kicked you off the team! The only reason I kept you on is because of your friend. That and because your limited presence on the team is equal to that of one of our average players, showing up every day. Regardless, that little stunt you pulled nearly made our team forfeit. We're near the end of our stride and I'll be damned if you do anything to jeopardize our victory. I expect you to be present at every practice. No excuses. We have one game left in the season and losing is not an option. Now, in position, Ryder." I line up with the others, with Storm being a couple players down from me. Coach Nickels confronts me, giving me close to no personal space. "I am so sorry that practice cuts into your precious 'me' time. Unlike you, they actually want to play. Where were you on the night of the game? Out getting wasted or whatever new trend you young kids do these days!" I open my mouth but close it automatically. "Now! Here's what we're going to do! And by 'we', I obviously mean 'you!' Everyone's going to take a lap and when you're done with that lap, take another! I don't want to see anyone walking or taking any breaks longer than five seconds! Doing so will result in punishment! Not just for you, but for the team! . . . Well, what the hell are you waiting for? Chinese New Year? Get going!" We do as ordered without hesitation. I find myself second to the lead, keeping my pace until I catch up to the runner in last place. I notice Chucky staggering left and right and slow down to his speed.

"You alright?"

He breathes heavily, pushing himself past his limit. "Inhaler." He mutters under his breath, but I hear him.

"Coach! He needs his inhaler!"

"He's welcome to come get it. If he wants to have the whole team suffer his actions! I'm not running a little league for toddlers! He'll get access to his inhaler when your laps are up!"

"But, Coach."

"Run! I want to see you sweat! No one gets anywhere in this world without a little struggle!" I help him for the remainder of the laps until Coach pulls us to a stop. "Water break! Baby Megee! Go get your inhaler!" Barely five minutes pass and we're thrown into exercises. "Let's go! Up! Down! Pushup! Run in place! Repeat!" I keep up with the pace, but the others look as if they're struggling.

"C'mon maggots! Unless you want to be running until your feet bleed, I suggest you hustle." My arms begin to tire, and Coach takes notice of this. "Having trouble there, Ryder? That's what happens when you skip out on practice. You get weak!" He presses his shoe into the underside of my arm, making me lose my form. I fall over to my side, holding my arm.

"Maybe if you joined us in the exercises rather than abusing us."

"What?" He speaks lowly, giving me a chance to change my response. "Pain builds character. If you had any, you'd have known."

"What better way to build character than to abuse us to the point of breaking."

"Is that what I'm doing, Ryder? Am I breaking you? I had no idea what a fragile little snowflake you were. Would you like a break? Perhaps a cup of tea? A teddy bear to keep from getting lonely? This is my team. That means that you are my property leading up to the point where you're not a part of this team anymore. Stop being a little bitch and do as told. Now!" He points to the track, "Everyone! Three laps. Whoever backs out doubles up on exercises next practice." When laps are done, we're forced into alignment. Coach Nickels walks with his hands behind his back as he silently judges us. "Ryder! Friezone! Turner! Zee! Get your asses up here! We part from the rest of the team, standing shoulder to shoulder, chins up, like soldiers in training. "You four did the best out of the bunch! Ryder! Though, you were a pain in the ass the whole practice, you still managed to best the rest of these pathetic wannabe athletes! As for the rest of you, let me just say . . . Your workouts were weak! Your attitudes were unacceptable, your appearances need work, and don't even get me started on the laps! I've seen more hustle in my dead grandmother's prosthetic leg! You are all weak! The sad part is, I don't think you know it, yet. You keep trying as if you have a chance out there in the real world."

"Bitch." I mumble under my breath. Unfortunately, it was in one of Coach's pause moments. I'm pretty sure he heard me.

"What was that, Ryder?"

He definitely heard me. "Nothing."

"Nothing, what!"

"Nothing, sir!"

"Do you see that, team? Ryder is what the outside world refers to as a pussy, and why? Because he only speaks ill of someone when thought to be ignored. When it comes down to confronting the recipient of the opinions, he cowers like the typical mouse."

"You can't speak like that, Coach. Language still applies on school grounds."

Coach Nickels stands in front of the messenger of that thought, which so happens to be Storm. "I can't speak like that? I just did! You're welcome to confront the new principal about my behavior towards the lot of ya. It'll just prove my point. That you're a bunch of spineless hermits who can't take a punch, as well as a few cruel words. Grandma! Get those cookies warmed up! Baby's comin' home!"

"Why do you have to be such a bitch?"

"What was that, Ryder?"

"I'm sorry. I'm sorry. What I meant to say is—why are you such a bitch, Coach Nickels?"

He gives a slight chuckle to my great surprise, "Look who's finally grown a pair."

"We're talking about me, right? Because, apparently, yours are taking their sweet ass time. Why are you like this? You act like an old man whose husband refused him a blowjob for the last eight years. You'd think you'd get used to the neglect, but, no. Your balls have been neglected so long that eventually, they disappeared, making you the bitch in every relationship."

"Do you wanna repeat that!"

"Do I need to? Given that you're asking in rage, I'd assume you heard me correctly."

The rest of the team stands in silence. I can see Storm to the side, biting his tongue, trying not to laugh. "One more outburst like that, then you can walk your ass off my playing field. In fact, you can walk your ass off this team! How do you feel about that?"

"Nothing would please me more."

"So be it. Leave. You are no longer a part of this team." I can feel my headache coming back. Coach's words echo with every syllable, until the echoing stops. Everything stops. When I come to, Nickels is lying on the ground, holding his nose. "Y-you broke my nose!" Blood streams down his chin, scabbing at his upper lip. "You have any idea how much trouble you'll be getting into!" I don't know what happened, but I'm not sorry. I might be a little concerned for my well-being. This has happened a couple times, but I'm seeing a pattern in what causes these temporary blackouts. At first, I had an idea, but now, I'm certain. I lean down to the coach.

"You're welcome to confront the new principal about my behavior towards you, but that'll only show me the pathetic hermit you are. You talk tough, but when it comes down to it, you can't take a punch as well as a few cruel words." I tap him, playfully, on the cheek. "That sound familiar? Do as you wish. Let it go, or dwell on the past like a bitch. Just a thought." I get up and leave the field, waving to Storm. "See ya later, bud."

I ride my bike in the direction of home when my phone buzzes in my pocket. I come to an abrupt stop on the side of the road to check my message: When you get off practice, meet me at Mt. View Park.

"I'm free. On my way. Give me 5 minutes." Jessyka waits for me by the swings. "Why'd you call me here?"

"You said you'd help search for Austin."

"Now?" She nods. *Great.* I lean on my bike.

"If we do it at night, we won't be able to see anything. Even with flashlights, our vision would be limited."

"I guess, but why start here?"

"Austin loves the park. He comes here sometimes to play his guitar."

"Listen, Jess. Do you actually have a plan for finding him, or are we searching wherever, hoping to come across him in our travels?"

She grabs my hand and pulls me in a direction, "Don't be silly. Of course, I have a plan. And that is to search everywhere I know he's familiar with. Obviously, the park is a bust. On to the next destination."

We stand in front of a run down, but still operating building. The sign reads *Gordy's Café*. What an original name, I know. The place isn't packed, but is, somehow, still in business. "I didn't even know we had a café."

"Understandable. Many people pass this place on a daily basis. Because of the broken-down exterior, many think it's just a run-down business. They don't even bother to look inside."

"What about when there's a different car out front. They have to realize this place is open by a few people coming in and out."

"They're most likely looking at the street ahead of them. And the cars parked outside could very well be for neighboring businesses."

We walk up to a heavy-set woman on duty. She turns to us and smiles a tired one at that.

"Wow, you look exhausted." Jessyka nudges me in the side.

She gives a weary smile, "Understatement of the day. Can I help you, Sugar?" She speaks it with a thick New Jersian accent. Leave it to a Diner to display the mainstream New Jersian waitress stereotype.

"Sorry about my friend. I was wondering if you've seen someone today," Jessyka says.

"Hun. You'll have to be a little more specific than that."

"Right. Um, has the boy I usually come in with been seen today?"

"I've been a bit preoccupied today. I barely remember a single face that has come in today. Ask Debby. Her shift is about to end. If your friend has been in within the last nine hours, she would've seen him."

"Thanks, Jenny."

"I take it, you've been here before?" I ask Jess.

She nods, "Austin and I come here before school sometimes. At least three times a week." We come across a thinner woman than the last. Jessyka taps her on the shoulder.

"Hey, girl. You're here awful late. Didn't see you this morning, so I figured you weren't coming today."

"Hey, Deborah. Can I ask you something?"

"Shoot. Fire away. Not literally, of course. We've had enough shootings in this Diner's history. And who is this?"

"Chance, Deborah. Deborah, Chance. Now that that's out of the way, have you seen—"

"You're cute." Jessyka turns her head and stares at me with disbelief. "What? I thought it, I said it."

Debby chuckles, "I'm flattered, really, but . . ." She raises a hand and wriggles a finger. At the base of her ring finger is a beautiful diamond ring. She leans in and gets a closer look at me, "I take it, you're the go-getter in your little environment."

"Go-getter?"

"How to say this, you're the babe magnet in your school. You've got the confidence to speak up because your looks don't hold you back. You can get almost every girl you want, yet you're unable to solely apply yourself in a whole relationship."

"Almost any girl?"

She chuckles, "Baby doll, looks aren't everything in a relationship. You're in high school. Wait a few years where everything is different. You've probably never been rejected. You've got the face. From the looks of it, you've got the physique. I'm gonna go out on a limb here and say, you're financially stable. You've got nice clothes. Your mom or dad must have a nice job. Am I wrong?"

Jessyka places a hand around my shoulder. "Right on the nose there, actually. You know that big house on the other side of town? That would be his place."

Debby goes wide-eyed for a split second, then regains composure. "You're kidding me. That's yours? How did you manage—"

"Sorry to interrupt, but, I . . . we came here to ask you a question."

Debby slaps her hand against her face, "Oh, shoot, yes. I'm sorry, dear. I totally get side-tracked. What'd you come here to ask?"

"Has Austin come in as of late?"

"No." Debby pats down her apron, "I'm sorry, but I haven't seen him since the last time you both came in here. Why? Is the poor boy in trouble?"

"That's a tough question. The thing is, I don't know. His mom is worried. He hasn't been to school in a few days. I was hoping, that if you saw him . . . I was hoping he'd keep some kind of routine. At least then, he'd be findable."

"I'm sorry, Hun. I'll make sure to keep a wide eye for him. I hope you're successful in your search. If I may intrude, are the cops looking for him? If he truly is missing, his mom must've put in the paperwork."

Jessyka leads me to the entrance/exit. "I'm sorry to bother you at work."

"Nonsense. None the bother at all. Oh, and Chance, dear, remember what I said. You mustn't rely on looks. They can only get you so far in life."

I nod as we leave the Diner in our rearview mirror, figuratively speaking. "That was a bust."

"Don't worry, Jess, we'll find him. When we do, I'll make sure to give him a good beating for worrying you."

"Thanks for helping."

"No problem. Hey, I've been meaning to ask. You've dated Ash for a little while, and you said Austin has been a friend for longer. Ash gets jealous over everything; has he ever, you know, been jealous over you two?"

"No. I didn't tell you because it wasn't relevant. Ash didn't have the right to be jealous over Austin, because, well, he is gay."

"Oh. He hid it well."

"Why? Because he doesn't wear a tuck in? He doesn't quaff his hair all elegantly? He's not a stereotype? He hated the stereotype gays. He'd always go on and on, saying that it's one thing to kiss a guy in public or to have pride in it, and it was another to flaunt it so publicly, like you needed to match the appropriate criteria needed to be gay. He was one to step outside of societal standards. He thought all this; yet, he refused to come out. No one knows he's gay, except me and maybe a few others."

"Why did he never come out?"

"Listen, you can't say anything about this to anybody, got it?" I nod. "He'd be furious that I blabbered to someone, especially you."

"Hey. What does that mean?"

"You really got under his skin. With you, he was at war. He'd say how sexy you are. What he didn't, or, doesn't like about you is how you are. You've got everything. To him, you lack struggle. You use your looks to your advantage. You play on what a girl loves, whether it be her hobbies or culture, and use it to reel her in. He doesn't like your manipulative side. And, as for not coming out, a lot of his friends are homophobic. They mock homosexuality."

"He's dated girls recently, right?"

"As a cover. He has to stand by and listen to his friends hate on 'queers', or 'fags', and has to try and become a part of the conversation to keep from standing out. He'd listen to them say things along the lines of, 'queers don't belong with the rest of us. They try so hard to be different, thinking they deserve special treatment. If people were meant to be gay, the bible wouldn't speak against them,' and such forth. He's told that it's a choice. He dates women, trying to change his sexuality. Sometimes, he cries himself to sleep. People just aren't mature enough to accept homosexuality into their social groups. The fucked-up part is, when it's a girl, it's totally justified. Guy on guy equals shun. Social outcast, except with other gays. Girl on girl equals rampaging hormones. Guys love to see that. I just don't get it. It's no wonder he keeps it secret. The truth is a scary thing.

Coming forth is a decision, one that, once out, can't be turned back. You really have to ask yourself if that's what you want."

"So, he hates me because I use women to my advantage; meanwhile, he uses them to change himself. What about you? You know who I am, what my intensions are, yet, you keep trying to get with me."

"Maybe, we're just two horny teenagers who look for release rather than a relationship." It hurts just how much that statement is accurate. We stare out at the vast series of trees that aim in every direction. "He comes here, too, and plays his guitar."

"How are we supposed to find him here? He could very well be anywhere."

"Looks like we'll have to search everywhere."

Great. This ought to be fun. We spend what feels like forever searching the woods for that blonde, hypocritical douchebag. Unsuccessful, If I might add. "We've been searching for a good hour. He's not here."

"He has to be here. If not here, then where? There's still so much ground to cover."

"And so many uncrossed paths that we can't possibly know."

She stops, "What do you mean by that?"

"If, in the unlikelihood, he is here, in these woods, who's to say he hasn't passed us and went on his merry way. There are many places in these woods, parallel to where we stand, that he could've crossed. If we keep moving, it could, very well, be for nothing."

"If we keep moving, and he is still here, he could be in danger. What if we arrive in the right moment to save him?"

"You said he's been missing for a while. If he was in trouble, what's the possibility that we'd stumble across it in time. It could've already happened, assuming he needed help in the first place."

Jessyka's eyes water, "We have to find him. I have to—you . . . you're right." She falls to her knees. "It's hopeless. It's a lost cause."

"I've never seen you like this."

"We've never really hung out. Austin's my oldest friend. He can't be gone."

I kneel to her height to comfort her. I hesitantly place an arm on her. She finishes my move by leaning her head in, under my chin, and onto my chest. "I'm sorry. I really am."

"You helped. We did everything we could."

"Almost everything." She looks up at me, "We can let the cops take over for us. Our job may be done, but the search doesn't have to be. They've got more connections than we do. They'll have more luck." She nods and pulls out her phone. My eyes narrow at something in the distance. I place my hand over hers, lowering the phone. "Does Austin play guitar with his fingers, or with a pick?"

"Um, both. Why?"

I walk over to a small, black triangle, partially stabbed into the ground. I pick it up. "Does he play with something like this?"

"He has at least a dozen picks of different colors, but the design definitely looks like his."

I spot a few faded footprints that wouldn't have been seen had I not been ground level, thanks to the generously given pick. This may be pointless scavenge, but it definitely wouldn't hurt. The footprints continue in an order that isn't consistent. The prints are all still a bit hazy and out of focus, probably because of the days between now and when these were made, and the night wind blowing dirt and leaves over them. Placed to the side, next to one of the prints, is a fragment of something. Another one can be seen a couple dozen steps away, same color. They're pretty big fragments. They look familiar. The markings give a hint of what this is, when the next piece closes the mystery of what this item could've been. "What color guitar did Austin have again?"

"Gray. Find something?"

I hold up a long, gray piece: the neck of a guitar. She gasps, holding her mouth. She reaches for the piece, and I give it to her. "This doesn't mean anything. That might not even be his—"

"You don't have to hold back. I'm not a kid that you try to keep the truth from. This is his guitar. If it's broken, then that means . . ." She buries her head into my chest again, wetting my shirt with her tears. "It looks as if our search has come to an end." I want to say something, anything, but she isn't wrong. The footprints continue for a few more strides, but that's it. There's nothing else to follow. We have come to the end of our road. I allow her to continue crying into my chest if it'll calm her down. I gently push her away, "It might be best if we go. Let the cops figure out what we—" She slowly leans in, readying her lips. I oblige, closing in, when she runs past me. *Wow, way to lead someone on.* "Ahh!" I turn swiftly, staring at a body that Jessyka found, tucked away in a bush. I run up to her side. In front of us lies a body without a head to recognize and arms without hands to print. She stares, mortified. Meanwhile, I take it all in, not in a sexual sense, but out of curiosity. I look down at the ground and see a string. I reach down to pick it up, feeling the nylon under my fingertips. No doubt is it one of the guitar's strings. The center piece of the strand is painted red. *Was this used to do the beheading?* The officers will definitely find the victim's DNA on it if it is, along with mine since I contaminated evidence. Some blood traces can be seen on the edges, too.

"Jessyka. We might want to leave this to the cops."

"We were too late. If I had come earlier."

"Jess, listen to me. Not to sound like a broken record or anything, but we don't know this is him."

"Open your eyes! His pick! His guitar! Now a body!"

"There's no head. No hands. There're not even feet. No shoes left behind. No shirt to identify. Whoever did this doesn't want his identity to be known. All the traceable features are gone."

"Not all of them."

"Jess! I'm sorry, but there's no point in fighting about it now. Assuming it is him—"

"Which it is. You might want to turn around." She slowly pulls down on his soiled briefs.

"Uh, what do you think you're doing?"

"Austin has this scar on his inner thigh. It's the only way to know for certain, even though I'm already dreading it." His briefs lower, exposing his dirtied skin, but there, exposed just barely, located mere inches from his privacy is a scar, like Jess mentioned. "There's your proof, Chance. Austin is, he's—"

"He's dead. I know it hurts. People die. Sometimes, you never get over it, but you will move on." She turns around and violently slaps me across the face. I feel the sting from the imprint. She continues abusing my body, until I grab her wrists. "Jess!"

"He can't be dead! He just can't!" She runs from my embrace into the direction in which we came from.

I pull out my phone and make the anonymous call. By the time they arrive, I'll be anywhere, but here.

A couple hours pass, and Jessyka hasn't returned my calls. My door creaks open and Mother's voice comes through, "Dinner's almost ready."

"Thanks."

"Everything alright?" She lets herself in.

"Yeah, just things at school, you know."

"It's so unlike you, to let anything as insignificant as school drama get to you."

"It's nothing like that, trust me."

"I see. Well, Dinner will be in a few. I won't try to overstep your boundaries."

"You're my mother. Overstepping my boundaries is what you're supposed to do."

She has a look of discomfort on her face. "I'll keep that in mind."

My phone buzzes in my pocket. One missed call: Jessyka. I push redial, but she doesn't answer. A message shows up on my phone: You were right. He is gone. You can refuse to believe the body was his, but you know the truth, as do I. You were wrong about one thing, though. There is something I can do. I will see him again ... Bye, and thank you.

"What! No." I jump up and into my shoes.

"Hun! Is everything . . ." Mother's voice fades the further I get. I hop on my bike and race to my destination.

Knock! Knock! Knock! The door opens, revealing a woman: Jessyka's mom. "Chance? What are you doing here?"

"Hi, Mrs. Sylva. Is your daughter here?"

"No. She left just a while ago."

I hop on my bike again. I have an idea as to what Jess is up to. I just hope I'm wrong. I come across a couple police cars, resting outside of the woods. It looks like they're leaving. This is the only place I can think of her going. I don't know why, or how she even got here without a ride in this amount of time, unless she gave herself a head start before sending the text. If she is here, then she had to get by the cops. Luckily, I don't. The cops leave the scene, so I enter the woods, hoping this is where she meant to go. I come across yellow caution tape, pinned on trees, preventing intruders. At least, caution tape is intended to keep me out. It does nothing against enforcing it. My ears pick up sobbing. I follow the noises when I come across Jess, in the same spot we found the body. She has a bag with her. She takes out a picture of Austin and pins it to the tree. Following are a few candles. From the looks of it, this seems more like a wake, or an event meant to reanimate the specified subject. Finally, she pulls a gun from the bag. Her hand trembles as she cocks it and aims it at her head. "I'm sorry."

I hop out of my hiding spot and rush her. As if in slow motion, her face turns to face me as I jump at her. I grab her hand holding the gun, releasing fire. I lay atop Jess. I get up to make sure if she's still breathing. Luckily, she is. "Idiot! You were actually going to shoot?"

"Of course, I was! Why else would I have a gun with me and no witnesses! What are you doing here, anyway?"

"I'm here to prevent you from doing anything stupid."

"What gives you that right?! I need to do this."

"Explain to me why it is that you must sentence yourself to death." She looks over at the picture of Austin. "No. That's not a good excuse. What happened to him is not your fault. Cry over him. Remember him. Love him. Do you think he would want you to kill yourself?" She shakes her head. "Exactly. Come on. We're leaving." I reach for her arm, but she backs away.

"He was the only one who got me. He's all I had!"

"That is where you're wrong. Your mother, from what I saw, loves you very much. Friends come and go. Love dies. Family is forever, no matter how you look at it. A family's love is unconditional."

"What do you know! You already have everything! You don't have the ordinary struggles of one of us."

"What struggles! Boys? Useless drama? Those aren't struggles! Does your mom hit you?" She shakes her head, no. "Do you get abused? What, in your life, sucks to the point of taking it?"

She pushes me away. "Go back to your mansion. You have no right in talking to me like that. You barely know me. We don't hang out. One way or another, I'll be with Austin again." She reaches for her gun. I leap onto her, both of us hitting the ground. I crawl atop her body and slap her.

"Snap out of it!" I realize what I did and slowly get back on my feet. "I'm sorry I—"

She grabs my hand and forcefully pulls me in, placing my hand on her cheek. "Do it again." Her chest breaths in and out.

"No. It was a mistake. I didn't mean to."

"I said, hit me!" She takes my hand and lightly taps it on her face, "but mean it."

"Jess. I can't just hit you for no reason."

"You're not hitting me for no reason. You're teaching me what I did that was in the wrong. Now do it!"

"No."

"Do it!" She slaps me. I do nothing to stop it. She raises her hand again and slaps me twice as hard. "Hit me, damn it!"

"Why do you ask me to do this? Why do you want to die so badly?" She drops to the floor in tears.

"Austin was the only friend I had. The only one I confided in. My other friends aren't friends. They are only around me because I'm popular. It's hard to be around a guy unless they're gay. All guys think about is sex. I need a friend. You, though. You're nice to people. You're the perfect hybrid."

"Hybrid?"

"You always have sex on your mind, but you know when not to act. You don't take an innocent girl, fuck her, then brag to your friends. You take her innocence under consideration. Unless she asks, you won't act. I like that."

"So, you need a friend. Go search for one. Don't just die."

She reaches for my hand again, "Please. Just this once."

I breathe in and raise my hand. Lightly, I slap her face.

"Harder. That wasn't a slap. Here, like this." She throws her hand back and releases force on my cheek. I do the same to her but hold back. "Harder . . . harder!" We take turns, each time harder than the last. She grabs me by the shirt and throws me into a tree. I grunt at impact. "Abuse me. Show me the fault in my ways." Her lips come crashing into mine. She presses her body into mine. My hands rest on her shoulders. I finally find the strength to push her away.

"We can't do this. Not in the state you're in. You need help."

She chuckles, "Help? I need help?" Heavily breathing, she strips herself of her shirt, standing in a black bra. "Then help me." Her body keeps me from moving from my spot, "Only you can." Her warm words linger in my ears.

I grab her shoulders with some force, pushing her back. I move with her. "I . . . can't." How can I take advantage of her weakness like this?

My body shudders as her hand forcefully grabs my crotch. She smiles in a way that makes me curious but scared. More scared of myself. "Feels to me, like you're more than ready." She pushes me to the ground and straddles me. Her hands run along my chest. She tugs at my shirt, allowing me to raise my hands so she can pull it off. Her eyes ogle at the sight. "Your scars are beautiful." Her lips meet mine in a violent manner. Her pelvis grinds against mine. I find it harder and harder to fight the urges, even though I know I should. I fight back a nearing headache.

"Stop!" I get up, pushing her to the side. I try to catch my breath.

"Oh! Was that not enough?" She unclips her bra, letting her perky breasts meet the breeze. I find it hard to look away. She charges me, ramming me into another tree. "Just give in. If there is a way to save me, then this is it." She bends down, pulling her pants down and stepping out of them, revealing a pair of black cheeky panties. They show off just how white and flawless her skin is. "Here. Maybe this will help." She tugs at my jeans, loosening them a bit. I break out of my mental prison and turn the tables. Now, Jess is in between the tree and me. She grabs my shoulders and jumps up, hanging on to my waist with her legs. "Do it." She whispers, then her tongue traces along my ear lobe. I lean into her neck. She releases gasps and moans as my teeth graze her skin. Her feet pull my pants and boxers down as they fall to my ankles. "I . . . want you." She gets to her feet and, with a couple fingers, leads me to the ground. She's hunched over me, her breasts in plain sight. My hands grab her buttocks, then I pull down on her panties. She reaches in between us, and grabs my shaft, aligning it. Without warning, she drops down on it. She lets out a quiet scream. I smile and flip us over.

"Your game. My rules."

"Yes. Anything you want. Just ravage me."

I grab her waist and help her move up and down. This continues for a little while. I'm about to reach my release when a flashlight lands on us. It takes an officer pulling us apart for either of us to realize them being here. We ride in separate cop cars to the precinct. Mother eventually shows up to bail me out. I stay quiet until we get outside. Jessyka's in the backseat. "You bailed her out?"

"Yes. She was with you, and you're my responsibility. It'd be unfair to her parents, otherwise." Mother adjusts the mirror, looking at Jess. "Where do you live, Hun?" We arrive at Jess' house. Her mother stands outside, awaiting our arrival. She doesn't look so happy, and why would she be? Jessyka hesitates to get out of the car. Her mom confronts the vehicle and extends a hand to my mother.

"I am truly grateful that you bailed her out. I promise, I will pay you back every cent."

"Don't bother. It was no trouble."

"You're too generous, really." She eyes me for a split second, "and as for you—"

Jess interrupts, "He had nothing to do with it. I was going through something and he arrived just in time to stop me from making a wrong choice."

"And you think fucking at a crime scene is the right choice! You are so grounded." She nods her head at Mother, and we drive off.

"You'll tell me everything when we get home."

"Yes, Mother."

Mother listens to what happened, bringing me a cup of tea in the process. She doesn't cut me off and only speaks when I finish. "I see. You're telling me that a girl her size, overpowered you?"

"Well, I wouldn't say she overpowered me. Made me weak to her beckoned call, more like it. She was persistent in getting what she wanted."

"You don't get what you want just by asking. Not in life. Not in the real world. Just because she asks doesn't mean you take it upon yourself to lose power over the matter. Perhaps, it was two-sided."

"What are you getting at?" I take a sip of my pumpkin spice tea.

"Nothing much. Just that maybe you wanted the same thing as her. She was just more out with it. Nothing wrong with that."

"So, I'm not grounded?"

"I've never grounded you before."

"I've never been in jail before."

"Touché. No. You're not grounded. On one condition."

Here it comes. "And that would be?"

"Try not to go have intimate fun in closed off crime scenes. That is all I ask." I nod my head. "Good. Discussion closed. Dinner is in the fridge. Personally, I think it's better fresh than microwaved, but, that's just me. I'll be in my room. Oh! And if you do go outside later tonight, try staying out of law enforcement's way."

"Will do."

In my room, I make sure no one can interrupt. I reach into my nightstand, discovering the mysterious phone that has miraculously made it into my possession overnight. I don't remember taking it, but then again, here it is. I press down on the side button, as the phone slowly turns on, looking over the texts and notifications. *He looks so happy in this picture. To think he also had a secret to keep. Our last confrontation didn't go too well, but I could never—*I look over the still visible, yet faded scars that are placed on my palms—*then again, who knows what I'm capable of?* I sigh, placing the phone down on my nightstand, taking notice of my medallion. I slowly pick it up, looking it over with concentration. *I wonder what secrets you hold.* I laugh to myself. "I'm overthinking things." I lie on my back, holding this medal above me, admiring the craftsmanship that has been put into it. My eyes shutter as I try to remain awake, but the overwhelming tiredness overcomes me, and I eventually close my eyes, drifting off until everything disappears from sight.

XI

Most of the lights are off, leaving the streets as dark and mysterious as the sky that bleeds onto its subjects. Officers patrol the streets like usual, not that that does any good. There are always blind spots and advantage points where you're not being watched. When those are covered, new ones are opened. That's how the world works. How? Who knows? I pass shady people on the streets who I try to avoid, but at night, that's when it's the most dangerous to be out, obviously. Most places have their streetlights, or convenience stores that light up. We aren't most places. Here, in Poshe, the only lights you can count on are the headlights of a passing vehicle. Sometimes, you wish the driver kept their lights off, because, at least then, you would've had a quick death. At night, it's difficult to know where the street and sidewalk part. You may think you're walking on the right side, when, *BAM!* You get hit by a Ford Focus. Who knows? You may get lucky and get hit by a Hearse. Drug deals are being made over at the Seven 11. There may or may not be a dead body in the dumpster behind Denny's. That's for the morning people to figure out. It's amazing, really, with how many people die nightly; yet, somehow, Poshe remains so populated. It's magic. If magic comes with a price, this is definitely it.

I hear something in the distance. A faint sound, quiet enough to make me question if it's real. I walk in the general direction of where it came from. Out of the shadows walks a tall, skeleton looking figure with excessive scarred tissue on his face. His eyes are lifeless. He pulls a girl out of the shadows with him. His elongated and bony hand encases her mouth so that she can't speak. "Chance, my dear pal!" He smiles a toothy cheek-to-cheek smile. "How the hell are ya!"

"Let her go."

"Straight to it. Buddy boy's not playing around. Hmm. You've changed. I can sense it in you. Not a lot, but enough."

"Who are you?"

"Who am I?" He holds in a laugh, "Who am I? Now, that just hurts. You think you know a guy." He holds the girl closer to him and wraps both hands around her throat. "I was going to let her go when you got here, but since you don't remember . . ." He tightens his grip.

"Stop! I know you!"

His hands loosen. "Prove it." He snarls.

"You . . . are . . . I know. Just give me a second."

"Nice try, but—" With one quick motion, the girl's head gets turned a good 180 degrees. A loud snap fills my ears. "You can't possibly know who I am. No matter the answer you gave, you'd have failed. Haha. Fun, right. Let's play another."

"You planned on killing her either way? You're sick!"

"Maybe, but that's beside the point. Haha." In an instant, he's face-to-face with me. "Come on, pal. I may look different, but who does my personality remind you of? You know."

"A psyche ward patient?"

"Cute, but NO! Think hard! Come on. I trash a party and you don't even know who I am. Quite frankly, I'm hurt." He pins me or tries to. "That's okay. I forgive ya. You may not remember me, but I'll always remember you. How could I not with how long I've played my little games with you? We're playmates, and it's about time you know the rules. Too long have I played alone. What fun is a game without a challenger?"

"My party? You didn't trash my party. Someone else gets that credit."

"Really. You think that after getting caught, and failing my objective, I'd keep the same face. Wrong! You keep getting away from me. Every time, I have failed. It's that hag you run with. She's why you don't remember me, isn't she?"

"Watch your tongue. I have no idea what you speak."

"You wouldn't. I'd tell you to ask her, but there isn't a next time. Not for you." He pulls out a gun from his pocket. "I know, not as cool or flashy as my usual dual blades, but it'll do the job." His finger twitches, about to pull the trigger, when he gets thrown back into a wall. "Ow. That's smarts. Remind me to get back the gear from my other body, will ya? Hehe. This one is weak."

"I'm afraid there isn't going to be a next time." A new player to this sick game has arrived, but is he a friend?

"Stealing my words, are ya? I have no business to deal with you. Leave me be and live to see another day."

"I'm sorry, but you get in the way of the one I serve. In return, that gets in the way of me."

Artemis grits his teeth, leaving that sick, rotten smile in plain sight, "So be it." He raises his gun-bearing hand but fails to fire. His opponent disappears, leaving a gaseous substance in his place, until he reappears a few feet away, charging Artemis. He grabs his wrist and with one swift motion, snaps it. Artemis drops the gun as he stumbles back in pain. "Who are you? . . . What are you?"

"If it's a name you seek, you won't find one here. I suppose you can call me by the one I control, Jessie . . . I know, not a suiting name for a body such as this."

"You're not human!"

"And you are? I know all about you, Arthur Reese, or do you prefer, Arti?"

"You know not what you speak, demon!"

"Struck a nerve? Haha. I've known about you and your endless mission. Sorry to disappoint, but the boy is mine."

I guess that answers my question on him being a friend. Apparently, there's a bounty or something on my head, but who put it up? I manage to stand by and watch this little feud carry on, unknowing as to why I haven't left yet. The demon looks my way, "Think I forgot about you?" *Kind of wish he had.*

"I'm sorry, but I won't allow it." Artemis lifts the gun with his working hand.

"If you know what I am, then you must surely know that using a mortal weapon against one as strong as I won't do."

"And if you, demon, know who I am, you must know that I've got magic on my side, along with a few supernatural tricks." Artemis whispers something into the gun and fires away. It strikes the demon center of the chest. It doesn't seem to be fazed at first.

It shows somewhat of a dead ass smirk, "When will you lear—" His sentence gets cut off. Purple veins start to surface up his neck as blood escapes his eyes. Such a gruesome sight . . . for the weak-hearted. It's forced to the ground as a type of smoke escapes the body, "What did you do!"

"Simple. I ended you. If I, did it right, you'll be going somewhere that isn't hell. Why give you the opportunity to come back? No variables left standing . . . a lesson I've come to enforce."

The demon fidgets throughout his body, slowly decaying. His body stiffens, and his hands stretch out to his sides, like he's praying for forgiveness. Veins can clearly be seen, popping out on all visible skin, and then a black storm escapes from his mouth. His hands tighten, as if he tries to grip the solid ground beneath him. His scream pierces the night sky as he manages to force out a few words before what I assume is the demon within, leaves the body completely. "YOU HAVE STARTED A WARR!!"

The body, once possessed, lies limp on the ground, until the former host forces out a cough, like he's been held under water and has been given CPR. His body looks as damaged as the demon left it, with the veins slowly receding back into their proper places and the blood drying out around his eyes. He shakes slightly, like he's having a mini seizure. The former host opens his mouth but is unable to force words. Instead, he gurgles the blood caught in his throat, choking between breaths. Paralysis is the state that the demon left this poor soul in. To be left in shock and agonizing ache and discomfort that leaves the body crippled in every sense of the word—well . . . that's just fucked up.

I run to the body and kneel, "You'll be alright. I promise." It's a lie, but an appropriate one. If he is to die, might as well give him final hope.

Jessie grips my shirt, stuttering as he forces out, "Where . . . am I?" His voice is hoarse. His hand automatically lets go of me, not having the strength to lift.

As I'm about to answer, a gunshot deafens me. I look down, watching as Jessie's shirt starts to get soaked with the flowing blood from the afflicted wound. The light, very slowly, begins to escape his eyes as Jessie fights to stay awake, failing after a few seconds, due to a bullet to the eye.

"You killed him, you bastard."

"He was already dead . . . Consider this a mercy killing. Funny how those around you seem to die, even the ones you aren't close to."

"It's you. You're the one that left me that note."

"I haven't the slightest clue as to what note you're referring to. Sorry to sound like a broken record, but this will be the last time you forget who I am. How should this go?"

"If you're referring to how I die, then I'm sorry to disappoint. I'm not going anywhere."

"Your devotion is admirable, but your naivety is childish. Don't worry, this won't be quick." His fingers on his good hand begin to spark out of the corner of my eye. "When they find your body, they'll be dumbfounded as to the cause. Any last words?"

"Monologuing is the key component to a second-rate villain."

He raises his hand, electricity traveling between his fingers. "This ought to be a shocking revelation to the one who solves the case."

"Puns are also a sign of second level villainy."

"I'm far stronger than that." With swiftness, he aims his hand towards me. Before I am able to dodge it, a powerful bolt of lightning strikes me, but that is all it does. I feel it surging through me as I suddenly drop to the floor. My body tenses up as strings of lightning trace through my veins. I am unable to speak.

"Breathe." The voice echoes in my head. It's soothing and reassuring, strangely.

Artemis chuckles as he walks up to my defenseless body. "You're really fighting, aren't ya? Never in all my years have I ever come across someone like you. To channel the power of a lightning bolt . . . it's astounding. Oh, how I wish I didn't have to do this, but orders are orders, am I right?" He kneels, reaching his hand out. "Good night, mighty soldier. You put up one hell of a fight, but in the end, it wasn't enough. It never is. As for your mourners, I'll stop by and make sure they have nothing to cry over." I take a breath, and hesitantly extend my arm, feeling every aching moment that comes from my tortured body. "Cute." My fingers extend outwards, as they near his face. He does nothing to stop me, as if he feels he's won this battle, as well as the war. Big mistake. The tips of my four fingers graze his cheek. I take another breath, feeling all the electricity in my body shift. I feel a powerful surge travel through my body, leaving no traces behind as the energy travels along the veins in my arm, leaving nothing but numbness in its place. My fingers tense as the pressure builds, like when your foot loses all feeling; yet, you try to stand on it anyway. By doing so, you can feel the stiff skin cracking apart with every forced step. That feeling is what I feel now as the electricity surges into my hand and into my fingers. I wince as the power leaves my body. Artemis freezes, trying to speak. His body uncontrollably shakes as I can see the pain in his eyes, yet he continues to smile. My hand drops to the floor, relieved of all the released energy. Artemis backs away, staggering with every step. Veins can be seen building up and his skin begins to tear apart slowly. It really is a gruesome sight, for most. To me, it's a bit fascinating to watch.

"It came from over here!" A man's voice can be heard getting closer. Red and blue lights can be seen in the corner of the ally. I look around for an escape, but there is none. Just a nine-foot wall and a dumpster. I suppose I can climb the wall, but I don't have the energy to stand, yet. The footsteps can be heard clearly, telling me that whoever is coming has picked up pace. Artemis is gone, which just leaves Jessie's deceased body and the one guy who will obviously get blamed. I scoot back, hiding behind a dumpster, just as a light gets shone at the wall, barely missing me. Two men confront the body. "My God. What monster could do this?"

That monster is nowhere to be seen and the only one who could say anything is hiding behind a dumpster, three feet away from the closest officer. As if two isn't enough, one of them calls in an ambulance, which means that I'll have to go unnoticed for a while. To my great mistake, I back up a little more. I manage to hit a crumpled can, as it crushes more so under the weight of my shoe.

"What was that?" the other officer asks.

"I believe we just found our monster."

"Or a mouse. It could be nothing."

"In which case, there's no harm in searching." The light flashes to my side, getting closer to me as I try to back further away. "Whoever you are, you have nowhere to go. Come out if you know what's good for you."

I get pulled out of the dark as I am forced out from behind the dumpster with a hand. "Gotcha!" The light flashes on me, focusing on my face. "Kid, you're in a heap of trouble."

"Would you believe me if I said I had nothing to do with this?" I hope that I picked up the stupid officers.

"Yeah. That would explain why you're hiding like someone who isn't innocent." He looks at the partner, "Call this in."

"I wouldn't."

"Is that a threat? If it is, you would be quite smart to shut it." My body shakes, but I am unsure as to if it's fear or adrenaline. I am hoping it's fear because nothing good happens out of my adrenaline rushes. Then again, fear is a form of adrenaline. "You have the right to remain silent. Anything you say can—"

I grab the officer behind me and toss him into the speaking officer like a ragdoll. My mind races, and my focus starts to delay.

I find myself breathing heavily. The sun is barely beginning to rise, and I have no idea how I got here. I appear to be a few blocks away from the ally where everything went down. I look down at my hands, feeling the substance in between my fingers.

"Hey, man. Are you okay?" A ragged man walks up to me. "Do you need—"

I face the grey stranger who reeks of cheap beer and cigarette smoke. He takes one look at me, seeing me, truly, for the first time, and turns on his heel, escaping the "monster" who is currently soaked in fresh innards, in which I assume he thinks aren't mine. "Hey!" I reach out for his arm, but what I do next is unexpected. I grab hold of his wrist and pull him towards me, instantly bending the weakling to my will. He falls onto his knees, his wrist dangling, as I have now just broken it. I hastily get behind him and wrap my arm around the helpless soul's neck. Before he is able to scream, he drops to the floor, a final thud being made as his soul leaves his body. I have just broken a man's neck, and what for? He was trying to help me, and I pay him back by killing him? Then again, he did start running, but that's no excuse. I hear something hit the ground; a soft tap compared to the dead weight of a 175-pound drunk's clumsy falling out. A little girl with pig tails shakes, tears swelling in her eyes. The sorrow of a woman— no, a girl, who has lost, not an unknown stranger, but a father, nonetheless. She doesn't run. She makes her way to me in a slow and steady pace, lowering herself to the man's body.

She grabs his hand in hers, "Daddy?" Dead men say no words, not unless those words are spoken through a true family's actions. This man was a drunk, but he also has a daughter. "Daddy, you can't be . . ." She looks up at me, letting loose the flood gates. Now, I do expect her to run, but she doesn't. She reaches out, grabbing my hand. "You killed him." She speaks quietly. "What makes a dad?" I'm confused at this. "Is it just being around. Is it not being a coward? Is it just a title? . . . My father ran out on me when I was born. He didn't have the makings to be a father, not in the ways that count. He may have a problem. He may have his addictions, but who doesn't? 'Father' is a title given through procreation. He was more than that. He drank. Sometimes, he forgets who he is, and I am around to remind him. At the end of the day, he comes home. He stays away long enough for the buzz to die. At the end of the day, his first priority is me. He loves me, despite his bad choices. He is around when I need him. He cares for me in more ways that my father never did, and that counts as so much more." Her words are mature, yet, she can't be much older than seven. She squeezes my hand tighter, "Where is your father? What brought you to committing such an act of despicable measures."

"I don't know." I speak under my breath, but she understands me. I am truly in aww. Not often, do I feel weak, but in this moment, I feel no mightier than those scum, rummaging through the night streets. How have I brought myself to do such a despicable act? I have killed, but this is the first time it's without reason, and it sickens me.

"I see. You never had a father figure, did you?" I'm taken aback at this. I have handled many things, but being told these things by a little girl? "What of your mother?" She reaches into her coat pocket and pulls out a locket. She opens it, revealing three people: a woman on the left, a man on the right, and a baby with light blue eyes, the same color as the girl who speaks. The man is recognizable. He's a younger version of the one I took down. The baby is, no doubt, her. "Mommy died a long time ago. I hear she was strong, but in the end, her body wasn't strong enough for me. I killed my mommy."

I kneel down, "You did not kill your mother. This is not on you."

"Now, you killed my daddy. I should be mad, but I'm not. You have a darkness and have succumbed to it in the moment. I only get to see my daddy when he comes home, when the alcohol has left him. In those moments of loneliness, I am not alone, not entirely. I look to someone else, something else." She reaches once more into her pocket, revealing a cross on a chain. "Daddy will always be with me, just as mommy has every day of my life." She extends her hand, shoving the cross against my abdomen. "Now, it is you that needs a light to guide your way."

"I don't know if—"

"Please. I don't need a cross to remind me that I am not alone. Take it." I reach out, and she places it into my palm. She leans in and, hugs me? "Let the light in." With that, she up and leaves, picking up the teddy bear she dropped in my discovery.

I find myself walking down a street, until I come across a familiar house with a light on. I grab a pebble and toss it at the window. The curtains open to reveal a set of eyes looking down on me. The sound of the door unlocking can be heard from outside. "Chance?" A girl in a pair of gray boy shorts opens the door with her arms crossed. "What happened to you?"

"You know. If you're cold, maybe you should dress in something warmer than those." I point downward at her legs, in case she doesn't get the gist. "May I come in?"

Danielle steps aside, allowing me entrance. "Are you going to answer my question?" She steps closer, grabbing my wrists, turning them skyward, so she can get a good look at the dry blood scattered on my palms. Most people would be cautious in letting a blood-stained guy into their house. Luckily, Danielle isn't everybody. Storm probably would have done the same thing, had his mother not been around to say no.

"Chance?" Sam steps into plain sight. Her eyes widen when she is able to see me, truly, and rushes towards me. "Oh my God. What happened?"

"Thank you! He hasn't explained, yet." They both stare daggers at me, awaiting an answer.

I can't tell them the truth. It'd sound made up. I don't want to lie to them, either. "I ran across some trouble."

"Leave it to you to do something as stupid as walking the night streets. Of course, you ran across trouble. Cops are useless. They're not stupid enough to do their job at this time. That still doesn't answer what we asked."

I give them a half truth, or as close to the truth as I can without telling them all the unbelievable parts. "I heard a noise . . ."

"And you wandered into that direction?"

"How'd you know?"

"It's kind of a given at this point. You are the curious type. If there is something that sparks an interest, you won't turn down the opportunity to uncover it. I swear, you're going to get killed one of these days. You're extremely smart, but you're extremely stupid." She motions for me to continue with what I was saying.

"Anyway, what I found wasn't what I was expecting."

"Is it ever?" Dani looks at Sam, telling her to shut up through eye contact.

"A girl was being tortured." Their looks change as I continue. Knowing that something is bad and hearing the exact details of the situation are two different things.

"You tried to help her?"

I nod. "I was . . . unsuccessful in doing so. When I got to her, she was practically dead already. I held her for a brief moment." I raise my hands as evidence.

"That blood is from her?"

"It is." What I'm saying is true, except for the blood being hers. There was a moment I blacked out, between the time I was caught by the police and that father that was in the wrong place at the wrong time. I believe the blood is his, but I don't know how the situation with the cops ended. I doubt they just let me go. Without realizing, I pull out the rosary handed to me out of support by a girl I wouldn't have expected such maturity out of. Is it maturity, or just a big heart? Sometimes, the two can be switched.

"Where'd you get that?" Danielle reaches for the cross, noticing as I slightly pull back.

"Sorry. What?"

"Are you alright?" She looks concerned.

"Yeah. Why wouldn't I be?"

"Well, for starters, you watched a girl die, and held her in her last moments. Other things may have happened that you haven't told us. I'd be pretty torn up about it."

"Death has never fazed me before. Why would it now?"

"Obviously, something is bothering you. Is it anything like that night when you were hearing things? When you had that little episode? If you're not going to tell us, you don't have to. Tell someone, though. Does your mom know?"

I shake my head, no. "I'm fine, really." I hold up the cross. "I was given this by someone. She thought it would help in moments of need."

"It's never wrong to look up to someone for help. Personally, I think it's wonderful that you're finding religion. Though, I don't know where this certain faith has come from, who am I to question it?"

"I don't know what to believe. I'll admit, I have seen things that add some perspective. Things that make me question myself. Who am I? Is there something that follows the life I'm in, now? Something that is determined, due to how I use the life I'm given. Like a test. One you can never truly be prepared for." A tear escapes my eye, out of pure surprise. This goes noticed by both girls. "Oh God. What is happening to me?"

Sam and Dani sit next to me on their bed. Dani reaches for my face and wipes the lone tear away. "I don't know."

"You've never been this open before." Sam joins in with her sister. "It's nothing to fear. Usually, you don't have much emotion in anything. Not to this level, anyway. I wish you'd share more often. I like this side of you."

"What? The weak state I'm in. Just these thoughts. The weight, pushing down. I don't like it. How do people handle this grief?"

Sam and Dani share a chuckle, "You sound as if you're more than human, or less. Some people are stronger willed than others, but everyone has a moment or two of weakness. Mankind isn't perfect. We aren't emotionless beasts. Even psychopaths have their drives. That which causes them to do what they do. They have their weaknesses, like the rest of us. Don't you think that, for a second, because you're having this moment of weakness, that you are weak. You are one of the strongest people I have ever met. I don't know if it's the bravery that helps you stand up to protect people, or the stupidity that keeps you from knowing when to give up. Who else can defend against a bunch of lunatics with guns?"

I smile. "I get what you're getting at. Thanks."

"Already. Dang. I had a whole couple more lines of wisdom to drop on you."

We laugh as I drop down on the bed, staring up at the ceiling fan. "Anyway. What are you two doing up at this time? Normal people would be sleeping."

Sam drops down next to me, rolling over to lie halfway on my body. "You're right." She jabs her index finger into my chest. "Normal people would be sleeping at this moment." She slowly closes in on my face, tugging at my bottom lip for acceptance, in which I happily oblige.

"What's brought you to do this?"

"Well. You're here. We're here. Why not have a little fun. I mean, while we're awake. Though, if you're too sissy to comply with these feelings, there's the bathroom."

"I never said that." I am highly confused as to how these feelings have shifted—how this situation has escalated in such a way. My hands grab onto her hips as I move her completely on top of me. Dani is hesitant, but slowly moves her way into the picture. I give a nice, hard slap to Sam's rear, causing her body to shutter, and her back to arch. Her breasts, for a split second, get pressed into my face. My fingers curl around the waistband of her sweats. I slowly pull down, freeing her cheeks from the confines of her sweats. I gesture to come forth, and Dani does as requested. The shy girl I met a while ago has truly left her shell.

"Chance Princeton Ryder!" The voice comes from outside of their house. I try to ignore it for a moment, as I continue to feel along Sam's perfect body. "Chance! I know you're in there." The voice isn't familiar. I peek out the window and see a kid, probably eight, standing in rags. "Come out here. I just want to talk." Something about the way he says that is off. I take a deep breath. Sam pulls her pants all the way up as we head to the door. "Do you know that kid?"

"Not exactly." They stay at the door as I exit the house to confront the kid. He isn't here. I look around for him, but he is nowhere to be seen. I turn to the girls when something grabs hold of me. The kid jumps me from behind, one arm wrapped around my throat and the opposite hand holding a knife to it. "What the hell?"

"Miss me!" I reach behind me and grab this little hellion from the back, chucking him over my shoulder with ease. He slams to the floor, skidding along the pavement. A loud crack can be heard, but the boy gets up as if he didn't just dislocate his shoulder. He grabs hold of it and quickly pops it back into place. "What a way to welcome someone with open arms."

His body, I have never seen, but his quips are familiar. "Arthur? Is that you?"

His eyes slightly narrow at the mention of that name. "Arthur is the name of someone who died years ago. You may call me, either by Artemis, or by the name of this sorry meat puppet—Dennis."

"How are you here? And why a child of all choices?"

"How are any of us here? Ask me a question that actually has an answer."

"Why me? Real question. What have I ever done to you?"

"Me? Nothing. The one I serve? Nothing. Yet."

"Fine. Be cryptic. But if you wanted to pose a threat to me, a seventy-five-pound runt may not be the way to go about with it."

"Surprised you haven't asked me a legitimate question. Like how I'm able to change bodies."

"Possession. Easy."

He laughs. "That would be a good answer. If it was correct." He reaches in his sock, pulling a knife out of it. "Curious. Have you ever . . . wanted to reach inside someone? See how the body works from a different point of view? Really observe the body. It truly is magnificent how the body is able to work. Alone, we are nothing more than a bunch of inanimate body parts, rotting: A heart, which is nothing without that to allow life; kidneys; a skeleton, immobile and lifeless without the appropriate bindings; and skin, which just acts as a costume of sorts. Of course, we can't leave out the blood, which is just a liquid by itself. Together, all those parts seem to allow us to live, like a switch has magically flipped. To walk. To breathe. Have you not ever been curious as to the magic that is life? We're nothing short of an anomaly."

"You are twisted. That's what you are."

"What would you call someone who confronts a police officer who's practically dead, fighting for his last breath? Someone's first reaction is to go look for help. Not yours, though. No. You observe in awe. You find death to be beautiful, do you not? Shame it is to kill you, really. I've always wanted a friend that sees the world how I see it. Who knows? Had we met under different circumstances, I could have come to see you as a son."

"Don't you, for a moment, think I'm anything like you."

"I have noticed that you're beginning to experience new things. Do you still find death to be beautiful? Do you cry? Those are weaknesses in the eyes of victory. Victory requires devotion. The will to do anything to win. Do you have the drive?" He plays with the weapon in his hand. "You know what?" He jabs the blade into my side, catching me off guard. "You are right. You're nothing like me. Not anymore." Red and blue lights can be seen in the distance, the sirens getting louder as a couple of police cars near Sam and Dani's house.

"Looks like you're out of time."

"You'd think. It's about time these bothersome interlopers learn to give up." I look to him in confusion as he walks towards the incoming police officers. He raises both arms, struggling as the police cars begin to levitate off the ground. Arthur's hands come closer together, as do the police cars, until they form together to make a big fist. The cop cars collide into each other, bending and crushing until they explode in the air. The noise definitely doesn't go unnoticed. Lights turn on in many households that align this street, as well as ones that don't.

"What are you?"

"Human, really. A better version."

"You're not human."

"If I'm not human, then you're definitely not human." Talking is heard as people begin to leave their houses. "Oh good. An audience." He grabs onto a piece of scrap metal from one of the cars and spins it, throwing it directly into a neighbor's house. A scream is heard, then vanishes as a man is caught in the impact. "And it's out of here!" He laughs like a little kid that has been told an extremely funny joke for the first time. He really is enjoying this, isn't he? "That's how the game goes, right?"

More sirens can be heard in the distance. People begin to run out of their homes in fear. Stupid move, really. Had they stayed indoors, they'd probably be overlooked. "Stop this nonsense. Aren't I the one you want?"

"My instructions never specified that you had to be my only target. As long as you go, who says others can't join? Besides . . ." He pops his neck and stretches his fingers. ". . . the ones who run are the best to toy with." He grabs a discarded tire from the vehicle wreckage and tosses it at an escaping target, "Yes! Did you see that?" He looks at me just in time to receive a fist to the face. I've always thought of punching a child. I thought it would be because of their terrible choice in everything. But this? This suffices. I like this. I throw a fist again, before he is able to know what has happened.

"Freeze!" An officer confronts me with his weapon raised as I kick the defenseless-looking child in the gut. I raise my hands, slowly.

"Listen. I know this may look wrong, but I am kicking the living shit out of this boy to protect you all." That may have been a poor choice of words, but perhaps, I said it that way on purpose. I've always wanted to be caught in a moment where I try to justify my actions using truthful, yet misleading dialogue that points me out to be the bad guy, mainly because it'd be funny to watch play out.

"On the floor, now!"

"Listen to me. He really isn't what he appears to be."

The officer's hand trembles as he slowly begins to aim the gun towards himself. Without a warning, the gun goes off, dropping a body in the process. The secondary police officer fires his gun at the sound of the first gunshot. I close my eyes, awaiting to be shot. I open an eye, once I realize I'm still here. A bullet appears to be levitating dead center between my eyes. Any closer, and I would have been a Halloween decoration. I look over at Arthur while he's extending an arm, blood coming from his nose.

"You owe me big time." He looks towards the officer who fired. "Should have listened to the kid."

"Paul!" The officer screams at his dead partner. "What are you?"

"A while ago, I'd say I was like you." The officer drops his gun, hoping it can't be used against him. "You're learning quick. Good. Still won't do you any good." The kid raises both hands, like he's holding on to something circular. With a quick jerk of a hand, the officer's neck snaps as his head faces away from us. His body drops like his early partner. I notice more blood coming from this kid's nose.

"So, this is the price for using these abilities."

"What happens when anyone pushes themselves? Eventually, they get hurt . . . Manipulation magic sure uses up a lot, though, as you can tell."

He stumbles a little. I walk towards him and kneel. "You're weak. But this doesn't change what you did." I put a good half of my weight into my fist as I punch the worthless brat in the face. I crawl on him, turning his head so that he could look into the eyes of the man who defeats him. Wrong decision, by the way. He slashes me in the chest as a resort to get away. "Gonna have to do better than that, kid."

"Well, if you insist." He charges me, aiming for the abdomen. He lands atop of me as he buries his finger into the open wound on my side. I grab him by the hair, trying to pull him off. "No need to hold back. Show me those killer instincts. Not like this boy is alive, anyway." He finally gets thrown back by a girl.

"Get the hell off of him, you little gremlin." Sam stands in my aid, Dani at her side.

"Take the fun out of a blood feud, why don't you." He lifts one of the officer's guns. "I'd say it's been fun, but you have been a total—"

He falls motionless to the ground as a woman stands above him. "You talk too much."

"Mother?"

"Get inside. Now!" I don't hesitate, with the girls following me into their house.

"Who the hell was that!" Danielle freaks out as we enter their home, slamming the door.

"Yeah, Chance! What the hell. Forget to mention the little detail that a gremlin was tailing you. He acted as if he knew you."

"This wasn't my first encounter with him, but I am as confused as you in terms of why he's going after me."

"Because you're the only thing in the way of the one he serves." The door opens and slams.

"Mother. You know him. You appeared to know him at the party. I never pried, but things are escalating. Who is this guy? How can he do what he can do?"

"I'm sure you have a lot of questions. Some, you may not know you have, yet. Allow me to tell you a story that may shine some light on the subject." We sit, like children awaiting a story. "Can you girls keep a secret? . . . Doesn't matter, anyway. Whoever you choose to tell would think you're nuts."

"We won't tell a soul."

"Does that mean I can't tell Storm?" I ask.

"I would advise against it, but I know he's your friend. Sharing this with him may put him in danger, but Artemis already has his eyes set on you three. He already knows your faces, so you're already in this situation. Girls, I am truly sorry for your involvement in all this."

"Well, we did tell Chance that he shouldn't go through what he's going through alone. I didn't think it'd be so literal."

"Okay. Try to keep up."

XII

Years ago, there was a kingdom, ruled by the great descendants of the one we've come to know as Arthur, the Noble. He has many names, as well as stories told, each one with a different origin; yet, many seem to end the same way. Not much is known of Arthur. Many believe him to be myth. An urban legend and nothing more. He was very much real, as was his following bloodline. Like any story, this all begins with . . . a baby—naturally.

They say that heroes aren't just born. They are chosen, specifically, by the universe. A bunch of hogwash, you say? Perhaps. But all it takes is one person to believe in something. If one person believes in it, eventually more will follow. Demons, for example, have been around longer than any tale. Every religion has its god, or gods, as well as its demons. Demons have been depicted as vile, grotesque things that creep in the shadows, away from the light of the good-willed. They've been said to deceive, lure, and steal bodies, using them as hosts in order to walk amongst us. No one really knows how true, or how false, these claims are.

Heroes may come with a specific purpose, but victory, like everything else, soon runs its course. It's never absolute. It's achieved through long, sometimes harsh, conditioning. Heroes come and go. Time is filled with them, but we aren't going to know every single one that ever walked this earth. Not everyone becomes a legend that lives eternally through the tales spoken throughout time. Like us, demons evolved. There is a fine line between religion and magic, but every so often, we get something that belongs to both worlds.

There was one who came to be known as Igneaal, a strong individual with an origin beyond our understanding. Times were rough enough as they were, but come coronation day, things were only going to get worse.

Dark times, they were. The king was sick, and only getting sicker as days passed. He had two sons: Chandler Rey Pendragon, being his younger of the two, and Ignitus Demorte Reese-Pendragon. Both stood by their father's side as he awaited his last breath. Both, filled with grief, listened to the words that would come to be known as his last.

"Boys? Come closer." The king orders, his eyesight failing him, and his hearing, not far behind. "It's about time we discuss one of you stepping up as the ruler of this land." Chandler tries to keep from tearing up any further. Igneaal, on the other hand, awaits his birth right as the oldest. "Igneaal? I never thought It'd be under these circumstances that you'd have to hear this. I should have told you years ago but couldn't bring myself to say it." Igneaal's smile slowly fades, awaiting the words he was never prepared for. "You, my son . . . will not be ascending to the throne. For this, I am—"

"What!" Igneaal is outraged, and a bit confused. "I am the oldest! I-I-why father?" His voice dies out.

Chandler extends an arm to Igneaal's shoulder, "Brother, it is alri—"

The eldest backs away, shrugging his brother off of him.

"You will always be my son, no matter where it is you come from."

"Where I come from?"

The king heavily breathes, forcing out words he's too weak to say. "You may not be blood, but your place as my own will always stand true."

Igneaal backs away in disbelief. "Are you saying what I think you're saying?" He awaits an answer but doesn't receive one. "Father?" He lightly shakes him but receives nothing in return.

Chandler stops his oldest brother, "Quit it! Quit it! He's go-ne." His voice stutters at the last second, due to the tears that uncontrollably well up.

"No. He can't be. It can't end like this!" Igneaal lashes out in rage, only to be apprehended by a couple of the guards.

"Put him somewhere so he can cool off." One of the trustees of the king speaks out. What seems like days passes when Chandler visits his brother in confinement.

"Brother?" Igneaal looks up as he hears the door screeching open. "Brother? Are you tranquil?" Igneaal nods, refusing to talk. "There's going to be a ceremony later today to appoint where I stand. I'd very much like you to be there by my side. Will you? You know, be there?" The eldest brother nods his head lazily as he's escorted out of the dungeon and back to his quarters.

Later that night, Igneaal escapes his room, finding himself just outside of the royal court. He places his ear to the door, listening in as all noise silences and the event commences further. "Can the two sons of our fallen king come up here?"

Chandler does as requested as the room waits a couple minutes for the other son's arrival. Chandler is saddened by the revelation that his brother might not make an appearance. Though upset, Chandler feels it necessary to continue with the ceremony and not wait any longer for someone who has already made the decision to not show up. "I'm sorry. I feel that my brother will not be making an appearance today."

"I see. How upsetting. We'll have to continue, then, without the presence of Prince Igneaal." Little known to them, the eldest prince was there that day, even if not in plain sight. "Being the youngest of the two sons, it is quite unusual to be marked runner up for the crown. Due to his age, however, a regent will be crowned in his stead. Prince Chandler will claim the throne on the day of his eighteenth birthday. Now to the question at hand, who will be the regent? Due to Prince Igneaal's absence, someone else will temporarily hold title to—"

"I am your new Queen." A woman stands, with long orange locks. She slowly steps up to the front, with elegance in every step. "Due to my

dear cousin's youth, bless him, I'll fill in for temporary regent, just until my dear Prince Chandler is old enough to fill the crown." She stands shoulder to shoulder with her cousin.

"You couldn't have waited a couple seconds?"

"What can I say? I've been waiting for this day."

"As you all have witnessed, you now serve our new Queen—Queen LaZilee-Gertrude ll." Everyone bows to their new Queen. Everyone, except Igneaal, who has left the scene moments before the queen was appointed.

The eldest is on his way to a new life, away from everything he thought he knew. For the first time in his life, he has no guards, no connections, nothing. He's forced to scurry for scraps, just to feed his aching belly. Weeks pass. He feels as if he's made a terrible choice by leaving, but how would he be able to face his brother after the way he left things?

Little known to him, his brother is suffering. The new queen is a tyrant unlike any other, who has an unquenchable thirst for power.

In order to live on the broken streets, Igneaal feels the need to find his own family, one that will support him, and one that will support the path that he has chosen. One that won't lie to him. He travels far and wide, finally getting a chance to see just how unjust, punishment is outside of the royal palace. Day by day, he evades the law, doing what is necessary in order to survive. Three months on the street, and he has already stolen from vendors and from people who had less than him. He didn't want to steal, but survival recommended it. A single year has shaped him, both mentally and physically. Though, only a year has passed, the selfish, dependent prince that had everything handed to him on a silver platter was no more. In order to move on and survive, he has to forget, or at least put in the past, what he once was. He is no longer a prince, but a street rat who works hard for his scraps, and will do anything, against his better judgement, to live another day. He hasn't forgotten what he once was, but he has accepted what he has become— stronger in every way. Along the way, he has met conflict, but has made a few acquaintances, too, including some encounters in Hereford and Oxon, but his most fateful encounter takes place in Sussex.

Igneeal, now known as Insygnia, is in the middle of hustling some cons out of their belongings when he hears a guard yelling. He's about to run for it when he notices it isn't him that the guards are chasing. A boy bumps into him in his attempt to evade the fuzz.

"Wait! Stop!" The law enforcement takes notice of Igneaal and adds him to their objectives. "You there, by the name of—" They aren't able to finish their thought, before Igneaal flees past them, knocking one of them over. He's able to lose them in the chase but comes across the boy again. He's in an ally, about to be apprehended by the ones he's been running from. He's thrown against the ground with unnecessary force. "You're at the end of the line, boy." Igneaal turns to leave but can't. He hears a sword being drawn by one of the guards.

"What are you doing? Our jobs are to apprehend him."

"But, if he were to disappear, what harm is there in that?"

"We were given a duty."

"What good does it do to lock up scum? You go in a murderer, you come out one as well. You go in a thief, you come out a tortured thief."

"That is not our place. We don't get paid to think. Deciding whether or not something is the right thing to do is not our purpose."

"As far as I see it," the sword lowers, "you are either with me or against me. Might I say, going against me wouldn't be the wisest choice. So, what's it going to be?"

The guard pauses in thought and sighs. "I guess I'm with you."

"That a boy. Trust me. We'll clean these streets of the filth." He lifts his sword again as the manipulated guard shakes, waiting for the dirty deed to be dealt. He feels the hilt of the sword being pressed against his abdomen. "I know where my heart lies, but yours, I am uncertain of. Use this and relieve me of my doubt."

"What! I can't. I won't."

"You will. If you do it, you will prove to me that you have what it takes. Can't have me being the only one who dirties his hands. How am I supposed to know you won't run off to the authorities with what you

have witnessed? Now, before someone comes, finish the task." The guard hesitantly takes the sword. "The first one is always the hardest. Believe me, this, newbie. It will get easier."

"I am sorry, truly, for what I am—"

"Just do it! No room for unneeded sentimentality."

The sword raises as the kid is held down against his will. Igneaal comes out in plain sight. "You know something, boys." The guards look to him. "Going against the king's wishes is punishable by death. Going rogue never ends happily."

"You! You're that fugitive!"

"Commence with what you're about to do, and I won't be the only one here."

One of the guards slowly steps toward Igneeal. "Might I say, you are a difficult one to apprehend. No one has been able to detain you. How lucky for us, and how generous of you to allow me this opportunity."

"Sorry to disappoint, fellas, but I have no plan on being detained. Not today, anyway."

One of them jumps at the opportunity to have the infamous 'Insygnia'. "Your reward money would pay my housing for months to come."

Igneeal dodges the advances, pushing the guard to the side. "If you wouldn't mind, the boy is coming with me."

"Like hell, he is!" He is rushed from behind, barely evading being shish kebabbed. Igneaal grabs the guard's wrists and with one swift action, breaks them. He covers the guard's mouth from behind.

"Shh. Don't want us to be found out, now, or do ya, ya naughty boy?" He knees the guard in the back of his knee, causing him to uncontrollably kneel.

"Please! Take the boy. Call this even."

"How weak. For you to simply give up your goal because you're hurt. That truly disappoints me." Igneaal runs his hand to the guard's throat with his other hand on the back of his head. "To think that I probably had guards going behind my back as well."

"*What are you blabbering on—*" Crack. *The body drops at Igneaal's feet. Footsteps are heard behind him as he swiftly turns, tripping the secondary guard. He flies, landing on his face.*

"*Where do you think you are off to in a hurry?*"

The guard's eyes are welling up. "*Please. I didn't even do the deed.*"

"*This is true, but you were about to. That, and . . . I can't have murdering a royal guard added to my list of crimes. Then again, that would spike my reputation now, wouldn't it? Close your eyes, young soldier. I'll make this quick and painless. You at least deserve that.*"

"*Please, I-I have a family.*" *In a split second, the guard's neck is cracked as his body falls limp.*

"*Don't we all, yet, here we are.*" *The ex-prince turns to face the boy who is frozen in fear.* "*You're welcome,*" *he says rudely, then turns to walk away.*

"*Wait. You're him, aren't you? You're Insygnia.*"

"*What's it to you, kid?*"

"*I was told you were evil. That you murdered in cold blood, yet, you saved me.*"

"*Rumours are a dangerous thing. I do what's necessary to survive. I suggest you do the same. I might not be there to save your hide next time.*"

"*Wait! Don't go!*" *Igneaal stops at this command.* "*You say you do what's needed to survive. You stepped in to save me, and you didn't have to.*"

"*Don't remind me.*"

"*Why did you spare my life, then? Why me, and not that guards?*"

"*People who commit heinous acts are one thing. But, ones in denial, ones who lie to deceive, to save their asses. That's a different story. Tell me kid. What are you wanted for?*"

"*It's embarrassing.*"

"*Fine. Don't tell me. I need to leave, anyway. It won't take long for someone to come searching for these two. It's best if we're not around.*"

"*I got caught stealing.*"

Igneaal takes a step, only to have the boy continue to speak. "What were you stealing for?" Knowing he's going to regret asking, he does so anyway.

"Mother was sick. She was the last of my family, and I had to nourish her back to health. She hated the fact that I had to steal for her, but it was something I had to do. That, and I was in the wrong place at the wrong time. Last year, someone died. I, the unlucky one, was the only one around when the guards showed."

"Sounds like an honest answer to me."

The boy looks up, "What?"

"You asked why I let you live. You stole to help your mother. That is why. You are honest. No matter what you do, you aren't in denial. You know who you are. The one guard practically admitted that he killed for what he thought was right. If it was truly right, then why would he lie to his superior about it? He was deceitful. Must I continue?"

"You are oddly composed for who you are. Do you mind if I ask what you were before this?"

"As a matter of fact, I do mind." Igneeal walks away, hearing the footsteps near him. He glances to the side, seeing the boy tail him. "Just where do you think you're going?"

"As a sign of my loyalty to you, I am, from this day on, yours to command. A life for a life, as they say."

"Seriously, kid. Go home to wherever it is you call home."

"I can't go home, even if I had one to go home to."

Igneaal stops in his tracks, breathing in, and finally sighs. "You spoke about your mother in past tense. You said she was the last of your family."

"Huh. You caught that." The boy tears up. "No matter how much I stole for her, it just wasn't enough. Besides my mother, you're the only one to ever stand up for my sake. I was ready to die, then you came along and showed me that people can still care. So, please." He grabs Igneeal in his arms, giving him a hug as he cries into his chest. The ex-prince tries to fight this advance but gives up. "If I can't serve you, then you saved my life for nothing."

Igneaal thinks it over and gives in, "Whatever. Do as you please. Just know that, if you slow me down in any way, I won't hesitate to leave you behind."

"Oh, thank you. Thank you. Should we exchange names?"

"You already know mine," He says, knowing that 'Insygnia' isn't who he is.

"Then I guess, it's my turn." The boy straightens up and lends out his hand. "My birth name is Arthur Reese. I am currently 13. And you are Insygnia."

"Reese?"

"Is something wrong with that name?"

Igneaal looks at the boy's extended arm and returns the gesture for a handshake. "Not at all."

"Mother used to call me 'Arti'."

"There is no way in hell I am calling you that."

And this is where the union between a prince who left his home behind, and an orphan who was at the end of the line, began.

Though, annoying as the boy was at times, the prince tolerated it. Even though, he failed to acknowledge this pact of comradery with the boy, he was somewhat happier with him than he was alone. Taking him under his wing and showing him the ropes, they were no longer surviving as individuals. They depended on each other. They were a family in the making. Not a family bound solely by blood, but one of purity, one that came from mutual trust.

Years pass, and Igneaal comes across news that his brother has become the new king of Wales. He is lost in confusion, for he was already under the impression that his brother has already taken on the role. By this time, he has already shared his true identity with Arthur. He never thought he'd return to his birth home, but he feels as if it is his right to grasp what has been unjustly taken from him. Arthur needs close to no explanation or manipulation to join Igneeal on this all-too-personal quest. For this man, Arthur's loyalty is boundless. Igneaal hasn't seen his brother in, well over, five years. His arrival would surely be an unexpected one, and his intensions even more so. It's a long quest back in the direction opposite they've been traveling these last years. They finally arrive in one of Igneeal's memories he wishes he'd forget, but his being here is fate. They enter, fitting in with those around them. Luckily, hiding their faces wouldn't be too difficult, since the night they chose to arrive happened in the presence of a wolf moon. Celebrations are held, and fireworks are displayed. Sneaking into the castle would pose some sort of challenge to most, but he knew this place in and out, including secret entrances no one knew about.

"Take care of yourself, at least for a while, Arti."

"What," Arthur objects. "We're in this together."

"Yes, but I feel you mustn't be a part of what's about to take place. I'll need you here for my return. Just know that, if I come back different, you are still my family."

"What's that supposed to mean?"

He embraces Arthur in a pure, brother-like manner, "You have surely grown in the short amount of time I've known you. I started my journey alone, leaving all hope of comradery behind me, but now, I can't think up a world where I never met you. You have given me hope, once more. Bye, Arti. For now. Things will change . . . I promise."

Igneaal sneaks past the guards and makes way to the throne room. Ridiculous, it is, to have a room meant for sitting and barking orders. He walks to the throne and feels the texture. Just as he remembered.

"May I help you?" The king steps into the room, asking with a slight rudeness to his tone, then again, why wouldn't he show some firm tone when someone allows themselves to your sacred room.

"On the contrary, my lord. It is I, however, who may be the one to help you." Igneaal turns around. Though his face can't be seen, he shows a look of pure smugness.

The king looks him up and down, noticing the hair that falls above the mask. "You seem fairly familiar. Have we, by any chance, met?"

Igneaal lets out a genuine laugh as he reaches for his mask. "Quite perceptive you are, indeed. Nothing gets past you, does it . . . Brother?" He removes the mask, letting his hair fall upon his face. "Even after all these years."

To Igneaal's great surprise, the king, his brother, shows an expression opposite to what Igneaal was waiting for. Rather than the anger he believed beforehand, the king, Chandler, showed an expression of happiness. "You have returned. After all these years, I was beginning to think that you wouldn't." *The king steps closer to his brother, only to have his brother step away at the same pace.* "Brother, you have been away. Your being here fills my heart with joy. Where have you run off to? Where have you been this whole time?"

"All this time . . . and you welcome me back with open arms?"

"What did you expect?"

"What did I expect? Are you serious? Why are you not furious? I walked out on you, all those years ago. And, on your big day, nonetheless."

"And I forgive—"

"No! You can't just forgive me after that. I came here today with a purpose. I plan on fulfilling it."

"And for what purpose other than amending our broken kinship have you returned? Unless . . ." *King Chandler backs away, slowly.* "You never planned on rekindling our bond, did you? You came here to reclaim what has been turned down to you."

"An act that you'll come to regret, Brother."

"That was never my call. I was as confused as you were."

"Were you really? Did you know? That we weren't related?"

"But we are."

"No, no. You know what I mean."

"Blood or not, that does not change a thing. I always thought you, my brother. We were raised as such. We've been through a lot. Too much. The fact that we're not blood means nothing to me."

"Either way, I hope you've enjoyed the throne and the power that comes with it, because after today, that duty will no longer be carried out by you."

"Guards!"

"Yes. Call them. I am here, which means I have already won." *The guards enter the room and push Igneaal to the ground, but he just smiles.* "Being carried away by guards? That takes me back."

"It breaks my heart to see you like this. Take him out of the kingdom. Make sure he does not return."

"What?" Igneaal struggles under the guards' combined weight. "Is that all you can do? I will come back. There is no keeping me out."

"Please, Brother. Go quietly. I am showing mercy upon you. You will be free anywhere, as long as you don't show your face here."

"How generous of you," Igneaal mumbles under his breath. Unfortunately, getting sent away goes against his plans. He pulls a blade out from under his cloak, as a last resort. "But, like I said . . ." He flips one of the guards, stabbing him in the thigh. The other two guards try to apprehend him but are no match. He rushes the king with the blade pointed out, "I will get what I came for!" The blade makes contact, but not with his brother. A guard, about a size and a half bigger than the other three, steps in front of the King, protecting him; yet, he has not fallen. He simply pulls the blade out of his chest and tosses it across the room. "Oh. You're a big one, aren't ya. No worries." He quickly uppercuts the oversized guard. The guard stumbles back but remains standing. The guard refuses to fight, and just takes the punches. "Why won't you fight? Scared, are ya?" He goes for one more blow but is unsuccessful in making contact. The guard catches his fist and slowly bends it back, as Igneaal kneels. The guard slams his fist into the eldest brother's sternum just hard enough to not kill him, but still get the message across. Igneaal rests on the floor, catching his breath. In this time, a few more guards show up, and immobilize the intruder.

"Take him to the dungeon. I am sorry, Brother, but you force my hand."

"Yes. Take me to the dungeon. Haha."

The king approaches Igneaal and lifts his head by the hair. "You're lucky I hold a soft spot for you. Even after what's gone down. Attempting to murder the king is punishable by death, yet, you're only serving time. Hopefully, you can appreciate that in which I've done for you."

"Very much so."

"I still hold hope for us, but it is obvious you're too far gone to change right away. Maybe, in time, we can reconcile and move forth with the life you've abandoned years ago . . . Take him away."

The guards obey orders, and Igneaal gets exactly what he wants. Months pass by as he serves imprisonment, eating off of scraps and conditioning himself, both physically and mentally. Being prince, he was able to persuade the king in giving him one act of special treatment, being books. Anything in the royal library, Igneaal is granted access to read. Being on the streets for so many years, he's picked up some knowledge, as well as rumors. He has also learned things about himself that he would have never believed, had he not witnessed them, himself. Night after night, he spent reading cult-related books. Some things said were hard to believe, but there were certain things that sounded doable. He practiced some of his discovered magic, while imprisoned until he believed it was time.

"Food." A tray gets slid to him. The guard is about to leave when Igneaal commences with his plan. He reaches for his food and takes a nibble, choking on the bit that gets caught in his throat. He begins to cough, making the guard look behind him. "Oh, for the love of God. Quit your foolin'. Your acting's about as terrible as you are a person." Igneaal continues to choke, banging on his chest, falling to his knees in the process. "C'mon. Quit it. You're just embarrassing . . ." He sees the tears in the king's brother's eyes and immediately rushes to save him. ". . . Nobody? You're not kidding." He rattles the keys, searching for the right one to the dungeon cell. He jumps to Igneaal's side and wraps his arms around him, saving him. Igneaal coughs up the scrap and catches his breath.

"Thank you, and sorry." Before the guard has a chance to respond, he's thrown across the room. He's pinned down and gagged, not going anywhere. Igneaal forces his hands inside the guard's mouth as he begins to tear away at his jaw, hearing a final crack as his head is split into two hemispheres, dripping red mess at his feet. He tears the flesh off the topside of the skull, making his own little sacrificial bowl of summons.

He gathers the appropriate bones needed for the specific task, unknowing of whether or not it would work.

"Perciel! You toying with the inmate again? You've been in there quite a while." The door opens as a guard lets himself in. "Perc—" What he sees before him is stomach-turning. The prisoner, hands red and dripping, as he messes with the left-behind remnants of Percy's body. "Guards!" Igneaal raises a hand as the guard flies into his grip.

With one squeeze, Igneaal, with all his strength, crushes the guard's body as it falls limp in his grasp. Unfortunately, he was too late. The guards are currently on their way, yet Igneaal is only a portion of the way into the communication process. The process didn't ask for a lot, but to the average man, it'd be too much to ask. For one, the process needs a bowl for mixing, made from the skull of an animal of some sort that's big enough to contain the needed ingredients. Technically, man is animal. Another ingredient, being the ground up leftovers from the skull, which includes every part of the head, excluding the part being used at the bowl. Those are the two easiest ingredients needed in the process. The next three ingredients are much more difficult: 3. Tears of the sacrificial lamb . . . 4. Personal blood that has been tainted by the forbidden fruit . . . 5. Lingering saliva. Having been kept imprisoned for nearly a year, Igneaal has done further research into the meanings behind what is wanted of him. The sacrificial lamb needn't be a literal lamb, but one who reflects innocence, like a child of sorts. They need to be bled of their tears, and then sacrificed. Easy enough. Step 4 was probably the one that confused him the most, but once it was looked into, he was disgusted, almost as much as he was the last step. Personal blood obviously means the blood of the user, being himself. "Forbidden fruit" has many forms, but all with the same underlining, being that in which you can't, rather, shouldn't have. He looked into many sins that define a forbidden fruit of sorts, but only one came the closest to what was specifically asked of him. The last step, he didn't have to research, more like think long and hard on the subject. Saliva is simple to come across, but "Linger" means to be left behind. The thought of drinking from the bowl disgusts him greatly, but he has already made it this far. By drinking, it allows a bond to be made:

between the summoner and the summoned. The final actual step in the process isn't really an ingredient, as much as it is an act. He must stir the ingredients with his finger and release a breath of life, meaning he must blow into his creation while stirring. This sets the act into motion, and once started, there is no retreating.

The guards rush into the room, but Igneaal is prepared. He leaps on them like an animal from a cage and tears them apart, leaving one immobilized and barely alive. A part of step 4 is the screaming of the one near death, which means that the victim has to be alive, even if barely, as he or she is being eaten. As it so turns out, cannibalism is the closest to forbidden fruit that you can get that matches the step to a T. For one, man shouldn't eat man. It's the only forbidden fruit that has to do with tainting blood. Plus, it includes the screaming of the victim as you're chowing down. Incestral rape is considered forbidden fruit, too, but isn't relevant to what needs to be done. "Where the hell am I going to get—" Igneaal suddenly hears laughter from the hall.

"Shh. They'll hear us."

"Right on schedule," Igneaal thinks to himself. For the last couple months, a couple of kids have been sneaking into the dungeon to mess with the prisoners. They must've found the secret entrance that Igneaal used to sneak into. One is a little girl, maybe around 8. The other barely ever talks, but occasionally, he shushes her, or tells her to quiet down. He sounds as if he could be an older brother, or a guardian. Igneaal has never met them, or even saw them, but has guessed their ages due to their voices. He puts his head up to the wall and speaks out to them, "Is that company I hear?"

The voices quiet down. "Shush. Don't talk."

"Hey, it's alright. I already know you're there. No point in hiding. What can I do? I'm in a cell."

"Let's go." The footsteps get further away, signaling that they're moving away from his door.

"Wait! What is it that you come down here for? And how? Is it perhaps a secret entrance that no one knows about?"

They stop. "If it's secret, then how do you know where it is?" the girl speaks.

"Oh, I used to sneak in when I was younger. In fact, I actually made that little blind spot."

"Yeah right. Don't listen to him, sis. We're going."

"Don't believe me? I understand. Not even my brother knew of that little entrance. I used to sneak out with it. See, I had limited access to the outside world, but I wanted to see what the fuss was about."

"You used to sneak out? That's preposterous. Only guards and royalty are allowed in here. And the prisoners of course, but given the location of the entrance, and the fact that you're still here, I doubt that's the case."

"Get in here already, before the guards hear you. Where you are isn't exactly soundproof, not when your voices bounce off the walls. In a hallway, nonetheless."

"We should listen to him, big brother."

"We've overstepped our welcome. We best get going before someone comes, like he said."

"Do you want to know who my brother is?"

"You've talked long enough. What are you even in here for?"

"Well, I'm not one to lie, so, yeah, I'll tell you. I'm here because I attempted to assassinate my brother for the crown."

"Now, why would we automatically trust you after hearing . . . Did you just say the king is your brother?"

"Yes, if you want to know more about—"

"That's it. Bye forever. C'mon sis. He's crazy."

"Wait!" Igneaal bangs his head against the wall. "Don't leave. I haven't had a visitor in the time I've been here, except for when my brother visits me from time to time. And let me tell you that's not been pleasant. Seeing him living the life that should rightfully be mine. It's infuriating. The truth is, I don't have much time left. I just want to have a nice conversation before I'm put to death. I promise, the guards won't be of trouble to you."

The door barely budges. "How do I know your words are true?"

"I'm locked in a cell in a room. I couldn't hurt you if I wanted to."

Igneaal stands behind where the door will open, to be unnoticed. "He sounds like he's in pain, Brother. Maybe, we should talk to him. Understand him."

The door opens slowly, as the brother takes the first step. "Stay behind me. We're coming in, but I'm doing this for my sister. Don't you even look at her in a way that makes me uncomf—" He walks in with his sister close behind, noticing that the cell is opened and empty.

Igneaal quickly closes the door behind them. The brother turns around, almost as quickly as the door closes, only to be hit upside the head with a blunt object. The girl begins to scream but is jumped. Igneaal straddles her, with his hand cupping her mouth. "Shhh. I'll let go if you promise not to scream. Deal?" She quickly nods her head. The prince lowers his face above hers, then lowers it more to her collarbone as he sniffs his victim. "My, my, you smell, so fresh. I was expecting innocence, but, mmmh, but not to this degree. Tell me. Girl, just how old are you?"

Tears flow from her eyes, leaving streaks down her cheeks. "S-six."

"Six? Perfect."

"W-why are you doing this, mister? You lied to us. We trusted you."

"There's your first mistake. Never trust someone who tried to kill their brother in cold blood. Tell me, child. Are you religious?"

"M-Momma always said that when days looked dark, that there were angels watching over us."

"Did you believe her?" She nods, the tears getting thicker. "Then there is good news, after all. When we're done here, you will get to meet an angel. I doubt a child as innocent as you would be cursed to damnation, so you'll be in a better place. Do you really want to live here? The death on the streets. The corrupt, demanding payment from those who barely hold value to feed their families, their kids, most of all. Right now, you live in hell. Don't you want to walk the streets of gold? Look upon divinity at its finest. Never get sick. I'm doing you a favor. I just hope you'll forgive me."

She turns her head, the tears dropping on the floor. "You're a m-monster. You lied to us when we tried to help. You're a demon, hiding in plain sight. But that doesn't mean you can't change. Even a demon can evolve."

These words touch Igneaal, but he has made it thus far. "You hold much maturity for one so young. It truly pains me to have to do this to one with potential in life. But, as it so happens . . ." He picks her up, and forces her back down, to where she is kneeling over the bowl of bone. "I may have to commit a few more monstrous acts before my road comes to a close." His hand tightens on the back of her neck as he holds her from behind, moving his hand from her neck to her mouth, then leaning her closer to the bowl. "I need your tears." His other hand reaches to her arm, and with one swift motion, he dislocates it. She screams out into his hand. The guard screams through his gag in the corner as he witnesses such cruelty. "I am sorry. I truly am." An idea suddenly strikes him, a way to kill two birds with one stone. The steps in the process never said they couldn't be connected. Maybe, and this was just thinking, but maybe, he could use the girl, as both a sacrifice, and a way to taint his person. To be sacrificed just means to die for a greater purpose. Technically, she'd still be sacrificed, but her death would just take longer than necessary. Igneaal wants to proceed with this idea, but then suddenly comes to realization. She's just a little girl. He doesn't mind killing extra if the little girl has a quick escape. She's suffered enough. There's no point in putting a little girl through so much, not when there's a body, yet to be tortured just lying in the corner. "You have served your purpose, my child, and I will forever be grateful. You will only suffer a little more, in order for the process to be recognized." He holds her over the bowl, his stomach against her back, as his hands hold her in place. One wraps around her throat and the other holds a blade up to her abdomen.

"Please, mister." She chokes on her tears as she attempts to speak. "I don't w-want to die."

"None of us ever do, my child." He jabs the curved knife into her stomach and unnecessarily turns it inside her as she screams out. Her body squirms as she bleeds out into the bowl of summoning. Due to blood loss, she begins to quiet down. Her body fails to move for her. She remains conscious, even if barely, but is unable to fend for herself. He

drops her to the floor. The blood begins to circle around her. The guard can be heard screaming through his gag from the corner, as he knows the fate that awaits him. The little girl continues to involuntarily squirm while she rests uncomfortably on the floor in numbing pain. Igneaal removes the knife from her person and decides to end her suffering altogether. "Sleep tight, my little angel." He breaks her neck quickly and kisses her forehead as a sign of good graces. His eyes then move slowly towards the next victim who is practically wetting himself as he waits for a most unpleasant death. The gagged guard shakes his head as he is slowly confronted by Igneaal—this demon amongst men. "I wish I could say this will be quick, but I can't lie to you like that. This will be most unpleasant, indeed, for the both of us." He kneels to the victim and runs his fingers along the victim's throat. "Where to start?" His hands run down his sides until he comes across the unappetizing love handles. The guard shutters and tries to get away but is thrown to the floor with force. He tears away at the clothing covering the sides of his unwanted, yet, necessary meal. He removes the gag and lowers his lips to the waist and wastes no time, as he takes his first bite of his own kind.

"Please, God. Make it stop."

Igneaal squeezes the love handles to make it easier to tear apart. Screams fill the room, but that doesn't make Igneaal stop. The raw stench of fresh blood and urine fills his nostrils. The prince moves on up his body, tearing away at the skin along the way. He makes it to the guard's throat and runs his finger along the Adam's apple. He looks into the guard's near-dead eyes as the victim shakes his head slowly, not having the will, nor the strength to move. He places the Adam's apple between his teeth and presses his lips to his throat with force, trying to fit as much as he could and bites down, feeling the penetration of his teeth surpassing the hard lump in the sad soul's throat—like a fresh apple, smaller in size, being bitten with impatience, as if the temptation is too much. The body drops limp to the ground, leaving strands of flesh between the prince's teeth, the distasteful aftertaste, making it a challenge to not vomit. Footsteps could be heard in the hallway, nearing his room. Grunts can be heard at his feet, as the deceased girl's older brother begins to awaken. He jumps to action as he picks the boy up, using him as leverage. The door slams open with five guards entering, armed to the fullest extent: arrows, knives, and all. "You can't hurt an innocent boy caught in the crossfire now, or can you?" Igneaal smiles smugly, but the smile quickly fades as the boy's body is pierced thoroughly, with the blade entering completely through his body, slightly striking the prince. The boy's body drops, leaving nothing in the way between the strayed prince and the guards. "You killed him?"

"Nothing is worth letting you leave. Given the scenery, you have proven to be more of a handful than initially thought out." The guard views the almost unarmed detainee, staring at the mess that surrounds his mouth and drips off his chin, staining the ground beneath him. He looks around, witnessing the few guards left dead, some in worse shape than the others, and the little girl that lies at rest, seemingly at peace. "Weapons up." Everyone does as asked and slowly steps closer and closer to the convict. "Stand down, and maybe this won't have to end with blood shed."

Igneaal looks down at the boy, "A little too late for that, wouldn't you say?"

"I'd listen if I were you. You are surely no match."

"As I was with the other sad victims here who had to witness my wrath. What's a couple more guards?"

"This is a fair warning. Take it and drop your weapon."

He steps back, "You wouldn't kill the brother of the king, now, or would you?"

"We weren't sent to kill you. We were sent to detain and immobilize you, by any means necessary. You can't fight if you're paralyzed, or would you like to try?" Igneaal nods his head and raises his fists. The guards ready their weapons as he drops his. "That may be the smartest decision you have ever made."

They move closer to apprehend him, but the prisoner seems to not be fazed. "I applaud your bravery, as well as your service, boys, but weapons are more for show. He opens his hands as the guards begin to lose balance, flying towards the ceiling. "You should have left good enough alone."

One of the guards forces himself to move his head as he is held tightly against the ceiling, "What are you?"

"Just a man with a duty." He throws his hands down as the guards drop, breaking their bodies on impact. Most of them die immediately, as one is left in a most uncomfortable state, with his head cracked, and his bones fractured. Igneaal kneels to his bowl of summons before he is interrupted any further, grabbing the blade that rests at his feet. He places the sharp edge horizontally to his wrist, cutting a little too deep as the blood flows fluently into the bowl. He begins to get a little lightheaded but shakes it off as he tears away at his clothing, having a nice strip to cover the wound. He wraps it around the deep gash and ties it. The blood mixes in with the ingredients as he stirs with his finger. He lifts the bowl to his lips and takes a big gulp as he places the edge of the skull between them and tilts his head back. The thick mixture of blood, ground-up bones, and tears enter his throat as he swallows, holding back the urge to regurgitate it all. He places the bowl in his lap as he sits on the ground, holding his hand to his mouth, feeling his stomach trying to reject his last meal. The contents in the bowl begin to stir as his surroundings begin to fade away, but not completely. Being left in darkness, with quick glimpses of reality flashing in and out, he begins to hear a voice.

"What do you seek out that's important enough to sell your humanity?"

"Power."

"Typical. You are all the same on the inside. Disgusting little rodents."

"Are you the one that is called Azazel?" Igneaal asks.

"Neigh. The one you seek is far too significant for the likes of you."

"Let me speak to him."

"Who are you to demand anything from me?"

"You listen here, you sorry excuse for a summons. I am beyond the point of return. I have done far too much to be reduced to speaking to an underling, such as yourself. I demand to speak to whoever this Azazel is."

"You speak with confidence. So sure of yourself."

"And why wouldn't I?"

"Very few have ever spoken directly to him and lived to tell about it. Why would you be any different?"

"There are things I can do that scare me. I want answers."

"You've come this far for answers?"

"No more questions!" The voice quiets down for a few seconds, making him unsure of whether or not he is still speaking to the other side. "Hello?"

"Who are you to summon me?" A different voice approaches, deeper than the last.

"Are you Azazel?"

"A-za-z . . . A-zul, and yes. I am he. Again. Who are you to summon me?"

"I am Igneaal, illegitimate child to—"

"Names mean nothing to me, boy. What is it you seek that requires speaking to me? Why not be stupid enough to speak to the prince of darkness, being Lu—"

"Lucifer can't help me with this. I'm pretty sure this name might have some significance to you."

"Proceed. And make this good. Insignificant intentions may pose a threat to your survival."

"I was supposed to be next in line for the throne. I was raised by the descendants of—"

"Pendragon."

"Yes."

"You reek of the pendragons, but not to the extent of being lineage."

"Yes. And I have questions that I request answers to."

"You surely are full of surprises, aren't you? But there is something about your scent that's foreign."

"Yes. I know. I am not a descendant of the Pendragons."

"You reek of Netherlands."

"Nether-lands?"

"You aren't from here. Your origins are completely unseen. This has never happened to me. This intrigues me."

"So, Azazel. You tell me. Is this conversation worth the effort?"

"Very."

"I can do things. Supernatural things."

"You don't reek of demonic possession."

"I can levitate things, amongst other things. I'd like you to give me answers."

"What does being adopted into the Pendragons have to do with you seeking my power?"

"I seek to become stronger, meaning I need you. Not just any demon will do."

"To think I'm a demon shows how little you know."

"I figured that having some connection with someone who has crossed paths with you would heighten my chances of receiving your help."

"Arthur Pendragon is of no kin to me. He simply held little power, given to him by my offspring. His scent only had minimal fractions of my own."

"None the matter, having just a slight fraction of your signature makes him related, as small and insignificant as that bond may be, whether you like it or not. I may not know how demons work, but I have some knowledge on the subject of ancestry. He's probably more along the lines of a removed child, isn't he? Like a fifth cousin twice removed, but on a bigger scale."

"That's hardly a significant bond at all."

"But the tree still connects at the moment where Arthur received your power."

"How dare you demand anything from me." Azazel is infuriated.

"Help me, please."

"Very well, but I'll have to understand you. The transference process may very well be the death of you, but it's also the only way you can receive even a portion of my grace, how diminished it may be. First, I'll need your eyes."

"I'm ready."

"So you say."

About a minute passes, and nothing happens. "Is it supposed to be this, uneventful. I figured by now—" Tension can be felt building up in his spine. The most uncomfortable and body shattering migraine begins to overtake him as he falls to his knees, arching his back as if his spirit is leaving him. A white noise screams out in his ears as he tries to cover them. "Please. For the love of—aah!" His fists clench, the sound making his ears bleed from the inside. Suddenly, everything stops. Though, he can't see, he can still feel, and what he feels in the moment is the stiffness around his eyes, likely the tears that are drying.

"You have survived. You are, indeed, a strong one." The voice is fuzzy as his mind is still recuperating from the intense pain that nearly melted his brain. "You have caught yourself in quite the predicament."

"I still can't see."

"But I can. Now shut it as I read you from the inside."

Flashes blind Igneaal as his life is spread out before him, including the exact moment he showed up on the doorstep of his adoptive parents. He knew as much, but what surprises him are the moments leading up to the drop off. He is in a man's arms, most likely his true father. "What is this? I don't remember any of this."

"You shouldn't. You were far too young to have memories. Now pipe down."

His eyes face skyward towards the unusual red clouds and winged creatures that dictate the discolored sky. Igneaal feels a tear hit his cheek as his father sheds them, but for what reason? "Bye, my little prince. Maybe, fate will allow us to cross paths someday." His father removes his necklace, and hands the gold locket to Igneaal. He's handed to a woman, most likely his mother, a beautiful woman, around mid-twenties, with elegant reddish hair and sun-kissed skin. Freckles spot the bridge of her nose. Love and sorrow shine in her radiant, yet unusual, eyes. One eye is a shade of ocean blue, while the other eye, is the most beautiful shade of gray. Like the male, she cries for him. The father figure puts both hands together, like he's grabbing hold of something that requires use of them, and begins to separate them, like he's tearing something apart. Veins start to surface along his body as he overexerts himself, tearing apart the area of space between his hands. Igneaal's body is lowered to a little girl with silver hair. She kisses his forehead as he is given back to his father, who then places a note on him. "You will be a true leader."

"Quickly! It won't stay open for long!"

The father extends out his body as Igneaal enters the tear between dimensions, the last thing seen, being a reptile—a dragon—closing in as new scenery begins to fade into his vision, a castle. He begins to cry as the doors open, revealing the king he has come to call "father." The king picks him up and automatically reaches for the note. "Igneaal. What a strange name." Everything goes dark once again, leaving him with the voice of Azazel.

"That . . . that was—"

"Fascinating." Azazel finishes. "That answers why your aura is foreign to anything known of this world. Because it isn't."

"What?"

"You're not from here. Not from this dimension."

"He called me Prince. There was . . . was a dragon or something. I came to you for answers, not to gain new ones."

"Watch your tone, boy. Maybe you, being prince, is the reason you were handed down to the pendragons, out of everyone who could have been chosen. There have been dragons that once roamed this earth. A couple brothers. They also smelt foreign."

"So, now, for my wish."

"Wishes are for genies. What I do doesn't come free. I grant favors."

"What! I did what was asked. I ate a man."

"You did what was necessary to contact me. That has nothing to do with what you ask of me."

"Then . . . What do you ask of me?"

"Guess, you'll have to find out. I'll reach out to you in the future and demand an order you'll have no say in denying. But power has its own price, apart from the one I demand of you."

"Two prices. Tell me how that's fair."

"I never said it was. The power will change you."

"How so?"

"*When one is born with the power, every decision is their own to make, but receiving it from someone else can be troublesome. It takes strong will-power to overcome the dark temptations. Taking on all this power will kill your fragile mind, since our auras are not compatible, but even a portion can alter you. You may not come out the same person you are now.*"

"*I don't care. I'll take that responsibility.*"

"*Let me hear the words, 'I accept.'*"

"*I accept, to the terms of this trade off.*"

"*Hehehe! Good luck . . .*" Vision starts to come back to Igneaal as his body begins to break, so it feels.

"*Aaaah!*" Again, he finds himself in excruciating pain, like his skin is tearing apart, nice and slowly. Minutes pass as his paralyzed body begins to return feeling. Heavily breathing, he notices a feeling, two feelings, grabbing his arms. He finds himself staring at a pair of feet, wearing a pair of familiar shoes. His head is lifted by the hair, as his brother's face comes into perspective.

Through the fading pain, Igneaal still finds the strength to laugh as tears well up. "*Dear brother, have you come all this way to see little ol' me?*"

"*Brother, what have you done?*"

He notices a good dozen guards surrounding him in the same room that he killed the poor unfortunate souls, but he notices a few extra bodies that he has no memory of murdering. "*Who are they?*" is all he can say, pointing out to the extra bodies.

"*Is that all you can say?*" The king kneels to his apprehended brother with anger, as well as sorrow, in his eyes. "*What have you done? You have changed.*"

"*But by how much? Hahaha.*"

He receives a hard slap to the face as the king grabs his shoulders. The backup raises their weapons as an attempt to keep Igneaal in line. "*For once, won't you be serious! You have attempted murder, amongst several first-degrees. There is no saving you from your punishment.*"

"*Sure, there is. You are king.*"

"Showing mercy on you at this point would resemble favoritism. What king would I be to my people if I allowed a mass murderer to live. You are my brother, which is why it pains me truly to sentence you to death." Igneaal is forced to the ground as a pair of heavy cuffs are placed upon his wrists, weighing him down. Knowing he is powerful enough to resist, he goes against his temptation, allowing his brother to win this one. A week, he spends in maximum holding, with his arms and legs chained to the walls. Besides the chains, a pair of weights are attached to his ankles in the slight chance of breaking free from them. Two meals are given to him per day as he awaits his demise. In that time, he communicates telepathically with his friend, his brother-in-arms. Though the first couple days were troublesome to his friend, he eventually got used to Igneaal's voice showing up in his head. The day arrives and Igneaal is moments away from his public execution. Crowds gather to witness the execution of a lost prince. Randoms, parents, as well as their children show up, but Igneaal isn't scared. The bigger the audience, the better. "You have all gathered to witness a murderer meet his end. A brother and a sister met their fates with this murderer. Some of you have been around awhile to know my father, as well as his two sons, being myself and, though at this point, it's sad to say, this man, my brother, this killer—Igneaal." This news receives quite a few gasps from the audience. "Through the years, he has called himself by another, Insygnia. Amongst the young siblings, many bodies have fallen, due to my brother's actions, which include a few of my guards, who met their ends a week ago. So, as a form of grief, I will be having one member from each victim's family come up here to express their pain."

"There is nothing you can do to help us forget what has been lost to us!" A woman from the crowd screams out.

"I don't expect you to forget, but I will allow you to punish, appropriately." The guard stands beside the king with a whip. "Leading up to my brother's execution will be three lashes each, given to my brother by the grieving member of each family."

"Only three! That's not nearly enough to—"

"*Silence! I understand what you are saying. Three lashes per person isn't worth a death, but there are far too many of you to allow ten lashes each. Doing so would kill Igneaal before the last person has a chance to release their punishment. Three each, then Igneaal will be beheaded publicly, then we can move on from this matter altogether. Don't you forget that my father died, now I have to witness my brother's death. You are not the only ones to suffer! Now . . .!*" *Igneaal gets adjusted with his hands tied to a post, and his knees planted on the ground with his back exposed.* "*Let the lashes begin!*" *He eyes his brother with Igneaal just smiling in a threatening way. A woman grabs the whip and stands behind him as she eyes his back with murderous intent. She raises the whip and fights through the tears. With one quick motion, the accused body jolts with force as the whip leaves a thin gash across his back, followed by two more. He undergoes this justified torture a good dozen more times, as his back begins to disappear under all the blood. Fighting to stay awake, his body drops. Three individuals grab him and readjust his body as his head is locked in a guillotine, his wrists being held down. The king walks up to his brother and meets him face-to-face.* "*Father would be mortified to see just how you've fallen.*"

"*Your father.*"

"*I'm done trying to convince you. Ready the guillotine!*" *He stands at his post above the crowd. His raises his hand as a way to signal when to drop the blade. Igneaal huffs as he readies himself, exercising his wrists. The king drops his hand and the blade falls, but it doesn't do the deed. Igneaal tightens his fists as everything slows. The crowd gasps as the blade stops, or rather, it falls in slow motion.* "*What is this sorcery?*" *The executioner holding him down falls with an arrow in his chest. The other two look around as another arrow flies through the air, targeting, yet, another guard. The last one is about to do the deed himself but shares the fate of the other two guards. A young man runs up to the guillotine with his face covered as he is chased along the way.* "*Kill him!*" *the king demands.*

The mysterious man shows some potential as he pulls a sword from his waist and holds back the challengers. He makes his way up to the king's brother and raises his sword, dropping it on the chains that immobilize him. Igneaal picks himself up and stares directly at his savior. "You have done well, Arti."

"Thank you, Brother. I live to serve you, after all." Arthur kneels.

"No need for that." He places a hand on Arthur's shoulder.

The king in rage, stands and points at the two, "Seize them. Whoever kills my brother and his accomplice will be rewarded greatly." The crowd disperses as everyone rushes the two fugitives.

"I think not!" Igneaal takes one step and swipes at the air, which results in everyone in that general direction flying back. "What, Brother! Do you not hold the jewels to come at me, yourself? What king hides behind his people?"

"Who said I'm hiding?" Chandler rushes his brother with sword in hand, ready to strike. "If you die, it will be by my hand!" He swings the sword at his brother but fails to make contact.

Igneaal dodges the weapon and catches Chandler under the rib cage with one powerful jab. "Where was this attitude mere moments ago?" King Chandler refuses to drop as he moves toward another attempt to end his brother, again, failing. Igneaal, having the power to kill him, refuses to do so. Instead, he toys with him. He captures the wrist that wields the weapon and holds it back as he uses his free hand to quickly give three blows, consecutively, to the sternum of the king. "You were never fit to be king. That should have been my place, my dear brother." He attacks Chandler between every few words with such anger in his voice.

"If you're going to kill me, then stop stalling. Just do it."

The stray prince shakes his head, laughing as if he is slowly losing his mind. Voices appear in his head, giving him suggestions on how to torture his victim. "No!" He speaks out, ending the voices. "You want me to kill you. You expect, me to kill you, which is why I'm not going to. I want you to suffer. You deserve to suffer." Chandler notices the change in his executioner's eyes, the way he looks at him. Igneaal stops everyone in their tracks as the scattered crowd stumbles to their knees. Everyone, except the king, who has been given the choice.

"*What has become of you?*"

"*I have simply found my calling. Everything you have . . . that's how you'll suffer. Look around. You will witness your kingdom fall, slowly, with me as the dictator. I have waited so long to see you like this. As of today, I am your king.*" *Igneaal waves his hand at the masses and slowly lowers his hand, watching as the citizens are forced to bow to their new leader.* "*It's up to you, Brother. Your decision decides it all.*"

"*I will never bow to you.*"

"*I thought as much, which is why . . .*" *He lifts his index finger as one individual, a child, stands above the ones who bow.* "*. . . I came prepared.*" *The boy's body begins to mangle and contort as his fingers, one by one, begin to bend in ways they aren't meant to be bent.* "*If you think I won't kill him, then you don't know me at all.*"

He feels a tugging at his clothing. "*I didn't think we'd go this far. Is there a way to do this, without hurting others?*"

Igneaal lets go of the boy. "*Arthur. I understand where you're coming from. That is why you aren't doing the dirty deed.*" *Arthur speaks up, but is slapped,* "*When I want you to speak, I will . . .*" *Tears well up in Arthur's eyes.* "*Listen . . . I'm sorry, but this is how things must be. You are my oldest friend. Won't you go on this journey with me?*" *He holds out his hand, waiting for Arthur to take it.*

"*Listen, kid . . .*" *King Chandler speaks up,* "*. . . he is not the same Igneaal that you knew. He has changed. Can you not see it?*"

Arthur looks into his friend's twisted eyes. "*He is my friend—my brother. I will follow him to wherever it is that he drags me.*"

A hand is placed upon Arthur's shoulder. "*We'll always have each other's backs. Now and forever.*" *Arti nods. The boy in the crowd is controlled again as he begins to scream in agony, feeling every bone become dislocated and rearranged.* "*It's up to you, Chandler. Make your decision. I won't stop at the boy, so, maybe you need some motivation.*" *A woman near the boy, most likely his mother, begins to weep as her son is slowly killed. Igneaal focuses on the boy and begins to slowly tear out his throat.*

"*Stop!*" *Everything stops.*

"My, my. Is this acceptance, I hear?"

Chandler slowly drops to his knees, "You will meet a most undesirable fate. I will tear you apart, myself, if it's the last thing I do."

"Until that day, I will be living on a full belly, with harems spread out for months at a time, and servants to do my bidding."

"You aren't my brother."

"Was I ever?"

Chandler lowers his upper body, fully bowing to his former ally. Igneaal has won. Weeks pass as his mind slowly begins to contort. Everything Azazel has promised is coming to pass, as his anger and dictatorship begin to manifest differently towards his brother, his true brother—Arthur.

"Arthur!"

A man enters the room, "Y-yes."

"Is everything prepared?"

"Yes, my king. Everything is as it should be. The prisoner is to be executed at nightfall, and your harem is scheduled to follow shortly after."

"Perfect. You are the perfect squire, Arthur. Is everything alright?"

"Yes, my king. Why wouldn't I be? You have given me the world. Everything I have is because of you. If not for that fateful day, I wouldn't even be here today."

"Yet, I sense uncertainty. Is this correct?"

"It's just that, the murdering, the bloodshed . . . there's too much of it. You stopped a lot of criminal activity when you took over, but now you demand so much from your people. People can't even leave the kingdom, or they'll be executed. I don't know. It just seems to me that—"

The king stands above Arthur. "You have a lot of doubts for someone under my protection. You are weak, but don't worry. I will shape you." He throws a punch at Arthur, knocking him to the floor. "With my help, you will be reborn. No more Arthur. You'll be someone else. Something else. Stronger. Doubtless. Without disobedience. A king's true right-hand man." Day in and day out, most of the king's focus is on Arti. Every execution is first-handedly past down to him as a way to shape him, to prove his loyalty. The first actual execution made Arti vomit, as did the second and the next several. Eventually, he was able to handle the sight of blood, even if barely. Soon after, executions became last resort. What took their place was torture, in which Arthur was forced to take up. He was forced to practice with knives, learning to aim them, as well as which body parts to strike without killing the victim. A couple years pass, and Arthur has changed, even if only a little. For every act of disobedience or act of doubt, he is personally handled by his king . . . his friend . . . his brother. Whenever a convict, or a criminal, is captured, rather than execution, they are put through intense torture by yours truly, being Arthur. That torture all depends on the crime. Sexual predators get tortured with genital anguish, leading up to mutilation. Before that, they are reduced to tears to teach them of the wrong, then, once they've seen the error of their ways, they are relieved of the very thing they have abused. Murderers get tortured by the family members of the victims, then again by Arthur. Any who attempt to help escape join in on the torture. The punishment is usually related to the crime, so once a murderer is humiliated publicly, over and over, they are put to death. Execution is also given to those, once all the cells are filled. The castle holds a lot of cells, spread out between a few dungeons. The inmates go through their torture day by day, publicly, and eventually, once all spots are full, if you are not released by that time, the inmate who has been in the longest finally reaches the end of their torture. Not often do all the spots get filled. Inmates sharing the same crimes share the same living space, to sort out their crimes amongst each other, until their due punishment. All in all, getting arrested puts you in the closest thing to hell on earth. A couple more years, and Arthur has been put in his place. No more doubts. Every night, he has spent going through his own torture by his brother. Morals have been forced upon him until his personality was practically no more. The shy, scared little boy that was saved all those years ago was now tortured beyond recognition. He now laughed at pain. He actually looked forward to it. He was allowed to improvise as long as the job was done. Not taught by Igneaal, Arthur has grown to love games. Toying with his victims before putting them to involuntary rest was a gimmick, his own special signature. His change was not limited to his love to take and conflict pain, but also in the way he reacted to certain things. In his eyes, Igneaal was no longer a brother, more of a father. Igneaal has completely recreated Arthur into something not to be dealt with, something that he wasn't before.

"I came as soon as I received your summons, Father."

"Arti. You have come a long way from that pathetic, scared, little embarrassment that you used to be." He focuses on Arti, trying to notice any flinch made as he says these things, but Arti stands upright, like the loyal soldier he has been molded into. "Tell me, Son. Do you doubt me at all?"

Without pause, Arthur speaks. "No. I do not doubt you, Father. These vermin need to see the error of their ways, by any means necessary."

"Right answer." A guard steps up, revealing a long rod with some kind of insignia, or crest, on the end. "Remove your shirt, Son, and kneel." Arti does as requested without hesitation. The king lowers the rod into a vat of lava for a good half minute, then takes it out. "You have proven to be quite worthy of my complete and undisputable respect. Do you accept this brand as a sign of loyalty to your king, to forever serve me?"

"I do, my lord."

"Then, from this day forward, that boy known as Arthur Reese is dead." He presses the branding rod into the soldier's chest, as Arthur takes it, biting his tongue till the act is done. "From Arthur's ashes will rise anew. You will now be known as Artemis. People will learn to tremble when they hear our names."

A couple more years pass and Igneaal has everything he has ever wanted. Never has he been more at home, then again, that may be the corruption acting out. As for his former brother, he is bound to the castle, and treated as a pet, being forced to eat on the floor as the king eats to his heart's content. Every now and then, he'll look out his window at the citizens, suffering to the wrath of a dictator far worse than his tyrant cousin, LaZilee. Chandler has sent his kingdom to the dark ages and has no power to make a change.

King Igneaal hears news of fortune tellers, three sisters, who live a day's trip away. He has heard of these sisters when he lived on the streets, but never paid attention to the rumors. He was never one to believe in absurd superstition, such as future-sight, but this was also long before he began to understand the full gravity of his abilities. Practically selling your soul to a high-level demon to gain a power boost puts reality into question. Who's to say what's real anymore? If magic can coexist with religion, let alone, science, then future-sight is nothing, right?

"Father. Where are you going?"

"I'm going to seek answers."

"You're just going to leave the kingdom to fend for itself?"

"Of course not." He turns around and places a hand on Artemis. "I am leaving this kingdom in your capable hands."

"I won't let you down, Father."

"I'm counting on it, otherwise, I wouldn't have entrusted you. I'll be gone for a couple days. Hopefully, in that time, I'll have the answers I seek. But for now, I bid you farewell, my most loyal of comrades."

He heads out on horseback, prepared for the worst of weather conditions. Along the way, he asks many random citizens of the whereabouts of these three sisters. It takes many attempts, as many do not know of these sisters, but he eventually comes across a couple of siblings who point him in the right direction. He stops at a cavern of sorts, just miles away from the next kingdom. Slowly, he begins to walk into the cavern, until he comes across a torch on a wall. "Hello! Anyone here?" The torches begin to flicker as he gets further into the cavern. "Show yourselves. I know you're here."

"You have traveled quite a ways, traveler." The torches die out, leaving him in the darkness. He turns around to see something shift.

"About a day's distance."

"We don't speak of Camelot. Your aura smells foreign."

"Who are you? . . . and how can you live like this? So dark."

"You learn to grow accustom to it after a while." A torch lights up in front of him, revealing three elderly women. "We are the three oracles—past, present, future—the sisters of fate."

"*Do you not have actual names?*" *Igneaal tries not to look directly at their faces.*

"*Aurora.*"

"*Bori.*"

"*Alice . . . What's the matter? Do you not like what you see?*"

Igneaal stares at the women's' gaping sockets. One of them holds something in their hand—an eye. "*You're blind.*"

"*If that's all you came here to say, then the exit's that way.*" *They all point in different directions.*

"*Sorry. I'm here because—*"

"*You come for answers. What other reason would there be? No one ever comes for a social visit.*"

"*So, you know what I wish to ask?*"

"*No.*"

"*I was told that you could see the future.*"

The three sisters chuckle. More of a cackle, really. "*Our abilities have been slightly overexaggerated. The future isn't something that can be seen, traveler.*"

"*But, I've heard that you've helped quite a few people with these things. Am I in the right place, or am I simply wasting my time?*"

"*Nothing is specific. We're never guaranteed a future. It is always changing with every decision made by yourself as well as those around you. We take a glimpse at the many possible paths that could lead to several different futures, but it is impossible to know for certain, exactly which one will be taken. Fate is the only one that truly knows all.*"

"*Then, let me speak to Fate.*"

"*Impossible. Fate is not a person, but the inevitable happening. Fate is something that can't be changed, no matter what decision is made.*"

"*Then how did you help people? Take a wild guess?*"

"*Precisely. By simply looking into their past, given their past choices, we took a wild guess to the most probable path that they would take. History repeats more often than not, but like we said, nothing is specific. We may see a glimpse of a future, but it is completely out of context.*"

"So, what you're saying is I have come here for nothing. Great." He begins to walk out in the opposite direction as the three.

"I guess this means that you don't wish to know the simple answer, that your end is met by someone far more capable than you."

Igneaal pauses in his tracks, looking over his shoulder. "What? I thought you couldn't see the definite future."

"Though, we can't know for certain, the exact future decided, we can at least take a glimpse of the most repeated death. One's true fate. Everyone dies. It's just one of those paths without corners. You can change the time and place, but there is no changing the result."

"What is this you speak of 'more capable'? I am all-powerful. I accept any challenger who believes they can best me."

"This need to be better, is precisely why you'll lose."

"Where is this challenger?"

"Not yet born, but he is not one to be taken lightly."

"Neither am I."

"Be that as it may, you can't fight this, even with your . . . origin."

"What do you know of my origin?"

"Enough."

Hours, they talked. Long enough for Igneaal to realize that there was no understanding the effects of fate, not completely, anyway. They spoke of fate, and how it differed from destiny. Eventually, this led to talk about prophecies, and how it differed from a simple future. As futures were shaped by the paths taken, prophecies were absolute. No matter which path is taken, they all, eventually lead to the bigger picture, with the only thing being changeable, the place and time, but never the result. Prophecies are a tricky subject, as there really is no point in meddling in them. They are specifically vague, making it impossible to choose a path that strays from it. The prophecy told, could very well be shaped by your constant attempts of avoiding it, but it won't tell you that much. Whether you know it or don't, it's built upon knowing what you know, meaning the prophecy knows that you're trying to find an escape. Confusing concept? Maybe.

Igneaal hears just enough about his death to want to stop it, though, it is unnecessary to try, given that, from the sound of it, it's still a while away. He rides back to his kingdom, kicking through his door. "Artemis!"

Artemis stands front and center, "Yes, sir. Have you found what you sought?"

"And so much more. Years and I've faced many challengers. I have defeated all who faced me, and I've grown quite bored with no one with the power to oppose me. Honestly, the challenge was the main source of my willpower, but there is no one left to stand, until now."

"You have found an opponent?"

"Indeed, I have, which is where you come in. I have a job for you."

"Anything, my lord."

"First off, I will need you to strip down." Artemis does as requested as Igneaal stands above him. "This may hurt a bit." He raises a hand skyward and rests the other along Artemis' chest. Thunder rolls in as streaks of lightning can be seen from outside. Everything begins to fade in and out, like flickering lights.

"Igneaal! What are you doing?" Chandler struggles to break free of his chains. "What is this madness?"

"I am simply doing what I believe to be necessary. Soon, we will see a new world." Igneaal lowers his hand, tracing along his sides as Artemis' body jerks, but he continues to stay put. Veins begin to surface and throb as something enters his body, a gaseous substance. Igneaal continues to mutter to himself. "Just . . . a little . . . MOREE!" Igneaal drops as a tidal wave of wind washes over the kingdom. Artemis holds his master as he recuperates.

"What was that?"

Igneaal stands and rushes to escape. "You have to leave. We only have minutes if I did things right." Artemis quickly jumps into his clothing and rushes to his master's side as he laughs skyward. "The deed is done! Haha."

Chandler escapes the castle and tackles his brother to the ground, "What have you done? You have killed us all!"

"Doesn't matter what I've done. There is no going back." Igneaal jabs Chandler in the side with his blade, as Chandler falls. "Don't worry. That will heal shortly enough." He faces his loyal subject, "As for you, you need to leave. You can't be here."

"What do you speak, Master?"

"You have been loyal to the end. Don't question me now. This kingdom will rise with your ashes, but you mustn't be in it when we fade. We live in you now." Artemis looks around at the fading scenery, then looks at his hand, as he begins to see through it. "There isn't much time. Go! Now! Find the one who is destined to end me and end him first. When the deed is finished, come back here, and resurrect what has fallen. Farewell."

"For now?"

"Forever."

Igneaal places his hands to his adoptive son's shoulders, and in an instance, Artemis finds himself just outside of Camelot's borders, just in time for the bang to happen. He flies with the blast, being left in a storm of dust. Once the storm clears, the home he's called Camelot is gone, completely. What remains in its place is a crater as big as the kingdom was. He falls to his knees, grabbing hold of the dirt beneath him. "Faaatheeerrrr!"

XIII

"When it came down to it, Artemis was just an innocent boy, caught in a toxic relationship."

"So, this thing, this assassin, is trying to kill me because of some sort of prophecy?"

Mother nods her head, "You get in the way of the one he serves. You are an obstacle that he must rid of."

"How do you know all this? Is it in some sort of book?"

"There isn't a book that knows this. It's all prophecy. Scribed in the Oracles' Library. It is fate."

"Just so I've got this, Deanne," Danielle raises her hand, "Some demonic entity from the past knew of Chance, hundreds of years before he came to pass, and has performed some kind of spell targeting him to stop him from what? And Arthur is involved in all this? Like, King Arthur?"

"He isn't a demonic entity. He is human, like us, for the most part. And yes, though the books on Arthurian mythology share some truth, there are many tales that differ, like Merlin. Arthur was very much real, but Artemis is not he."

"And I'm just hearing about this now? When were you going to tell me? Or were you planning on not? Aah, this is too much. I mean, I've come across some indescribable things, but this?"

"Indescribable, how?"

"Well, uh, like a demon that was set out to end me. The whole astral projection thing. Still figuring that shit out! But, King Arthur? Merlin? Supernatural and Magic? Isn't there, like, a confliction there?"

"I understand, Chance. But, it's all real. And you have it?"

The room grows silent for a few seconds. "I have it? Magic? Supernatural powers? Please, by all means . . . elaborate."

"You have magic. Is that what you want to hear? I'm surprised at you, that you haven't figured this out on your own. Haven't you ever done something amazing, maybe due to an adrenaline spike."

"So, the nightmares?"

"Related. Yes. But I'm afraid that whoever it is you may be having conflicts with in these nightmares, isn't Igneaal."

I stand up, rubbing the back of my head, "Jesus Christ." I try to remain calm and collected, but this is too much. "There are just too many secrets. I mean, I figured you were keeping something from me, but . . . Did you know this all from the get-go?" I ask as if I don't know the answer, already.

"Please, sit down. I'll tell you all you need to know."

"You must be telling me all this for a reason. Is there, like, a deadline? Is that why this is all happening now? My head hurts."

"I should've told you from the start. I know I've made a mistake. Please, sit down."

"Is this all? Is this all the secrets you have for me? Please, tell me."

"There are some that you must find out on your own."

I pace in circles, trying to collect all the thoughts roaming in my head and filing them into their like-cabinets. "I'm sorry, Mother, but I need time to process."

She nods in acceptance, yelling after me, "I'll be there for you if you need anything!" My friends follow as I close the door behind us.

Danielle and Samantha stare blankly at the wall opposite to them. None of us have the slightest clue as to how to start off a conversation. "Well, that was—"

"Too much. It's difficult to take that all in, though, if I have been given these facts, one by one, it wouldn't be too much to handle. Having them all thrown at me in one go, well, that's too much to ask of anyone."

"Chance, you seem, on edge."

I look towards Sam, "Why wouldn't I be? With that bombshell."

"It's just so unlike you, to lose your composure. You're usually calm in certain situations."

"So, you think I'm weak to be so . . . so—"

"No. I never said that." Danielle reaches towards my hands and slowly lowers them, "What I mean is, you're human. No one expects to be strong all the time. Every now and then, someone has to comfort you."

"I'm not used to these feelings. I don't know if I like them."

"Trust someone who's felt hurt and doubt constantly. These feelings suck. I won't lie, but, in the end, you'll realize that you've grown from it. Do I wish certain things never happened? Of course, but the fact in the matter: it happened. It's all in the past, even if barely. It's how you deal with these things now. If you ask me, I like this side of you. The side that shows emotion, even if only a little."

"Are you not at all wondering about the whole Arthur thing? I thought you'd react differently to that."

"I'd be lying if I said I wasn't shaken by this revelation. Personally, I don't know what to be more surprised at. The reveal of King Arthur and Merlin, or the reveal that you're somehow connected to them. But none the less, we're in this together."

"You're still with me?"

"I never left. We said that we'd be there for you, and we plan on following through. Your entire world has just been turned on its axis. What kind of friends would we be to leave you to deal with it on your own?"

I open my mouth to speak, but she takes initiative, pressing her lips against mine, wiping away the tear that snuck past my emotional defense system. "Danielle?"

"Shh. Don't ruin the moment with words. If you're hurt, let me heal you."

"Hehe. That'd be a moving sentiment if it weren't completely wrong. Emotional pain and physical pain aren't—" She shuts me up again, with her hands pressed firmly into my broad shoulders.

I lay her body down, leaving trails of kisses up her stomach, leading to her breasts, as I bind her wrists with her shirt. "The road might be dangerous."

I feel a secondary pair of hands unbuckling my belt, tugging at my waistband. "And we'll be ready for it." Sam's hands latch onto my stomach, one moving towards my chest and the other into my briefs, as she gently bites down onto my neck. For the moment, everything begins to fade away as I lose myself. My vision begins to haze in and out as the moment begins to split between scenes. One moment, I'm above Dani, and the next, Sam is pinned against the wall. It's as if you take a movie and delete a bunch of random scenes until only a portion of the movie remains, in clips.

My eyes slowly open to the streams of light that enter through my blinds. I grunt as I shift the blanket, letting my legs hang off the bedside. I glance at the clock on my nightstand. 7:47 a.m.

I make my way down to the kitchen, grabbing a bowl of cereal when she yells from the living room. "There's stew in the fridge if you want any." I pour the milk into my bowl. "I came into your room last night, but you were all passed out, so I got back to their parents. Are you ready to talk about last night?" I toss my bowl into the sink and leave out the front door, hearing her call after me.

I pass by the school and come across the public library, stopping by for a visit. It isn't that busy, but the library never really is. The woman at the counter takes notice of me and automatically opens her mouth, "Isn't there somewhere you should be right now?" I look at her and shrug my shoulders in confusion. "She glances at the clock on the wall, then back at me, "It's school hours. Is someone playing hooky?"

"Oh, that. No. I have a hall pass for the morning. I'm able to leave school grounds."

"May I see it?"

"See what? Oh, yeah, that. Sorry, I'm usually more aware than this."

When she notices I don't have one, she sighs, "Right. Well, be sure to stay quiet. This is a library, after all."

I nod my head, "Oh, do you know which aisle I can find mythology in? . . . You know, like Arthurian, or biblical? Pretty much any kind." She stares at me with her dead eyes, like she's annoyed. That typical librarian glare. "You know what, never mind. I think I can manage."

I make my way to the back, skimming the aisles until I can come across what I need. "Don't mind her." I look to my left to find a woman with a wagon of books, placing them in their appropriate places. "She's been here for nine years. She's never been one to talk much, not as long as I've worked here."

"Oh, so you work here?" I pause, realizing just how stupid I sound, "Sorry. Stupid question," I say, taking notice of the wagon and literally the last sentence she said.

"There are no stupid questions."

"Do you really believe that?"

I can see her form a smile from where I stand. "You're a smart boy. This much, I can tell. You're just having an off day. Is there anything I can put at ease for you?"

"Uhh, no. It's a personal matter. No need to get you involved." I leave out the part where this personal matter may sound fictional to the ears of someone who hasn't witnessed.

"The books that you seek are in the second aisle to the back."

"Thanks. By the way, how can you sense I'm a"— I turn to talk to her, but she's gone—"smart boy?" I notice the woman at the counter glaring at me with her finger to her lips. I awkwardly turn and walk towards the back aisle. I come across the books, passing authors, such as Hamilton, Lewis, Gaiman, and Bulfinch, amongst other well know myth-writers. I come across a book that looks promising. *Le Morte d'Arthur.* Sir Thomas Malory? Never heard of him, then again, I've never been one to read into mythology, or religion for that matter. I don't know why I'm reading into this Arthurian myth. Real or not, how could I take some author's word for it, especially when the book is labeled fiction? I'm out of my wits here. I sit down and place the large book out in front of me, including a couple shorter books of Merlin, which were in the same group. A couple hours of turning pages and I'm beginning to understand what type of person Arthur is, or was. There are a few things, quite a lot actually, that contradict with some things I have been told. I knew it. This is pointless. Even if King Arthur was real, how would a fiction writer come across him, when his existence is still a rumor? I run my hands through my hair and close the book, placing my cheek against the hard leather. *Ugh, I wouldn't even know which Arthur book to take seriously. There are a couple, or a few, origins to his tale.* I place the books back in their designated spots, taking notice of an author I could have sworn I have come across: Bayonette. Sounds familiar enough. I reach for the book and stare at the cover. *Fact or Myth.* Another of his books reads *From Father to Son.* "These aren't myth." Must be in the wrong aisle. I glimpse at the clock. I've been here long enough.

I walk past the school again, on my way home, and hear some shouting. I walk into the office at the front of the school where students usually log in when they're late, but no one is there, so I just let myself in. "Kick his ass!" I haven't even come across the event, but I can already visualize a fight, and I needn't guess who's at the center of it. I see Storm in the outer layer of a bunch of students raising their phones up.

"Not again."

Storm takes notice of me, "Dude, did you just get here?"

"Walking by."

"You need to start coming to school. I'm surprised they haven't sent a letter or called your mom, or something."

"Mother said that as long as I keep my grades up, I can do whatever I want."

"Your mom's lenient."

"I know. Why do these people just stand here and rant on? It's despicable."

"People love a good fight."

"It's only a fight if the other person stands a chance. This isn't a fight. It's a fuckin beat down." I force myself into the circle, pushing past people who refuse to move. Laughter and gasps deafen me the closer I get. People shout and videotape, while others stand aside and just witness. There are some people that don't enjoy this. I reach the scene and still fail to understand why they're so amused. In the center of the circle is a boy with medium brown hair. Two lackies hold him in place as Ash gives him one in the gut. Kyle just takes it, staring at the ground, biting his tongue. The crowd seems rather pleased. A bunch of pathetic ingrates who amount to nothing more than specters. I slowly make my way to the floor when it happens. Laughter, chuckling, snarky remarks, and reason for mor phones to be lifted. The two students back away as the deed has already been done. The damage, irreparable.

"Where do you think you're going?" Ash says, proud of his desperate act of superiority. There, unguarded and humiliated is Kyle, frozen in panic with his drawers around his ankles. "Wow. Now, there's no coming back from that."

I grab the wrist of a student who has his phone lifted and slap it out of his hand. "Hey, man. What the hell do you think you're doing?" the bystander says, a bit ticked. I ignore him.

I walk casually to where Kyle is and guard him, "You alright?"

He stares down towards the ground, heart beating quickly. "I didn't ask for your help." Rather than a thank you, he tries to push me away.

"You didn't need to. Make yourself decent and scram."

Kyle pulls up his pants and undergarments, avoiding eye contact with anyone as he leaves the picture. "Why am I not surprised? Chance! Who are you to get in the way of my fun? Let the boy defend himself for a change. You think you're saving him? You're just making it more the obvious that he can't do shit to protect himself. Weak, helpless Kyle. Spineless, limp dick coward who can barely speak for himself. But why would he need to, when his mom is here to back him up. How is that, when you're the one being fucked with, you show no interest, not as much as the interest you have in someone else's affairs. What I see are the lame attempts of standing up as a hero of sorts, acting all high and mighty, when no one asked for it."

"Are you saying you're any better? Your acts here, right now, are insignificant. Whatever image you strive for yourself here won't help you in the world out there. Here, you're nothing but a petty highschool bully whose gratuitous acts are nothing more than the obvious, ill-willed and pathetic. There's no weight behind anything you do here. You're a dick for the sole purpose of being a dick. Aiming to achieve petty high school popularity through the misdeeds done to weaker underclassmen . . . you can't control me, and that pisses you off. You look for someone weaker to inflate your overly compensating ego while, in the meantime, you continue to attempt your sorry advancements at me. Quit with the childish tantrums, and grow up. By the way, how's the arm?"

That did it. With every forced step forward, he heavily breathes. Storm's words are heard from the crowd, "Chance, you're better than this! You made your point!"

"That's the thing, Stormie. I don't think I'm better than this. Holding back just means a repeat is bound to happen. It's best to get it over with."

"You don't think that."

"Don't I? I always thought I was better than this. That fighting was stupid, but the truth is, I might even like it. Not for the attention, but for the mere pleasure. Kicking Ash's ass last time helped put that into perspective." Ash stands to the side, cracking his knuckles and readying himself for a fight. "I may be calm on the outside, but lately, I have slowly been becoming mad. It's loud all the time. The only way to calm the noises is to succumb to them."

"Maybe, but doesn't that explain us all? We all have urges. Sometimes, it feels impossible to turn away, but we do. That's what keeps us from the animals. We know when to hold back."

My hands tremble, then start to ease. I take a deep breath, then another one. My meditating is interrupted by Ash, lunging towards me in a fit of rage. I fall back, shaking it off. He lunges at me again, sloppily if I might add. I sidestep ever so calmly. Phones are still raised, but the banter has reduced. Rather than the obnoxious pests they were, moments beforehand, they now observe, patiently waiting to see how this plays out. Ash tries me again. Rather than another side-step, I lunge into his advancements, landing a held back blow to the abdomen. He falls back, holding his gut.

"I'm tired, Ash. Of this whole charade. You. Me. Us. This whole situation can be fixed. There's no need for this unnecessary feud. So, why? All it takes is for one of us to take the first step. Someone to admit defeat and be the bigger man. I know you won't do it. You're not like that, so let me be the first . . . you win. I'm sorry. For whatever caused you to fill this role, can't we just try? We don't have to be friends, but we don't have to be enemies, either."

"What are you sorry for, exactly? I want to hear it in your words, Chance."

"You know. I'm sorry . . . that, uh."

Ash looks away, "Even when apologizing, you refuse to admit what you've done. Do you have so much fucking pride in yourself, that you are incapable of acknowledging your own flaws? Your own misdeeds? I'm not pissed at whatever you think I'm pissed at. It's you. You're infuriating." He lands a hit to my chin, and I let him. He keeps landing blows between conversation. "I don't know what it is about you, but it pisses me off. You accuse me of having an ego as if yours isn't there at all. You've got to have the biggest ego I've seen. Your false sense of justice, but as long as you're happy in the end, am I right? Between the relationships you've ruined, the girls you've fucked, and the fucks that you give, which in case your pride makes you incapable of admitting to, is none, I don't know what it is that makes you believe so highly of yourself, you self-righteous, overly-invasive prick . . . sure, I may be whatever it is you called me, but don't make it sound as if you're any better off." He wipes the sweat from his brow and flings it to the ground. "I'm not the only degenerate here. Look around. A bunch of clueless, nobodies who have nothing better to do than to observe. Fuck. Half of the school is trash, anyways, from the easy harlots to the teachers who don't step in till the last minute. It's a concoction of freaks and closet-deviants who have their own drama. Why do you act as if everything revolves around you? You asked why I have a problem with you. Don't undermine my reasoning and make it sound as if a reason as petty as something that happened in junior high could still be of any relevance today. I didn't see it back then, but now, it's all clear and damn well in my face. Your arrogance. That pride. The look in your eye. You're not a saint, you know!"

He throws another punch, one I manage to catch and refuse to release. "You think I don't know that? When did I ever say I was? I'm human. I have emotions. I'm with flaws. I admit that."

"Where the fuck was that emotion when a kid died at your house?" Everything goes silent. Students cringe and back away an inch or two. "I must've watched that video a dozen times, and each time, I had to hold back my disgust and force my eyes to observe. Look for any trace of terror or horror in your eyes but guess what. There wasn't any. You cracked jokes. You added inappropriate humor and shrugged off a dead body as if it was nothing more than hitting a nerd. What part of that is humane? You and that sociopath mom of yours are freaks. If she were to die right before your very eyes, you'd laugh it off, wouldn't you?" I reach slowly for his face. "For all I care, you can both fuck o—"

I grab him by the throat and begin to push back. He slowly succumbs to the pressure as he attempts to pull my fingers from their grip.

"Chance! Chance!" Storm reaches for my shoulder, but as I look at him, he suddenly recoils his attempt and backs away. This causes me to back off. I remove Ash's throat.

He coughs and gasps, trying to talk through it. "Did I strike a nerve?" His eyes show a glimpse of fear; yet, he refuses to shut up.

"Let's go, bud. He's not worth it." Storm grabs my arm and leads me away from this situation.

The crowd slowly disbands as I get near them, when suddenly, "I wonder. Is your mom as easy as you are?" I stop in my tracks. "I mean, there's no daddy in the picture. One would have to assume she's getting dicked somewhere. Who's to say it's only one man?"

"Chance?" Storm tries to get through, "Ash, shut up!" He tries to make me budge, but his attempts are futile. "Chance. Your eyes. What's happening?" His voice begins to get drowned out by static. I sense another presence, watching me amidst this commotion. All I see is red. The thought of tearing him apart. In this very moment, I want nothing more than for Ash to swallow his words, starting with his tongue. I feel the weight of my rage strangling me. I charge Ash and pounce on him, dragging him by the throat along the pavement, hearing his pleads die away along with the blood being smeared behind us. I then pick him up, one handed, and tighten my grip, harder and harder, until the blood can be seen around his bulging eyes. He kicks, but his attempts don't weaken my hold. Suddenly, he smiles, and his face begins to look a lot like mine.

"Do it," he says. I begin to loosen my grip when he insists further, "Do it! You are weak. You will always be weak. You will never amount to anything so long as you refuse to be anything other than who you are . . . just do it!" He reaches for his stained face and slowly buries his fingers beneath his eyes, scooping them out without an ounce of restraint. "Look. I started the deed. Now finish it . . . Your mother never loved you. You're an obligation she had no choice but to care for. You're a burden she'd walk out on the second she's given the chance. That's why she's not concerned when you're put in danger. She prays for the day you slip up and eat it. Your death would spark the light that hasn't held flame since the day you burdened her life with your existence."

"Shut it!" I plunge him into the ground, a sudden crack blessing my ears as his words become no more. The damage doesn't stop there. I ball both fists together, hammering his skull until it becomes putty under my skin. "Shut up! Shut up!" Storm grabs my arm. I look at him, but his eyes are unsympathetic to say the least.

"Face it, bro. Everything said is true. You are nothing. Let it out and quit lying to yourself by stating otherwise."

"Storm, what are you saying?" I back away in disbelief, running my bloodied hands through my hair.

"Open your eyes, bro. You're a monster. Stop acting as if you're this pariah sent to help others who never asked for it. You take what you want and care none to the consequences." He pulls me in. "Take any of these qualities Ash has pointed out for you and ask yourself. Do these sound like the qualities of a hero?" I look around at all the shocked, twisted faces of my surroundings and see mother.

"You are unraveling," she whispers. Everything begins to spin. Reality begins to strike. Before realizing it, I take Storm's head and smash it into the bloodied ground beneath my feet, the ground in which Ash's flesh was used to mop away the gray. His head bursts on impact. Even after death, his lips continue to speak. "That's it. Don't hold back. Let it out."

I grab my head and scream, an act that causes unforeseen repercussions. Bodies get blown back and the ground beneath me crumbles. "What do you want from me!" I continuously slam his face into the curb, next to Ash as his head begins to soften on impact, making a sloshing noise with every plunge.

"I just want you to be honest with yourself. Who are you?" I reach into his mouth, tearing away at his jaw with both hands, silencing him once and for all. I run my hands through his blood and begin to smear it on my face, tasting it on my upper lip.

"Why did you have to go and say all that, Storm?" I ball up as my name can be heard, continuously calling out to me. Suddenly,

Storm's innards begin to rewind, and his death becomes undone. I wake up . . . in a sense.

I'm staring into Ashton's blackened eyes. He's out of breath but continues to attempt pushing me off him. "You gonna eat me like you did that criminal?"

"How—"

"Small town. You're worse than I am, Ryder. See it, or don't. I may be some pathetic bully, but you . . . you're a closeted psychopath, spiraling out of control. How do you live with yourself? How do you stay so calm in circumstances such as the ones that have been handed to you? It's because you are a monster. There's no other explanation. The only reason you could be that calm is because no matter what gets thrown at you, your darkness overshadows theirs. There's something going on that you are covering up, and I fear that. But I'm not going to back down, till I find out what you're hiding."

I grab his face, whispering, "Stay away from me if you know what's good for you." With one quick push, I slam his head into the pavement.

He cries out, "You cracked my fucking head!"

"Not scared of a little blood, are ya?" The horror plastered on everyone's faces as I grab Ash's shirt and pull him towards me, head butting his face. "In a way, this is all your fault. I would've walked out, but you had to show your chops. You had to be superior." I pick him up by the throat with one arm and tighten my grip. He chokes on his own words as he tries to tell me to stop. I drop him as he lands on his knees. I grab his hair and force his face down to my knee. I toss him aside and place a foot down onto his ankle, slowly putting all my weight into it. His hands tighten, trying to grab onto the ground. His eyes open and close as he begins to lose consciousness, due to blood loss. I hold his eyes open for him, so he can witness it all. "Can't have you fall asleep." I straddle him, throwing punches left and right across his face until I hear Storm behind me.

"Chance! Stop! You're killing him!" I look up at my friend, and the new principal standing beside him. I study the expressions of my peers. When this started, they were smiling, laughing, and enjoying the humiliation. Now, they are frozen with fear. Some look as if they're about to vomit.

I sit quietly in the Principal's office as she sits across from me with her legs crossed. My fists feel stiff from the blood that has had time to dry. "Are you aware of what you have just done? A student has been sent to the hospital because of you. For your own sake, you better hope he doesn't die in the E.R. Chance? Chance! Are you listening to a word that I say?"

"Uh, sorry. I've been spacing out."

"Yes, I could tell. What's happening to you? You have changed. I have never seen you like that."

"Principal Skyy?"

"What."

"Is he alright?"

"Funny how one shows concern in these types of moments. Do you surely care about his well-being, or are you only asking to gain sympathy from me?" I just sit here, calmly with my hands on my lap. "Look, Chance. I'm the Principal of the school, and regardless of your view on me, I understand what goes on. I understand that Ash is a troublesome kid and quite the troublemaker, but that does not give you the right of way to hurt him in the way you have done so. He, like you, is my student at this school. As long as that status remains, you are my responsibility to the point where you graduate."

"Then why have you not intervened?"

"Excuse me."

"I think you heard me. You said you understand what goes on in this school, but do you? The harassment, the remarks, the bullying. Do you take notice of that, or just in moments like this? Do you take notice of the fact that Mr. Lite practically harasses his female students with excessive amounts of very uncomfortable ogling? The fact that he stares at their asses as they leave the classroom, then leaves shortly after everyone is gone and heads directly to the bathroom for about twenty-five minutes of break. Every single fucking day, as if it's a routine. God must know what he does in there every day for that amount of time after getting an eye full. Do you notice that the coach for the football team harasses his players as a way to sharpen them up? I notice these things. As for the fight. I know it was wrong. Hell, I almost walked out. I understand that I was in the wrong, but that doesn't dismiss all that Ashton has gotten away with. This isn't the only fight that has happened this year. Ash constantly bullies Kyle, but I doubt you noticed. You either didn't notice, or you just didn't care. What form of protection do you apply to this school . . . Principal Skyy?"

Principal Skyy sits there calmly, "I understand where you're coming from. That is why I am listening, rather than interrupting your thoughts. I feel our time is done. You may leave." Slowly, I stand, waiting for a catch. "Go straight home. I contacted your mother. Make sure to keep your phone at your side. You may need to answer questions."

"So, I am going to jail?"

"That all depends on the outcome."

Once I get home, I close the door to my house, trying not to slam it. "Is that you, Baby?"

"Yes." I clear my throat. I pass the living room to see her sitting rather calmly on the sofa. "I'm going to my room."

"Just hold on. I received a call. I think we need to talk. Please, sit down."

"Like I said, I'm heading to my room."

"I said sit! Please."

"Can't this just wait! Please, God!"

She's taken aback at this unusual outburst. "You have changed."

"Yes. I've been told that." I take a breath to calm myself. "Sorry. I just need some time. Do you think, maybe, we could talk tomorrow? I'm tired."

"We can talk now if you wouldn't mind. You put a kid in the E.R. You expect me to just stand idly by?"

"Isn't that what you do? I cause a panic and you clean up after it?"

She looks hurt. "Chance. I've never felt the need to punish you, but you're going too far. Have I kept secrets from you? Yes. That doesn't give you permission to go moody and act like a child having a tantrum. We are going to have this talk whether you like it or not."

"So now you act like a mom."

"What? I will not have you speak to me like that. From this day onward, you are grounded. That means no games, no phone, and no friends."

"Oooh, a grounding. Least you're stepping up to the role."

"Go to your room."

"Excuse me."

"Go to your room!" She's to the point of tears.

"Fine."

She grabs her coat and heads for the door, "Now, if you'd excuse me. I have to deal with your problem."

"How do you figure to manage that? The deed is done."

"The same way I have your entire life. Room, now. We'll speak, later."

I close my door and immediately drop dead on my bed, unable to move. My phone buzzes a couple times. A couple messages from Storm and Dani.

XIV

Mother has set off to bed long before the need to sleep overpowers me when suddenly, my eyes open to the sound of a silent thud and a shush. I make my way to my door and slowly open it to listen in to the voices of three people trying to make no noise.

"Did you hear that?"

"It's just your mind playing tricks on you."

"I don't know, man."

"Jesus Christ. This house is nice. These people must be fuckin' rich."

"Of course, they're rich, dumbass. You think you could afford to live here on minimum fuckin' wage. I think not."

"Who lives here? A fuckin' doctor?"

"Nah. Just a punk ass kid and his mom. Funny, though. With a house like this, you'd think they'd be big news, but they keep to themselves. They're not high profile or anything. I've passed this house a lot on scavenges. The mom's always here, and when she's gone, it's not for long."

"You're saying they're probably home?"

"It's fucking 1 in the morning and the car's here. How stupid can you be? Of course, they're home."

"Shh." A third voice silences the other twos' dialogue. "We're here on a fuckin' job. It'd be of great help if the two of ya would pipe down. Yes, they're home and most definitely asleep since no one's shown, yet. I plan on them staying like that. So, shut the fuck up . . . Men. You can't work with them."

I slowly try to sneak past my door without opening it any further, but it makes a creak. "There it is again. That noise."

"Jesus. If you heard something, check it out. Try not to make a ruckus. It'd be a shame if we had to leave with our hands dirty. I just bought these gloves."

I leave my door as is and rush back to my bed, getting under the covers. I hear heavy footsteps as my door creaks further open. *God, this door sure makes loud creaking noises. Just how old is this house?* The thing about creaky doors, is that, in the mornings and afternoons, the door doesn't seem as loud compared to the dead silence of night where that's all you seem to hear. One swift motion is needed to make sure the creak happens as fast and quietly as possible. I feel a presence above me. Even through my eyes are shut, it's as if the darkness just became darker. "Sleep tight, kid. I'd stay here if I were you. We'll be out quickly." The thick scent of rum runs off his breath as he speaks quietly above me. I hear his footsteps grow distant as my door shuts behind him. I should stay put, but I can't. I make my way to the door and with one swift, tiny motion, I pull the door open just enough for my body to sneak through. As I move my foot forward to escape, my eyes meet the narrowed eyes of one of the intruders. I open my mouth as his big, ape-like hands crash against it, silencing me. He steps into my room, closing the door after him. "Just couldn't resist, could ya?" His eyes aren't what I'd expect. They almost seem sorrowful. Given the scent of his breath, I'd say he's near drunk. Buzzed at the least. He's a bigger, husky ape of a man, about 5'11" with an estimated 52 waist. His exceptional strength is fitting for one who resembles a barrel-shaped Italian Mob boss, if that boss had a reddish goatee with thinning red strands holding his hair piece together. He moves me to my bed, practically throwing me to it, and pins me down with both of his hands slowly tightening around my throat. "You should've stayed in bed, kid. I'll make this quick." A kid of my size holds no challenge, nor poses a threat of any to a man built like a mini gorilla. All I know is, no matter the size, every man shares a weakness. You've just got to know how much force to throw into it. I angle my knee as he continues to relieve me of my final breaths and thrusts it up as it crashes into the bigger man's jewels. Instantly, he releases me with his eyes widened. The first moment I get, I push up on his chest, trying to get his weight off me until he crashes to the floor. The other two most definitely heard that. I jump on top of the bigger man and quickly knuckle him dead center in the throat with enough force to pass through a few layers. He suddenly throws me to the side like nothing as he coughs up blood into his palm, stumbling into my dresser. Out of the corner of my eye, I see another man enter my room.

"Butch!"

"Don't. I got this." The ape, known as Butch by the smaller thief, pushes the dresser to the side as he wipes the blood from his lips. "You've got spunk in you, kid. I've never had one your size get the best of me."

"I'm not done, yet."

"Why can't you be a normal kid and scram?" He rushes me, and I do the same. He extends his arm, preparing a punch as I duck under his fist. "Nice maneuver, kid, but if you think—" I climb on his back the moment his fist misses me and slam both of my fists onto both sides of his face. He backs up into a wall to rid of me as he takes a knee, cupping his face.

"Hurts, doesn't it." The face is fragile, especially when you get targeted on both sides of it, simultaneously.

"You bitch."

"Butch, is it? Just leave. I'll ignore the damage done to my walls and even forget your faces. I don't want to hurt you."

"Believe me. The feeling is mutual." Slowly, he makes his way towards me, clenching his fists.

"What's your objective, here? Money?"

"Like I'd tell you." He punches a chip out of the wall as I evade contact.

Wow. That would have killed me, probably. "Listen. You're obviously the brawn. I heard a woman. She sounded like she could've been your boss, or at least the leader of this operation. What's she paying you? I can pay you more if you just leave."

"For someone in your position, you sure talk a lot." I avoid another punch thrown, and another.

"Seriously, man. You caught me on a bad night. Let's not do something we'll regret."

"I have my orders, and I'll follow through whatever the cost."

"Is it that woman downstairs? She the ringleader?"

"You don't know the half of it."

"By all means, I'm all ears."

"You're fucked up in the head, you know that? A normal kid would have called the cops, but you haven't once reached for the phone. Just what are you planning?"

I slide past him, kicking his knee in as he loses balance. "Now, who's talking a lot?" He grunts, holding on to his leg for support. "I'd like to see you charge me now."

"Jesus!"

"I'll be damned if I'm bested by some petty homewreckers. After all I've done. I didn't kill my principal, nearly kill Ash, and be put in the position I'm in to be killed off by some powerless nobody on some worthless home invasion mission." I take a deep breath, realizing what I said. "What's happening to me? How messed up must I be to think these thoughts?" I turn away from Butch. "I've gotten away with so much shit, and have I payed the consequences? No. I'm just getting worse." I wait a couple seconds, turning to face this man on the ground. "Well, aren't you going to finish the job? Why haven't you moved, you worthless sack of—"

"You're hurting . . . You're on the verge of unraveling."

"What would you know? You couldn't possibly understand what I'm going through."

"You're right. I'm a coward. Always was. I'm not violent in nature. Never saw the point."

"Then why are you here?"

"Would knowing that really lighten my punishment? I'm not doing this without reason, and I don't expect to come out unscathed . . . but, that's besides the point. What is this about killing? You can't be serious, or are you?"

"It's complicated. You wouldn't understand."

He gets a little closer to me, without the intent to kill. "Maybe not. Or maybe, I just might. Keeping this stuff bottled is never good for you. You can go years, shouldering this, but sooner or later, you will snap. Considering where you stand, you don't have years to waste. I'll listen and try to understand. You don't seem too far gone to at least make a difference."

"First off, I don't fully understand this. I'm supposed to know everything there is to know about me, but I don't. Mother kept me in the dark for far too long, and now, I don't think knowing would change the outcome. It's too late. There were moments where I lost control and almost killed others, too. I don't know what's happening. There's something dark inside me. I know it sounds over exaggerative, but it's there." I don't know why I'm telling him this, but something about him, despite his actions, doesn't scream cold-blooded murderer.

"Blood lust. I've seen it first-hand. I, on the other hand, don't have it. Some people are born fucked up. Others grow up in a bad environment that makes 'em that way. About that principal, do you attend Cambridge High School? . . . I see. I heard about that incident. I don't know why, or what brought you to it, but I am sincerely sorry that you had to do something so brutal at such a young age."

"I don't seek your sorrow. I am simply explaining what I've done, nothing more. Why are you showing sympathy, anyway? You came here with your mind set on killing me. Now you're apologizing after hearing what I've gone through?"

"I didn't . . . I don't want to kill you. I told you to stay in bed. We came here to do a job."

"What job?"

"I don't know the full story, but we're here for a weapon. Anything else, we can have. He just came out of the shadows and recruited us. We've been chosen for our strengths. The woman has leadership to keep us in check. I am the brute strength. That doesn't really help if violence disgusts me. He latched on to my weakness, and I volunteered. Not like no was an answer that would allow me to live, afterwards. I have killed, but I have regretted every single one. I haven't just taken a person. I've taken someone's brother, their sister, a parent—a loved one. The one who came in here to help me? He's a killer, through and through. He does the job when I won't. I never wanted this life."

"What was the weakness that made you succumb?"

"Do you have a sibling?" I narrow my eyes at the question, then shake my head. "I see. I have a sister. We grew up in an abusive household. I wanted to escape to make something of myself. She wanted nothing more than to stay by my side. My father would constantly rape my mother in front of us, then he'd head to work. My mother was too weak to leave, so she took her anger out on us when it was just the three of us. Eventually, I couldn't do it, anymore. I took my sister and we left. We were homeless, but as long as we had each other, we had enough. Eventually, she got sick. She's dying. She's currently in the back of a long wait list, but I fear I don't have the time. She's very weak. Every day is a risk. So, I don't want this. But, what else could I do?"

"All you need is the money. I'm terribly sorry about your sister. How much is needed? You can have the money and leave. Leave this whole life behind you."

"Wish it was that easy. I can't leave. Not without this weapon."

"What is this weapon? You can have it."

He opens his mouth and tries to speak through his tears, but suddenly drops as a loud bang fills my ears. I watch as a puddle forms around Butch's head.

"My god, he's weak. What a waste, too. I leave for a couple minutes and he shares his life story. Oh well. If you ask me, three is too many people to retrieve a weapon." He holds the gun up to me with a serious look on his face. "Where is it, kid?"

I stare at Butch's limp body. "Seriously, you just made a big mistake."

"Doubtful. I will have you tell me the location of this weapon."

"I have no idea what you're talking about."

"Don't play stupid with me. You have to know where it is."

"Sorry."

He presses the gun up to my throat and slowly moves his finger, then stops. I close my eyes, awaiting my death, but it doesn't come. The gun gets removed from my person. "I wish I could mop the floor with you, but that wasn't the mission . . . Though killing you would be delicious, I have no plans of dying, myself."

"So, you're the crazy one?"

"Butch talks too much."

"He's a big man, yet, I took him. You're half his size. If you're not going to kill me, then what exactly are your plans on winning?"

"Breaking your kneecaps is an option. Prying off your fingernails. Pulling out your teeth, one by one, with a wrench. So many options. Gotta love loopholes."

"You're one sick bastard."

"So, I heard you killed your principal. If that's true, then I'd say there's more than one cold-blooded killer in here. You have no right to judge me when your hands are dirty, themselves."

I jab forward, knocking him to the ground. He drops the gun, wiping the blood from his nose. "After hearing Butch's story, I actually felt sorry for the sap. For you, a killer, I'd find no trouble putting you in your place."

"That's quite a jab there, Boyo. What other surprises do you hold?" He jumps up and lashes out at me. I manage to catch a fist in my palm as I bend it back, slowly, causing him to kneel. "This . . . pain. I want more." He kicks my feet out from under me, crawling on top. "You are a gem in my eye. I'd love to mount you to my wall, oh, but sadly, you're forbidden. Maybe just the hand."

"Like hell." I press my feet to his stomach and throw him back. I rush him, countering his attacks.

"You're pretty quick there. So unexpected." I palm him in the face just to have him step off as I pin him to the floor. I grab his wrist and slowly begin to press my fingers into his surfacing veins. His back arches, and he grits his teeth. "You're quite the sadist. At such a young age, too. Please, allow me to mutilate you. Anything. An arm. A leg. Something you won't miss."

"How fucked up can one be? You disgust me to the highest point of the definition. This world doesn't need you."

"Does it need any of us? Think about it. We're all working together to kill this planet, with the false idea that we're saving it. Think the garden of Eden. It was beautiful until Adam and Eve came along. Come to think of it, that's when the first sin occurred. Did it not?"

"I highly doubt that eating an apple counts as a sin."

"Isn't it, though? To be told not to, but to have the urge to disobey. That's lust. Lust needn't be sexual. It's just the unfightable desire to attain something. That, my pupil, is called lust, and lust is one of the seven deadly sins. But the angels adore us because of our flaws. That's what I call unconditional love. To love someone, given all their flaws, without asking them to change. They love us. God put us here; yet, at the same time, our flaws are killing his greatest creation: Mother nature, herself."

"You're not just crazy. You're textbook-delusional."

"Flattery won't get you anywhere." I have my hand against his throat and press up, with my knee pressed into his crotch. His face is pain-stricken, but at the same time, enjoying it. His hand grabs my arm and slowly pushes it back. He grabs a knife from its sheath and comes at me with it. "I have decided. Hand, it is." He swings the blade without aim and corners me into a wall. "Can you try, and act scared for me. It's no fun when you're like this."

"Sorry to disappoint."

"No worries. I'll just have to cut deep until you show me the face I so crave."

"If you have no intention of killing me, then why did your little queen down there say that it'd be a shame to dirty your hands?"

"What do you think I'm doing now? She never said the word 'kill' because we can't. We can still make you bleed."

"Ah, I see. And to think you'd kill me."

"Excuse me."

"You can't take my life, and that is why you're not leaving this house alive."

"You speak big words. I like you."

"Glad to hear, but the feeling's far from mutual." I push him back into a wall, feeling small cuts form on my skin, due to his blade. I grab his hand with the knife as I make him drop it. "Goodbye." His smile slowly fades as he realizes the secondary blade I have managed to pierce into his abdomen. I twist the small weapon in place, hearing his insides turn and the blood gush out in spurts. I take the knife out and thrust it back in, only to repeat the cycle a few more times. I drop the bloody weapon to the floor, inserting a couple fingers into the wound, wriggling my fingers about. He bites his tongue. "I thought you liked pain. A shame to find out you lied." He tries to clout me, but I quickly grab his arm and throw him to the ground. I retrieve the lost blade and plunge it into his eye, feeling some tension until the blade pushes through it. Some of his blood manages to spray my face. His body shakes until his movement comes to a halt, with his one good eye staring blankly, right at me. I stand up, feeling the puddle beneath my bare foot, nearly slipping as I make way to my door. I make my way to the living room, where the third intruder is most likely waiting. I haven't a clue as to why she has not encroached or intervened on my blood-thirsty episode. It's dark, so I can't make out anything. I flick the switch near the wall's corner only to be jumped from behind. I feel the sharp edge of a weapon being held against my throat. How many times in a day can I be put into this position? The switch suddenly gets switched off.

"To think a kid could overpower those two idiots. You are something."

"Wish I could say the same. Might as well put the knife down. I know you can't kill me."

"Those two talk too much. I guess now, I know why you're to be kept alive. He must want you to himself."

"He?"

"Demons, living amongst us. Who knew? I never thought I'd witness that power in my life. Come here for a stupid weapon, he said. In and out, he said. At first, I was like, why, but after what was shown to me, this weapon must be the real deal. I can't even touch it with my own hands, ha."

"And you say they talk a lot."

"No need to be rude." She shoves me against the wall with both my hands behind my back as she whispers into my ear. "You'd make an adorable pet. How old are you, boy?"

"Like that's important."

She pushes me into the wall harder, bending my arms. "Answer my question." I feel her teeth graze my lobe, then I'm turned around to face her, leaving less than a couple inches between our faces. "Seventeen? Eighteen?"

"Sixteen."

"Still going through puberty. Have you ever been with an older woman?" Her tongue trails along my cheek. "Ooh, looks like I hit a nerve. You know . . . I can do things you've most-likely never witnessed from a high school bitch." I can see bits and pieces of this woman in the darkness. The closer she is to me, the more I can see her. She has auburn hair. This much I can make out. Her eyes are light. Her figure is shapely as I feel her rather large breasts being pressed into my chest. "So, you game?" She grabs my hand and presses it against her breast as my hand involuntarily squeezes.

"Why are you doing this?"

"I'm just having fun." Her face nears mine until our noses are touching. She's beautiful. To suddenly sleep with a woman who is your enemy? It's true that I find her beautiful, but I try to fight the urge. She's a woman in her mid-twenties, maybe twenty-seven. "Tell me," she whispers into my ear. "Where is the weapon? There's no point in hiding it now."

"Like I told them, I don't know of this weapon you seek." Her hand circles my stomach, then suddenly grabs me by my erection. Her eyes widen, and a smile forms.

"Is this the weapon?"

"You know damn well, it isn't."

"For someone in your state, you're really holding back. I applaud your effort."

"I'm going to ask nicely. Please leave. I gave them the same option. Butch almost took it. This is seriously not the night to mess with me."

"Why? Girlfriend broke up with you? Flunked an exam?"

"You're moments away from regretting finding out."

"I have no intension to leave. A lot of money comes with that weapon. With those two out of the picture, that just means more for me. Besides, I already took the job. Leaving without it is not an option. Failure results in a certain someone, staring into the eyes of her maker."

"If you don't leave, then I'll kill you, myself."

"You're not a killer . . . Well, I guess you are."

"The other two were the ones who carried out certain dirty deeds. You're the smarter one, I take it. Are you as violent as them?"

"I don't resort to violence, but if I must. They do the dirty work. I'm, what you call, a seductress. I can seduce almost anyone, women, and men alike. There're more ways to get what you want than to kill. Killing is so messy. How do you think certain people get into office? Women take work, but men? Once the tent is pitched, there is very little you can do to fight that urge. That's why men are weak. Succumbing to their sexual needs. It's so primitive, but it does have its perks." Her hand squeezes as her lips take hold of mine, tugging at the bottom lip as she pulls away. "Looks like you'll need extra motivation." She grabs my hand and reaches it around her, placing it upon her hindquarters. "You like that? I can tell. It's fine if you don't hold back. You can have me all to yourself." She sways her hips as my hands cup her shapely buttocks. "You've got quite the sexual aura, yourself. You're fighting the urge quite well. If I didn't know better, I'd say you were part incubus, yourself."

"No." I pull back and force her off me. "I won't succumb to your siren call."

"Siren? I like that. But, how can you fight the urge, with that post, still throbbing between your legs. It's got to hurt by now."

"Stop talking erotically. No one speaks like that."

"They do when they're making love. It's to set the mood. You feeling anything, yet? . . . Are you, by any chance, a virgin?"

"Not in the slightest."

"You're acting like one. Are you scared? Or—Wait. Are you gay?"

I force her to the ground, landing on top of her. Ringing occurs in my ears as the familiar headache comes back to me. "I'm not gay." My lips clash with hers as her hands rub my back. I unbutton her top and lift her bra, revealing her pale melons in sight.

"Yes. God. Take me. We both want this."

"I can't. I won't. How old are you?"

She turns the tides, sitting on my crotch with her breasts exposed, "Never ask a woman her age. I cannot stress that enough. And you're sixteen. What do you have to be scared about? When you turn eighteen, it's not like you're going to think any differently than you do now. You're doing this now. When you're of age, can you say that what we're doing now would've been any different? No. You'd make the same decision, so don't even act like I'm taking advantage of you. Maybe this will help." She tugs at my pants, releasing me from them. "Yes. I'll do this, then I'll search while you're sleeping."

"You're stupid, ya know that? A gun was fired not too long ago. You think the cops won't be here in a bit?"

"I'm counting on it. Bad things have happened in this shit town, and the cops haven't showed. We live in a place where violence is the only way. I'm actually surprised you haven't come across people like me before, searching for gems or whatever you have in this luxury home. Now, back at it. I'm going to take this, and I'm going to use it as I please. You killed my two men with ease. Why are you holding back with me? Because of this guy. Typical man." She tosses her top to the side; her bra follows. "I'm eager to see just what you can do with this weapon."

She's right. I can't fight it. I want to, but I can't. Is that all I am? How can I kill so easily, but fall prey to a pair of perfect breasts? And the feeling of her round assets. This feeling is all too familiar. If she was out to kill me, I guess she would've succeeded. Or, am I only falling victim because she can't kill me? The thrill of doing this because I'm to live by her hand. I never thought of how my sex addiction would be applied in this situation. I feel a sudden tightness, then her cries of pleasure. My eyes haze in and out. One moment, I'm atop her, then the next, she's riding cowgirl. Suddenly, I have her leg raised over my shoulder as I'm feeding on her moans. Scene by scene, I find myself in a different scenario. I come to my senses as the headache fades. I have her arms held back with her body pushed forward and her derriere slamming at my pelvis. I release her as she drops to the floor, heavily breathing. I turn her to face me. She shows a tired smile as her body trembles.

"How can you . . . continue on like this? You're a fuckin' child."

"Funny. I strictly remember that not being an issue with you." I bite down on her neck as she claws at my back, her body jolting. I finally lose stamina as it goes flaccid over her stomach. I drop down on top of her. We both try to regain our breaths.

"You are full of surprises, aren't ya? In all my years . . . You have bested my top moments."

"Then, I guess you have to try harder with the others or find better qualified slaves. Now, about my proposal. I'm willing to overlook this."

"I can't." She sighs, "Like I said, I'll be killed if I leave empty-handed."

"Why in the hell would you take a job like that?"

"I've stolen from many people. I thought, maybe, how hard could it be to steal a stupid knife. The fact that you could take those two? That was a fucking shock to me." She chuckles, "I guess these are my last moments."

"If I knew of the weapon you're searching for, I'd give it to you. But, I don't."

"Just my luck. That's that, then."

"Maybe, there's another way."

"Look at you, trying to think of a way to save a woman you would've killed a couple hours ago. How time flies. May I say, you'll make a woman very happy someday. Whatever these killer instincts of yours are, try to kill them. You're a good kid. You shouldn't be caught up in this world of ours . . . perhaps, a peaceful life was never in the cards for you."

"Why are you talking like these are your last words?"

She grabs the unique knife and places it in my hand, holding it point down in her direction. "It's easier this way. He'll make my death slow. At least like this, I can die with a small sliver of final happiness, here, with a man as caring as you. Hehe. Listen to me blabber on. You never know what your last words are going to be until that time has come."

"Shut up. You're not dying."

"May I have your name?"

"Um, Chance."

"Well, Chance, I hope you live a happy life." Before I am able to say anything, she pulls me down to her body, with my hands on her belly, and the knife firmly implanted inside her.

"What? No." I release my hands from the weapon, as her blood oozes out and smears against my bare skin. In her final moments, she smiles, as her chest compresses. Her veins pulse and surface, her skin growing paler with every second. Suddenly, she stops. Her head tilts to the side and her hand, grabbing mine, falls to the floor. Even in this moment, I can't quite bring myself to cry over her. Something gets thrown at my back as I look behind me.

"Go shower." Mother stands across the room from me, averting eye contact.

"You were here the whole time? What the fuck. You didn't do anything."

"I felt that you could handle them."

"What kind of excuse is that from a mother to her son? People died, and you tell me to shower?"

"I understand your anger. Please, put the towel on. You must shower before the cops arrive. It's been a while, so I feel they should be on their way."

I wrap the towel around my waist. "We need to talk."

"I agree."

"What?"

"You said you'd talk tomorrow. Well, it's tomorrow. Just go shower. We'll handle the police, then we'll talk. We have some things to discuss. Some secrets I must relieve myself of. You may even hate me after, but I need to do this."

I stare at her in disbelief, then walk by her to the shower. I drop the towel as I step into the warm shower, feeling the droplets ricochet off my shoulders. My hair falls over my eyes as I spit out water at my feet. I feel a presence with me but am not certain until I feel something graze my back. "You haven't forgotten me, have you?" I turn around, but no one's there.

"Who is it? Show yourself."

"I'm not a ghost."

"No shit. Who are you?"

"Your soulmate."

"Seriously."

"Seriously. I aim not to lie to you. I only want to get closer to you. I did make a promise, didn't I? No matter what, we'd find each other."

"If you're not a ghost, then why can't I see you? Wait, are you—?"

"Remember me, yet?"

"Why are you here?" I receive no answer, so I ask again. Again. No answer. I can hear small talk coming from downstairs. I make my way to the living room, where officers await me.

"Are you Chance Ryder?"

"I am." *Who the fuck else would I be?*

"We'll need the two of you to come with us to the precinct to answer a few questions."

"Um," I look at Mother and she just nods, "Okay."

Down at the precinct, Mother and I are questioned in different rooms, probably to make sure the stories add up. She didn't tell me what to say, so I assume she wants me to tell the whole truth to an extent. Leave out the details that could make me sound guilty, like how she's probably leaving out the part where she knew what was going on, how she just sat back and watched. She'll probably say she was asleep and woke up at the last bit, which means there's probably nothing to compare to her story. Just to be safe, I should tell the truth on all parts that make me sound like the victim.

"Chance Princeton Ryder. Lives at 676 Monroe Boulevard. Attends Cambridge High School. Hm. You seem to skip school a lot. In the last three months, you've attended, maybe half of that time. Playing hooky can get you in trouble, you know that, kid? Surprised they haven't visited your home. It's a big mistake on your mom's part for allowing this."

"We live in a pretty fucked up place. My attendance at school should be the least of your problems. Aren't we here about a different matter?"

"You've got some balls on you, kid. Talking to an officer like that. You're either brave, or too stupid to know otherwise. You are right, however. So. The intruders. I want to hear your side of the story. Your mom was pretty chatty in her sitting. Your story better match up."

"What? My mother was asleep."

The officer sits back in his chair as I hope I didn't say something wrong. It is the truth, after all. "Right, you are. She said as much. Wanted to double check that. If you would have continued, then that would have meant that one of you are lying. She did, however, say that she walked in around a certain moment. You may not have a story to compare to but try to refrain from lying. Your story should end around the time your mom walked in. Okay. Let's hear it."

"I was about to fall asleep when I heard something. I opened my door to listen in and heard a few voices."

"So, what did you do when you heard them?"

"I was about to sneak downstairs to get a closer look."

"A closer look? At the intruders? Are you that stupid, or does danger excite you? Just know that all answers are being recorded as we speak. Don't let that stop you. If you're innocent, then you'll be found out as such."

"You sure about that? Innocent people have been found guilty before. Anyway, yeah, I was about to sneak downstairs, but one of the guys heard my door creak as I did so. I got back in bed as I heard one of them come into my room. He said something strange though, like he knew I was awake and trying to warn me against acting."

"And like the little curious ball of wonder you seem to be, you couldn't resist."

"That is correct. I got up when he left, but he was outside my door, ready. He apologized beforehand."

"Now, why would a cold killer apologize for doing what he does best?" The officer stares, not knowing whether the story sounds real or not. To be honest, it does sound ridiculous. It sounds more like a filler plot in a story to make it last longer, like a little side quest.

"He hated doing what he does or did. He told me in his last minutes." His eyes narrow. "No, I didn't kill him. He said he was doing these jobs because of a sick relative, but the jobs only made him feel worse. He needed the money."

"Okay, I'm on board. If you know that much, then you're speaking at least a little truth. We did background checks on the three. The one you're talking about is named . . .? If he told you as much about a dying relative, I'm guessing he had to at least give a name, or maybe you heard someone call him by it."

"Butch. Well, he was giving me this talk. He even cried a little. I asked him how much he needed."

"You offered him money?"

"Yes. If you're not aware, I have quite a bit of it. I felt sorry for him. I wanted to help him."

"So, instead of donating to a cause for the better, you offer a criminal money? Because you're sorry. I'm sorry. No one is that nice. You're lying."

"Assuming is dangerous, officer . . ." I glance at his badge, ". . . Freeman. I wanted to give him money to help his sister. I'm telling you what happened. I have no reason to lie because I didn't do anything wrong." He gestures with his hand for me to continue. "Before he could respond, he got shot in front of me by his partner. His partner had a few screws loose. I didn't get a name. He said that Butch was weak, and that the operation didn't need three."

"You said Butch was shot? Because his body had more than a bullet in the head. He had bruising. His kneecap was shattered."

"I did that."

"You said he was telling a story. How'd that happen if you weren't fighting?"

"Before he told me about his sister, we were fighting. He was hesitant a bit. There were a few times where he missed me when he should have hit me. I fought back."

"Against that man?"

"I can handle myself. The psycho who shot him had a go at me. We fought for a while, but it ended up with me, um—"

"You, what?"

"He almost had me, but I found an opening. When it came down to it, I chose my life over his."

"You killed him? In the beginning, you said you did nothing wrong."

"Is defending yourself wrong? I said I did nothing wrong. I didn't say I didn't kill. I got downstairs and she was waiting for me. The third. She was more flirtatious than violent. She tried to seduce me."

"Tried?"

"In the end, we did sleep together. It was her way of getting what she wanted without the need for violence. She said that when it came down to it, all men couldn't resist their lustful urges. She ended up not getting what she came for and killed herself through my hand."

"Excuse me." The officer pinches the bridge of his nose, trying to understand any, if not all of this story.

"She was dead either way. If she left without the objective, she'd be killed by the woman who hired her. She said that at least, this way, she could die on her own terms. She placed the knife in my hand as I was over her. I was refusing, and before I knew it, she plunged the knife into her body."

"That's around the time your mom came in. Okay. The story connects, but it sounds absurd." I did it. I told the officer everything, well almost everything. I left out the part where they weren't supposed to kill me. I feel that if I told the officer that they were specifically supposed to keep me alive, it'd make the case that much more difficult.

"So, are we done?"

"On the contrary. You're a very . . . evasive little guy. You attend a school where your principal was killed. A killer interrupts a certain party, and the cops who were sent to that case have nothing to share of your connection. A movie you just so happen to attend gets targeted. The list goes on. Care to share what the deal is with that? How is it that a simple high school kid came out unscathed and most importantly, mentally intact after all that has happened. Something's going on in this already fucked up little town, and I don't know why, but something tells me you're not far from the center of it all."

"Big accusation from a small-time badge."

"You saying you have nothing to do with these coincidences?"

"I didn't say that. I do, however, know that until I'm of age, you can't force me to say anything without the proper permissions, and a lawyer to oversee it. You could go and get it, but I know I'm in the right place to leave. So, if you have any other questions or accusations, you'll have to wait till I have no choice but to answer. Well officer, am I free to go?"

Mother and I wait in the waiting room for about an hour when we're confronted by a female officer.

"You two can leave. You will be visited a few more times at random to make sure the story stays consistent. Your belongings are with that officer over there."

Back at home, we immediately get down to business. "I'm going to make us a couple sandwiches, then we need to talk."

"Talk? Oh, right. That."

I lay on my bed, looking over to my dresser. Secrets are everywhere. From Austin's mystery phone to the medallion received on my birthday. The scars on my skin and my history that isn't without its missing footage. This house. The money I seem to have, but no job to back it up. I never thought about these specifics. I've lived with what I had, without questioning how it is I've come to be. Obviously, I have memories, but nothing's for certain. For once, I wish I could have a normal life, like Storm, Dani, or Sam. To worry about acne instead of this bullshit.

"Okay, come out!" Mother shouts from the living room.

When I confront her, she's sitting on the couch, holding a picture frame with our sandwiches to the side. She pats the seat next to her, motioning for me to sit. I do just that. I take a glimpse at the frame, and the picture that resides within it. I show a small smile, "Mother?"

"That word." She slightly trembles at the sound. "Who'd have thought that word would make this that much more difficult?"

"Are you alright? You look upset. I'm sorry, really. I know I've been different, lately. Maybe a little difficult to handle. I don't know what's going on with me, but—"

"It's not that. I already know the reason, but that's not the subject we need to talk about."

"What is it then, Mother?"

"Please." A tear escapes her eye. "Don't call me that."

I look down at my lap, unknowing of what to say. I glance at the picture of Father and aim to change the subject. "Do you miss him? Father, that is."

"Your father was loved greatly, as you are, which is why I need to tell you this. Prolonging the inevitable will only make things more difficult later . . . if that's possible."

"If it hurts you so much, then, you don't have to say it. I understand that people have secrets. Even mother and son."

"I said not to call me that."

"Why? Why can't I call you that? I've always called you by that. Would you prefer mom?"

"No. That's worse." She pulls out a picture, well, a torn half of one, anyway. Her thumb is pressed directly on the face."

"You said that you lost that piece."

"Another lie. That's all I ever seem to do, lately. I've had it all these years. I knew that one day, I'd have to tell you. Keeping it hidden for so long has just made it harder. I don't know why I had you call me Mother. Maybe, it's because I wasn't quite a mom. I knew of the secrets I'd be keeping, and a mom doesn't do that. I couldn't have you call me by my name either because that would look bad. It'd sound bad." Tears continue to stream down her face. "I figured Mother was best, but in time, it's made me realize, or remember, who I have taken from you. Who I've replaced." She removes her finger from the face on the severed picture to reveal a beautiful young woman, looking as happy as she could possibly be, with her hand on her inflated stomach.

"Is that—"

"Your true mother. Her name is Beverly. You were the light of her world, even before you were born. I've never seen someone be so happy." Mother looks down, her smile fading. "I meant to—"

"You kept this from me?" I say under my breath.

"What?"

"How could you keep something like this from me! You're not my mother? Then, who the hell are you! Did you take me?"

"No. Of course not. It's not like that. I did nothing illegal."

"Then, why? You adopted me? You could've told me that from the start. I would've understood!"

"Please, sit."

"Uhh! I can't handle all these big bomb shells you seem to have tucked away! It's—It's too much. You know how bad this makes you look?"

"I know!" She suddenly stands, shouting, with a hand over her mouth. "I know. I've wanted to tell you, but I couldn't."

"Why'd you have me call you Mother? We're not even blood."

"Please, lower your voice. Sit. There's m—"

"There's more! Is that what you were going to say?"

"Please. If you'd just sit."

"I need time to think. I'm sorry, but I can't even look at you."

"Where are you going?" She reaches out an arm, trying to grab me.

"Don't fucking touch me! You've lost the right to do anything a mother does with her kid. I don't want to hear your voice! I don't want to see your face! I can't even be near you!"

She's practically on her knees at this point, sobbing. "Please . . . Please. I can change. No more secrets. I promise . . . Please. Don't leave."

"Don't wait up." I open the front door, closing it behind me before she has a chance to respond. I hear my name, faintly, through the door that separates us. Seeing her like this pains me, but I don't know what to do.

I'm out front a familiar house, as I make way to the door, ringing the doorbell, disregarding the time. No one answers. Of course. I give a light knock on the front door, awaiting a voice. I hear light footsteps coming from inside, then the door opens, revealing a black man in a robe and slippers. "Chance?"

"Hey, Mr. Friezone. Sorry to wake you."

"No. I was just doing some light reading. What brings you here so late?"

"I was wondering if I could spend the night, or a few nights."

"Of course. You're always welcome. You are family, after all. Storm should be in his room, probably playing a game or something." Storm's father steps aside, allowing me entrance into the house. "Please. It must be cold out there. Where is your jacket?"

"It's fine."

"Did you walk here?" I nod. "That's a good way to get something. Where's your jacket?"

"Didn't bring one."

"Obviously. Are you alright?"

"Yeah. Why wouldn't I be?"

"Storm told me what happened at school. Obviously, I don't know the whole story, but I've heard enough about this Ash kid to know he probably deserved it. I'm not going to lecture you on the stupidity of violence, but please, next time, try not to go so far. From the looks of it, he hardly touched you."

"I didn't allow him to."

"Anyway, does Storm know you were coming?"

"No. I kinda just showed. Sorry."

"No apologies. Just knock first before you go in. It is late after all and, well, I shouldn't have to tell you the specifics. Just try to keep it down. I'm heading to bed."

"Understood. Good night, Mr. Friezone."

"Good night, Chance. If you want breakfast in the morning, it'll be ready around eight or nine."

"Thank you."

I knock on the door that has light coming through the cracks and hear his voice from the inside. "Come in."

"I open the door and Storm is just on his bean bag, playing a first-person shooting game. "Hey, sorry to come uninvited."

"Chance? This is surely unexpected." He pauses his game and turns to face me, patting the beanbag next to him. I plop down onto the red beanbag as he hands me a controller. "Wanna play? I'll reset it to multiplayer."

"Uh, yeah. Sure."

"So, man. What brings you here? I mean, it's nearly two in the morning for crying out loud. What would you have done if everyone was asleep?"

"Oh, please. You're never asleep this early. If your dad didn't answer, eventually, you would."

"Why didn't you call?"

"This visit was kind of sudden."

"What happened?"

"What?"

"If this was so sudden that you didn't even call, something must be going on. Tell me, man."

"Something at home."

"Really? You two are never arguing. You're like the perfect mother and son."

"Yeah. About that." I explain the revelation of secrets that has been thrown at me in one go. He just sits back in awe. His eyes widen, and his lips pucker the moment I explain that my mother isn't my mother. "At this point, I don't even know what to believe anymore. We were always close. She was always a good friend. We talked about everything. Now it makes sense. It's easy to be more of a friend to your son when you're not even their mother. You don't have that motherly love getting in the way."

"Let me stop you right there. I know you're smart enough to not believe that. You're just not in your right mind set at the moment. So, she's not your mother. Did you give her a moment to explain herself?"

"Well, no, but—"

"You've got to allow someone at least that. There could be more than what's being said. Never accept a portion of a story, man. You should know that. That's how misunderstandings happen."

"I hear you."

"Tell me that when your mind's cleared. First, school, now this. You used to allow someone to explain themselves. I've noticed that you've been steadily changing. The nightmares. The episodes. The violence. I don't know what's going on with you."

"What happened at school was completely unintentional."

"That's what freaks me out. The mere fact that you didn't even have to try. I looked into your eyes. You were lost. You were drowning in your own rage. What divides us from the monsters in the world is restraint."

"So, I'm a monster?"

"No. I didn't mean that. It's just that, you used to be so composed. Relaxed. You do have your moments, but now, you're unrecognizable."

"Yet, you still put up with me. Why?"

"I'm your friend, no, I'm more than that. You're like the brother I always wanted. I'll always be there if you need me. To talk, or whatever. That's what family does. They share with each other. They help each other in times of need. I always thought that, you had no emotions. Hell, you even began to believe that bullshit yourself. Did it ever occur to you, that, maybe, just maybe, you do have emotions? That you've repressed them in an attempt to appear strong."

"No. I'm not faking anything. If I don't show emotion, then it's because there's nothing to feel. I'm not drowning it out."

"Either way, you're starting to show them now. Maybe they were there. You just didn't know it. Now, it's all manifesting at the same time. You're a time bomb. Who knows how long until that last tick?"

"And what do you suppose would be at the end of the ticking?"

"There are many options. Murder is one of them."

"I would never—"

"You already have. You've witnessed things that someone our age shouldn't witness. Hell, no one should have to."

"Anyway, that's not all she told me. That's just one secret."

Storm puts his controller down, crossing his legs. "What else could there be?"

XV

I'm looking into a pair of eyes I've seen all too many times, a face I have come to recognize, as my own. His bangs hang in front of his eyes and a hint of blood can be seen in the corner of his mouth. He stumbles slowly towards me, like a zombie, only, more human. He opens his mouth, but no words come out. I can clearly see tears escape from his bangs' territory. The familiar stranger extends an arm, as if begging for help. I stand still as he struggles to make his way to me. He, then, grabs my wrist, tightening his grip. A breeze comes out of nowhere, sweeping his bangs to the side, revealing a pair of green eyes. The color in them begins to fade, and a darkness begins to take over. Not the type of metaphorical darkness that's used as an artistic depiction of one's anger and morality, but the type of darkness that follows the sun's removal in the sky, only darker. A black gas-like substance begins to consume us, like we're lost in space without the company of the stars to light the way. This other person, the other "me", has a smile on his face, small enough to be barely counted as a smile, but big enough to be visible. Bit by bit, he disappears in an ash-like manner, like the release of a loved one's ashes in the wind. Eventually, I'm alone, floating in a void, with my thoughts as my only company.

"Depressing, isn't it?" A voice comes out of nowhere, but it's different. It's not as if someone is actually speaking to me, but something present in my mind, like when you hear things. When you know the voice isn't real; yet, you can understand every syllable spoken, as if it were.

"Who are you?"

"We've had this conversation. I'd say this is our seventh, maybe eighth time, going over this. It gets tiring. I left you signs. I hoped you'd remember. Then again, most don't remember their dreams, not fully. You'll have an idea, whether it was scary enough to wake you up or not, but you won't have the memory to try to relive it."

"What do you want?"

"Again. Redundant. How did you get those scars on your body?"

"The hell does that—"

"Answer me."

"I don't know. I woke up with most of these. Sometimes, I get hurt in my dreams, I guess. When I wake up, it's as if the injuries sustained in the nightmare followed me. It's odd. It's not 100 percent."

"Meaning?"

"I've been hurt many times in dreams. I don't always wake up in blood. It's like, it's random."

"Don't give me that. Nothing is random. There's got to be something in this head of yours that remembers something. Anything. Those times you woke up injured. Was there, perhaps, something that was consistent? One thing that led to each moment." Images flash in my mind. The only thing that has been constant in my night terrors has been this specific being. "That's a start, I guess."

"I never saw his face, except these eyes that were like nothing I have seen before."

"That's not true. I'm not the only one you have seen with these eyes. Dreams are magical, are they not? They're a gateway to repressed memories if you have any. They just sneak up on you. The thing about dreams is, once you realize where you are, you become the owner of it. Dreams tend to guide you in most cases, but only when you're unaware it's fake. Even in the most bizarre dreams that couldn't possibly be real, you never really think of those things while going through it. Suddenly, you wake up. You don't memorize everything, but then, you're like, 'How the hell did I not know that was a dream?'"

"What is the purpose here? Suddenly, you're my psychiatrist? Wait, are you—"

"You're really stupid in these dreams, aren't you? Out there, you're in control. You were, anyway. You're beginning to metamorphose into something beautiful, something pure."

"How the hell do you know that?"

"Another thing about dreams. Though it isn't real, your knowledge will always be limited to what you already knew. In other words, you're not going to become three times smarter, and know things you never knew just because you're dreaming. It doesn't work like that. It's possible, however, for something you saw, something you read, even if it was a glimpse, to show up in dream form. It's very possible that I'm not even here. You just think I am. Who's to know? You could just be talking to someone whose knowledge is limited to your own."

"Stop. I don't understand. I get that I'm dreaming. Why am I dreaming of talking, though?"

"If you're bored, change it. If you just sit back and enjoy the ride, the dream will lead you. You can choose what to do from there. If you want to change it, you can choose that option, too, but what fun is it if you call all the shots? It is thrilling when you're unknowing of what's to come. That's enough with the lecture, though. I need you to succumb to the power that is eating at you."

"The power?"

"The sudden rage. The anger. Don't hold back who you are. That is how you got here, isn't it? Sometimes, the best way is through. Live through the rage. Do what you have to do in order to feed that hunger. Some serial killers calm down with every kill. It's a part of them. It's like a drug. If someone's genetic wiring is to kill, then kill is what you must do. Going without slowly starts to eat at you. Give in."

"I'm not a killer."

"Of course not. You just handle blood like anything else. You killed a principal. You nearly killed a kid at school, and without thinking about it. Don't get me started on that little break-in incident. Three people went in. None came out—not alive, anyway. Deny it all you want, but that is what it's like to hold back the beast. That's why psychopaths are at their best when they don't hold back. They don't have all that unneeded tension that's built from being contained. You are just like me. Just give in, and clarity is what you'll receive."

"I think I remember exactly who you are now. I'm sorry to disappoint, but the answer is still no. I will not become your little puppet."

"You have me wrong. We're the same. I don't see you as a puppet. I recognize your potential. All I need is for you to stop fighting these urges. Maybe if you just followed where the current took you, you'd have less blackouts. Don't you hate living in a broken film, only remembering portions of the story. This tends to happen when you have an extreme emotional jump, does it not, such as adrenaline."

"You know about that?"

"Of course. I know everything, from your hobbies to your unusually high sex drive. I am you."

"Repeating that isn't going to make me suddenly join you. I believe what I believe."

"Is that all? You believe. It must suck, not to know. Especially with these ongoing secrets that keep getting thrown at you from the shadows. That surely must piss you off."

"So, what now? You going to kill me? Because, here I am, refusing your offer."

"You're right." The voice is different. It's the same sound, but different. I turn to face a man in the shadows. This man is no longer the voice in my head. Something begins to grow in his hands, a weapon. A sword with two snakes wrapped around the hilt. "Gotta love dreams, right? I wish I truly had a weapon such as this, but here is as good as any."

"What are you talking about?"

"All you had to do was give those three idgets a weapon, but you seriously don't know where it is. That makes things troublesome."

"You sent those three? Wait, how? You're not real. Because of you, three people died."

"Well, two people and one monster. I hardly see the issue, here."

"Monster?"

"It was a surprise that you couldn't sense a succudemon when you saw one. Part succubus at least. Your mind is muddled. Probably due to all the times Dora scrambled your memories." I try to visualize a weapon, like the one he manifested, and find myself holding a blade. I can't see his face, except for the green eyes and the shadowing of a smile. He refuses to move as I make contact with his skin. The blade inches its way into his side until a pain overtakes me. I back away, dropping the knife, pressing my hand into my side. A warm sensation floods over it as I can feel the comforting warmth span between my fingers. It's like I've been stabbed, but he didn't get the opportunity. So, how can I be feeling this while he stands as if nothing happened? "Hurts, doesn't it? I know all too well."

"What are you blabbering on about?"

"I know you're not fazed much at the sight of blood, but you don't have to act like you don't feel it. I've been there. It hurts like a bitch, but you're not going to give me the satisfaction of watching you in pain. That's one of the many things we share."

"Kill me, already. If you can."

I get pushed down by a force as a feeling holds me in place, like chains wrapped around my throat, pulling back as I continuously try to push forward. The only thing that does is deprive you of oxygen faster. I feel the point of his sword jab me in the stomach as he pins me down, his body above mine. "You know," the weapon backs away, but he stays put, "Usually, I'd give you two options: to join me, or die: but lately, you've been changing. I was beginning to think you were a lost cause. What do I think now? Hehe. I'm not going to kill you, not when you're so close to being pushed over the edge. I must tell you though. Friends. Family. They're holding you back, or maybe, they provide opportunity. If secrets can make you this vulnerable to the dark urges trying to rip their way out, imagine what having them taken from you can do. Fair warning, little urchin. Ditch the drawbacks. Unless you want to be like me."

"You're making no sense."

"I will. Heed my warning. It'd be a shame if you were to witness all you cherish, burn."

"You even think about—"

"You'll what? You know what happens if you touch me. Friends or survival? Your choice."

"Who are you?"

"We'll meet short enough. The more we converse, the more I feel like we're brothers. I've always wanted a brother."

"This is a dream, yet, I feel like this is real."

"This is very real . . . I must be going. Consider what I've said. In the end, no one can be trusted. No one, except yourself."

"You can't leave! I've still got questions! Hey!" I'm left alone, again, with my thoughts. I hear something shatter like glass, then I'm falling. Hard to tell, since everything's black. My hair whips at my face as I try to retrieve my oxygen. I come to a harsh landing, one that should have killed me. Instead of a splash landing, it's more like hitting a wall. I say wall instead of ground because, initially, I was falling like I was skydiving, belly down, when suddenly, I find myself slamming into something vertical. I get knocked on my ass, rather than slamming onto my stomach. I pick myself up, staring in front of me. The black void that hasn't left my side begins to ripple. Have you ever skipped rocks into a river? Yeah, like that. Like ripples from a lake, the void begins to swirl. I extend my arm forward, watching it disappear into the void. I pull it back into view. Slowly, I step into it, finding myself somewhere slightly lighter. Again, I find myself staring at myself. A lot of "my selves." Each one shows differences in their behaviors. The one in front of me just stands there quietly, smiling. A regular smile, not a creepy one. He holds his hand out, but something's in the way. I reach out, expecting to feel his hand, but end up touching a surface, like a mirror. He breathes on the surface, writing into the fog, "Help." My hand rests on his, when suddenly, I begin to sink into him, inside the mirror. I try to fight the suction, losing balance as I fly into this other realm. I try to move around but can't. I bang on the glass in front of me, but I'm trapped. Out of the shadows comes another individual. He stares into my eyes, adjusting his bangs, like he can't see me, but is staring into our reflection. He tries different angles, making sure his appearance is perfect. The fact that we share a face isn't coincidence. This is my dream, but I'm not able to control it. This must be where I keep all my different sides. It's obvious that the one I'm in front of now is my conceded version, the self that puts appearance above all else. His eyes narrow at me. He gets closer to the mirror that contains me, like he's checking for a flaw. I know it's useless to try to talk to him, since he can't see me or hear me. He walks away, looking pleased with himself.

I hear a bang, not like a gunshot, but something smacking into the glass. I turn around to see a body pressed up against the mirror, being held up against something. This person isn't me. This is a woman's figure, being pinned by a stronger force. I see a couple hands press up to the mirror, being placed on both sides of her legs. I see his face and am not shocked. Those lustful eyes. A woman appears behind him, kissing his neck. This must be the version of me that cherishes the desire to fornicate. I'm forced to watch myself make love from a different perspective. What's the point of all this? Subjecting me to witness the many shades of Chance Ryder. The many versions of myself.

A banshee-like scream fills my ears, making me drop to my knees. I feel a hand grab my shoulder and pull me out of this state of imprisonment. I slam onto my back, staring up at the man who saved me, but his face is as if I just ruined his life. His teeth are gritted, his eyes wide with anger. He pins me down, getting a good crack at my jaw. He continues to slam away with his anger. His rage. Something comes into view. A crowbar smashes this other Chance's jaw bone. The angry Chance has been dealt with, but who do I have to face now?

I turn around, staring at the bare feet of the next individual. I haven't seen his face yet, but I don't need to guess who it is. I already know. His feet are covered, almost wholly, in what can only be looked at as blood. His feet are too covered for this to be his own. It doesn't look as if his feet are damaged. It's as if he has stepped into a puddle of someone else's. I look up slowly, following the blood that's splattered along his thighs. His chest is marked in it as well, like camouflage. His eyes are dead, showing no emotion. His lips are flatlined, neither showing anger nor happiness. An object drops from his hands, landing in front of my face. A blood-splattered butchering knife. He kneels to face me, face to face. The topside of his hand wipes the tears from my cheeks. Tears, I didn't even know I had. His hand lowers to the wound on my side. My body jolts as he spreads the gash with his fingers, plunging them into the open wound without hesitation. I nearly bite my tongue at the sudden pain. My veins surface as my muscles tense up. The sound of my heartbeat pulsates in my ears. The warmth of the blood flowing through my veins becomes known. It's like I'm on a major acid trip. Like synthetic marijuana, spice, filling me with the need to die. I can't die. Not here. He removes his fingers from the stab wound, raising them to his lips, slowly licking off the blood. His body begins to change, not physically. Like a glitch in a game, he begins to phase back and forth, being overlapped by after images of himself. You ever have a video game glitch? Like, let's say, you're in the middle of a fight, and everything freezes, but not completely. A better example would be when your computer screen crashes, and you do everything you can to unfreeze it, like, let's say, click nonstop, 500 times until the screen fixes. By the time it does, it starts to catch up with every single click you've enacted, until you start to see many different pages open, with others simultaneously closing. That's practically what's going on here. This guy constantly shifts, his head rotating left and right, like he's possessed by 8 different spirits trying to take hold at the same time. Suddenly, everything stops.

I hear crying. The man is gone. I get up and follow the next voice. This one sounds like a child. I see the back of someone knelt down at a graveyard. He's smaller. I walk up to him, this kid, and notice the gravestones: Merida Jubilee Hackett—Beloved friend, good inventor; Stormie Raye Friezone—Best friend, brother.

I come across a few other names: Danielle (Dani) Sera-Lee Ferom, Samantha (Sam) Casey Ferom, Angel Leah Lancaster, Ariel Cosette Lancaster, and others. Some, I don't recognize: Beverly Laine Hilton-Hillz, Miles St. James Hillz, Tirek St. James Hilton, and Dora Macbeth Carrington. Dora's grave is the only one covered in dust and cobwebs, like it's older than the rest, and has gone without care. The one this kid is standing in front of, however, is none other than Deanna Margarette Winters. I kneel next to the kid, noticing his features. His eyes. His jawline. It's me. I hear something coming, then see a wrecking ball hanging from nothing flying at us. I take the kid and rush out of the way. Mother's tomb stone has been demolished. The kid lays there, tears escaping his eyes, but a look of absence in them too. "We killed them." I back away from the kid, hearing these words come from his lips. "Chance? That doesn't sound right. Who am I?" His lips tremble. With every word, he chokes. I feel something dripping down my chin, noticing the large gash left on the kid's throat. A part of it is missing. Suddenly, I taste something in my esophagus. Something fatty, yet hard and stringy. Metallic. I lift my finger to my bottom lip, staring at the blood that comes off it. "Why? Why?"

"Shh. Don't speak."

"Monster." That's his last word as his eyes close and his body falls limp.

"Everyone you come into contact with, will eventually die. When will you learn to let go?"

The boy disappears. I turn to face no one. "Face me, you coward."

"Who's the coward?"

"You killed them. You won't even admit it."

I feel hands press onto my face as I look into the eyes of the man whose face I have never seen. It's mine, naturally. "You're too modest. I didn't kill them. We killed them, together. Feel proud."

"I won't hear this."

"I don't like you like this. You're too emotional. You'll come around. It's a matter of time." He fades away. It was me? Only different. My face, but with those peculiar eyes. He shared my scars. Even the gash on my side. He had it.

"Chance?" I hear a voice come from the darkness. "Chance."

The voice is familiar, but not mine. "Storm?"

"Chance?"

"Wake up, already." A man stands in the corner. His welsh accent. He's an older gentleman, with the same eyes as the dark me. "You've been here long enough."

"Who the hell are you?"

"Too soon. I'll be back when you need me. The medallion holds the answers you seek of me. For now, it is time you awaken. Seek what has not been asked. The time is upon us."

"Hey, come back!"

"Chance!" I feel arms grab my shoulders. "Chance! Wake up, man!"

My eyes pop open, the darkness fading away as Storm's face comes into view.

CUTSCENE (XV.V)

It's been a few days since the nightmare. I ended up telling Storm the details. That, next to what I told him earlier about the details that Deanna told the girls and I, put him slightly on edge. No secrets. That's the compromise we made. The girls, too. There was going to be nothing hidden between us. I'm okay with that. Mother, or should I say Deanna, hasn't contacted me in the last few days, since I walked out, leaving her broken. She must know I'm here. She's just giving me time. I can respect that. Storm's parents haven't been bothered by my being here. They never even questioned. My phone suddenly rings. It's Mother. At least, that's what caller ID notices her as. I let it ring, not answering it.

"Who was it?" Storm sits in the beanbag next to me, playing his game.

"Nobody."

"With that answer, I wouldn't say 'nobody.' Is it her?"

"Yeah. Nothing gets by you, does it?"

"Why didn't you answer?" he asks.

"I need more time."

"Okay," Storm pauses the game and turns to face me, "We need to talk. Now."

"About?"

"Your problems with your mom."

"She's not—"

"Please. Let me finish. I know you say she's not your mother. From what you told me, that is true. She's not your mother. That much has been said, but it pisses me off to hear you badmouth your 'mom'. That's what she is. She's your mom. Nothing less. Accept it."

"But she's not. Even moms don't keep stuff like this from their kids."

"Did you ever think, maybe there's a reason? I understand that there are secrets. Some pretty, fucking big ones, but still. We've seen a lot of shit, man. I'm still trying to deny the fact that I may be crazy. If there is shit out there, like demons, then it isn't too much of a leap to even consider that your mom may have good-hearted reasons for keeping certain secrets from you. From the sound of it, she may even know about the existence of them."

"That thought has crossed my mind. These secrets she keeps. They're not your normal secrets. They may very well be intertwined with the existence of demons. She's keeping something else from me."

"Exactly."

"She knew Artemis. That unto itself is disturbing. Why the hell would you keep from your son? The fact that I'm being hunted like an animal to be mounted."

"Maybe, she felt you were out of harm's way. If she truly believed that, then there would be no need to worry you any further. Why tell you something that may never come to pass."

"Yeah, but after hearing the story of him. She initially told me that he tried to kill me as a baby. That may be true, but now his motives are completely inconsistent. I don't know what to believe."

"Ask her."

"Like that'd get me anywhere."

"Dude. I've had it with this whole drama thing you're putting off. I know this is all very new to you—the whole emotions thing. Call her for Christ's sake. She tried to reach out to you after three days. She must need to talk. Like, really talk. If you feel she's keeping more from you, now is the time to come clean, while you're already pissed. From here, things can only get better. The chance to milk her of her last secrets has presented itself to you. Now's the chance."

"First of all, never use my mom in that sentence again. It's hard to hear that. Secondly, you're right. I have been childish."

"She's your mom either way. She loves you. That much is obvious. These secrets mustn't have been easy to contain. Come back when you've resolved your differences."

"She left a message."

I go to my voicemails and click on hers. "Hey, honey. Sorry. You probably don't want to hear that. Even now, you probably don't want to talk to me, or even hear my voice. I understand this." I can hear in her voice, the uneasiness. "I have tried to do the best I could in raising you. Even now, I still love you like you are my own. I have failed as your . . . guardian. That much is obvious. Hear me when I say, whatever happens is not your fault. You needn't blame yourself. I take it all. From here, things will only get more difficult—more intense. It saddens me that I may not play a part in your life anymore, but you can always turn to me. In my eyes, you are my son—nothing has changed. I don't hate you. I do not blame you for a thing. I understand that you're going through change, but whatever the voice commands of you, don't succumb to its evil. That's not who you are. We make our own choices in life. We determine where we go from here. You have questions, and I am ready to answer them all. I've sheltered you from the truth in a naïve sense that, by not coming out, it'd be as if the secret were nonexistent. I must come to terms with the fact that you're no longer my sweet . . . baby boy, but a man, now. You're starting a new passage in life—a new chapter. I just hope you'll allow me the opportunity to see how it pans out. When you are ready, I'll be waiting for you. I Love you, with all my heart." The phone clicks, the end of her message.

"See, man. She misses you. What you're doing is torturing her."

"I need to call her."

"I'd have slapped you if you didn't come to that realization."

Her phone rings, but no one answers. I hang up on the voicemail and call back. Again, no one. "I've got to go."

"Completely understand. Don't come back now, you hear. Not until you two are closer than you were."

I make it to my house. The car is here. I make way to the door, pushing it open. "Deanna?" I look around the living room, noticing some things out of place. "Deanna? . . . Mom! I know you're here!" Her door is slightly creaked. A scent fills my nostrils. One I've stumbled upon on multiple occasions. "Mom?" I slowly open her door, but what I see makes me freeze. The walls are scratched. The bed is in ruins. The entire room looks as if it were hit by a mini tornado. A pair of legs hang off the bed. I cup my mouth as I stumble slowly towards the body. Scratches, like from an animal, are visible all over her body. I stand over my dead mother, my mom, as her eyes stare up at me, blankly. Her chest has been mauled, ripped open. The blood is fresh, covering her bare body from head to toe. Never has the sight of blood been so sickening to my senses. I drop to my knees, next to the bed, and find myself facing a box, neatly wrapped. The corners of the package are soaked. I tear at the wrapping, and what I see makes my stomach turn. What is this feeling? I've never been one to stir at the sight of blood, but this is unsightly. It's distasteful. Placed in the box, is a heart. A human heart. Mom's heart. I choke up as I vomit next to the box, holding my stomach. Tears mix in with the taste of the moment. A note is placed in with the heart. I reach in, feeling the mess, as I open the note. The writing is smeared, due to the dampness.

"Love can be testy: the struggles foreseen,
but none quite as messy as the one before thee . . .
—This was a test, and you failed. It's best to learn
from these failures as to not repeat them."

I crumple the note in my hand, balling up. The tears come, and there is nothing I can do to fight them. My mom is dead, and why?

These secrets killed her. No. It's more than that. These secrets were to protect me, but in the end, protecting me cost her life.

In the end, it is I who is to blame. I killed my mom and now, I must live with it . . .

(To be continued in: DEVIANT)

INSIGHT

(Just a glimpse into the author's thought process after the fact)

When Life hands you lemons, write fanfiction.

If I ever get old, and that's a big IF, given I don't commit suicide in my thirties, I better not be a burden to anyone. If I'm constantly drooling, or my mouth just hangs lazily open, if I've got various health problems, if my stomach sags to my knees as I try to push myself in a three times too small mobile chair, or if I have to be monitored 24/7, just kill me. No joke. Abe f****** Lincoln me. Doesn't even have to be an open theatre. Please, for the love of God. I may not say it, or I may gain a form of retardation that comes with age that makes me unable to see the great misfortune that has become my life but rest assured; I am highly depressed. I may fight it, which is why you must be stronger. Thank you. I'll see you in Hell.

To anyone who says that the sex was too quickly paced, I'll say this. Highschool is an orgy of emotionless sex. Whores who know the reputations of other whores don't hold back any subtleties, and therefore, sex doesn't really need an overly extended prologue that builds up to it, so long as context is present and accounted for. So no, I don't think the sex was unnecessary. If anything, I did you a favor. I wrote the scenes in a way that told you what was happening without the completely uncensored visuals and vulgar dialogue. You're welcome.

AUTHOR PAGE

J. M. BLOODWORTH is a poet who writes songs and fan fiction in his free time. He is a long-time fan of cartoons, anime, and books and has been writing since he was twelve. He hopes to eventually attend the California Institute of the Arts and become a voice actor, game designer, and lyricist. He currently resides in Arizona with his family.

www.ingramcontent.com/pod-product-compliance
Lightning Source LLC
Chambersburg PA
CBHW030706190726

48286CB00001B/195